PRAISE FOR HEART MASTER

"Drawing on the rich tradition of classic fantasy and sword and sorcery by the likes of Fritz Lieber, Robert E Howard and Michael Moorcock, Nikolas Everhart brings something fresh and new to the genre. Heart Master may be his novel debut but it certainly won't be the last time we see this writer's name on the front of a fantasy novel. A very impressive debut." —*Joel Meadows, editor-in-chief* **Tripwire**, *co-creator* **Sherlock Holmes and The Empire Builders**

"A promising series opener that carries all the hallmarks of great epic fantasy; featuring an engaging cast of characters in a richly-built world. Draven proves a worthy hero with a compelling journey of action, danger and redemption. The world of Heart Master remains inventive while still paying homage to classically beloved aspects of epic fantasy that will keep readers returning to these well-paced pages." – *Leanna Renee Hieber, award-winning author of the* **Strangely Beautiful** *and* **Spectral City** *series*

"I was sucked right into this world, as much a pawn of the gods as the team hunting their relics and racing against the evil threatening to blot out the world. The stakes were high, the tensions solid, and the conclusion a perfect launching point into what I have no doubt will prove to be a riveting series." - *Krista Walsh, author of* **The Meratis Trilogy**

"HEART MASTER offers complex characters navigating high stakes in a compelling fantasy setting, resulting in a story that represents all the best aspects of classic fantasy while approaching the genre with a compelling modern sensibility." —*Dirk Manning, author of* **Tales of Mr. Rhee, Nightmare World, Write or Wrong**

Heart Master

Nikolas Everhart

Dragon Street Press

A Dragon Street Press Book

PRINTING HISTORY

Published November 2023

This is a work of fiction. Names, characters, businesses, places, events, locales, and incidents are either the products of the author's imagination or used in a fictitious manner. Any resemblance to actual persons, living or dead, or actual events is purely coincidental.

Library of Congress Control Number: 2023948841

FIRST EDITION

1 3 5 7 6 4 2

ISBN-13: 979-8-9867714-1-0 (Hardcover Jacket)

ISBN-13: 979-8-9867714-2-7 (Hardcover Laminate)

ISBN-13: 979-8-9867714-3-4 (Trade Paperback)

ISBN-13: 979-8-9867714-4-1 (eBook)

Cover art by Jay DeFoy. Provided by Nikolas Everhart.

Printed in the United States of America

For all those who dream.

Contents

1

Prove Your Worth

A DISHEVELED BARD FINISHED his latest ribald tune, and Draven roared with laughter, slamming his goblet on the table harder than intended. Burgundy liquid sloshed over the rim, coating his hands in sticky alcohol. He licked it off like a cat cleaning its paws. A dark-haired Mektwin beauty curled around his chest like a second skin favored Draven with a winsome smile. He winked at her, knowing full well she cared only for his coin. A worthy trade. The Mektwin's fingers stole downward, seeking the purse at his belt. He pulled her hand away and pressed it to his lips.

It was rare for any Mektwin to be free, but he admired the fierce pride she carried herself with in spite of her race's notorious reputation. Once their empire, commanded by the Mad King, had stretched the length of the continent. Only the combined forces of all the gods could topple him. Or so the story went.

"I'm not that drunk, my sweet. Give it an hour." He smiled while she pouted. She traced a fingertip down his neck to his chest, content to bide her time.

Draven emptied his wine cup and called for another. "A toast to Draven, the greatest thief to prowl the proud city of Sharazin!" He raised his cup, praising himself for his latest haul, a stolen wine shipment that netted him enough to pay his dues to the thieves' guild for a season.

They can wait. I've better uses for the money—like the beautiful lady at my side.

She laughed, but not everyone found mirth in his jest. A knife flew in his direction. Draven plucked it from the air and drove it onto the top of his table. The woman at his side scurried away at the prospect of violence. Identical scenes played out around the rundown tavern. Fools like him were ever ready to gamble away their coin for moments of raucous abandon.

She'll be back. He tapped a finger to his chin, wondering whom he might have insulted this time.

Draven turned his head, looking for the owner of the jewel-encrusted knife wobbling on his table. It didn't take long to find his mark.

"Katay." Draven rolled his eyes. He placed a finger on the quivering knife to stop its movement. He considered plucking it from the table and returning it to its sender in kind.

"Lying moon-faced jackal!" A swarthy face appeared from behind the rabble, which quieted, eager for a bit of bloodshed.

"I prefer 'Draven the Deft'." Draven attempted a smirk, but his heart wasn't in it. The man at the end of the room had stolen the joy he'd reveled in only moments ago.

"Ha. No one calls you that. 'Draven the Daft', mayhap." Katay strode through the crowd, short of stature, but broad of shoulder. Dark eyes peered at Draven from a visage marred by scars and a patchy beard.

Really? He gets a name like Katay the Cat's Eye, and I'm stuck with 'daft'?

Draven wiggled the dagger out of the table, flipping it in the air. The polished blade threw glints of light across the room. "I'm sure you'd like to have this fine blade returned." An evil gleam communicated Draven's intent.

Katay laughed. "Keep it. Not as if you could ever steal such a blade on your own." The tavern laughed with him.

Draven frowned, and an angry twitch of his wrist sent the jeweled knife into the floor between them. "It's not worth enough to spark my interest, cat's belly."

Katay rose to Draven's taunt, launching himself at the younger man with a bellow of rage. Knives slid from well-oiled sheaths and the pair met in a clash of metal on metal. Steel snaked out, glinting in the guttering lanterns of the dingy tavern. Draven spun and ducked under a slash, his blade coming up under Katay's guard to score the front of the man's tunic. Then Draven rolled back, laughing as he went, and came up resting on the balls of his feet, ready to strike again. Katay bellowed another insult, but did not charge again. He dabbed at a spot of blood on his ruined tunic.

"First blood. That's the rule." Draven held up his dagger, wiping away a faint trace of scarlet.

Katay grumbled something unintelligible but shoved his knives back into their sheaths. "You're fast, I'll give you that. But that doesn't mean you've earned your rank."

Their audience reacted with nods and Draven scowled. As if they knew what made a master.

"Have I not defrauded merchants from one end of the city to the other? Have I not taken jewels from ladies' ears without arousing … their suspicions?" Draven leered at Katay, chewing on his words. "Have I not picked nearly every pocket that had so much as a silver piece in the whole of Sharazin?" He executed a perfect bow, never taking his eye off his enemy.

"Lies and chicanery. You're a master of common thefts, but common is all you'll ever be." Katay spat on the floor at Draven's feet. "I dare you to name one item of note you've stolen. Margat the Bold once stole a priest-king's jeweled slippers from his feet with the man none the wiser. That dagger I lobbed at you hung from the girdle of a wizard who didn't know it was gone till I was half a day's ride away." Katay crossed his arms over his chest, looking down his nose at his rival. "They will forget your name the moment you exit this den of ilk. What will be your legacy? Spilt wine and loose coins."

Draven puffed out his chest and pointed a finger at Katay, only to realize he might have a point. True, he had amassed a tidy hoard, but he preferred easy marks and guaranteed profits.

I don't care for risk. Risk leaves someone dead and me running in shame.

"Your silence speaks volumes." Katay sniffed and dabbed at the scratch Draven inflicted on his torso.

"Who needs some priceless bauble he'd never be able to fence?" Draven folded his arms across his chest, wilting as every eye now turned to him. Even his evening's entertainment joined them in silent judgment.

You'd think my coin would buy loyalty.

A fresh voice called out from the throng, one that he recognized and that cut him to his core. "People who claim to be master thieves. Who would hold themselves above common footpads and rogues."

Draven's head turned so fast he feared his neck might snap. This new critique came not from the quarrelsome Katay but from his own mentor, Laresh, who had taken him in when Draven's world had collapsed a few years ago.

That loss still ate at Draven, still framed his days with guilt, and this fresh reminder nibbled at his bravado. He shook his head free of cobwebs and turned to face Laresh, but kept one eye on Katay.

"You too, Laresh? I thought at least you might have my back."

"You've done passably well since I helped you out of that spot, but it's time you either learned your place or made your mark. You want to boast you're a master? Then you need to steal something of note and register it with the guild." Laresh put a hand to Draven's shoulder in a fatherly gesture, but the glint of steel in the man's eyes betrayed his true motivation. There was no love there. Only a serpent looking for an angle.

Draven shrugged his hand off.

"So you can claim that all I know came from you? Well, it didn't. You may have taught me some tricks, but much I already knew before you apprenticed me, you old sot." Draven gritted his teeth, willing himself not to ball up his fists as anger boiled his blood.

Laresh's hand strayed to the dagger at his waist as Draven's words hit home. Draven sneered and laughed.

"Try it, old man, and I'll gut you where you stand. No first blood. No second chances." Draven froze the older thief with an icy glare.

Laresh looked at him with a mixed expression, calculating the odds before letting the dagger fall back into the sheath and crossing his arms.

"Are you going to let this upstart rail on like this?" Katay bounced, eager to restart their squabble.

Laresh held up a hand to Katay, motioning him to silence and then clucked his tongue, eyeing Draven up and down. "You've missed your calling, boy. Mayhap you're more assassin than thief. You've got quick hands—not deft, but certainly quick."

The insult cut Draven to his core, but he wouldn't give Laresh the satisfaction of knowing how deeply. He shifted his gaze left and right, noting every eye in the tavern was now glued directly on him and the spectacle he'd become. The wrong spectacle. He'd need something grand to walk out of this place with his dignity intact.

"I'm no killer." His words were barely audible, even to him. "You want something of note, old man, then you'll have it. Mark it, before the season's out, Sharazin will see the boldest theft in its history. You'll all know its architect." He bared his teeth. "The eyes of the city will be blind, but the Eyes of Nerys will be on her favorite son."

Katay scoffed, but Laresh said nothing and only glared at Draven.

"Oh, and Katay? You misplaced this." Draven launched the gem-encrusted dagger at his rival. Katay attempted to catch it, but missed, and it sank into the beam he leaned against.

Draven swept out of the tavern, wondering how in the hells he would steal the jeweled eyes of the Goddess of Luck and Death from her temple without bringing the entire city down on his head.

2

FREEDOM

FRESH TAPERS BURNED IN brass candlesticks on the worn oak table. Seguris focused his hate-filled gaze on them rather than looking into the eyes of Caldor, his current owner and head artificer to one of the lesser priest-kings.

Owner. The word disgusted him.

Guards held Seguris's arms, the chains jingling. Corded muscles tensed under dusky skin, ready for any chance to strike.

"How many times, Seguris? How many times must we repeat this before you're broken?" Caldor's spidery hand scratched something in a ledger while appraising his property. Seguris glared hatred back, shaking his head like an angry lion. Perspiration flew from his dark curls. The only thing Caldor did better than inventing new weapons for his master was devising new tortures for his unfortunate slaves.

"Eleven..., in case you haven't kept count. I have. And this time you've killed one of my servants." His quick eyes seemed to regard Seguris as a failed investment.

Which I am.

"I see you are still proud. Don't think you're the first Mektwin scum I've broken. You are a single grain of sand in an endless desert. You will pay the price for your mad-king ancestor. Khyris tilted the world into chaos, and his mad blood flows in your veins." Caldor waved to his men and rose, closing to the tome. "Bind him to the ring."

Seguris's chains were connected to a stout iron ring mounted to one of the ceiling beams. The metal was pitted from years of use. Seguris knew it well.

I swear this will be the last time the lash tastes my back. He'd spoken the oath a hundred times before and he believed it now as fervently as he did the first time.

"Your chains may bind my flesh, but you will never master me, Caldor. The Mektwin will rise." Seguris spat on the floor and got a punch to the ribs for his trouble.

Caldor produced the lash and ran the handle along Seguris's back while the guards withdrew to the corners of the room. The slave heard the rip of fabric as his shirt was torn. His owner was strong for such a willowy man, but Seguris wondered what it would take to snap that slender neck.

"No. I'm afraid this won't do. You have scars back here. I just don't think the barbs are getting through to you as they once did." Caldor turned the chained slave and brought the lash down across his midsection.

Seguris exhaled, but gave no other sign someone had struck him. Years of beatings provided him with a high threshold for pain. He flexed his arms, testing the chains, but no matter how he strained, they held. His efforts earned him a chuckle from the slave-owner.

"Damn your eyes!" Seguris thrashed, willing every iota of hate into his master.

"Oh, Seguris, will you never learn? Your shackles are designed for that. No, I think the lash needs a break. Let's try something new."

What additional torment awaits me this time? The pens were rife with tales of the cruelties Caldor visited on his slaves. Seguris had endured so many lashings he scarcely felt the lash any longer. His wrists ached from the cuffs digging into the scar tissue every time he strained against the bonds. Seguris opened his eyes once more, looking for any opening he could exploit.

Ghedryn, my god, give me the strength to shatter these bonds and carve out the heart of this contemptuous bastard.

Caldor walked out of his field of vision. The guards stared at him with undisguised horror.

Pity? That's a first.

Burning pain stabbed between his shoulder blades, and this time he screamed. Beyond the pain, he heard the sizzle of his flesh. The scent of his own burning flesh turned his stomach. The brand, or whatever it was, dug around, burrowing beneath his flesh, and Seguris imagined it would burst from his chest. White light blurred his vision, and a new sensation blossomed within him. Fire. White and hot.

He writhed, hearing Caldor call for another iron. He had lost all concept of time. Even when Caldor removed the brands, the fire inside him continued to grow until he imagined it would consume his whole body.

"Release him." Caldor's barked command resonated in Seguris's ears.

Thank Ghedryn.

The two guards rushed to comply. When they released one of his manacles to pass the chain through the ring, he crumpled to the floor. His muscles twitched in response to the fresh burns on his back. They tried to lift his arm to reconnect the cuff, but Seguris's hand remained trapped underneath him.

"Hurry with that. Get him off the floor." The clank of a branding iron punctuated Caldor's words as it dropped against the metal of the brazier.

My last chance. He tensed his muscles, resisting the fumbling hands that tried to get to his freed arm. His sweat-slick skin hampered the guards' efforts. As one knelt, Seguris exploded into motion, shoving him back to topple over a table. The other guard struck him hard across the jaw, but Seguris gave it little heed. He rose and drove his forearm into the man's face in one fluid motion. The guard reeled out of his view.

"Damn you! I'll kill you this time. I swear!" Caldor ripped the iron out of the brazier and swung it at Seguris, who blocked the blow with the length of chain dangling from his wrist. Seguris snarled in response, kicking his owner in the stomach. Caldor leapt out of the reach of the swinging chain before the empty cuff could connect with his chin.

The two guards, who had regrouped, rushed forward. Seguris's anger overwhelmed his pain, and he hefted a wooden bench to cast it at the oncoming men. One man went down under the weight of it. The other drew a short, stabbing sword and edged forward. Seguris side-stepped a slash and sent him sprawling with a meaty fist to the side of his head, following it up with a kick to the mid-section. The man's sword skittered away.

Fire bloomed in his back again. He whirled, catching the iron rod halfway up the haft and ripping it out of the slave-owner's hand. Caldor crumpled when Seguris backhanded him. The guard behind him was crawling on his knees to retrieve his sword. Seguris swiveled and brought the long piece of iron down on the back of his head. Blood flew up, painting the ceiling with an arc of tiny droplets. The other guard, who was just now coming around, received the same fate.

"Please—stop! Guards will come and kill you if you don't stop now!" Spittle flew from Caldor's mouth and tears mingled with blood coursed down his face, coloring his gray beard.

Seguris, regarding his former master, reveled in his long-denied victory. For years, as he languished in cells or labored in quarries, he had dreamt of this day.

Would the bastard honor a deal if I made one for my freedom? No, he would cut me down like a rabid dog the moment I released him.

Seguris kicked Caldor to the ground, relishing the entreaties from his "master." With calm efficiency, he looped the chain around Caldor's throat, and pulled with strength born from decades of labor. The burns on his body rebelled, attempting to steal that power and sending echoes of agony up his spine, but he gritted his teeth and pulled harder.

Time spiraled into eternity until he thought he'd been pulling his entire life. He allowed Caldor's limp body to fall back to the floor with a wet thud, and hurried to the door, slamming the bolts a moment before someone crashed into it from the other side, shouting for Caldor to answer.

"He can no longer hear you, but I'll be happy to greet you once I find a proper weapon." Seguris hefted a dead guard's short sword.

Not a proper desert sword, but it will do.

He had no illusions. Exhausted by torture, he didn't stand a chance. This room had but one exit. He might not make his escape—but he'd at least die a free man. He found the key on Caldor's belt and shortly the other manacle fell from his scarred wrist. The chain he had looped around his wrist provided a poor shield, but it might allow him to fend off a slash without losing a hand.

"Fight for me or die a slave." The voice boomed in his mind, and he involuntarily fell to one knee.

"Whoever you are, I'll fight any battle you choose so long as you don't chain me. I will never be a slave again." Weight crashed against the door and the wood cracked.

Seguris braced himself.

The air shimmered fire, and a grim-faced titan appeared from nowhere. Even in the center of the room, his golden helm touched the ceiling. A long beard fell past a face as craggy as the mountains. Ghedryn extended a hand to Seguris.

"The God of Conquest has heard your prayer. Take my hand and fight for your destiny."

3

THE ARENA

REALITY SHIMMERED BACK INTO view; Seguris stumbled but didn't go down. He stood in an ancient coliseum of crumbling stone along with dozens of others, bristling with weapons, who all looked as confused as he felt. Seguris tightened the grip on his purloined short sword, readying himself for anything, but not a single person moved. He tried to step forward and instantly understood why. Some invisible force was holding him in place. The same must be true for the other warriors arrayed around the sandy pit.

He flexed his arms, surprised to feel no tightness in his back from the wounds inflicted by Grand Artificer Caldor. He checked with his free hand and found only smooth, unblemished skin under his touch.

Blessings of the god. So we're all to fight to the death for Ghedryn's amusement?

The air at the center of the great pit shimmered and before their eyes appeared a raised dais of basalt crowned by a throne of gold and brass. Ghedryn, the God of Conquest, sat unmoving on his lofty jewel-encrusted perch. He held something in his hand that glittered even in the dim light of the arena.

The prize?

Whatever it ended up being, Seguris didn't care. He possessed the only reward he'd ever sought: his freedom. Anything more would just be icing on a festival cake... not that he'd ever tasted one, just seen them from afar.

"Warriors! Hear me! You have been assembled by divine purpose to determine which of you is worthy to lead my armies against the remainder of the Twelve who sit idly by while suffering is visited upon the world." Ghedryn rose, growing in stature till he barely fit on the dais. "In my hand, I hold The Fist of Heaven, a relic invested with my power, to help you conquer the world in my name."

Murmurs sprang up around the arena as the same question arose from many mouths. "What must we do?" "How can we prove our mettle?" "Who shall we kill?"

Ghedryn silenced them with a wave of his hand. "Only one may claim this gauntlet and become my champion. Only one may lead my armies to victory and hold rein over the world. How that person is selected is up to you." He followed this ominous statement with a guttural laugh that made even Seguris's knees go weak.

Then the invisible force holding him went slack, and Seguris found he could move once more. He looked to the other contestants, who had also tasted their freedom. Seguris tested the weight of his blade, swinging it in the air. The chain he kept looped around his arm with the manacles dangling. He smiled a grim smile: he knew he'd be the only one to leave this pit alive.

It took mere moments for chaos to erupt. Some ran for the raised dais, only to be rebuffed by that same invisible force. Evidently Ghedryn had no plans to allow his gift to be obtained by speed or guile. The rest attacked each other. More than a dozen must have fallen in the first moments of the battle.

Seguris nodded. This was as it should be.

He twisted just in time to fend off the blow of a heavy longsword. The edge of the other blade skittered to his crossguard and caught there. He pivoted and drove a series of blows into his opponent's midsection until he heard bones crack. All the breath went out of his opponent, who sank to his knees. Seguris drove his sword into the man's neck. A splash of blood sprayed Seguris' face, and he licked his lips, relishing the taste. He imagined every warrior in the arena as one of his hated oppressors.

He ducked an overhead slash and drove his short sword up to the crossguard into the chest of another man dressed in long, flowing white robes. When the man fell to the ground, Seguris scooped up the long, curved sword from the man's slack fingers. Now that was a blade fit for a Mektwin desert fighter. Seguris smiled, slicing into his thumb with its fine edge and painting whorls of blood on his face as his ancestors did before a battle, back when the Mektwin were still free.

Then he ran forward, lashing out at a wild-eyed harpy of a woman with the chain hanging from his other hand, cleaving her with his new-found blade when she dodged, severing her torso. He sprinted to his next victim before her body even hit the ground.

Next, he came upon a soldier, in the livery of a Vellerian priest-king, dispatching his opponent with quick, efficient blows that spoke of military training. Seguris raised his sword to end the man's life before they could even turn, but something in that man's posture gave him pause. The soldier turned his head, raising his longsword to target Seguris, and then his mouth formed an oval of surprise. Seguris nearly dropped his own sword in response.

"Ethan? Can it be you?" Seguris raised his blade across his body just in case the man failed to recognize him in return.

"Seguris, you old dog! Never thought I'd see a familiar face in this gore-splattered blood pit." Ethan spun and disemboweled a man who surged at them, trying to take advantage of their seeming inattention.

Seguris took Ethan's measure. Ethan was older and grayer, but he was still the man who'd taught Seguris to use weapons, though it had been against the law for a Mektwin to even hold a weapon. Ethan had been one of the few lighter-skinned men who had ever shown him a measure of decency. And Seguris would likely already be dead on this sand if not for the lessons Ethan had shared with him during the long nights they'd spent sparring together while the others slept.

"I'm not game to cross my blade with you, old friend. What say you? Should we work together to gut the rest of this rabble?" Ethan gave him a wink as he shook the blood from his longsword.

"And the prize?" Seguris asked, ever wary of betrayal.

"It should be worn by a king. If I remember, you often claimed to be of royal blood. I refuse to be a captain of the priest-kings anymore—but I'd serve such a king as yourself. Mayhap you can revive your lost kingdom with Ghedryn's trinket."

He held his blade up in a gesture Seguris took as a salute.

Seguris flourished his blade in the same manner, dreams of an empire dancing before his eyes. He would keep an eye on this one, but if Ethan was genuine, it wouldn't hurt to have someone watching his back. And if not, Ethan would die like every other light-skin beneath his curved blade.

They set out across the field, working in tandem with deadly effect. Months of sparring together in the wee hours of the night allowed them to mesh into an effective unit. Ethan flanked his left side, protecting Seguris from all attacks on that side and allowing him to focus on driving forward like a berserk titan. His blade rose and fell with uncanny speed and certainty 'til Seguris was sure the God of Conquest was guiding his every movement.

Another deft cut and a wild-haired woman bearing twin daggers sank to the ground with a cleft skull. *Do they all feel the god moving within them, or is it just me?* Ethan blocked an overhead strike with a shield he'd taken from a dead combatant and lunged forward, impaling a man and kicking him away with brutal efficiency.

Against all odds, they not only seemed to be winning but also attracting followers. One man, Bastus, who labored alongside Seguris once in a quarry, fell in on Seguris's other side with nary a word. Bastus bore a broadax, and though he lacked Ethan's skill, his sheer strength and brutality made up for it. Soon, two became six, and they cut through the opposing contestants like a scythe through ripe wheat.

It made him wonder if he really was destined to lead. They deferred to him, shadowed his movements, and killed as if mirroring him, and Seguris thought there might be some divine force balancing the odds in his favor.

He shook such thoughts from his head. There would be time enough to think on these things later once he'd claimed Ghedryn's favor.

A blade met his in a violent collision, sending a shock wave down his arm. The wielder was a brawny man clad only in animal skins who even towered over him. Seguris snarled, lashing out with his free hand into the barbarian's midsection, dropping him to one knee. Then he grabbed the barbarian by the throat and squeezed until the man's eyes bugged out of his head. A lusty smile creased his lips as the barbarian's neck snapped.

On and on his team worked, 'til only a score stood between them and the end of this interminable struggle. He bled from a dozen wounds, including a long, angry weal of red that ran diagonally down his chest to his hip. His motley crew of four remaining followers all bore similar injuries, but for the most part they were whole. Only two had fallen, and they had died well.

Seguris gave his remaining compatriots a wolfish grin. "The god's purpose is our purpose. We are all free brothers. Drink deep of their blood so we may claim our destiny." He uttered a guttural war cry as he imagined his Mektwin ancestors must have done and surged forward. Ethan and the rest followed without hesitation.

Seguris's last opponent was a small, swarthy, rat-faced man bearing a rust-pitted longsword and wearing an oilskin cloak. The whisper of a beard decorated his pox-scarred face. He wielded his blade like a bolt of lightning, and it left a bleeding gash on Seguris's cheek. Seguris parried with all the speed he could muster after what must have been hours in this blood-spattered arena. On and on they went, trading blows and parrying swings. Seguris received another wound, this time to his leg, which hampered his movement, but still he drove onward, casting a net of steel with his curved sword.

Fortune smiled on him: the rusty longsword snapped during one of their exchanges and Seguris's heavier sword dug deep into the man's side. A quick rabbit punch to his opponent's throat left him gasping for breath. Like a fish out of water, the man flopped about on the sand, dying at Seguris's feet. Seguris smiled and stepped over his body to cut down the man Ethan grappled.

With the last man dead, Seguris stood side by side with Bastus and Ethan, facing their god.

"Only one may approach." The god extended his hand, proffering the golden gauntlet.

Seguris regarded his comrades. Ethan shrugged his shoulders in response. Bastus went to one knee, showing he had no interest in the prize. Seguris strode forward, wind whipping at his sweat-drenched hair. Liquid dripped from his face, and he couldn't tell if it was perspiration or blood.

The god of conquest looked down on him and a thin, tight smile turned up the corners of Ghedryn's mouth. "You are the one."

"I am the one." Seguris raised his hand, fingers outstretched. He knew his heritage as a direct descendant of the Great King Khyris, Emperor of the Mektwin, and now he would make his dream a reality. His people would be free once more and they would raise him up as their king.

No, as their emperor.

Ghedryn did not move, but a glittering gauntlet of shining brass rose and floated through the air to settle on Seguris's outstretched hand. A slight ripple of power echoed through the now silent amphitheater. He curled his hand into a fist, reveling in the thrum of energy.

"Go forth in my name and claim your kingdom, warlord."

Seguris nodded.

It begins.

4

THE EYES OF NERYS

GUTTERING TORCHES ILLUMINATED ORNATE stone walls decorated with tapestries and friezes depicting the goddess of luck and death. Light spilled out in wavering circles against the darkness cloaking the room. Polished pews of smooth, planed dark wood stood empty of supplicants. A blue velvet banner on either side of the burled wood lay unfurled, depicting interlocking circles. There was only one thing out of place, and that was Draven climbing the statue of Nerys.

One arm of the deity rose to the heavens. The other bore a silver cuff. Even in the gloom, the cuff reflected glints of brilliance. At her throat glittered a ruby brooch, shining like an angry star. Pinned at her girdle, a gold shield larger than a man's hand represented the protection she offered.

At the base of the statue stood a plaque with the standard curse for anyone who stole from the Goddess of Luck and Death:

> The hands of men will turn against the thief.
> The mind of the thief will warp.
> The heart of the thief will shrivel.
> The flesh will slough from his bones.

Bugger that! What does a goddess need with jewels?

Draven's attention was arrested by the eyes, twin gemstones of different hues. A radiant sapphire gleamed with the calm serenity of the sea beside an emerald as green as the fertile plains to the east. Their facets caught even the smallest flicker from the torches: the Eyes of Nerys.

Draven gazed up in wonder, his mouth going dry while his palms perspired. He was finally here. In the temple.

Undiscovered.

Draven was about to pirate the treasures of the goddess herself. With just one theft the guild would never question him again. Despite his anxiety, he remained still. His mind free of all fear, Draven dried his palms.

Everyone will know the name of Draven, Master Thief.

With a practiced hand, he snagged the cuff from the statue's outstretched arm. As he touched the half-circle of metal with a heart emblazoned upon it a shiver ran down his spine. An eerie blue light flashed before his eyes. Perspiration dotted his brow.

Draven fought for breath. His skin burned, and he almost fell. Visions of a past not his own swam before his eyes.

A massive destrier carried a knight in battered cerulean armor into battle against red-robed mages throwing fire and lightning. Demons rose up behind them while the knight wielded a saber more blue than his armor and wreathed in flames, burning white hot. The man on horseback cast his helmet away with one mailed hand and stared directly at Draven. Long hair whipped in the heated, dust-riven wind and he whispered, "Heart Master."

The vision faded, and the darkened temple rose around Draven once more.

"Ghosts and demons." He wiped at his brow with the heel of his hand. Could there be something to the curse? The ornate silver cuff went into his bag, and the weakness passed.

Damned ghosts.

He pulled the gold buckle from the statue, his fingers light as a summer breeze.

Silence.

The ruby brooch came away with a subtle clink of metal against stone, and he froze for the third time since he had stolen into this sacred room. Somewhere far off he heard metal on metal.

Now for the eyes.

From the pouch at his belt, he withdrew a thin pick lipped at one end. The eyes were a bit of a stretch, but he squirmed higher.

Thank Nerys, her statue was bolted to the floor.

He paused to appreciate the irony of praying to a goddess he was robbing.

The pry tool sounded like a chisel on granite as he worked it back and forth to free first the sapphire and then the emerald. Not until the second gem fell into his palm did he breathe a sigh of relief and drop to the floor like a phantom.

A voice growled behind him. "Thief!"

"Oh, hells!"

He turned, shoving the tool back into his pouch with a practiced gesture. He slipped the gems into a shallow breast pocket. A long knife appeared from its sheath like magic. Before him stood a stout man in red silk robes, bearing a torch in one hand and a bottle of thick, green glass in another. In a heartbeat, the clamor of running and shouts came to Draven's ears. The man stared at him, hands shaking, face white with shock.

"Will you just run, damn it? I have no desire to gut you where you stand." Draven extended the knife before him and flourished it in the air, describing deadly arcs.

This was all the encouragement the portly priest needed as he dropped his bottle to the floor. It hit and rolled, coming to rest against the toe of Draven's soft leather boot. Off the man fled, torch bobbing over his head, a banner of flame, while he bellowed for aid. Draven couldn't suppress a soft laugh before he turned to make his escape.

The fat, old bastard ran off in the same direction Draven had entered. Draven elected to head in the opposite direction. As usual, he chose poorly; two men appeared dressed in pale cassocks. They were empty-handed, but one grabbed an unlit torch from a nearby sconce while the other grabbed a heavy vase filled with lilies and pitched it at Draven.

Draven side-stepped and the vessel shattered off to his left. He brandished his knife at the men but they stood their ground.

Damnation. Draven wiped the heel of his hand along his jaw, weighing his options.

He feinted toward the torch-wielder and sent a fist crashing into the other man's temple. That blow landed, crumpling the man to the floor. The remaining priest swung the unlit brand at him, which Draven caught with ease on his long dagger while he kicked the holy man. A whoosh of breath left the man's body. It was a simple matter to bring the hilt of the knife down onto his skull. The priest sank to the ground, unconscious.

Two down, only a couple hundred to go before I'm free. Or dead. Fishing the gems from his pocket, he kissed them, then clutched them in his fist.

He sprinted down the hall, praying to all the gods and goddesses he could remember to get him out of this thrice-damned temple. As usual, they were deaf. The clamor of armed men reverberated ahead of him. Massive gongs rang in the recesses of the building, loud enough to call Nerys herself. Draven skidded to a halt as half a dozen armed men pounded down the hall.

"Stop or die!"

Draven cursed, hearing movement from behind him. He upended a brazier full to the brim with holy oil in their direction. The sound of armor clanging together mixed with shouts as the men tried to find purchase on the slippery floor.

His relief died as he encountered more soldiers. Their faces blanched in surprise, and he crashed into them, shoving one to the ground as he scrambled past. He was through them in a heartbeat, continuing his flight. Turning a corner, he ran headlong into a burly man-at-arms who knocked him to the floor with a sweeping blow of a mailed arm, then looked down at him with a gap-toothed grin.

Draven struggled to draw in a breath as the gems went flying. They arced through the air, and his eyes could barely track their descent.

No Goddess, please. Why didn't I put them back in my pocket? Damn my eyes.

The glittering emerald skittered against the wall and ricocheted around the corner. The sapphire came to rest just feet away. Relief flooded into him, but disappeared as a lumbering mountain of a man-at-arms stepped on the jewel with a heavy boot. The unmistakable sound of broken glass resounded even over the tumult. Draven and the guard both froze. The big man looked down, his face ashen.

Hells, they were fakes! He'd stolen worthless glass. He laughed out loud and took flight.

A large window loomed at the side of this hall and he dove through, hoping he was still on the east side of the building. Time stood still for the briefest moment, then his heart was in his throat as he fell for interminable seconds before crashing into dark water. The impact stole all the air from him. His lungs burned to breathe, but Draven fought the temptation. Cold seeped into his skin, and the sodden leather jerkin threatened to drag him down.

Now I just have to find some way to explain this mess. Nothing to pay the guild with, and the church will want a noose around my neck, at the very least.

Dreams of becoming a master thief floated from Draven as the bubbles of his breath rose to the surface. He kicked his legs and swam for his life.

5

CONSEQUENCES

DRAVEN ROSE THE NEXT day with sunlight scalding his eyes. He shoved the bed linen aside with a grimace and thought about the night before as he scrubbed a hand across his cheeks.

Disaster. His grand robbery couldn't have gone any worse.

The cool tile sent a shiver up his lower legs as Draven swung his feet off the bed. He threw on a silk robe with an ermine collar and took in the room's rich furnishings, wondering if he'd have to give it all up.

How many people saw my face? Once news reaches the guild, they'll send assassins.

He checked his thieving leathers where they hung by an oak-topped desk. They were dry, as expected. He'd wondered for years if they were enchanted. Magic left a foul taste in his mouth, but it had its uses, like his satchel that could hold his entire room.

A light knock sounded at the door.

Draven froze, then relaxed. It was too light to be a city guard.

"Yes?"

Instead of an answer, the door rattled again. "Draven? You never shoot the bolts. Are you well?"

He rushed to let her in after he heard a familiar voice. A blond woman, Maren, stood holding a tray in her slender hands. Clear blue eyes regarded him above pouting lips. Draven returned a well-practiced grin.

"Rough night. I planned to sleep in, but the sun woke me." He plopped down on a divan opposite the bed.

"It's half-noon. You accomplished your goal." Maren smiled, set the tray on a small marble inlaid table, and offered him a plate with bread and cheese.

"Is it now? I thought it was still early." He furrowed his brow, wondering how far the news had spread.

"You look like you spent the night in a sewer." She wrinkled her nose. "And you smell of it, too. I take it your business didn't go well last night?"

Draven returned a wan smile. Maren was one of the few servants that knew him for a thief rather than the merchant he claimed to be.

"It could have gone better." He took the plate, slapped the cheese on a hunk of bread, and wolfed it down. She proffered him a cup of sweet mead, and he drank it in a single gulp.

"Hungry?" she asked, a finger caressing the side of his neck as she joined him on the divan.

"My appetites are vast." He wiped his mouth with the heel of his hand as Maren slid her hand to his chest. His heart jumped, and he scooted back on reflex. She pouted.

"You don't favor me?" Her pout turned to a frown, palming a few silvers from a side table.

"It's not that, Maren. You're beautiful." He looked down but didn't comment on her theft.

"Then why? You've never tried so much as to kiss me."

Draven chuckled as her fingers crept back to the side table.

"Once a woman captured my heart, but I betrayed her trust. She haunts me."

"A noble woman?"

He laughed. "She was noble, but not royal." Draven took another bite of bread and chewed. Memories of a different woman clouded his vision.

"She broke your heart? And now you won't risk it for another?" Her words teased him.

Maren's dangerous. One wrong word from her and I'll have guards and gods only know who else at my door.

"In a way." He sighed, wondering how he'd fallen into this snare.

"I'd like to know what kind of woman causes you to spurn me." She traced a finger up his knee.

Memories he wished he could forget came flooding back. A torrent of images besieged him. *Nellonah...*

"I was foolish. There was an ... accident with one of her proteges, and they... died. It was my fault." Draven sucked in a breath and exhaled. "It was easier to run. Still, I see her face, her smile, and I hear her laugh." His breath caught in his throat, wondering what might have been if he'd stayed.

"Poor man. Well, one day you'll forget her, and maybe I'll still think you're handsome. I wouldn't wait too long."

Draven nodded, all too conscious of the fact that her interest probably had as much to do with his purse as it did his features.

Maren leaned back on the couch and smiled at him knowingly. "It was you, wasn't it?"

"What was, dear heart?" Draven shoved more food into his mouth.

"The temple robbery. It's on everyone's lips today." The silky smile began to sour.

Draven laughed, scratching his forehead. "Temple? No, never rob a priest. They're all mad."

"It's not wise to mock a goddess." She shot him a reproachful glance. Her soft features tightened into a look he didn't care for.

"A jest only. I pay my tithes to Nerys like any good believer."

This satisfied Maren: her blue eyes twinkled, echoing her smile.

"Whose temple?" Draven asked, hoping to glean a bit of information from her.

"Nerys. The rumor is a dozen armed men barged in and made off with the very eyes of her statue."

A dozen? Damned priests. And the eyes weren't even real. Stupid, sodding fakes. Must be in a vault somewhere.

"Maren, dear, you know I always work alone."

"There is a manhunt for anyone involved."

"A manhunt? For a gang of thieves? Good for them."

"Truly," she said as she rose, gathering up the tray in her arms. "Still, get your affairs in order. Word is they'll finally crack down on the guild of thieves. That this is the final affront." She gave another demure pout before turning to leave.

"Certainly." He let his gaze wander to that backside as she disappeared through the door before shaking his head and throwing off his robe.

Hells. Not only did I miss the prize, but now I've led the guard and church to blame the guild. They'll never forgive this.

He lost no time in shrugging into his familiar brown leather jerkin, pants, and boots. His heart hammered in his chest as he hurried about the room, gathering weapons, tools, and anything else of value that would fit into the enchanted satchel.

He stood, taking a last look around his rooms, wondering if he would ever return. Marble tiles that shone like a mirror reflected the dark silk curtains that would have let him sleep the day if he'd remembered to pull them. Furniture of the richest oak and mahogany littered the space with little thought to function. Draven collected pieces that fancied his eyes, with no real idea of what he'd do with them. He'd spent a small fortune on this ruse. Anything to distract him from his humble beginnings as a street beggar with no family to call his own.

Ah well, the goddess gives, and the goddess takes away.

6

A Pile of Junk

Draven didn't dare risk trying to pass the trinkets on to any reputable shop. A brisk walk found him before the false front of his favorite fence. Draven gazed up at the freshly veneered sign for Ronell's Imports. He strode in with confidence and milled around the shop while the proprietor dealt with another customer in the back room.

♥*Turn away.*♥

Draven whirled to face the speaker, but the shop remained empty. In the rear, Vistan haggled with an unseen patron. Other than that, Draven stood alone.

♥*Turn from this path. It holds naught but pain and dishonor.*♥

Again Draven spun, but still there was no one. He would have heard the door. It squeaked like a dying rat.

He recalled the curse on the statue.

Superstition. He repeated the word over and over, yet it didn't keep his heart from rabbiting. Heat burned his hand, and he dropped the brass candle holder he was examining, only to see its symmetrical lines marred by the imprint of his hand.

He did not see that. He was *not* cursed. He kicked the candle stick under a shelf.

"Draven!"

The thief's knees went weak, and his heart beat faster. He turned on shaky legs to see Vistan. Another customer in a red leather tunic hurried past.

"Come on back." Vistan stood in the doorway, his fingers steepled in expectation. Spidery hands extended out of the voluminous folds of a burgundy robe. Narrow, ferret-like eyes appraised Draven beneath a heavily lined brow.

Goddess, what's wrong with me? I didn't even bother to steal anything. Draven straightened his jerkin and strode back. Shaking hands wiped away perspiration from his forehead.

Vistan chuckled, clapping him on the back as they sat down at an oak table. Deep set eddies of the wood grain shown through where years took their toll on the finish. A few strips of fraying velvet ran the length, dangling over the sides.

"Vistan." He nodded to the older man and put on his best trading smile.

"So, what do you have for me? Maybe the eyes of the goddess?" The wiry old man cackled, his long, wispy beard fluttering as he spoke.

♥ *You may not profit from the divine.* ♥

Hells take you. I don't need a conscience. "If only." Draven swallowed a lump in his throat and pulled the satchel around so it sat on his lap. He shoved his hand in and pictured the items from last night: the filigreed cuff, the ruby brooch, and the golden buckle. The magic tingled pins and needles along his hand. Vistan sighed loudly. Draven shoved his hand further into his satchel. The tingles crept up to his elbow, till the pieces came to his hand. Draven smiled back at Vistan. It had never been this hard before.

Another electric shock stung him, and he bit his lip to stifle a cry. Fire lanced through his wrist, running up his arm till he wanted to scream. Something smooth and cool ran along his skin, soothing the pain. Draven withdrew his hand, holding the buckle and brooch. The cuff now decorated his forearm. Blood seeped around the edges, running in rivulets around the silver-inlaid iron. The thief's eyes opened wide as he stared at it. He dropped the other items on the table as if they were on fire.

♥ *Impossible.* ♥

Draven continued to stare at his arm. An armored cuff now ran from his palm to his elbow. Iron and silver work mingled in intricate swirls. At the very center of it, elaborate chains encircled an ornate heart. Tiny drops of blood ran along the inlays in a delicate swirl pattern. Aghast, he looked back to Vistan, ignoring the voice in his mind.

The fence raised an eyebrow. "Well, that's an interesting trick."

Draven shook his head, then wiped nonexistent perspiration from his brow, and he flashed a weak smile to Vistan. *I am not mad.*

♥*This simply cannot be. The greatest treasure of all the gods on the arm of a thief?*
'Tis madness, footpad.♥

I am no footpad, you thrice damned — He choked off the thought when he realized he was talking to the voice in his head.

♥*I am no mere voice. I am Ansalon, knight of valor, the handpicked chosen of The*
Twelve.♥

Draven shook his head, denying the voice. Pinpricks of lights danced before him and the room spun. Vistan's thin, poxy face swam before him. Draven couldn't tell what was real and what was some maddened fever dream.

"Is this a joke?" Vistan glared at him, hands flat on the table. A sour smirk turned his mouth downward.

"What? A gold buckle, a ruby brooch. That's a hundred crowns or I'm a pauper."

"A prisoner you'll be, then. These are from the temple. I've seen them myself on Nerys' statue." Vistan flicked a finger at the brooch as if afraid to touch it.

"So?" Draven tossed his hair back, trying to ignore the numbness in his hand and the lead weight of the cuff. He wondered if he'd ever be able to lift his arm again.

The voice echoed laughter in his mind.

♥*You cannot encompass the weight you now bear... but you will.*♥

"It will be ages before I can move these. A fortnight, at least. Even my contacts won't touch them." Sweat beaded the brow of the fence, and his hands shook. His eyes darted back and forth between Draven and the jewelry before him, as if he couldn't decide which scared him more.

Draven knew exactly how he felt.

Vistan blew out a breath between pursed lips. "Let me look closer." Out came a round glass set in a round wooden frame and the fence peered at the golden buckle. Then came a file that he rasped along an edge. Vistan gave the brooch a similar appraisal and placed both pieces carefully back on the table. "Fifty silver."

Draven relaxed, knowing Vistan was finally ready to deal.

They haggled, and haggled more. Draven found himself haunted by visions of him dancing at the end of a noose, or even worse, handless, begging in the streets with only stumps for arms and legs. His pulse pounded in his throat. Sweat stood out on his palms. He wiped it away, but it returned as he dickered with Vistan.

♥ *Destiny is calling and you dither over coins.* ♥

The voice ticked away in his head, a constant drip.

My only destiny is a fast boat and a new city. Pain ran up his arm. His joints ached.

Vistan proclaimed the deal done as he poured silver and a few gold pieces into a bag and slammed it down on the table.

"Nice doing business with you, lad. Never come back."

Draven nodded and turned to leave, grabbing a silk robe to throw over his leathers. He waved a hand at Vistan, the strange cuff catching the light, and Draven tossed a coin over his shoulder, chuckling. He couldn't tell if it was born of humor or madness.

The knight's voice remained silent.

7

Discovery

THE SMELL OF FRESH baked bread warred with the heady scent of exotic spices. White puffy clouds rolled overhead, breaking up a crystal blue sky, while white and gray shop faces gleamed in the light, polished to a reflective sheen. Well-dressed patrons idled by perusing dazzling fabrics or lighting upon exclusive eateries. Draven had done well here.

Nothing like the bazaar. The markets of Sharazin offered anything and everything, and it was his for the taking. It made for a thief's paradise.

He smoothed out his silk tunic, which he had thrown over his leathers and cinched at the waist with an elaborate belt embossed with dragons and griffins. A breeze whispered through the street. Draven chuckled to himself, feeling like an impostor in the opulent surroundings. If discovered, he would face a stern fine and at least a night in the Magistrate's jails, but he never was. He excelled at going among the wealthy undetected.

Draven slipped into a restaurant dedicated to the sumptuous food of the East. Sharp and tangy spices assaulted his nostrils as he entered. He walked straight to a table facing the window as if he owned the place. He stood before the table and beckoned to the perturbed servers. His mouth turned down in displeasure.

"This table is filthy. Have it cleaned, and the chair, too." He gestured to his tunic. "This is silk." It never failed to astonish him that acting like an ass was always the perfect disguise.

♥*It's not an act. How could Heart Master have bonded to a common thief?*♥

Draven ignored the voice, wondering what Heart Master might be. The cuff? Was it alive somehow? And why was it haunted by a self-righteous knight? He yanked the sleeve of his robe down.

Within moments, a pair of servants scurried over, cleaning the table, chairs, and even giving his tunic a good brushing. It took all Draven's willpower to resist breaking into a smile. He waved them away, gathering up the base of his garment as he seated himself at the now immaculate table. He slapped coins on the table and ordered.

Just watch the gold. He needed to do some reconnaissance. According to that silly girl Maren, they were looking for a gang. He should be safe.

Should be.

♥ *Whether by the hand of man or goddess, you will pay for your travesty.* ♥

Draven snickered.

"Will sir be eating?" A trim, neatly attired young man stood waiting for his reply.

Draven nodded in assent and ordered pastries stuffed with tangy fruits. He stared out the window, glimpsing a troop of soldiers wandering by with a member of the clergy in tow. They stopped people on the street, interrogating them. He gulped. If people in this quarter were being so roughly treated, then the search for him was serious indeed. Draven's expression soured even as a plate appeared on the table as if by magic. His appetite left him as his stomach knotted. He took a sip of wine, eyes riveted on the scene outside.

Draven's head ratcheted at the click of the door opening. In strode a tall, thickly built captain of the guard, followed by a weasel-faced priest. He cast a quick glance over at the pair, and his blood froze. Unless his wits had totally abandoned him, it was the same cleric he'd punched last night. Draven took great interest in his food, stealing the occasional glance to determine if the priest recognized him.

♥ *The will of the goddess will not be denied.* ♥

The pair talked to patrons as they passed tables and beckoned to a server. A clipped conversation ensued that Draven couldn't make out. Draven leaned in to catch a few words, craning his neck as far as he dared.

The guardsman did all the talking in hushed whispers, with the priest nodding. When the clergyman turned, Draven could see the ugly bruise on one side of his mostly bald head. That was him, all right.

He hunched over his meal, dissecting the pastry with the meticulous nature of a surgeon. He flagged down a server as an excuse to turn his back on the pair. Still, he tracked their progress.

♥*You should join them, not flee, craven one. If the relic has awakened, a great evil has arisen.*♥

Draven ignored the barb, biting his lip, and called for another cup of wine. A thin trickle of perspiration wound its way down his temple. He cupped his forehead in his palm, shoving bits of pastry around his plate while his mind raced.

A hand settled on his shoulder. Stifling every natural urge to tense up, Draven half-turned without looking up. As if by magic, the sleeve of his robe slipped down, revealing the cursed cuff.

"Pardon, sir. We will ask you questions about the robbery in the temple of Nerys."

Draven gazed up at them through slitted eyes, trying not to make eye contact. He shook his head but deigned not to reply.

"This is a waste of time. We will not find bandits in a market, Captain." The priest fumed while fidgeting with the edge of his sleeve, looking everywhere but at Draven.

For once, the gods are smiling upon me.

♥*I doubt that.*♥

The cuff heated his arm. Draven clamped a hand over the metal to stifle its pulse and sighed. "This is highly irregular. Can a man not dine in peace?"

The captain muttered apologies to Draven and turned to the priest. "This is High Dremsa Blus. He is assisting with our inquiries into a theft at the temple of Nerys."

"Heathens," Draven swore aloud. "Is there no sanctity in our city?" He took a quick glance at the men, but they didn't notice him.

"Were you, or any of your household, about last eve? There was purported to be a band of six." The captain removed his hand from Draven's shoulder and tucked a thumb into his wide leather belt.

"I was abed. I can't say for my staff, but I will interrogate them when I return. You never know what servants get up to while a man's sleeping." He couldn't resist raising his face to the captain with an expression of mock outrage.

His gaze locked with the priest. An eon passed between them in that uncertain moment. The priest's face reddened before freezing in place. The captain turned to the priest. His mouth opened to ask a question when Draven slammed a plate into it, spattering the guard with the remains of his dessert. Blood or jam dribbled down the guard's face.

The captain wasted no time in going for his sword.

Draven followed up by slamming the brass goblet he'd been drinking from into the man's chin, splattering them both with wine. *Damn. That was a nice robe.*

The captain went to one knee. The priest grabbed Draven by the arm. Bewilderment lit the man's face as if he did not understand what to do with this advantage. Draven suffered from no such dilemma. He forced his arm downward, using leverage to bring the man into a crouch. Draven's knee came up into the priest's jaw, dropping him to the ground. He almost felt bad knocking him out twice in two days.

♥*How dare you strike a priest?*♥

The guard captain shook his head and rose. His broadsword, jerked out of its scabbard, wavered before the thief, while his other hand found the table to steady himself.

This was too easy. Draven brought the heavy wooden chair down onto the captain.

The chair crashed into the captain's sword arm, driving the blade back against his throat. Blood ran, staining his tunic scarlet as he fell motionless. Panic surged from Draven's stomach as he bent over to make sure the man still lived. The guard still breathed, and the gash wasn't deep.

It'll scar, but he'll be able to brag that he almost nicked Draven, the Master Thief. He chuckled to himself and turned to regard the patrons. At the end of his arm, the cuff thrummed, and he saw it glow.

Pity it doesn't have any powers. You'd think it should be good for something. Damned magic is never good for aught but ill.

♥*As if I'd let refuse such as you command Heart Master.*♥

Draven smiled, addressing the captain and the gawking patrons. "He's fine. I'd love to stay and rob you all, but it looks as if I have other matters to attend to."

A woman screamed. Then a whole chorus of voices arose, calling for more guards. Damn, rich people were touchy.

He vaulted over a table where a pair of diners shrank back and sprinted for the stairs. He plowed over someone in his haste. This time it was a dowdy serving woman carrying a stack of plates. He could still hear the crash of breaking dishes when he found an open window and shot through it. He grabbed a cornice as he went and hoisted himself up handhold by handhold to the relative safety of the roofs.

He turned to look down. Nearly everyone on the street stopped to stare and point in his direction. The troop of guards assembled in loose knots, muttering to themselves and barking orders.

At least they don't have bows. He turned and ran. His legs pumped with the vigor of youth, propelling him along the clay tiles. He angled his way away from the merchant quarter, jumping from roof to roof.

Time to lose myself in the thieves' quarter. Surely not everyone wants to kill me.

8

GOD-MARKED

IN THE HIGH, WIND-SWEPT mountains of his birth, Kell awoke in his cave, startled, heart pounding. Sweat plastered his pale blond hair to his scalp as he gasped for breath. It came to him in uneven gulps, and his chest burned as if scalded. Grunting with the effort, he threw off his furs and sat up, putting a muscled hand to his chest to check for a wound.

Nothing. His skin was clammy, though, and inside he still ached.

The light of morning outside cast feeble rays through the hide-covered entrance. Dust motes drifted in the air like dancing stars. He propped his broad back against the cool, uneven rock of the cave wall as his breathing returned to normal, and the pain diminished. He would have to see the healer. Something wasn't right. Perhaps the mountain god was speaking to him; perhaps he had angered Regnir somehow.

Last spring Garmak had talked of a burning in his skin that would not abate. Fire raged within the warrior; eventually he had gone mad and fled. He took nothing with him, raving all the while that Regnir called him to a great destiny. The next season, on a raid beyond the far hills, Kell spied his furs among a pile of carrion. He would never forget Garmak's blackened bones crawling with vermin.

"Regnir, spare me," he prayed to the mountain god. "Let my time come in the heat of battle with my blood hot and my mind clear."

He pulled on breeches and coarse leather boots. His fingers moved with dexterity while his mind careened through possibilities. He toweled the sweat from his chest and donned a plain shirt. He left his weapon harness next to his sleeping pallet.

Kell moved with slow deliberation. At his throat dangled a hawk pendant. Every warrior chose a totem with their first kill. The thrumming in his chest increased, but now it was not with pain—it was with need. Rather than crippling him as before, it filled him with a sense of the righteous mountain god.

"I pray Martok can sort this out." He thrust the crude covering aside and stepped into the light of morning. Rocky peaks rose around him as the path sloped down. Hazy gray clouds obscured the sun. Down the slight incline to the village proper, women and a few men went about the mundane chores of the Vale Stone tribe: cooking, drying, weaving, tanning.

He ran a hand through his hair, mindful of his footing on the slight rise to his cave. Leather lean-tos provided shelter to keep the sun from the workers who made and repaired the goods necessary for the tribe's welfare.

He followed the loose scree down, avoiding the main encampment, and climbed a winding path that led to the cave of the medicine man. It wasn't a visit he was looking forward to.

Martok delved deep into the mysteries of the gods. Every ear bent to his words. One omen from him could make or break a man's standing—and Kell had never been in Martok's favor.

"Damn it." His steady stride carried him higher up the path, and the dwelling of Martok came into view. It was a spacious cavern with a wide opening, and it stretched back three or four times as far as his own.

The only one who held greater standing was the chieftain, and even she gave deference to the gods and, by extension, Martok. A wooden overhang had been erected before the cave to give shelter for two rough-hewn tables on which fetishes and powders were scattered. Kell dawdled, fingering the bits of bone and feather as he worked up his courage.

What if he had some sickness? Would he wither and die? Go mad like Garmak? He sighed, eased around the table, and strode into the cave. To his surprise, the old snake was nowhere in sight. Torches burned in brass sconces, sending oily smoke into the high roof of the cave. Trophies and religious trappings of all sorts hung on the walls. Some were from the tribe, others plundered from raids.

The shining silver starburst of Velleris sat next to the triangular icon of Ghedryn the Conqueror. Thick furs and rough wool blankets covered the dirt floor.

A girl with hair even lighter than Kell's worked a mortar and pestle. He turned to leave, but a sudden pain welled up in his chest, dropping him to his knees. The girl looked up from her work, a note of concern creasing her smooth features. She set down the mortar and rushed around the table to help him to a stone bench.

"Easy, warrior. What ails the pebble who would be a boulder?"

"I am—" He stopped, then started again. "I don't know. There is pain, first like an avalanche, then sometimes just a thrum in my chest. I.. I feel a pull. Words are meaningless."

The girl regarded him without skepticism.

"This could be many things. Could be heart-sickness. Do you cough? Spit blood? Lose teeth?"

Kell shook his head. "I need the magic man. Wait. I know you, don't I? You are Neelah."

"Almost right. Nala. I am apprenticed to Martok. He's away on an errand to Regnir."

"More likely sleeping off too much wine where no one can see."

She looked at him with a level gaze that left him feeling like a hunted animal.

"Let's see what troubles you. I'm not without my own gifts." She pushed him back, her hand hot against the skin of his chest. "This brand? I don't recall seeing it before. How long have you born it?"

He told her he had naught but a few scars. Looking down, he saw his chest now sported a circle with flames radiating out. Red inflamed edges surrounded white puckered lines. He jumped up in shock, shoving Nala to the ground, ignoring her outcry.

"By the gods, what is this?" He touched the marks, expecting pain, but felt only a mild warmth where the lines marred his otherwise smooth skin.

"Keep that foolishness up, and you'll find a curse rather than a cure, you big lout."

He murmured a brief apology and helped her up to sit on the bench. He joined her there, rubbing his chest.

"I've never seen this before. Not even Garmak had these scars. Am I cursed?"

She laughed as if he had told a grand joke. "If I suspect aright, you are more than blessed. May I?" she asked, and he nodded his assent even though fear wriggled like a worm in his stomach.

She laid a hand on his chest, and her fingers glowed, illuminating the cave. Something in his chest throbbed in answer. He squirmed away, but her other hand clamped to his shoulder and the strength drained out of him. Nala pushed into his chest, and pain lanced all the way to his spine. Still, a peace came with it that lulled him like a cup of warm mead on a cold night.

Images filled his mind. Skulls floated on the wind. A titan of a man astride a huge stallion. Then a dark-haired woman in shining armor; and a wiry man whose arm glittered. Armor gleaming too brightly not to be of the gods, a bracer of iron inlaid with silver, a gold shield, a blade of blood, and a dull brass gauntlet.

She released him. "You aren't cursed, but you might wish you were when it's done." She gave him a grim smile.

"Am I—am I god-touched?" he asked, trying to keep the fear out of his voice.

"Not exactly. Not how you think. You will not go mad."

"Then what?"

"You have been called to the service of Regnir."

"Regnir?"

She nodded in assent, her expression serious. "Tell no one but Kaissa. This is between you and your god."

"But why? Is this not cause for celebration? I am called." Suddenly, he felt jubilant: of all the men and women of the tribe, he was summoned. "There should be a feast. And an offer of others to join me in my quest. It will be glorious."

"Martok is mad and jealous. He's more likely to damn you. Seek counsel only from those you trust. If Regnir meant for you to lead men, he would have told you. Seek out the chieftain immediately. At the very least, she needs to know she's losing one of her best warriors."

"Destiny." He spat at the ground, expressing his opinion of fate, his dream of leading warriors of the tribe falling to ashes.

"Try to ignore it, but the gods will not. Regnir may even punish us if you reject him." Nala raised her eyebrows at him.

This gave Kell pause. His brow furrowed as he considered her words. He rose and turned to go just as the magic man appeared at the head of the cave.

"What's all this?" he croaked, a slight stumble to his gait. "You need healing? Come back later." Even from several feet away, Kell could smell sour spirits on the man's breath.

"Nay, he drank too much last night. I gave him some of your powders. He will be well." Nala glanced a silent warning to Kell.

The old man grunted and shuffled to the rear of the cave. Kell left without another word.

He had much to ponder.

9

REFUSING DESTINY

T HE WEIGHT ON KELL'S shoulders overwhelmed him. The god-mark twisted a burning knife in his chest. His shirt hid the raised wheals, but the material chafed against the fresh scars.

From the healer's cave, he strolled to the center of the village, loose rocks crunching under his feet. People of the tribe passed on either side of him as the village sprang to life.

Old women with gap-toothed grins wove fabric while men fletched arrows, sharpened spears, and tanned leather. He sidestepped a group of youngsters enacting a daring battle with sticks for swords. Despite his grim mood, he smiled at their antics.

The echo in his chest throbbed its own heartbeat. Kell's joy at being chosen turned to melancholy as he realized the mark would tear him away from his people. He stalked past his own dwelling and wound his way toward the sparring rings. He needed something to hit, to attack—anything to quell his fear.

A few warriors exercised there, honing their skills for the next raid. That would do.

He shouldered a young man out of the way, selected a blunted sword, and proceeded over to one of the wooden dummies erected to perfect slashing techniques. Kell imagined Regnir's craggy face at the center of the oblong, wooden log sticking out of the ground that was nearly as tall as him. He tested the weight of the blade, giving it a few practice swings first to get his timing, then brought his sword into contact with the hardwood, chipped from hundreds of blades.

The hollow thunk did little to ease his mood even as the shiver of the impact ran up his arm. He shifted his stance and hit it again. A wood chip flew from the wooden post to land at his feet, along with countless others from previous sessions. A bit of yellow wood now peeked through, and for some reason, that angered Kell more.

He attacked that spot, widening it, until his blade flew faster than his eye could follow, sending great chunks almost the size of his fist from the target. Perspiration beaded his forehead and sweat ran down his back, plastering his shirt to his skin.

His fury only grew with each strike of his sword on the inert log. Whispers sprang up behind him, wondering at his behavior. Kell rarely spent much time here, preferring instead to hunt or help the artisans when not out raiding with the other warriors. He believed learning as much as he could was paramount to becoming a good leader. How else could he hope to understand the people he would one day rule?

A pang ran through his chest: his future was being stolen from him by a spiteful god seeking to derail his dreams for some probably pointless battle in a foreign land.

An errant chip of wood flew, hitting his face and leaving a slight cut. This finally broke Kell from his battle reverie, and he dropped his sword, panting. He leaned against the now nearly ruined sparring post and sucked in great gulps of air. He heard laughter from behind, and the anger crept back into him, this time from shame.

To his surprise, the others in the training area had tripled in size and now included artisans and workers as well. Sagat, a burly warrior ten years Kell's senior, strode out from the throng with a sour expression on his bearded face. A scar crept down from his forehead, giving the veteran a perpetual leer.

"Would you have words with me, Sagat?" Kell rubbed at his chest, his breathing easing back into a normal rhythm. The mark now throbbed so hard that it was difficult to stand.

To the hells with the god and his damned mark.

"It seems you lack the capacity for words, Kell, only chopping away at a target that can't fight back. You've all but ruined that dummy. Another will need to be cut and sunk. How about you try a target that can hit back?" The older man scratched at his patchy beard, eying Kell up and down like a recalcitrant child.

Without another word, Kell launched himself at Sagat like a bolt from a crossbow. His shoulder collided with the other man's midsection. To his credit, Sagat only gave a few inches, wrapping beefy arms around Kell's middle as the man attempted to throw him off. Every muscle in his body tensed against the bigger warrior as Kell kicked his legs out, dropping his center of gravity.

Sagat grunted, tightening his grip on Kell's body to drive the breath from him. Kell gritted his teeth, coiling his legs and arched his back, pulling Sagat up and over him. Kell was rewarded by a grunt as they crashed to the ground in a cloud of dust, with Sagat bearing the force of the impact. The younger man refused to give up his advantage, ratcheting blows with his elbow into the soft midsection of his opponent.

Sagat gave another massive grunt and wrenched Kell around, driving his face into the dirt. Kell exhaled, blowing little plumes of dust out and tasting dirt on his tongue. Sagat released his grip, so he could drive his fist into Kell's ribs.

They grappled back and forth, trading blows, neither really gaining any advantage but taking enough punishment to remind them they truly lived. Sagat finally got both feet against Kell's chest and sent him sailing across the ring. Kell landed heavily and rolled to his feet. His body ached from dozens of scratches. Sagat lumbered to his feet, a little slower than Kell, sucking in air like a worn-out bellows.

Kell prepared to launch himself at Sagat again, but noticed that they'd amassed even more onlookers, some of whom were taking odds on the winner. He also noticed Sagat didn't look at him so much as past him, though he didn't dare take his eyes off his opponent.

"This isn't over, Sagat." Kell rubbed at his chest where the god mark hammered at him.

"I wager it might be." Sagat rubbed his jaw where Kell had ground it into the dirt. "You have an appointment with a higher power." He turned his back to Kell and lumbered off amidst grumbling complaints from those who had wagered on the fight.

Kell turned to see Kaissa, garbed in doeskin boots, a leather girdle, and a simple shirt of coarse wool, his chieftain somehow looming over him despite their difference in height. A single gold hoop dangled from her nose and her red braids fell past her shoulders. Her face was unreadable. With a toss of her head, she indicated Kell should follow her.

His head full of cotton and his heart beating at the god's message, Kell followed. A reckoning approached, and he could guess what form it would take. She gave favor to none, imposing a rigid yet fair discipline. To his surprise, she didn't lead him back to the central cavern where she normally ruled over disputes.

Kell kept his lips sealed, regretting the decision to leave his weapons back in the cave. Kaissa wore a longsword across her back and her infamous curved daggers at her waist.

They wound their way away from the camp until it took all Kell's strength just to keep up as they climbed over the loose scree. Kaissa showed no hint she found the going difficult. But then, she wouldn't. She was the chieftain. She had to be perfect in every way.

They ascended until the valley shrank beneath them. When they reached a wide ledge overlooking their home, she stopped and turned. Her gaze was hard and made his guts shrivel.

He tried to return her look with steel. Kaissa's face showed no sign he was succeeding. She resembled the grim gray stone that rose above them on the right and fell away to their left in deep chasms.

Wind roared down from the mountain top, whipping his blond hair into his face. Kell tried to show no fear. Regnir's call pounded in his chest, thunder only he could hear. He stood rock-still, even when Kaissa whipped the longsword from her back and threw it in his direction. It clattered to the rocky soil just inches from his boots.

Kell made no move to pick it up: he knew this was a test.

Then she drew her long daggers and rushed at him with a blood-curdling scream. He braced himself, but didn't leap for the sword. He prayed to Regnir; he correctly guessed her intent. Kaissa stopped a hair's breadth from plunging a dagger into his chest. Instead, she used the tip of her blade to score his shirt till the mark of Regnir became visible. How had she known? Nala? Or did she truly see all that transpired in her tribe?

"Well, at least you're not a complete fool. What did you think you were doing in the sparring ring with that muscle-bound oaf?"

"There is a weight on my heart I can't bear. It calls me to leave."

"We answer the call. That is our way. Whatever it may entail." Her gaze weighed on him.

"I fear if my feet leave the valley, they'll never return." He bit his lip when his words ran out. He hadn't meant to give away even that much.

"And what would guide those steps, warrior?"

Kell didn't answer, only bowed his head.

Kaissa rocked him with a blow to the side of his head that caused Kell's head to snap around. He staggered back a step and glowered at her.

"Fine, damn it! I've been called by Regnir!" He spat the words like a foul-tasting poison.

"Explain." She crossed her arms over her chest with an eyebrow raised. He was certain she needed nothing explained. Somehow, she knew.

"I awoke to this." He pulled the shirt up to display the sunburst of scar tissue. "A pounding in my chest pulls me. I saw Nala, and she claims it is a call to the god. She said I must follow it wherever it leads me."

"Yet you do not leave. Instead, you rage like a toddler." She ran her finger over the curious marking. "What do you think?"

"I think it is otherworldly."

"So, you threw a tantrum?" She flipped her hand up to his chin as if inspecting a piece of meat.

"My life is here. My world is here. I don't give a damn about the gods."

Her hand delivered another a jarring blow to the side of his face.

"I've drawn and quartered men for less, boy." She turned her back on him and walked to the lip of the cliff. "Do you see that mountain in the distance, the one that smokes and steams?"

Kell nodded.

"Regnir is the god of emotion. The last time one of us disappointed him, his ire caused fire to belch from the earth." Kaissa pointed to the mountain in question.

"That's a legend." If the elders were to be believed, Regnir's outbursts had formed the mountains out of shapeless dust eons ago. Any who attempted to take up residence near that smoking peak died, and no plants or trees grew at its base.

"Many legends are born from truth."

Kell shook his head. "Yet I fear if I leave our cliffs, I'll never return."

"So?"

"So? I don't wish to die in a far-off land for a god that treats me like a game piece!"

"We are all game pieces of the gods. You are Regnir's—and you are mine. Everyone belongs to someone."

"You think I should leave the tribe? Never return?" Kell couldn't hide the riot of emotions on his face.

"If you don't, I have to throw you off this cliff. Take your choice, cub." As his pleading eyes looked on, the set of her shoulders slackened and she turned to face him. Her voice softened for a moment. "I don't want to lose one of my best warriors.—but when the gods speak, we listen."

"But—"

She silenced him with a look.

"The world is immense. This is only one insignificant piece of it. Your destiny lies beyond these peaks." She looked almost envious for a moment, resting her hands on his shoulders.

"That's your last word?"

"Unless you wish to learn the art of flight." She smiled, but there was no dismissing her meaning.

He swallowed hard. "Regnir willing, I'll make our clan proud." He picked up the longsword and handed it back to its owner, bowing his head as he did so. She nodded as he turned away from the mountainous peaks that towered over her. She stood as impassive as the stone itself.

"Don't despair, warrior. I don't send you alone." She waved her hand, and Kell half expected the Mountain-Father to appear riding a thunderbolt.

Instead, Nala came up the path, lugging two packs behind her. Kell recognized his ax protruding from one of them.

"She has done nothing wrong!"

She grinned. "Always looking for a sword to fall on? I'm not punishing her. She told me of your calling. Nala has learned all she can from Martok, and asked some time ago if she could study in Merrakka before replacing him. Her experience will guide you on your path. You are to respect her. Nala, you have my leave to dump him in a gully if he does not." Nala grinned at them both, and Kell laughed despite himself.

"Now, on your way. I've better things to do than play wet-nurse to the god-touched. Our god has chosen you. Act like it."

Kell took his pack from Nala and slung it over his shoulder. He took one last look at the mountains and his impassive chieftain. He picked up a stone the size of his fist and rolled it over in his hand, then walked away. Nala fell into step beside him.

10

YOUR TIME HAS COME

A WARM GLOW RADIATED through the stained-glass window that depicted Velleris, the Goddess of Justice. Dust motes drifted in the sunlight, falling across Helena's face. Eyes closed, she embraced the stillness of the small chapel and the peace it brought her. The outside world ceased to exist. No time, no violence, no killing. In this one place, war could not find her. She committed herself body, mind, and soul to the Goddess. Her mind unwound while her heartbeat slowed.

She sensed her time grew short. Soon she must fulfill her purpose as a knight of Velleris. It both excited and terrified her beyond rational thought.

Helena opened her eyes. A familiar heat blossomed behind her, while before her stood a statue of the goddess, sword in one hand, shield in the other. Chiseled stone reflected the peace of the divine, poised to dole out bloody justice. The heat grew in intensity until a bonfire raged at her back. Helena rose and turned to behold her goddess.

Helena fell to her knees as her eyes fell on the radiant figure swathed in layers of different colored light. Her face pressed into the floor of the temple. The coarse stone dug into the tender skin of her forehead as her plain cotton robe spilled all around her. A braid of dark red hair fell to one side. A single delicate finger caressed her head, then lifted Helena into the air. Her whole being lightened. Helena's mind reeled, and every care fell away.

"You are called, my child. I require your strength of arms." A slight grin illuminated the face of the goddess.

"I am yours, Velleris. Where you point, I will strike." She clutched the plain iron star with the eyes of the goddess dangling from her neck. She clenched her fist till the points dug into her palm, drawing blood and allowing her thoughts to focus.

"Your piety is duly noted. One thing I have never faulted you for is your faith." The goddess's body sparkled in a kaleidoscope of colors as the two drifted in the air.

The rough white robe fluttered around Helena. Her stomach churned, unaccustomed to dangling in open space.

"Thank you, my lady." Helena breathed out a pent-up sigh, casting her eyes downward. It pained her to look at Velleris when the goddess shone so brightly. Velleris faded out of sight altogether, only to return an instant later.

Helena parted her lips, eager to ask a dozen questions.

"You do not have to inquire, child. It is time for you to depart." Velleris favored her with a knowing smile that caused the young woman to blush.

"I am ready. I will not disappoint you. Your enemies will feel the bite of my mace." Helena bit out every word of her oath.

"The time for combat is not quite nigh, but it will be soon. Ghedryn, God of Conquest, has blessed a cursed Mektwin with a holy relic and given him an army. You will locate him, recover the relic, and kill him. Put the Mektwin under the ground where he belongs. He is called Seguris."

"As you command, Goddess." Rage at the ancient enemy of Velleris surged in her.

"But beware: it is no ordinary relic. Seguris bears The Fist."

"The Fist of Heaven?"

"Verily, created by Ghedryn. It conveys enormous power. And he shall seek Blood Thorn, the cursed blade forged by my brother Regnir to be used with the gauntlet. Combined, the two relics are unbeatable. You cannot allow this to come to pass. Mind you also, Blood Thorn feeds on anger. Its power is compelling but dangerous."

Helena nodded, committing this all to memory, wondering at her own battles with the rage that she endured daily.

"If you can, find Heart Master. Prior to the rise of the Mektwin dynasty, all twelve gods forged it. Its power is unsurpassed if used by the faithful. But, again, beware: its power is guarded by the soul of its first wielder, one of the legendary knights of valor."

"Where may I find the relic?"

"Its location is unknown even to me, but the priest who bound Ansalon to Heart Master may know. Kethek moves constantly, but he currently resides near the coastal city of Risell. Make him your priority."

"I will see to it, Velleris." Helena's mind already turned, planning routes, and devising strategies.

"I am not without resources, however. This is Hallowed Verity." A teardrop-shaped shield appeared from the ether before Helena and hovered in the air. The face of the shield depicted a mammoth tower in gold and silver with rose blooms from base to parapet. It slowly sank to the floor of the chapel, gleaming in the rays of light streaming in through the stained glass. "It will protect those balanced in mind, spirit, and body. It will serve you in your mission."

"I cannot express how you have honored me, goddess." Tears gathered at the corners of Helena's eyes, but she held them back. "I will leave at once."

"Proceed alone, my child. You must move with haste if you are to overtake Seguris and locate Heart Master. These battles will be decided between champions, not armies."

"I agree. The faithful will rise when the time is nigh. I know it." She bobbed her head in religious fervor.

"Now, child, you will come across followers of other gods. You may work with them, but do not stray from the path of law. They lack your faith. Use your own judgment whether they may serve your cause or hinder it."

"Yes, my goddess." She swallowed again, knowing her faith might face its ultimate test in the execution of this task. "One thing, how do I invoke the magic of the shield?"

Velleris frowned. "Each object behaves differently with each champion. In the past, they have evoked Hallowed Verity through absolute stillness. I hope this does not prove a challenge for you. Your anger has always been a blessing and bane. Relics respond to temperament as much as alignment. Rein in your anger and it should protect you from any evil."

Helena bit back an angry retort, knowing it would only add credence to Velleris's words.

"May you say where Seguris will seek Blood Thorn?" Helena wondered how the legendary sword could work in tandem with her shield, then chided herself for greedy thoughts.

"Blood Thorn will be found at the Tower of the White Rose."

"And where is this tower?" Helena's own boldness shocked her, but she did not know if Velleris would come to her again before she faced Seguris. *Get all the details you can before she disappears.*

"Some things you must learn for yourself. I will not spoon feed you. Kethek should know how to find the Tower of the White Rose. He designed its construction to guard secrets not meant for mortal eyes."

Helena bit her lip, wondering what secrets those might be, but she dared not ask. Velleris was known for her temper as much as her largess. "I will not fail you."

Velleris exploded from view, and Helena dropped to the floor. A knot settled between her shoulders as she straightened. She stood slowly, tugging at her braid, looking around at the stone walls and stained glass. These low wooden benches had known the weight of hundreds, perhaps thousands, of the faithful. Dread tingled along her spine that she would never see them again.

Finally, she scooped up the shield and ran a hand over its scalloped top edge and down the embossed front. The craftsmanship was divine. She rapped it with her knuckles, but no sound returned. The metal offered no hint of its power. Helena took the straps, hoping to feel the divine power flow through her, but was again disappointed.

For all its beauty, Hallowed Verity appeared no more magical than any other shield.

I can see this will take some effort. Something to meditate on… but all things come to the faithful in time.

Shoulders squared and jaw set, she turned and strode away from the icon of Velleris.

I am chosen. This is my destiny. The Bright Lady will not desert me.

She prayed reality would echo her hopes.

11

FLIGHT

Draven moved with a slight rustle of canvas and leather. He'd lost count of how many days had passed since his botched robbery of the temple. A week perhaps, no more than two. His arm ached from the steady pulse of the cuff digging into his skin. No matter how hard he tried, he could not wrest it from his arm.

Then there was the voice. That constant, self-righteous, nattering voice belonging to someone named Ansalon, incessantly chattering about Heart Master.

His hope of eluding pursuit until the clamor abated was short-lived. The longer this went on, the more people waited in line for his head. Proclamations for his arrest were posted in every market and tavern where he sought refuge. The church hunted him. The city guards hunted him. Even his own guild had joined the chase.

Heavy footfalls suddenly echoed behind him, followed by the thrum of bowstrings and the whistle of bolts. Angry murmurs arose from the merchant quarter of Sharazin.

"There! He's there!"

"Crossbows!" another voice called, disturbing the stillness of the dark streets.

Draven tossed back the hood of his heavy cloak. Days of stubble at the start of this mess had matured into a full beard.

The time for stealth had passed. He lengthened his stride and ran, hoping their aim would be poor in the dim light. Crossbow bolts clattered against the stone walls. Nerys continued to both punish and favor him.

More footfalls suggested more pursuers, followed by still more shouting. He stopped for a moment to listen, praying the commotion aroused the guard. He was rewarded by the ring of steel on steel. Well, at least they still hated each other. The gray walls of a residence rose beside him, balconies of wood and stone jutting out every ten feet above the pitted granite. It was perfect for his needs.

He withdrew his climbing tools from within his jerkin and sprang, snagging the hooked metal claws into the soft mortar between the stones and hoisting himself up the walls. Well-trained muscles responded, as he drew himself up higher and higher. Not wanting to risk awakening the residents, he worked himself up to the next ledge when he heard a familiar whistle, followed by pain in his lower back.

The breath exploded from his lungs, and he nearly fell. Dangling from one hand, he reached around and wrenched the bolt out. It had barely penetrated, but it was enough to send fire racing through his torso. He blessed the thick cloak and jerkin that had saved his life.

More projectiles whistled in the darkness. He spared no time in leaping again, biting his lip against the pain, climbing for his very life. Barbed shafts continued to thud all around him. Crossbow bolts clattered against the pitted stone or sunk into weathered wood. Draven climbed. Hand over hand he went, making his way to the rooftop with less than his usual dexterity. He spared himself just a moment to catch his breath from the hurried climb before rising on unsteady legs to survey the pitched roof of scalloped reddish clay tiles. It wouldn't be an easy run, but he thought it would take a few minutes before his pursuers could gain the roofs.

And here Draven was king.

♥*A staunch champion would never run from a fight with mere footpads.*♥

"I never claimed to be a champion. More of a chump, if I'm honest. Give me a magic shield or wings and we'll discuss it." His own voice sounded alien to him after so many days of silence.

♥*I will never allow you to command Heart Master's power.*♥

Draven dismissed the voice as he began to move, running for his life and pushing away the madness assailing him. His soft-soled boots made no sound as he raced along the uneven surface. A scarlet bolt of light flashed across the sky, and he flattened to the clay. His breath came in quick gasps. Draven clung to the pitched edge of the roof, mind racing and back aching from the crossbow bolt. Sticky warmth trickled down his side.

Quiet descended, and he rose, quiet as death. He wrapped his thick cloak about him to ward off of the chill. The rooftops offered a measure of safety, but he couldn't remain here forever. The nights grew chilly, and another night spent sleeping on rain-slick roof tiles might be the death of him.

He lit off at a sprint again, leaping from building to building with a grace born of long practice despite his wound. He couldn't help wondering why his robbery at the temple had caused such outrage. The gems weren't even real.

And if the voice in my head is to be believed, no one even knew about this cuff.

Yet clearly Draven had burned too many bridges. No one would risk the wrath of the guard or the church, much less the assassins of the thieves' guild, to help him. The slanted roofs of the merchant quarter fell away as he moved into the poorer section of the city. The buildings here were lower, of squat design, with roofs less friendly to footpads. Broken glass and crude spikes littered the flat stone to dissuade the criminal element.

He stopped on the roof of a deserted building and picked his way carefully across the hazardous surface until he was on a side bordering an unlit alley. A flick of his wrist dropped a three-pronged, spiked device into his hands, perfect for digging into the soft stone or old wood.

Draven flipped himself over the lip of the roof, avoiding the jutting wooden spikes meant to skewer travelers such as himself. He worked his way down the wall in complete darkness until he came to an open window. In he slithered, seeking a dark corner to weather the night.

No light greeted his questing eyes, but the room reeked of urine and offal. He took a moment to listen. Absolute stillness. For now, he should remain safe from detection. At least until dawn came, and this cat-and-mouse game started anew.

His wondrous satchel provided a short, thin taper, which Draven lit with a tinder on a wax cord. By the thin, guttering flame, he located some foul-smelling burlap which he stretched across the opening he came through. He secured it with a few throwing spikes.

Draven probed the inside of his jerkin, and his hand came away sticky with blood. The wound wasn't deep, but it would require attention soon. Out of the pack came a length of cloth that would serve as a bandage. He wadded it up and shoved it against the wound to stem the flow.

The fetid odor of despair wafted up to his nostrils. He took a moment to gaze around his sanctuary. There were heaps of rags, stacks of broken furniture, and decaying food. Bones littered the corners. Even rats avoided these haunts because the lost souls who frequented them were not choosy about what served for food. He tied a sash across his face to block the stench. Shoving as much of the filth out of the corner as he could, he relaxed for the first time in days.

♥*How long?*♥

"What?" Draven shook himself awake, but realized it was just the knight again.

♥*How long have I slept? How long since the dragons burned Coriolis?*♥

"If you won't help me, why should I tell you anything?"

Fire raced up his arm, and the damned cuff flared with blinding blue light.

"All right, all right. How would I know? It's just a story. Probably more than a few generations, if it ever really happened." He waved his arm to relieve the lingering pain.

♥*Oh, it happened. I assisted Lord Varial in destroying the dragons and chaining the Mad King. Then I slept until the magic of Heart Master awoke me again.*♥

"Sleep sounds good."

♥*You* must *return me to the temple. If Heart Master has awoken, then war is coming.*♥

"Hard pass. I'd be gutted, flayed, or worse. Besides, you're a Knight of Valor? You serve Velleris? What's your connection to my goddess?" But he sensed nothing but frustration from the cuff.

♥*I did. I renounced Velleris for her unjust treatment of the Mektwin people over the actions of a few. Not that it concerns you.*♥

"Forgiveness from the Goddess of Justice? That's rich. So that's how the Mektwin met their end."

♥*Their* end? *They no longer exist?*♥

Fury rolled off the cuff, and the glow intensified until Draven was certain it was visible from anywhere in the city.

"*I* didn't do it. Settle down. Mostly they're slaves. Some roam the desert as nomads. Hard to wipe out an entire people, even for a goddess." Draven tugged at the cuff again, but the barbs only dug deeper into his skin. "Look, I'll make you a deal. I know someone who may have the skills necessary to separate us. If you quit with the beacon, I'll find a way to return you to Nerys. Then I'm bound for another city where all hands are not raised against me."

♥*You will relinquish Heart Master to a real champion?*♥

"Gladly. Yes. Please."

Suddenly the light of the cuff faded and grew dark and still. Draven bound it up with another cloth from his satchel just in case. He waited, but Ansalon had nothing more to add.

Sleep, when it came, brought nightmares of knights and gods, with him caught in the middle.

Light crept by degrees through Draven's ramshackle refuge. He stretched, weighing his limited options. There were only two: he could flee the city or face capture and execution. His eyes roved over the gray haze of early morning. Despite his plight, his heart was heavy. This city was his home. He couldn't imagine a life anywhere else.

"All right. Enough procrastinating. It's time to get out while the getting is still good." Odd to think he had burned through an entire city, but at least his escapades were now the stuff of legend. He wouldn't be forgotten any time soon.

He doffed his canvas cloak, rolling it with care into his voluminous pack. The satchel was the one bit of magic that he allowed himself.

Unless I count Ansalon—and I'll be damned happy to be rid of him.

Frowning, he pulled down the burlap from the window and pocketed the throwing spikes that had held it up. He hacked at the moldering cloth until it was a rude cloak. Then he smeared a little of the dirt and offal on it for good measure. It was all he could do not to choke from the stench.

Looking out the window, he observed the way was clear. Only a few early morning ruffians crept by street merchants, setting up their wares. Waiting for a beggar to amble past, he dropped to the ground and limped to a certain alehouse that he hoped still housed his old paramour. It irritated him to move with such caution when all he wanted to do was flee as fast as his feet would carry him.

I wonder if Nellonah will receive me with open arms... or a knife in my back.

12

CALLING ON AN OLD FLAME

THE CITY SURGED TO life as stall keepers opened for business, guards took up their posts, and a new day promised life or death at the end of a blade. Draven would miss this. He loved watching the bustling city awaken in fits and starts. Mornings were the best when you were a poor thief looking for food. Sleepy-eyed merchants rarely noticed the odd loaf of bread vanishing.

He shoved past the beggars as the shingle for the Final Fortune came into view. Though the bright colors had faded, Draven could still make out a skull with dice in its eye sockets.

After waiting for two groggy guardsmen to swagger by, he cast off his foul-smelling cloak and slipped inside. The tavern interior resembled the weather-worn shingle. Worn oak floor boards in need of a fresh coat of finish creaked underfoot. A few drunks snored their ale away while a single server moved about the common room, making a token effort at cleaning the spilled blood and alcohol from the night before.

A slender man with wispy blond hair and a jagged scar running from his forehead to his chin was wiping a rag across the top of the bar. On seeing him, Draven froze. The man looked up, and Draven saw that a black silk patch covered one eye. Recognition bloomed in the man's other eye, and Draven wanted to slink away in shame. How would he ever escape from his past?

"Loken." Draven struggled for words and found his usual wit absent. "I thought you died."

Loken stared back at him, red-faced and seething. "She said you'd come back, but I didn't believe you had the spine."

Before Draven could reply, Loken's hand dipped below the bar and a knife hurtled in his direction. Draven sidestepped neatly, despite his fatigue, and the blade shuddered as it struck an oak timber. Loken vaulted over the bar with a cudgel in one hand. Draven noticed the knuckles of each hand bulging like an old man's. Loken's left leg was bent at an odd angle, but it didn't slow him in the least.

Draven braced himself and threw up his hands against the inevitable blow. A dull roar deafened him, and Loken sailed back from an invisible force. The cudgel spun away and rolled to rest by Draven's foot.

"What? How?"

♥ You asked for a shield. ♥

But against a cripple? Demons, you don't think that's overkill? I need to be careful what I wish for!

He moved to make sure Loken was all right. He pulled his former friend up, barely evading a fist to his face, ducking his head and pulling Loken's arm behind him and twisting.

"Now that I know you're not dead, I don't want to hurt you. Don't make me."

He shoved, and Loken collided with the bar, staring daggers at Draven. A few men hustled down the stairs, pointed at Draven, then hurried back to wherever they came from. The common room filled with noisy whispers while hands crept to whatever weapon they had at hand. Draven held up his palms, pleading for peace. Loken looked in both directions, his body coiling to spring.

"Stop."

A wave of light followed the feminine voice. Draven fell to his knees while Loken sagged against the bar. Somewhere a glass shattered, and the air reeked of burnt ozone. Illuminated on the stairs in a corona of pale green light stood the woman Draven had once loved. Still loved, if he was honest. Heart Master pulsed waves of pain up his arm, causing him to bite down on his lower lip.

Nellonah flung back amber-colored hair as she cocked a hip and pointed at Draven. Green fire still danced along her fingers. Hazel eyes bored into him, and it took him a moment to realize he was still on the floor. Clad only in a simple green dress belted at the waist, Nellonah still looked every inch a goddess in human form.

"You. Come." She beckoned at Draven, then pointed at Loken. "You—rein in your temper and remember why we're here. Everyone else, a round on the house. And if word of this reaches anyone outside this tavern, you won't see the sunset." Nellonah flashed a toothy smile and everyone hurried to comply. It wasn't wise to disobey the witch of the Final Fortune.

♥ *There is an echo of the goddess in this place. I may have misjudged you.* ♥

"What?" Draven got to his feet on shaking legs. The cuff throbbed even stronger, and he pulled the covering tighter in case it glowed again.

Nellonah turned in a swirl of green fabric and ascended the stairs. Draven followed, dragging his scuffed leather boots. A sinking feeling replaced the throbbing in his arm as memories flooded back to him. He traced his hands along the smooth plaster of the walls, reveling in the texture even as he dreaded the destination.

Nellonah glided past the room where they had shared more nights together than he could count to the study at the end of the hall. A twinge at his back told him his wound had reopened. Sticky wetness slid down his skin under the jerkin. Well, that was the least of his worries.

♥ *You said she would help you.* ♥

She may help you. *Me, I'm not so sure of.*

A soft laugh escaped him, and Nellonah turned to glare in his direction as she settled into a seat behind a broad oak desk. Upholstered leather ran the top of it, capped with brass nails a finger's width apart.

"Sit."

He fell rather than sat in an armless chair opposite her. The unyielding wood dug into his aching back. Pain flared, but he clenched his teeth, ignoring it. Looking into her face brought a riot of emotion. Her eyes were still hard and cold, but Draven thought he detected a softness on her lips.

"Nellonah, I didn't know. I thought he died. I thought I would not be welcome." He tried to stammer out some form of apology, but the words trailed into gibberish.

"I have not said you are." Nellonah's slender fingers rose to either side of the desk. She plucked a delicate silver dagger from its resting place atop a stack of papers. It traced circles in the air. An opal in the pommel riveted his attention.

"I know what I did was unforgivable. That's why I left. I knew there was no way you could look at me after I caused Loken's death." He hung his head and sucked in a breath. "I would not have returned if the need were not great. I will pay any price."

Nellonah frowned back at him. The tip of the dagger described another circle in the air. Draven jumped when the door slammed shut behind him. She licked her lips and thrust the fine blade onto the top of the desk. The hilt trembled as she released it. A subtle hum of power tickled the air.

"Your presumption is as ever, boundless. Leaving Loken to fall to his death I could have forgiven. In time. What you did? Desertion? Leaving this mess for me to clean up? Gods, Draven." Nellonah put her elbows on the desk, and her head sank into her hands. "Did we mean nothing to you?"

She took a tremulous breath and looked up, fixing him with her gaze. Her anger he could bear— but not this.

"No! No, of course not. I couldn't accept what I'd done. I know taking Loken to steal from the baron was too soon, but I was arrogant. He seemed so agile. I thought he'd be fine on the rooftops. Almost as good as me." Draven looked down, his eyes drawn to the crude bandage on his right arm, wondering if it all started on that thoughtless, fateful night. "Then when he fell, it was at least a hundred feet. I was sure he must have died. To know I left him there bleeding? Gods, Nell."

"Never call me that again."

He rocked back in his chair so hard his wound seeped fresh blood.

"No. I know. You're right. This is different. I'm not asking for your forgiveness. I know I don't deserve it."

"Then why are you here? I know there's something different, and it's not just desperation. You reek of magic—holy magic."

The words hung in the air like an accusation.

Draven sighed and leaned forward. He traced the little studs covering the leather top of the desk with a dirty fingernail.

"Do you really think we'll hide you? Buy your way out of the city? Save you?"

"You might." He unwrapped his right arm, wincing as the ornate band came into view. "You might want this." The glow was gone, but the silver filigree still sparkled in the light and throbbed with unearthly power.

Nellonah stared at the cuff. Fury overtook her delicate features.

Oops. I didn't think she could get any angrier.

"Is this real?"

"You know what it is?" It wouldn't surprise him if she did. Information had always been her business.

She snatched up the dagger before he could react and stabbed his arm. Draven clenched for a blow that never landed. Instead, a milky blue substance flowed from the cuff and formed a hard shell, shattering the dagger. The cuff and his arm remained whole.

"You could have protected me before, you rotting ghost!"

♥*Heart Master protects itself. I would have let you bleed.*♥

"Good to know." Draven looked back to Nellonah, whose mouth formed a perfect oval.

"Goddess Nerys," she whispered to herself, not even acknowledging the conversation Draven held with his inner voice.

Hells, for all I know, she can hear him.

"That's why I'm here. There's a ghost haunting this thing, and he says war is coming. Gods or some like. I need your help to get it off, so it can go back to the temple, and I can go anywhere but here. No offense."

"There's no need for the temple. I have already named the champion. We just need to get this off you and onto her."

"You can do that?"

"Perhaps." She took his hand, running her fingers over his palm and tapping the milky shell.

He shuddered, not expecting his body to still react to her touch. Head down, brow furrowed, she was still the most beautiful woman he'd ever seen.

"You really are an idiot."

Draven sought an argument, but pinpricks of light danced before his eyes. Nausea crept up from his stomach, strangling his voice. He pitched forward into blackness.

13

WAKING IN THE FINAL FORTUNE

Draven awoke alone to guttering candle light in a windowless room he didn't recognize. His mouth tasted of metal, and the goddess only knew how long he'd been out. Heavy blankets weighed him down, but the heat felt good after so many freezing nights on the rooftops. Sitting up sent a lightning bolt through his lower back.

Beside the bed, he found a wooden plate with bread and cheese. Next to it rested an earthenware jug. Gritting his teeth, he swung his legs off the bed, fighting nausea. He sniffed at the jug. Water. When the plate and pitcher were both empty, hunger still gnawed at him. Gazing down at his bare legs, Draven wondered where they'd hidden his leathers.

His brown hair hung in damp clumps. He probed at his side, finding new bandages crisscrossing his torso. Blood no longer seeped from the wound. Running a hand along his cheek, Draven found his face smooth, so he'd been shaved too. That was a good sign.

Rubbing his hands on his thighs, he stared at the cuff. No glow. No voice in his head. Maybe Nellonah had removed the enchantment while he was out.

Draven tugged on it, but the same telltale teeth bit into his arm, refusing to release him from its curse. (Or blessing, if Ansalon was to be believed.) He tapped at it with the fingers of his left hand, wondering what powers it held.

"Ansalon." He spoke the name aloud, feeling foolish.

The wide cuff resonated in response.

♥*You don't have to speak. I can hear your thoughts.*♥

"This was bizarre enough already." Draven rubbed his jaw with the heel of his hand. "If the cuff protected me from Nell's dagger and Loken's cudgel, why not the arrow that skewered me?"

Draven thought he heard laughter in his mind.

♥*There are two reasons. Heart Master can only protect from attacks it, or rather you, perceive.*♥

He let this sink in a moment. "And the second reason?"

♥*The longer you wear the relic, the more powerful the bond and the better it can protect you.*♥

"Why do I suspect that also means it will be that much harder to get rid of?"

Ansalon remained silent on the subject, and Draven took that as an affirmative.

"Great." He sighed as an even greater weight settled between his shoulders.

The door opened. He perked up, hoping to see Nellonah, but Loken's twisted visage leered back at him. He carried a tray with more food on one side and bandages on the other. The cudgel was nowhere in sight, but there was a long, curved knife strapped to his good leg. A single ruby glittered on the pommel. Draven knew it well.

He still carries the knife I gave him. Maybe so he can shove it in my chest someday.

"You're not dead. I suppose that's something. She said it would be more complicated if you died."

Draven tensed, ready for another attack, but Loken only pulled up a chair.

"Relax, I'm not going to kill you." Loken grinned, but the ragged scar and bulging jaw bone on the left side of his face ruined the effect.

"You had murder in your eyes when I came in. How many days was that?"

"Two." He cracked enlarged knuckles, never taking his eyes off Draven. "It was a shock. I'll admit that. I might have broken a leg, or a hand, but that's all. I'm no murderer." Loken laughed at some internal jest.

"Two days." He repeated the words more for his benefit than Loken's. "You should want me dead for what I did. I had no idea you survived."

"I didn't. I died. Lady Nellonah brought me back, but even her magic could only do so much. She could not restore my body. The goddess of luck and death extracted a high price for me to continue breathing." He laughed again. "I should thank you."

"Thank me? Gods, for killing you?" Draven could barely work his mouth.

"I idolized you. I would have followed you anywhere. Any mad caper and I would have been at your side. I may have lost a leg and an eye, but at least, I learned not to want to be like you. I gave up thieving to serve as Nellonah's chief spymaster."

"Then you still steal. It's just information rather than gold." He tried to deflect the sting of Loken's words, but his own rang hollow in his ears.

"I serve a cause. You serve only yourself. That was the lesson I learned that day, Draven. You will only ever look out for yourself." There was no anger or malice in Loken's words. Just truth.

Draven bit back an angry retort, because he knew the boy was right. Though, looking at him, he realized there was no boy left in Loken. He was five years younger than Draven but he looked older by a decade.

Yet another price for his resurrection?

♥ *The gods demand a heavy price for their favors, even for an aspect of the goddess.* ♥

"I still wish I hadn't taken you that night. I should have listened to Nellonah when she said you weren't ready, but you were so nimble. I can never give you back what you've lost, and I'm sorry for that."

"Yes. You were arrogant, and you still are. You learned nothing. But I gained wisdom I've used ever since then. I may hobble, but you are still on the rooftop, looking down at my corpse. Which of us is the more pitiable?" Loken stood and shoved Draven over, unwinding bandages, dabbing him with foul unguents and re-bandaging his wound with disapproving snarls.

"Eat. You'll need your strength." Loken shoved the plate onto his lap.

"Why isn't Nellonah here? When will this thing come off my wrist?"

"She isn't ready to see you yet."

"But she'll help get this off my arm?"

Loken shook his head. "You don't see what a disaster you've caused, do you? The knight's wisdom hasn't made you see what you've done?"

"Other than angering the entire city? No." Draven chewed on salt pork, turning Loken's words over in his mind.

"There is a war brewing between the gods. It's been brewing since the last Mektwin king devoured the High-Father, ruler of the gods. Nellonah spent years looking for a champion to represent Nerys, and you have turned all her plans to dust days before she planned to retrieve the relic for the knight-commander. *Days.*"

Draven choked on the meat. An icy dread crawled up his back, around his side, and strangled his heart. He swore, looking down at the cuff. The cold silver took on an even more ominous air.

"I wasn't to know. How could I know? Yet another reason for you to hate me." Draven fell into sullen silence, stewing in his own thoughts.

"You know, I should, but I don't."

"What?"

"I think of you with nothing but animosity and yet you are still my brother. I even changed my name to be similar to yours."

"Lock was a silly name for a thief anyway, more so for a spy." He offered a quick smile that was not returned.

"I might as well hate a force of nature, for that's what you are. Unmindful and ignorant of the wrongs you do, or the damage you cause. I love you. I hate you. Still, at the end of each day, we'll always be brothers." Now Loken smiled, showing flawless teeth that looked incongruous in that cruel visage.

Draven sagged with guilt, trying to take some measure of hope from Loken's words. A dozen arguments whirled in his brain, but he knew they were moot. Loken spoke truly. Draven rarely thought about the people he wronged, stole from, or hurt. He had even rationalized that Nellonah was better off for his absence, not because it was true, but because it was easier.

"I... I can change." Draven uttered the words without knowing if any truth backed them.

"Anyone can. Depends on how deeply you wish to. I think you like the way you are. You haven't lost enough yet. But you will."

Draven scowled, and Loken barked out a laugh. It was time for a subject change.

"Where is this room? I don't recall seeing it before." Draven frowned, looking down at his bare legs, shivering now in the damp cool air.

"Used to be the cellar. We needed you out of sight of everyone. Nellonah hid the entrance behind multiple glamours. You're of no use to her if you're taken before she can get Heart Master back. And I suppose she might still have some affection for you. Deep down."

"Where are my leathers?"

"Probably burned. They were ripped in a dozen places and smelled like a sewer. There's some clothing in the chest. She's making up another set. Not that you deserve it. Your pack's there, too, along with your never-ending satchel, but the weapons are gone. She said they needed replacing, too."

"When do you think she'll be here?" Draven quirked an eyebrow as he looked toward the chest Loken gestured at.

"Has to be soon. There's no time to waste, the way she and the knight-commander talk."

"Good. This thing needs to be someone else's burden."

♥*Heart Master is an honor, not a burden.*♥

Draven scowled at the cuff then looked back at his long-lost brother, but Loken only shrugged and turned to leave.

Once he'd gone, a key turned from the other side of the door.

"Locked in by Loken. Can't help but appreciate that." He rose on shuddering legs and dressed in the ill-fitting garments, grimacing at the stiffness in his back. "Let's hope her magic works better for me and Heart Master than it did for poor old Lock."

14

REUNION

Draven paced the small room, tapping the enchanted cuff against his leg as he walked, weighing his options for the hundredth time. He guessed it to be midmorning on the third day of his incarceration in Nellonah's cellar, but he had no way of telling time here. Draven regarded his pack sitting on the chest in the corner, then the single locked door leading to freedom.

He could pick the lock. That would be child's play. But what then? No point in escaping since the Final Fortune was his only haven from the church, the guild, and the city guard. Even with the wrinkle of Loken not being dead, Nellonah was his best bet for getting rid of Heart Master and Ansalon.

"The question is, does she truly hate me?" Draven drummed his fingers against his leg, did another half circle, walked the length of the room, and rested his forehead on the uneven plaster of the cool wall. "Will she just turn me in once she has what she wants?"

♥*Have faith in the goddess.*♥

"Having faith in the goddess is one thing. Having faith in a jilted sorceress who may want me dead is another thing entirely."

♥*They are the same.*♥

"They aren't one and the—wait, what?"

♥*They are the same. She is of the goddess.*♥

"Wait, you mean like we are all the goddess, or she really is *of* the goddess?"

♥*Any secrets she harbors are not mine to impart, but this Nellonah resonates strongly with Nerys. If she is not a shard, then she is at least connected to the Goddess of Luck and Death.*♥

"Shard? What's a shard? Isn't that something to do with pots?"

Somehow, the spirit inside the cuff sighed. A shiver ran up Draven's arm that made his entire body tingle.

♥*You are truly hopeless. Shards are aspects of the gods that are divided from them so that they may visit the mortal realm without causing destruction wherever they trod.*♥

"Like children?" The shiver in Draven's arm turned to a dull, throbbing ache of annoyance.

♥*No. They are fully formed beings with most of the goddess's knowledge. They exist for short periods, then cease to exist when they become part of the goddess again.*♥

Draven shuddered. Nellonah could disappear? He shook his head, denying the possibility. Nellonah was a force of nature. She would always be here. He refused to accept it.

"That's ridiculous. Whatever you sense. It's not that. Sure, she's got magic and can do amazing things, but she's not a sliver to a goddess."

♥*Shard.*♥

"Whatever. She's not that. She will not disappear. Nell just isn't." Draven shook his head again to cement the denial, refusing to believe what the dead knight suggested. "She may work for the goddess. That's all." Despite his rebuttal, a tingle of dread remained. Though he'd walked out on her years ago, he couldn't deal with the concept that she could just wink out of existence like a phantom.

The key turning in the lock shook him from his reverie, and his attention snapped to the door. Loken stood framed in the pale light of Draven's candle, bent as always to the left on that misshapen leg. Nothing about the man suggested he couldn't move like lightning, though. His stance still contained the same sureness he possessed when Draven knew him before. Before Draven killed him.

Damn magic. It confuses everything it touches.

♥*Or you're just too easily confused.*♥

Draven cursed, earning him a quizzical look from Loken.

"Nothing. Voice in my head."

Loken raised an eyebrow, but chose not to reply before stepping into the small room and looking Draven up and down.

"You look better. Almost presentable to our Lady."

"You really call her the Lady?" Draven laughed but stopped when it was clear he was alone in his mirth.

"That's who she is. She is the Lady of Nerys. Lady of the Final Fortune." Loken spoke with a reverence that stunned Draven: to him, she would always just be Nell.

"I think I'll stick with Nellonah for the time being until she declares herself a goddess." He shook his head again, trying not to provoke Loken. "No food. Does that mean I'm allowed back upstairs?"

"She wants to see you on the roof." He jerked his head and turned to lead the way. Draven again noted the odd angle of Loken's left leg. It must be some kind of peg leg.

They walked through a series of cramped lower halls, some of which Draven recalled, before coming to a hidden spiral staircase that twisted up to the roof. He remembered it well. It accessed every level of the Final Fortune. The entrances remained hidden behind a series of panels, so a person could go up or down without being seen by anyone else in the tavern. How Loken could navigate the narrow, twisting stairs was beyond him, but the odd leg flexed as needed, giving him a surprising agility.

When they came out into the open air of the roof, Draven released a breath he hadn't realized he'd been holding. Torches burned at regular intervals, illuminating the broken pieces of stone and mortar. One section he could remember breaking off when he first learned to run the rooftops.

Nearly fell to my death at that time.

♥*More's the pity.*♥

Draven bit back an annoyed retort as Nellonah came into view. She sat in a sultry pose on a mahogany chair built for someone twice her size, wearing a form fitting black garment. She'd changed her hair to match. It fell straight over her shoulders and was even darker than the night. A spider web of black lines crawled around her eyes. She was famous for changing her appearance the way most women changed their attire.

"Nellonah." Her name sprang off his tongue like a lover's kiss.

Loken rolled his eyes and disappeared without a sound.

Nellonah gestured with her hand at a chair opposite hers. A narrow table littered with food sat between them. She plucked a pastry from a plate and popped it into her mouth, chewing slowly, regarding him as if he was on the menu as well.

He straightened his oversized doublet and took the offered seat. His stomach growled. So he boldly scooped up a candied apple and took a bite.

Nellonah said nothing as he ate, only continued to stare at him. Her gaze felt like a nest of bees. He tossed the core on the tray and gave her his best sheepish grin.

"Are we here to talk or play games, Nell?"

"I told you not to call me that." The corner of her lip turned up in a snarl.

"Kill me then."

"Damn you, Draven. Do you have any clue what you've done?"

"Loken filled me in."

"Ten years, Draven... for ten years I have sought the champion, secure in knowing that Heart Master was safe in my temple. Days—literally days—after choosing her, you ruined it all."

Draven fought to keep his face neutral. He wasn't sure he was entirely successful. The words "my temple" bothered him.

"How was I to know? If you didn't keep so many bloody secrets, I would have known not to steal the cursed cuff."

Nellonah smacked her palm on the table, rattling the plates. "Draven, I can't protect you from what's coming."

"Why would you even care after what I did?"

Why is she playing this game instead of getting this thing off me?

♥Likely because she cannot.♥

The thought froze Draven where he sat.

Nellonah folded her hands and frowned back at him. "I don't hate you, Draven. Angry, goddess, yes. Hurt? Disappointed? All those things a hundred times, yes. Even with your abandonment, I would still spare you this war."

Her words felt like a spear through Draven's midsection, and he sagged.

"Look, I'm sorry for that, for what happened to Loken, and most of all, for not returning sooner. When you've made a mistake, it's all too easy to keep moving forward rather than returning to face up to the damage you've done. Loken called me a whirlwind. He's not wrong. I've lived only for my own desires for too long. Maybe what happened in the temple that night was fate."

"A thief wielding Heart Master. The gods must be thrilled." A soft laugh escaped her throat. "Give me your arm. I have little hope, but we should at least attempt it."

Draven shoved his arm on the table between them, pushing several plates aside with a clatter. He rolled up his sleeve to give Nellonah better access. "Will it hurt?"

"At the very least. Yes. It will hurt."

Draven thought she took a bit too much pleasure in that admission.

She moved her fingers over the cuff. Dancing green light flowed from her fingers, only to be met by the blue glow from Heart Master. Ansalon said nothing, but skepticism rolled off the cursed relic in waves.

The spines securing it to his arm dug in tighter. He clenched his teeth as they drew fresh blood. The two different sources of magic met and swirled together in a beautiful, if angry, combination. The color reminded him of the ocean at sunset.

Smoke began to curl from his arm as Nellonah grimaced. The cyan hue of the magic turned an angry red. Draven fought to hold still, swearing under his breath as the cuff grew to cover his entire forearm and turned into a vise that threatened to crush his bones. He fought the urge to pull his arm back and curl in on himself.

Then the warring magics exploded, throwing them both in opposite directions.

Draven found himself on his back. Steam rolled off his skin as he looked down at it. His whole body ached. With no little difficulty, he got to his feet to check on Nellonah. Somehow, she'd remained seated, but her head was down. Blood seeped from the corners of her eyes like tears.

He raced over, taking her head in his hands, checking for signs of life. Nellonah sucked in a deep breath, and he sighed in relief. Hazel eyes opened to regard him with a softness he thought he'd never see again. She coughed, and he backed away to reclaim his overturned chair. The wood looked singed, but it still held his weight.

"That could have gone better." He held his arm up to the light. The cuff didn't even appear scratched. A bit of blood dripped from the edge, but the spines had loosened after the detonation of magic.

"Ansalon, you still alive in there?" Draven shook his forearm as if to wake the knight.

♥*If you call this living. My mission remains intact.*♥

"Cheery as ever. Heart Master seems fine." He looked back at Nellonah, who had recovered her wits.

"Your mastery of understatement appears intact." She smoothed an errant black lock behind her ear. "I doubt I can do aught else. All twelve gods forged Heart Master. There is little I can do to affect it, and calling on the goddess could have dire implications for us both."

"What? You can do that? Call on a goddess?"

"You might say Nerys and I have a special relationship." She smiled, but sadness lurked behind her eyes.

"Ansalon said you might be shared with the goddess? Is that true? You're not human?"

♥*Shard. Not shared. Shard.* Shard. *How thick are you?*♥

"The wording is off, but she created me from a piece of herself, yes. It would mean the end of us both if she could do it. Me for disappointing her and you for ruining her machinations."

Draven blew out a breath, processing the implication. "We'll leave that as a last resort. Before you even suggest it, I am not losing my arm. I'm not." Even he didn't dare risk the wrath of a goddess—and yet he'd stolen from her temple without a second thought.

"It might be better than becoming the champion of Nerys." Her eyes twinkled in jest.

"I say we cut off his arm."

That voice. Draven turned to regard the speaker. She stood a head taller than him with long hair like blood on wheat. Even without armor, her frame was nothing short of intimidating, and he would have known her anywhere.

"Fairoaks? Are you mad?" He leapt from his chair, turning to Nellonah for confirmation.

"Draven, meet the real champion. Elisah Fairoaks, knight-commander of Sharazin, and the only hope for our world." Nellonah held her hand out to show off the imposing woman.

Draven knew her already. Elisah Fairoaks had tried to capture him more than once. He hoped she wouldn't manage it this time.

Stars above, can this get any worse?

15

What Now?

Draven stared down the imposing female warrior with all the bravado he could muster. "You are not taking me in, Fairoaks, not now, not ever. You'll have to kill me first."

"What a lovely idea." The knight-commander shook her head. "The world may end, and you're worried about your petty crimes?"

Draven crossed his arms, glaring daggers at her.

"No one is killing anyone, Elisah," Nellonah said, scowling at the newcomer.

"The world could be ending. You said it." The knight-commander rested a hand on the pommel of her sword, raising an eyebrow at Draven.

"My magic failed. That doesn't mean we don't have other options."

"Such as?" Draven arched an eyebrow, a sinking feeling growing in his gut.

"There is a priest further down the coast. He knows more about Heart Master and the relics than anyone living. More even than some gods. His name is Kethek."

The cuff flamed into blinding light on Draven's arm.

♥*Impossible. Kethek still lives? If any can separate you from the holy relic, it would be him.*♥

Draven put a hand on his hip. "Ansalon agrees. He's surprised the old man is alive, but he's sure if anyone can fix this, Kethek can."

"See, the fight is not yet lost, but there's no time to waste. The enemy is on his way to the tower."

"Tower? What tower?" Draven's head swam, trying to keep track of everything. "Kethek is going to the tower? I'm lost."

"The Tower of the White Rose. Nellonah believes Seguris will most likely go after the blood sword. It's supposed to be linked to the gauntlet he wields. But he could just as easily be looking for Heart Master." Elisah rolled her eyes.

"It's a gamble, to be sure, but it's our best chance. If Seguris chases after Heart Master rather than Blood Thorn, then all the better." Nellonah looked down at the table as if it displayed a map only she could see.

"Wait, who's Seguris?" Draven imagined himself as one of those silly birds he'd heard of that mimicked whatever their owners said.

"A former slave-turned-warlord, and supposedly a direct descendent of the Mad King. Leads a band of rogues. According to Nellonah's spies, he seeks to resurrect the Mektwin empire. Ghedryn gifted him The Fist of Heaven, a relic of Ghedryn's. He's displayed a knack for strategy. His Free Riders, as he calls them, appear and disappear like ghosts raiding settlements, with only token opposition."

"Former slave? Raiding doesn't sound so bad." To be honest, Draven thought it might be interesting teaming up with a company of thieves, taking what they needed from rich caravans.

"If anarchy and the return of the most reviled empire in history sounds appealing to you, then you are more of a blackguard than I imagined."

"I'm a thief. I'm proud to be a thief. And I can't wait to get back to being a thief. You're just irritated you could never catch me on your own." He beamed a wide grin in the knight-commander's direction.

"If my lady did not protect you, I would sever your arm now." Elisah's hand twitched on the pommel.

Draven's head pounded.

"She calls you 'lady' too?"

"Of course, I do. She is the Lady, the living embodiment of Nerys."

"Elisah!" Draven could tell by Nellonah's expression that she'd spoken more sharply than intended. "It's not wise to invoke her name, especially in my presence."

Elisah bowed her head, meek as a schoolgirl. A gauntleted thumb clicked back and forth over the hilt of her sword.

Draven whistled. *She's even cowed Fairoaks. I shouldn't be shocked, but having a knight-commander in your pocket is something, even for Nell.*

♥ *You do not comprehend even a single piece of that puzzle.* ♥

What? I mean, if she's divine or something, I suppose a holy soldier would obey her.

Once again, the cuff shuddered with something like a laugh. Both women looked at him with eyebrows raised.

♥*Elisah was old when I lived as a man. She taught me all I knew about being a knight and a champion. But that's not my tale to tell.*♥

Draven held his arm up and shrugged at Elisah and Nellonah. "Chatty cuff. Guess I'd be too if they trapped me in a hunk of metal for two hundred years."

He shook out his hand to dispel the pins and needles the cuff had brought on. Quicker than his eyes could follow, Fairoak's sword leapt from its scabbard and sliced at his arm. Almost of its own accord, his hand rose just as fast and grasped the blade, wrenching it from the knight-commander. A flick of his wrist sent the sword clattering across the roof. Draven looked down at his palm, expecting blood, but all he saw was that eerie blue light dancing on his skin like static electricity. Elisah gazed at him, mouth agape.

"Fairoaks." Nellonah spat the name like a curse, and magic coursed along her arms.

Elisah shrugged her shoulders in way of response. "It was worth a try."

"Are you mad?" Draven inquired, as he ran his hand over his arm, checking for injuries. "If I knew how, you'd be roasting in blue flames right now."

♥*I will allow no harm to the champion.*♥

Draven scowled at the cuff.

"I warned you that Draven was to come to no harm." Nellonah's voice carried a hard edge that Draven had never heard before. Emerald electricity arced along her skin. A corona wreathed her hair, which ran from black to red to sparkling green.

"But why, Lady? He's just a thief. He betrayed you once at least already, and will most likely do so again." Elisah went retrieved her sword. Slamming it back into its scabbard, she turned to look at both Nellonah and Draven. "And I'm not sorry, thief. You've caused us no end of misery with one stupid act. Were it not for Heart Master, I'd gladly see you rot in my cells."

Nellonah showed no sign of backing down. Even more magic danced around her.

♥ *You must stop this, thief. Companions should not fight. Especially over someone like you.* ♥

Goddess, what am I even doing here? Draven shook his head. Loose hair fell in his face. "Nell, stop. Attacking her won't solve our problem, and if speaking the the name of the goddess is bad, then invoking her magic is even worse. And you, Fairoaks— anytime you want to square off, I'll happily plant my boot along your jaw. Champion or not, I don't fear you." He was lying, of course. Everyone feared the knight-commander, but his bravado invigorated him.

He couldn't be sure if his words had reached her, but Nellonah's magic faded and Fairoaks relaxed enough to sit beside the table. She flipped her cape out of her way. Nellonah let out a long breath, resuming her seat as well.

Draven put his palms down, hoping this wasn't just a lull in the festivities. When both women relaxed, he took a seat and looked between them as he picked at a sweet. It was a divine miracle that someone had not upended the table and its bounty in all the tumult. It reminded him of the ill-fated day when he'd run afoul of the guard.

Was it truly only a week, mayhap two? It's as if that life belonged to another Draven.

"So," he said between bites. "Kethek, old wizard-priest guy." He looked for any reaction from the women, but they remained wrapped in their own thoughts. "What makes you think he'll help us?" For a moment, he thought they'd maintain their angry silence.

"Kethek is a founding member of the Order of Twelve." Nellonah spoke the words as if they should make absolute sense to him.

"Pretend at least one person at the table wasn't alive back then."

Elisah threw down a lump of pastry in disgust and massaged her temples. "The Order answers to no single god. They are dedicated to serving all and protecting humanity. Kethek is the last, at least that we know of. He will hold to their tenets. If it's in his power, he'll want Heart Master entrusted to someone who will not abuse it." She eyed him in a knowing manner.

Nellonah murmured but offered no rebuttal.

"Hey, I'm not all bad. I've never murdered a man." The moment the words left his mouth, he regretted them. "Much. Kind of."

"Not for lack of trying." Nellonah gave him a hard, disdainful glance.

"Loken aside, you're a thief." Elisah glared at him with clenched teeth. "Will you swear you won't abuse Heart Master? Will you stand shoulder-to-shoulder with me and battle this Seguris? Do you even care about the people who will die in this conflict?"

Elisah's words slapped him harder than any blow could have. Yet he wasn't sure how to care about people he'd never met, people who had no care for him. The idea of him facing off against a bandit warlord, magic gauntlet or not, seemed laughable. And yes, he would use Heart Master for his own benefit. Who wouldn't? The world offered no favors, only took them from the unwary.

"I care about Nell, and believe it or not, Loken. I can't speak for folk I've never even seen. How can I? I'm just a thief. I care about thrills, treasure, and the challenge of the next job. I've never looked beyond that."

"Typical." Elisah shook her head.

"But I'm no heartless rogue. I can't believe I'm saying this, but I'll do what must be done. Join with you to seek this wizard. Fight if need be." He detected something stirring in Heart Master, but he didn't think it was Ansalon. Once again, he wondered where Heart Master ended and the caged knight began.

"You will fight? Against Seguris and whatever nightmares Ghedryn has unleashed?" Nellonah's voice was little more than a whisper, but her words went to his heart.

"For you? Yes. And... maybe for me, too. If coming back here has taught me anything, it's that I've left a trail of suffering in my wake. Maybe this is the goddess telling me to do something about it." He looked down, uncertain if it was him, Heart Master, or the knight who spurred those words.

"Trust me. If the goddess knew even a tenth of this, we'd all be dead. She who must not be named created me to enact a specific plan and this—" she laughed, "is certainly not it."

Elisah clearly was fighting to contain a chuckle, and Draven grinned too. He thought he sensed Ansalon fuming deep within the ancient metal of Heart Master. A feeling welled up inside him he couldn't identify.

Pride, or maybe hope.

Always wondered what it was like to be one of those fools with some divine purpose. Guess I've finally joined them.

He laughed, knowing there would be much to cry about soon.

16

TROUBLE IN THE RANKS

SEGURIS STARED INTO THE twisting flames of the fire, thinking about his life. He rubbed the scars on his wrists from years of being chained. Seguris had to remind himself that he was now free. More to the point, he commanded a growing army. He flexed his right hand, watching the crackle of power from The Fist of Heaven.

Beside him, Ethan was roasting a hunk of meat. Brown hair fell into Ethan's face, and he shook it away. He rotated the meat and turned to look into his leader's eyes.

"You could just smoke this with the glove. Save me sweating over the fire."

"I doubt Ghedryn intended his relic to cook your dinner."

"Priests, pigs, little difference to me." Ethan turned the meat again and judged it fit to eat. He pulled it back and winced when it was too hot for his fingers. Swearing, he stuffed a hunk into his mouth and chewed with care.

Seguris chuckled, appraising the man who had quickly become his chief lieutenant. He still wondered, out of all the other contenders, why Ethan had chosen him to follow.

They'd amassed a hundred men to date, and more trickled in daily. It didn't take long before the warlord of the band they'd named The Free Riders became overwhelmed by the logistics of all these soldiers and their needs.

Growing up in chains, Seguris had only an inkling of feeding, arming, and housing a band of thieves and mercenaries. Fortunately for him, Ethan had experience in both fighting and administration and was more than happy to put that to good use for Seguris.

"At least show a little reverence. If not for Ghedryn, we'd still be in chains."

"Or dead." Ethan tore off another bite of pork and chewed with his mouth open. "I was about to be hanged for striking a priest of Velleris when Ghedryn came for me."

"And I was about to be skewered by a dozen guards after killing my enslaver. And yet here we are, free men in command of an army." Seguris looked down, dreading his next line of inquiry, but he had to know. "This brings me to something that's been bothering me. Out of all the fighters who could have landed in that pit, how is it that you, Bastus, and others known to me came to be there? It troubles me and makes me wary of trusting this."

Ethan stopped chewing and swallowed hard as if the pig flesh were the worst-tasting dung. He tossed the rest of the piece into the fire and licked his fingers. All hint of mirth drained from his long, lean face as the flames blackened the meat, its juices sizzling away.

"I was afraid you might ask that."

"So, not chance then."

Ethan looked down at his feet, his expression pained. "We were handpicked, at least some of us. I can't speak for the others, but it gave me the chance to fight for a man fit to conquer the known world. Given how fed up I was with serving priests, I leapt at the offer, especially when I was told that it would be an old friend."

"It was all a farce?" Anger warmed Seguris's face, but he couldn't bear to direct it at Ethan, who looked like a whipped pup, cringing before a blow.

Or a whipped slave. How often did I tense up in exactly the same way?

"Not all. There were plenty of fighters in that pit out for our blood. Whether there were more chosen ones, I cannot say, but the fighting was real. It was just tipped in your favor."

"No doubt because of my royal blood." Seguris suddenly smiled, stroking his chin.

"You really believe that, don't you? How would you know?"

"I've always known. I may not have known who sired me, but it's always sung in my veins like a fire I can't quench. My blood speaks to me when magic is near. It strengthens me when I am weak. It whispers of the reign of Khyris and his father's father and what was and should be again." Seguris's voice trailed off as that fiery blood drew him once more into fantasies of a kingdom and a world under his guidance.

Ethan shook his head, bemused. "I suppose that's why you're a king and I am a soldier. I don't feel any greatness in my future besides watching your flank."

"You'll do more than that, old friend. You'll command this growing army, train them, and become their general. Then sit at my right hand. I will never take your loyalty for granted." Seguris dipped his head as if doing so would bring the future into being.

Ethan nodded his head. "Not all are as loyal."

Seguris followed Ethan's eyes to Bastus, who walked by whispering to two big men clad in skins. Bastus noticed Seguris and Ethan looking on and steered his cohorts away, still chattering away in a voice too low to be overheard.

Subtle. I don't need to hear your words to know the treachery in your heart.

"I'm afraid I'll need to kill that man. Pity, he was of great use in the arena and would make a suitable commander with his taste for blood." Seguris let his gaze linger on the disappearing form of Bastus and his fur-clad minions. He didn't know those men, but he was sure Bastus filled them with ideas of how they could take charge of this growing army.

"'Tis better to put down a dog before he becomes rabid, Warlord." Ethan followed Seguris's gaze, tapping a finger to his cheek.

"You keep saying warlord. Why is that?"

"Well, you are not a king yet, but you are certainly no slave. You're a warlord till you wrest the crowns from the priest-kings and fashion one for yourself." Ethan smiled as if he'd come up with something clever.

Seguris barked out a short laugh. "I do like the way you think. I'm pleased I didn't kill you."

"As am I." Ethan turned his gaze away from the disappearing traitor. "So aside from dealing with Bastus, what's next for our army?"

"The god of conquest wishes us to seek a Vellerian stronghold called the Tower of the White Rose. Legend has it near where the last Mektwin empire flourished."

"The desert is a big place."

Seguris nodded. "Ghedryn suggests we will find a clue to its precise location in a keep to the south of Coriolis."

"Still vague. There is a great deal south of Coriolis."

"It will be good practice for the men. A test of your training."

Ethan spat into the fire. "It would be nice if he could be more specific. Waste of time, traveling around looting all the keeps south of that priest-infested city."

Seguris laughed. "It's not wise to question the will of the gods. We fought in the arena, and we will fight again for our own nation."

Ethan grumbled some more, but Seguris knew it was mostly for effect. His lieutenant was eager to test their army and get a measure of revenge.

"When will you deal with your serpent in the garden?" Ethan inclined his head in the direction Bastus had disappeared.

"There's no time like the present. The longer I let that cur draw breath, the more men he may infect with his poison. I trust I can count on you to guard my back." Seguris put a hand to the pommel of his blade.

"With my dying breath, but the day I can't hamstring a couple of furry barbarians is the day I hang this up for good." Ethan put a hand to his own blade, slid it out a hand span, and let it fall back into the scabbard with a whisper of metal on leather.

"Good, let's take a stroll and tend the garden."

The pair set off at a brisk pace following Bastus. Seguris's blood whispered in his ears as it always did in the direction he needed to follow. They came upon their quarry sitting on a log, whispering treason to the wild-eyed men Seguris had seen him with earlier. Now a half dozen other men stood or lounged about. It cut Seguris to the bone that so many had already fallen under the man's sway.

All conversation ceased as Seguris and Ethan strolled up to stand opposite Bastus and his barbarians. Seguris leveled a fierce gaze at the man, who returned a guileless smile.

"You've been busy, Bastus." Seguris rested a hand on the hilt of his blade. "If only you'd been as busy when we knew each other before, I'd have fewer scars on my back."

"What news from our god, Seguris? More orders only you can hear?" Bastus stood, his stance bristling with menace.

"This has nothing to do with Ghedryn. This only concerns you and me. Not even a season out from the arena and you already whisper betrayal in the ears of my army."

Bastus leered back, putting his hand on his own weapon. "One name is as good as another. The only thing that sets you apart is that gauntlet. Who's to say you deserve to wield it?"

"Ghedryn for one, you miserable cur. My royal blood for another. Ethan has told me what transpired with the god."

"Your race is dead. It's high time you joined them." Bastus nodded to his men, and weapons slithered from their resting places.

Seguris gestured with The Fist, and men went flying. Ethan drew his blade and stood at his warlord's flank, daring any of them to make a move. One leapt up, heedless of the power Seguris commanded, but the warlord skewered him before the man could so much as raise his blade.

Bastus got back to his feet and drew his ax. "Just like the coward you are, to hide behind the power of our god."

"This will change nothing." Seguris slid the gauntlet from his hand and shoved it into the wide belt at his waist. His gleaming sword slid from the scabbard in a fluid motion.

His opponent's ax whistled at him before he could even raise his blade. Seguris side-stepped, letting it crash to the ground beside him. He slammed his fist into Bastus's jaw, rocking the big man back on his heels. Seguris lashed out with his sword in a wide arc, and the metal rebounded from the wood of his opponent's ax.

Like immovable titans, they rained blows on one another that would have broken the bones of lesser men. Bastus moved like an avalanche, his ax crashing down again and again against Seguris's guard. The warlord moved with more grace but just as much strength, driving the bigger man around the clearing to avoid his lightning quick blade.

Eventually, Seguris's endurance won, and he was rewarded by a slice to Bastus's side, dropping Bastus to his knees. Bastus panted, the ax falling from his hand to thump against the earth. Seguris looked at the men that followed his enemy, but they seemed to have lost their taste for treason. He slid the gauntlet back over his hand and relished the thrum of power that it brought with it.

"I yield. I will serve you. I swear it." Bastus gazed up at him with those calculating eyes.

"No, Bastus, I'm afraid you won't." Seguris reached out with his gauntleted hand and grasped Bastus by the throat. A single thought channeled the power of his holy relic, and Bastus burned. Smoke sizzled from the big man's skin as it enveloped him in scarlet light. Bastus screamed, and Seguris roared. Clothing burned and flesh sloughed off of Bastus's gigantic frame until nothing remained but smoking bones, and even they crumbled to a fine ash.

Seguris dusted off his gauntlet and eyed the men who had followed Bastus. They looked at him in abject terror.

"Thus is the fate of traitors." Seguris struck The Fist of Heaven against his chest.

17

IN THE WILDS

HELENA RODE THROUGH ANOTHER burnt village, her relic shield Hallowed Verity clanked against her saddle horn. It irked her. No matter how long she meditated, it remained an inert hunk of metal.

Could the goddess have chosen incorrectly? Perhaps I am not the right person to stand for Velleris. Maybe all I'm good for is killing.

Helena banged her fist into the embossed shield, stinging her knuckles, but not so much as smudging the radiant shine of the metal.

Infuriating scrap. Helena smiled wistfully that any gift of the goddess could anger her to such an extent.

The remains of thatched huts, smoldering buildings, and tumbled walls sapped her resolve. Helena reined up as she saw a handful of soot-covered men and women putting out fires and carrying away bodies. They glared at her as she drew near. A man dropped the bucket he held and picked up a length of wood, brandishing it at her as she came to a halt. His hands quivered, and his legs looked as if they might buckle beneath him. Helena shook her head.

She held up a hand, showing she meant no harm. Her heart thudded in her breast at the carnage. The dead and dying lay everywhere, mostly unattended. Days ago, this must have been a thriving farming community. Now it lay in ruins.

How can this ground ever grow life again?

"Hold. I mean you no harm. I am a knight of Velleris. Can I help you?" She swung down from her horse but kept a hand near her mace.

These people are desperate. Goddess only knows their intentions. Who could blame them if they turned to sin after all they'd lost?

"Where was our goddess when we prayed to her? Can you resurrect the dead? Can you raise the burned buildings or the crops we lost to the bandits?" The man shook his makeshift cudgel at her, tears carving channels in his dirt-smeared face.

"You know I cannot. I wish I'd come sooner, but that doesn't mean I can't help you now." Helena dropped her hands, nervous fingers pulling at the fabric as she smoothed her robes to hide the turmoil simmering in her heart. The man waved the stick once more before letting it sag to the dirt, defeated. The anger in his gaze gave way to weariness.

"I'm Maldon. I'm sorry, but we've had a rough time." He looked about with red, watery eyes. From smoke or grief, it was unclear to her.

"Was this Seguris and his Free Riders?" Self-righteous indignation welled within her.

"Him, or men intent on joining him. They called his name, and Ghedryn's. Does it matter? Who can tell one evil from another? Do we care who does the stealing and killing? Their deaths won't feed us, or bring back our dead."

The man sagged, and she darted forward, catching him in her arms. She noticed how thin he was, how thin they all were. *How long have they been living like this? If this can even be called living.* She eased Maldon to the ground, regarding the rest with a calculating eye. The villagers appeared tired, scared, and wasted, even for peasants.

"I'll do what I can." She said a prayer, and a soft light radiated from her, extinguishing the fires, and gave the ravaged farmers a sense of peace. *Should I leave them to their fates, or stay and help? Goddess, guide me. I know my mission is paramount, but these people can't last much longer.*

Daughter, you shall meet Seguris in the tower. Spread my word and do what good you can for these people.

Helena blinked in surprise, not expecting an answer. Her heart swelled with love for Velleris.

"Let's prioritize any buildings we can save. Those who are sick need shelter. But first, I have some food; not much, for I am a knight on a mission, but enough to feed you for a few days. After you get a bit of sustenance, then we can put your homes to rights. After that, we will bless the dead, speeding their journey to the next world." It took all her resolve to keep tears at bay.

♥♥♥

Later, they sat around a roaring fire, made up of the debris of homes. She ate a thin soup made from the dried meat from her provisions. It was meager fare, but the villagers didn't seem to care. She'd have to restock at the next town assuming there was another town left standing, but it was worth it to see some life come back to these people. Their eyes still bore the horror of what they'd been through, but for now, hope blossomed. Maldon sat across from her with a woman called Sharl. He gnawed on some hard tack as if he'd not eaten in weeks.

"I do not know what we would have done without you." He took another bite of the biscuit and looked almost guilty to be eating it.

"After the last attack, we despaired of making it another day. The last group took every bit of food we had left, and any coin went to the Free Riders. All we could think to do was journey to another town, but some of us wouldn't have made it." Sharl hung her head as if speaking that much exhausted her. She was older than Maldon, and bandages covered her lower legs. Helena doubted she could walk to the end of the village, much less to the next one. Greasy gray hair hung over Sharl's eyes. Helena healed those she could, but her powers had limits.

"I vow I will make them pay. The vengeance of the goddess will be legendary. I know that will not help you survive, but I can remain a few days. Each day, I can heal your people a little more before I continue on my mission. My provisions should hold out that long." Helena rubbed at her face, wishing that she could do more.

Damn it, Velleris. I am made for war, not healing. I am useless here. She bit at her inner lip, trembling with emotion. Helena craved an enemy to smite, but all she saw were these tired, hungry souls in need of more than she could give.

Peace, daughter. Your time will come and the survivors will recall the knight of Velleris who succored them. Our renown will grow from this brief pause in your quest. The time for vengeance will come. Practice patience. Velleris's warmth reminded Helena that her presence helped these shattered people.

"Your pledge means much to us, honored knight. Knowing others will not suffer our fate heartens us, and thanks to you, we will survive. If not here, then as part of another village." Maldon's eyes were moist as he spoke, but the knight could sense a renewed optimism in him that was absent when she first rode in.

"Did the Free Riders mention where they were bound or what they wanted?" Helena shifted in her makeshift seat, eager for a change of subject.

Sharl forced a wan smile. "Our church had an icon. It could promote growth. Any food or plants placed inside would double. While we had it, our village never went hungry. They took it and anything else of value. Hells, even things that had no value. It was as if they thrived on our pain."

Helena didn't doubt it. They served Ghedryn, the god of conquest. His power grew with each victory of his followers, even over simple peasants. They offered pain, and he drank it in, just as Velleris thrived on justice.

Maldon scowled and threw more wood onto the fire. "The murdering scum said little, but they kept asking about a tower in the desert. As if we know anything about towers. We could teach them volumes about growing vegetables. Alas, that information was of little interest."

Helena considered asking him to join in her quest, but others would need his passion to keep them safe. *Would that I had a companion... someone who shared my anger, my mission, my thirst for holy reckoning. I don't know if I have the strength to triumph on my own. The faith of the goddess guides me, but am I enough? I spend my time in cloisters or fighting the enemies of the church. I am not a saint or a healer. Helping people ravaged by warfare is something I have no experience in.*

The goddess remained annoyingly silent. Helena favored Maldon with a wry grin and tossed another broken table leg onto the fire.

"Words enough, friends. Let's get some rest. Survive tomorrow, and know I will avenge your fallen." She clenched her fist and renewed her vow to bring Seguris and his devils to justice.

Somehow, I will redress these crimes even if it costs my life. Even if it costs my very soul.

18

EMBRACING DESTINY

A FEW DAYS' TRAVEL brought Kell and Nala to the base of the Veil Mountains. Kell turned, gazing at the peaks he'd called home his entire life, and offered Regnir a silent prayer. Nala continued, oblivious to Kell's regret. Wiping the sweat from his brow, he hurried to catch up to her. They walked in uncomfortable silence unless Nala commented on an unusual rock formation or the healing properties of some plant. He breathed out a heavy sigh. Beside him, Nala huffed.

I wouldn't care to have me as a travel companion, either.

He knew it should honor him to be handpicked by their god to complete some monumental task, but he couldn't care less. The farther they got from home, the more uneasy he felt.

Regnir's god-mark thrummed within his chest, and his heart seemed to beat faster and faster while a chilling void gaped within him.

Nala squealed, darting off to kneel before a tree as wide as two men side by side. He gave her a sidelong glance as she took a knife from her belt and collected a new specimen. It amazed him there was any space left in her pack. Kell tapped a finger on the knife at his belt until she rejoined him. Nala went on a rambling discourse about how it would stave off skin disorders when ground into a paste.

Shadow of Regnir. How much of this can one man take?

The pair continued on, Kell dreading his quest, while Nala pointed this way and that. The flat ground spread out before them unnerved him. He imagined enemies lurking behind every tree. Living so long in the mountains made flat land seem unnatural.

Kell kicked a loose stone just to hear it skitter over the ground before coming to rest in the underbrush. He smiled at his act of defiance.

"Are you always so dull?" Nala stopped and turned to him, eyes bright, her snowy hair billowing in the wind.

Is it wrong that her spirit infuriates me?

"I'm not dull."

She gave him a knowing look.

"Fine, I'm not usually this dull."

"So, being favored by a god is an occasion to mourn all the glorious plans you had to take control of the tribe and forge your own destiny?"

"Hells, Nala." Kell stopped, dropped his pack, and slid down the bole of a wide tree. Pulling a long blade of grass, he stuck it in his mouth. He chewed it, savoring the sharp, acrid flavor on his tongue.

I suppose this is where she tells me this plant is poisonous and I have only moments to live.

True to form, Nala plopped down beside him, yanking the blade from his mouth with a pout. "That could make you sick if you swallow the pulp, perhaps kill you." She turned the plant over in her fingers, squinting at it with one eye closed.

"I'm a dead man walking. You notice how all the legends involve the hero dying. I don't fear it, but I'm in no hurry for it either." He grabbed a small rock and tossed it, ricocheting it off two trees before it came to land somewhere in the foliage. A gentle wind tugged at his hair, tickling his cheek.

"You're hale to be a dead man. There are also stories about heroes who return covered in glory. Or become demi-gods to serve at Regnir's side. That's probably better than a chieftain."

"It is." He rolled a small stone across his knuckles, trying to distract his warring thoughts.

"Then what ails you?"

He cleared his throat and licked his lips. "The... uncertainty?"

"Not knowing if you'll return?"

"Not so much that. I don't even know what I'm supposed to accomplish. Kill a demon? Lead an army? Recover a treasure? It maddens me to be called into service with no idea of what I'm to do, and no clue other than this damnable mark that tugs me like a puppet."

She chuckled. "You don't like not being in control."

"Of course not. Who would? Dying is one thing. Stumbling along like a blind man is something else."

She nodded but made no reply.

"What of you? Did you always want to leave? Were you ever happy in the Veil Mountains?" Kell tried to recall Nala, but he'd only glimpsed her a few times and then only from a distance. It was odd that in a tribe of a hundred, this woman could have gone largely unnoticed by him.

"Gods, no. The first time Martok took me to a city, I was terrified. When we left the peaks, I thought there was too much air, and my chest seized. He had to tie me to the horse to keep me from fleeing back to the caves."

"How old were you?" Kell plucked another stone from the ground, rolling it between his fingers, committing every pit in the stone to memory.

"I don't know. My parents perished when I was a babe. I found myself passed around different tribes until Martok took me in as an apprentice. Not over twelve summers, I think."

"You must have been terrified." He whistled between his teeth. He couldn't imagine being traded like property.

"I was until we reached the town. Everyone lived in houses made of wood and stone on flat ground. I saw colors I didn't know existed before. Food I'd only heard people talk about. I learned to read, and another world opened up for me. Now I can't envision a life in just one place. Every time I gaze at the horizon, I wonder what might be over the next rise."

"Sounds like you'd be a better choice for Regnir than me." Kell offered her a thin smile.

"I'd wager you're better with a sword than me, and perhaps that's why Regnir chose you."

"Because I'm better with a sword? To be honest, I favor an ax."

"No, oaf. Because you need to see more of the world. You were too comfortable in the mountains. To be a leader, you must know how to see beyond what's before you."

Kell blinked, letting her words sink in. She could have a point. He had never been more than a few days' ride from their village. Anything beyond that filled him with a touch of dread.

"If Regnir keeps your task from you, then you may have much to learn before you can face it."

Kell chewed on the thought, chagrined that talking to Nala about this made him feel like a whelp who knew nothing. "Would you care to have your destiny hidden from you?"

"Destiny is always hidden from the gaze of mortals. We can't know what the next day will bring. Martok's whim could make me a slave again tomorrow. Another tribe could take me. I could fall from a peak and crash on the rocks, or I could become the greatest healer of our time. The uncertainty is something I enjoy."

Kell shook his head, thinking her mad. "Would that I had your confidence. I'll end up dead in some foreign land with no one to recall my name."

"I swear to you I will always remember your name. I took a part in your destiny. I shall not forget." Her gaze softened, and his heartbeat doubled in its cadence.

"And what if you are wrong? What if this is just some fever? What if I'm just mad?"

"Then you do not differ from the rest of us. You'll still be no worse off for seeing a bit of the world. Besides, it will give me an excuse to practice my healing craft." Nala winked at him and poked his broad chest with her finger.

"You certainly have a fire for adventure. I hope your knowledge frees you from your shackles."

"Maybe I'll join you on your next quest. I have no fear that you will return from this one."

Kell chided himself for being a fool. Nala was right, and he saw it clearly now. He reached into his pack, withdrew a water skin, and took a long drink, then offered it to his insightful companion, who drank her fill as well.

"You are wise beyond your years. I don't think I feared my destiny as much as losing my place in the tribe. And if that happens, I'll win it back." Confidence rushed in to fill the void left by his insecurities.

Nala handed him the skin and sprang to her feet. "Now that's settled, we have leagues to cover before we reach Merrakka."

He rose without a word, stowing the skin in his pack. The open horizon in front of him now looked both threatening and inviting. Nala's words heartened him but could not completely dispel the unease that continued to grow within him. Regnir's mark thrummed in his chest as he took another step toward his uncertain destiny.

19

PARTING

KELL LEANED ON A makeshift staff as they finally entered the city of Merrakka. Splinters from the newly skinned branch dug into his palm, stinging his skin. Breath rattled in and out of his chest as he fought to put one foot in front of the other. Nala's hand circled his waist, bearing some of his weight. It wasn't much, given their discrepancy in size. His chest burned with each breath, the god-mark an angry wound.

"Do we need to rest?" Nala placed a hand on his shoulder.

People streamed by on either side of them. So many people. There were more people here than Kell had ever dreamt of. They pressed close, shoving each other. He wondered how there could be enough air to breathe with so many people crowded together.

Buildings of stone and wood crowded either side of the street. Harsh angles jutted everywhere. And the smell. Kell fought to catch his breath. There was so little open space. His heart hammered in his ears, and it was all he could do to keep his feet. He sucked in a breath, fighting disorientation.

He willed his breathing to diminish. "No. I can go on."

Kell struggled to his feet with an effort of willpower and hobbled on at a feeble pace. He tired of the sound of his staff on the pavement with each uneven step he took. People veered away, their faces mixed with fear and irritation. He didn't blame them. Kell's ears burned with shame, tears ran from his eyes, and he couldn't tell if it was from embarrassment or anger.

Why has my health failed? Was I not chosen by Regnir? How can I be his warrior if I can't even walk? Nala believes it is because I fear I am not up to this task and my body is failing because of it. How do I fight my mind?

Minute stacked on tortured minute until the pair arrived at an inn. A brightly painted boar's head decorated the shingle. The squeak of the chain on rusted hinges was audible over the hustle of people rushing past. Kell slumped down on an uneven bench, sucking in a deep breath. Nala dropped to a knee beside him.

"Will you be fine while I secure a room?"

"I am a warrior. Do you need coins?" Kell raised his head and tried to focus on her.

"I've my own. Probably more than you. Remember, slow deep breaths. Concentrate on nothing but the rhythm of your existence." She winked at him and patted his leg, her white-blonde hair dancing in the wind as she hurried away.

He followed her instructions, but the riot of input from all around him made it nearly impossible. All he wanted was to run as far and as fast as his legs could carry him to some wide-open space empty of people and their voices.

He sucked in another shallow breath and tightened his fingers around the staff, willing strength back into his sagging body. He fought to find a core of bravery within him to fill his yawning chasm of emptiness that unmanned him.

When he looked up, Kell noticed a man staring at him. The man was bigger than him, with brass armor beneath animal furs. A long beard cascaded over his chest.

Kell shivered as a fresh tingle of fear wriggled its way up his spine. He leapt to his feet and instantly regretted it. The ailing warrior clutched the staff to keep from falling. When his sight cleared, the man was gone, and a word floated on the breeze.

"Hubris."

Kell shook his head, wondering if his mind played tricks on him. He didn't know the word, and his ignorance added to his growing anxiety. A hand fell on his shoulder, interrupting his thoughts.

"Ready?" Nala looked at him, brow furrowed.

"Yes, cramped rooms must be better than crowded streets."

"Still your breathing until we get to the room. If they think you're ill, they'll toss us out." She patted his brawny back.

"And if they try?"

Nala shushed him, leading the way. The walk through the crowded common room took an eternity. His eyes watered, and the brand on his chest raged, yet somehow, he made it up the stairs.

Nala bustled out of the room. She returned an age later with boiling water and prepared another noxious brew that Kell was sure would ravage his taste buds beyond recovery. He stashed his gear and staff in the corner, placing his ax next to him on the pallet. Kell's chest still burned, and that word kept rattling around in his brain.

"Do you know what hubris means?"

Nala settled across from him, scattering herbs into a wooden cup. "Hubris? That's ironic, given your demeanor." She quirked a smile, thrusting the cup under his nose. "Breathe in the steam before you drink."

"So, it means confidence?" He choked while inhaling the vapors.

She laughed. "Excessive pride. Vanity. Why do you inquire?"

Kell frowned, embarrassed by her laughter. Even though she knew Regnir called him, he still felt foolish relating the reason for his question. "I think our mountain god appeared to me while you were inside. I heard that word on the wind." He sniffed the cooling tea again and hazarded a drink. He didn't quite choke, but it was a near thing.

"The ways of deities are murky. I believe it couldn't hurt to finish that. Lay back and meditate on what it means to you."

Kell grumbled but did as she bade. Exhaustion had robbed him of his strength, and although the straw poked at him through the thin covering, he drifted off immediately. Blackness enveloped him as blue and red fire danced in his mind.

His vision cleared, but instead of the dank little room, he beheld a grassy meadow. Regnir sat on a rock opposite him with an amused expression.

Kell sputtered, attempting to find words and failing. A void opened in his chest, and his hand rubbed Regnir's mark. Unsure of the protocol when meeting a god, Kell went down to one knee. The icy tingle of dread gnawed at him, sapping what little confidence he'd mustered.

"What do you fear, boy?" The god leveled him with an iron stare, withering Kell.

"A warrior does not fear." Kell mouthed the words even as his hands shook, and he prayed Regnir would not discern the lie.

An inhuman roar erupted from Regnir, causing Kell to shrink back, nearly falling on his rump. He threw a hand over his eyes as his god glowed like a thousand bonfires.

"Liar! You dissemble before the god of emotion while you kneel before me, hollowed out by *fear*?"

Kell hung his head, his whole body shaking before the heavenly rage. The light faded, to be replaced by a feeling of calm empathy. Kell dared to raise his eyes to see Regnir leaning forward with a hand on one knee.

"You think warriors do not fear? You think bravery comes from the absence of fear?"

"It has always been this way." Kell's brow knotted in confusion, trying to find the right words.

To his surprise, his god laughed for a long time, then sighed and beckoned him forward. Kell rose on unsteady legs and limped forward, trying to steady his tremors and failing utterly.

"Sit." Regnir motioned with his hand and a low stone bench rose from the ground.

Kell dropped onto it, shuddering. He didn't know how much more his battered senses could take. "I never feared before. Combat came easily to me. I never questioned that I would prevail and another would die. Since your mark appeared and I left home, I am frozen with it. Everything from the open air to the people in this town to knowing I may never see the Veil mountains again—everything paralyzes me. I am failing you before this quest even begins." Moisture gathered at the corners of his eyes, and he squeezed them shut to keep from shedding the tears of his failure.

Regnir offered him a knowing smile before answering. "Kell, everyone fears. This is the reason I chose you. Everything has come too easily to you. Yes, this will be a challenge. One that doesn't involve swinging an ax but involves the courage of sacrifice and understanding the world is bigger than you envisioned."

"But how can I face this when I can't breathe, when I can't move, where my every heartbeat is a labor?"

"You must understand your fear. You must acknowledge it exists."

"And if I don't understand any of this? How can I be your champion?" Kell's head slumped into his hands.

Regnir grabbed a lock of his hair and yanked upwards, putting them eye to eye. Only inches separated their faces. "I will set you on the proper path, as the mark was meant to. Then, like all mortals, you must learn, struggle, fail, and succeed."

"I still don't understand the first step. How do I take it? I desire to serve you. I just don't know how." Kell rubbed at his thighs with his hands as if the friction could ease the war within him.

Regnir patted him on the cheek like a consoling parent. "Control is your problem."

"I know I can't control my fear. That is my problem." Kell restated it, wondering if the god missed his point.

"Nay, you seek control. You need it. You strive to control every situation. It's natural. Your first step is accepting that you control nothing. Not only will you learn to confront your fear but also gain wisdom."

Kell's mouth opened and closed, framing a dozen replies but then going silent. His understanding deepened and his chest loosened, allowing him to take his first deep breath in days.

"For the first time in your life, I forced you to deal with the unknown. You had to put yourself in an environment that made you uncomfortable and face a quest you couldn't fathom. It's natural that frightens you. You need to accept the fear rather than let it consume you." Regnir sat beside Kell, clapping him on the back with the force of a thunderbolt, and the god shimmered.

"Wait!" Kell waved his arms, and to his surprise, Regnir's wavering form solidified. "You haven't told me what I'm supposed to accomplish yet."

Another laugh. Another broad smile. "Follow the mark. Your world is on the brink of war, and only your wits, and perhaps other god-touched, may avert it. Your heart will guide you. I would not have chosen you if I didn't think you had it in you to triumph."

The god of emotion disappeared in a blinding flash of light, and consciousness faded.

Kell sat up in the bed so swiftly his head spun. He cursed and wiped his brow. The thrum in his chest remained, but he no longer struggled to breathe.

"Gods." He gazed on Nala's sleek form, dozing in a stiff-backed chair. At his exclamation, she woke, regarding him with gentle concern. She shifted in the chair and yawned. The curve of her neck set his pulse going again.

His face burned with embarrassment. He shook his head, trying to make sense of his attraction to Nala. A week ago, he barely knew she existed, and now he couldn't imagine a life without her.

"How are you feeling? I was worried you would never wake up." She went to a basin, collected a rag, and wiped perspiration from his head and chest. Kell relished the attention.

"Better. I dreamed of Regnir. Or mayhap he came to me in my dreams. He helped me understand my fear and its cause." He took the cloth from Nala and took over. Sweat-drenched hair clung to his scalp. Kell was sure he must smell worse than the tribe's midden heap, but Nala did not wrinkle her nose.

"And what is the mission?" Nala raised an eyebrow.

"Would that I knew. 'Follow the mark.'" He blew out a breath and looked at her, expecting a jest. "Perhaps I am mad."

"If you are mad, we are all mad. Mayhap you are waking to your calling." She tossed him a comb from her pack, which he dragged through his matted hair.

"It's possible. I've only ever worried about my flank. This quest must mean there is a danger to our home, perhaps even the entire world." He hung his head.

Nala took one finger, pressed it to his forehead, and shoved till he met her eyes. "You're a lout, but now you understand you're a lout. That is a start. Regnir would not have chosen you if you were unworthy. I'll not lie. You are selfish and can be manipulative, but even in our brief time together, I've seen you be kind." She caressed his cheek then pinched it till he squealed. "Master your heart, Kell. I won't be around if this happens again."

Kell rubbed his cheek and smiled back at her. "Understood. I will try to be more worthy of Regnir's favor ... and your own." He cupped her cheek in his calloused hand. "Your friendship means much to me. It will be a hard parting to journey on alone."

Nala blushed at his compliment. "We both have our destinies. Though they diverge, there is nothing to say they may not reconnect."

Kell grinned at the thought. For one brief, shining moment, he knew peace. The only thing that marred it was the steady, throbbing call. He nodded to her and rose, stretching his limbs. "The god-mark calls me, and though my fear is not gone, at least now I understand it. Some. I think I'll need to be on my way."

Nala frowned, and Kell wondered anew if there might ever be something more than friendship between them.

She's unlike any of the women I've known. So forthright, yet delicate. But would that ruin the bond we've forged? Kell couldn't decide if it was worth the risk.

"Thank you for getting me this far. If I live ... I hope to find you again." Kell bit his lip, dreading parting with her as much as the uncertainty of his future.

Nala stood as well and smoothed her skirts, changing the subject. "I have volumes of healing to learn, and maybe some to teach these fools. I may be green to their eyes, but they know little of the healing properties of common herbs. It's all about vapors and magic."

Mighty Regnir, is there any woman like this in all the world? Though she's not a warrior, she fears nothing.

They gathered their belongings. After a quick meal, they set out into the city. Kell marveled at the buildings rising like little mountains.

Brightly colored banners dazzled his imagination. In the Veil mountains, everything was gray. He saw more people than he'd ever seen in his life. They were everywhere. They milled about like ants scrabbling over crumbs, scurrying back and forth with absurd haste, yet they accomplished little, at least to his eyes. The press of their bodies still made him uneasy.

"You get used to it. This city is tiny by comparison, but it has excellent schools, not to mention the food. You can't imagine all the different ways they can prepare fowl." Nala twirled her hair as she walked.

"Don't you miss the mountains? The hills? The silence and the wind whistling through the crags?" Kell attempted to keep pace with her, though the sensory overload made it a chore.

"Sometimes. I've never been in a city for more than a few days. While you are swinging your ax for Regnir, I'll be finding new ways to heal our people. Ask me in a fortnight." Her laughter rang out.

His mark pulsed, and he realized this was what he should fight for. The quiet moments between the clang of steel. He nodded.

"I'll do that. By the time I return, you'll be miserable and begging for a day without this stench." Kell clapped her lightly on the back, and she touched his arm.

"And you'll come back with a gleaming, golden sword or armor that's too bright to look upon, and we'll bow down to you." She mocked him, but this time, instead of embarrassing him, it made him proud to have such a friend. A chink opened in his armor, but it didn't make him feel weak.

"My weapons serve me fine." He thrust his head back. So impressed with himself, Kell almost didn't note Nala had stopped in her tracks. A rare frown bent the edges of her lips. Turning to follow her expression, the warrior realized why.

"I'm here," she said, gesturing around the city. "You know, I'm not exactly expected. We could spend a few more days getting to know the city." She patted his chest, and he found himself smiling.

"Nala, it tempts me, but it's high time I found a horse and started chasing this quest. Then I can be done with this god business and back to my life."

Nala laughed and shrugged. Kell suspected there was a jest he missed. "Truly. The offer tempts me more than you know. Yet I wager Regnir would not allow it, and if the need is great, I should not tarry."

"You likely speak the truth." Nala bit her lip, gazing up at him. She pulled him down so she could kiss his cheek, and his heart skipped a beat. "I never thought I would be sorry to see you go, but you are proving to be more interesting than I first guessed. The world is in excellent hands."

"I hope you're right. I may not be the only champion." He adjusted the ax at his back and held her pack out to her. "I've found something worth protecting." Kell gave her a sly wink and turned to find his destiny. He wanted to look over his shoulder to see if she watched him leave, but a feat of strength kept his eyes glued on the horizon as Regnir's mark showed him the way.

20

HISTORY LESSONS

Draven lay on his pallet, staring up at an oak beam stained to resemble mahogany. A crack ran down the length. He longed to spring up and pull at the splinter, wondering if it would come crashing down like the rest of his life.

I'm getting positively maudlin.

He extended his arm, watching glimmers of magic crawling along the enchanted metal. "Flames!" He clenched his fist, aiming at the beam, willing fire to shoot from it with all his might.

♥*Are you serious? You really wish to burn down the tavern?* ♥

"I'm bored."

♥*You think Heart Master exists to entertain you?*♥

Draven sighed and shook his head. "Just passing the time. Imprisonment in this cellar is testing my sanity."

♥*The hardships you endure are truly arduous.*♥

"You don't like me much, do you?" Draven flicked a nail against the cuff, imagining it was Ansalon's ear.

♥*My opinion of you is clear. You may not be evil, but that doesn't make you noble.*♥

"There's not much noble about the nobility. I'd not be one, and piety only serves priests. What do I owe a goddess? They sold me at five summers to a baker with wandering hands. My only escape was the streets. Nellonah was the first hint that all humans weren't dung, and now she turns out to not even be real."

A knock sounded at the door, and Draven turned and swung his legs off the cramped bed. He realized his back no longer pained him.

Huh. That healed fast.

Before he could stand, the door opened to reveal Loken. Draven wondered if Loken had become his shadow. Looking at him still sent a pang of guilt through him. Those twisted features and black eye patch made him shiver.

"My lady wants to see you again."

"Jealous?" Draven couldn't resist a jape at Loken. Instead, he should beg forgiveness, but teasing was easier. It didn't require delving into his recriminations about that night.

Loken said nothing, just turned, leaving the door ajar. Draven frowned at the void he left. The distinct thump-click of Loken's characteristic stride dwindled, and all grew silent once again.

♥*Insults where you should ask pardon? And you wonder why I despise you.*♥

Draven ignored the dead knight. He leapt from the bed and made his way after Loken to the hidden spiral staircase to see what Nellonah wanted this time. One thing was certain, it wouldn't be something he'd enjoy.

He arrived on the landing leading to Nellonah's study, tugging at the ill-fitting tunic. Draven missed his form-fitting thieving leathers. This borrowed clothing chafed him. He'd almost rather be naked. Her door stood ajar, so Draven walked in, head down, already dreading what was to come.

Another scolding.

♥*Well deserved.*♥

Draven banged the cuff on the door frame as he entered and took a chair opposite Nellonah. He found himself surprised that neither Loken nor Elisah joined them. Somehow, being alone with her unnerved him more than the bellicose knight-commander.

"You look surly. Wake up on the wrong side of the cellar?" She smirked as she flipped through a pile of papers, initialing some, ignoring others.

"You took my proper clothes and stuck me in the cellar for a week without so much as a book to pass the time. I'm going mad. Madder, if you count the voice in my head criticizing my lifestyle." Draven plucked at the hateful garment as if it burned his skin.

"Your last leathers had more holes than leather. Your knives were nicked, dull, and nearly worthless." She waved a hand in the air and pointed to a chest in the corner. "I had these made up for you. They should serve where we're going. And if you put important items like clothes in your satchel instead of mountains of loot, you could have worn your own clothing."

Draven rolled his eyes as he hurried to open the chest without looking like he was hurrying. Two lacquered boxes rested atop a fine jerkin, pants, and boots. The leather was so supple it felt like silk in his hands. Opening the boxes, he found a heavy-bladed falchion in one and a sturdy sword-breaker in the other. Both gleamed in the sunlight streaming in through the double windows. Testing their balance, he found himself pleased.

"Nellonah, I'm speechless! Many thanks." He took his seat again after stowing his new gear back in the chest. "I don't deserve these. How did you even know to have these made?"

"I knew you'd return one day. They've waited for you a long time." She pursed her lips. "I hoped you'd come back for me."

"Sometimes it's easier to keep running than accept what you've done. I know I should have come back sooner."

"I didn't ask you here to dwell on the past. There's something I need to know, and if you lie, I will know. I always know."

"I'm an open book. I'm literally at your mercy."

"What you said on the roof. Was it true? Or was that just talk?"

Draven looked her in the eyes for what seemed like an eternity before turning away.

"Your guess is as good as mine. I won't lie. I'm selfish and want no part of a war, yet I can't sit back and do nothing with what you've told me. Once Elisah has this in her possession, I will stay and help you if I can. I owe you that much.

Nellonah tilted her head. "You owe yourself at least that much. I wish you could see that."

Draven frowned, not understanding her meaning. He couldn't fathom how following her off to some faraway conflict would serve him at all.

"For your life to have meaning, you must eventually stand for something. Your lot was bad, but not as bad as others. Neither the world nor the gods owe you a destiny. That is for you to decide."

Draven stared at her, stunned. His mouth moved, but no words formed. His world inverted, again.

"I'm trying." The words rang hollow in his ears. "No one can expect more. A month ago, my only worry was paying off the guild and keeping out of the docks. Now I could be responsible for the world ending. At least give me a moment to catch my breath."

"In this, you may have a point. How can you understand the extent of the danger without the proper context?"

Draven crossed his arms, nodding. "Right, like this Seguris. How is he so bad?"

"My reports are incomplete, but he aims to resurrect the Mektwin empire that enslaved much of the continent centuries ago."

"Revolutions happen all the time."

"Not always to the benefit, and were Seguris not being backed by a god who thrives on conflict, I might not disagree. If my sources are correct, Seguris is of Mektwin royal blood and raised in slavery. He escaped somehow and now gathers followers. Many followers. By all accounts, he is seeking vengeance for every wrong ever visited on his people."

"How many is 'many'? Ten? Twenty?"

"Try hundreds. And yet the monarchies either don't consider him a threat or can't find him. When Khyris came to power, he learned to kill gods and take their power. If Seguris gains Blood Thorn, we could see the same madness play out again, but this time we may not be able to stop it."

Draven nodded his head, not understanding her meaning at all.

"And this knight-commander, she is our best hope for ending the conflict before it begins?"

"Elisah is old, Draven, ancient. Her origins are unknown, but she's hundreds of years old. Legend says she appeared one day, dressed in rags, wielding a broadsword."

"Sort of like you?" Draven scowled, looking at Nellonah with a raised brow.

"She is older, far older. I am not much older than you."

"But you appeared one day, just as you are now."

"Not quite, but close. When gods give birth to shards, we know all our god knows. With time, that fades. We gain fresh memories and experience. Usually, shards are short-lived for specific missions, but in my case, my creator wished for an ongoing spy she could trust implicitly."

"But you don't tell her everything?"

Nellonah pursed her lips and steepled her fingers. "No, I do not. I enjoy my existence. I have no desire to be reabsorbed by her, so I report what I can. Also, to protect those I care about, like you and Loken." She frowned, rubbing her temples. "I had to swear that Loken was important to the prophecy to be allowed to bring him back and even then, not fully. If she learns you have Heart Master and are not the chosen champion, I fear for us all."

Draven looked down at the cuff, wondering what it would be like to be wiped from existence. He found he could accept his own death easier than he could picture Nellonah being wiped from existence. He whistled through his teeth.

"And this Blood Thorn, it's worse than Heart Master? Or this Fist, whatever that is?"

"It's certainly one of the strangest relics. It feeds on anger and blood. Created by Regnir, the mountain god of emotion, it takes anger and turns it into pure power. Ghedryn created The Fist of Heaven so that it would enable the bearer to control Blood Thorn rather than being consumed by it."

"So, The Fist is useless without the sword?"

"Far from it. The Fist channels ambition into various kinds of destructive force. That's why it works so well with Blood Thorn. Separately, they are devastating; combined, they convey near god-like power."

Draven scrubbed at his hair, overwhelmed by it all.

"And this thing?" He tapped at the cuff. "Why is it such a big deal?"

"Blood Thorn, Hallowed Verity, The Fist, and the Chaos Masque—all contain the power of singular gods. It took the power of all twelve gods to forge Heart Master."

"Twelve? There are only ten gods. Everyone knows that."

"*Now* there are only ten. Khyris learned to bind gods and—" she shuddered, "consumed them. Somehow."

Draven swallowed hard, wondering at the mechanics.

"Can—can any Mektwin do that? I heard they are magic, that they're born wizards."

Nellonah shook her head. "No, but they have certain abilities. They covet magic, particularly enchantments. They're drawn to them."

"So that's why the war god employed a Mektwin to start his war."

"Now you are learning." Nellonah looked at him with the gentle compassion he hadn't seen on her face since his return.

"Anything else? Like, can they throw lightning bolts or crap fire?"

"They're the reason Ansalon changed allegiances from Velleris to my creator."

"Why? The Mektwin don't worship either, or at least I didn't think they did."

"When the Mektwin were overthrown, Nerys argued they should be allowed to atone, but Velleris commanded their deaths. Every one of them." She twisted a lock of hair around her finger.

"I take it the knights... didn't like that?" Draven felt like an imbecile.

"They thought it unfair to punish an entire race for the crimes of some. A select few became guardians of relics. The rest..." She spread her fingers across the desk as if throwing sand on the wind. "The rest are still slaves today. Knights like Ansalon and Elisah broke faith with Velleris and took new patrons. Even two centuries later, the tensions run high."

Draven shook his head in disbelief. "This is much to digest. Any idea why this thing chose me? I assume Heart Master isn't supposed to bond with just anyone, especially with Ansalon inside it."

"That even I do not understand. It's supposed to choose only anointed champions. Yet despite your selfish behavior, I've always believed your heart was good. Noble even."

Draven cracked a grin, tapping the cuff again. "Ansalon doesn't seem to like me much. Maybe a few hundred years have driven him mad. I know I'd be losing it. And then it chooses me right under his nose." The thief wondered if he could really be a champion.

♥ No. ♥

Ansalon's annoyance cheered him even more.

"I should go back to my hole. I have much to think about."

"And I have to finish booking our passage. Ready your sea legs."

Sea legs? I've never even been on a boat before.

21

SETTING SAIL

THE MUSTY AROMA OF dust, hay, and manure wafted into Draven's nostrils as he followed behind the impressive figure of Elisah Fairoaks. He marveled at how any woman could be so big and graceful at the same time. Her arms were as thick as his own and her shoulders even broader, yet she picked her way to the stables with a grace he envied.

Guess she's had practice. Like... a thousand years of practice.

"I still don't understand." Draven hurried to keep up with her long stride.

♥ *Your lack of understanding could fill a library.* ♥

Draven ignored the voice of the cuff and tapped Elisah's massive shoulder.

"It's not my job to educate you." Her reply was more grunt than words.

"You are stuck with me until this thing comes off." He banged the cuff on the stall. "Maybe longer if I choose to stick around and join the quest."

Fairoaks whirled, leveling him with a gaze that froze his blood. "It is my job to stop Ghedryn and Seguris. I don't have a hundred years to train you. You have no part in this."

"This holy relic says otherwise. You may not like it. Nellonah may not like it. The ghost sure as hell doesn't like it. But this happened for a reason. I'm sure of it."

"Fine. I don't like it, but I have accepted it." She turned, putting a hand on her hip. "What don't you understand?"

Draven still couldn't get used to her without the armor. *I thought her size was all those layers of plate mail, but no, she's just as imposing underneath it.*

"We are going by boat, correct?"

"By ship, but yes, we'll sail to the coast to find Kethek."

"So why are we picking out horses? You can't take horses on a boat. Can you?" The question seemed logical to him, but he sensed nothing but disdain from Ansalon.

"You know even less about horses than you do about ships." Elisah shook her head, trying not to laugh.

"I live in a city. I run across the rooftops. What do I need with a horse?"

"And boats? You live in a port city? How can you live in a port and know nothing about ships?"

Draven rolled his eyes. "Never left the city. I may have rummaged around a few at the docks. Everything I ever needed was in Sharazin." He crossed his arms, daring her to argue with his logic.

"We'll need horses after we disembark for the ride to the tower. So, we take horses we know. Horses we can depend on. I've ridden the same charger for years. He knows me, and I know I can depend on him in a fight. The last thing you need in the middle of battle is a horse that's going to bolt."

When she put it like that, it made sense. He couldn't get the picture of a horse swimming out of his head.

"Okay, fine. We need horses. Known horses. What do I look for since I've never been on one?"

"Oh, for the love of the goddess. You've never ridden before?"

"No." Draven kicked at the straw until he cleaned a spot down to the floorboards. "How hard can it be? After all, anyone can do it."

The stable resounded with the echo of Elisah's laughter. Draven's face colored, and he dipped his head.

"Two hundred years and we might make a warrior of you... I'm sure there is a well-broken nag in the lady's stable somewhere. Maybe a pony."

Draven grumbled as Elisah went off in search of the stable master. As if by magic, Nellonah appeared beside him, laying a hand on his shoulder. The touch reminded him of a time when they were more than whatever they were now. Beside her, Loken lanced him with a jealous glare.

"He's coming too? Thought he'd need to stay and run the business." Draven jerked his head back toward the Final Fortune.

"I won't need the Final Fortune after today. I doubt I will return. It's up to Loken or you, whether either of you wants to return."

Loken glared. Draven ran his tongue over dry lips, suddenly realizing that everything he had ever known was ending. He stiffened his spine.

"We're coming back. This is my home. We're not just going to abandon it." He crossed his arms and glared back at Loken. "Are you sure he won't be a problem?"

"Try to keep up with me," Loken said.

Draven threw his hands in the air. He knew better than to argue with Loken.

"Elisah, make certain they use the black saddles with the oak leaves." Nellonah hurried up to Elisah, leaving Draven alone with his brother.

Draven put a hand to his falchion and regarded Loken. The spymaster had donned thick leather armor. A heavy-bladed cutlass hung from a wide, red sash at his waist. A thin braid now held back Loken's wispy hair. Across his back hung a stout ash bow carved with symbols Draven could only guess at.

"So, you're up for fighting gods, too?"

"I fight my lady's enemies."

"You used to be a better conversationalist. You used to be fun. Not everything needs to be a world-ending crisis."

Elisah and Nellonah returned with three horses each. Elisah swung up onto the saddle of a massive warhorse. Loken took a chestnut mare next to hers, his fake leg giving him no trouble. Draven whistled as Nellonah led a mount to him. Draven hoped the animal had been well-trained. It took a few tries, but he clambered into the saddle. The horse didn't so much as move an inch. Nellonah slid up hers like a spider.

"Who are the other horses for?" Draven tugged his reins this way and that, but the horse continued to ignore him.

"Provisions."

He rubbed his head, chiding himself that he had given no thought to food or shelter. He was used to taking what he needed. Then, there was always his satchel if times got lean. The food he stashed there never spoiled.

"Stop in the name of The Twelve! Dismount and prepare to face justice."

Draven craned his neck to see a white-robed priest holding a large gold staff. Behind him were at least a dozen armed men. He calculated his odds of controlling the beast he sat upon, but church men blocked both exits from the stable.

At least it's not the one I punched. Funny, that the goddess's shard is getting stopped by priests to keep her from a holy quest.

"I told you I would handle the thief." Elisah guided her steed past Draven and Nellonah's as if by mental command alone.

"There are rituals to follow. Knight-commander, you may be, but until anointed, you cannot bear Heart Master. Where is it?" The imperious priest eyed Draven suspiciously.

Nellonah swore in at least three languages. Loken laughed, clearly enjoying Draven's plight.

Can't say I blame him.

♥*Surrender. It is inevitable.*♥

Draven scanned the buildings next to the church soldiers. He could make it, but it would require abandoning Nellonah and the rest. He chewed at his lip as he considered jumping from his horse to the roof.

I could make it, but what then? If I stay, I face imprisonment or worse, but it would mean abandoning Lock and Nell? I can't do that again. He gritted his teeth and looked down, praying Nellonah could handle this, putting his faith in another person for perhaps the first time in his life.

"Stay on your horses." Nellonah's voice rang out like a gong. Even the imperious priest took a step back. "Your instructions were simple. Fairoaks is the champion. I will see to her and to Heart Master."

"No, you will not. If you can't observe the rituals, the church will name its own champion. Give over the thief for justice and Heart Master." The heavy staff banged on the cobbles. The priest motioned to guards on either side of him to proceed.

"You leave me no choice." Nellonah raised her hands, magic spooling down from the heavens, engulfing her in the green light. Before Draven could even take a breath, the light exploded. He blinked to clear his eyes, and the churchmen were gone. In fact, the entire street was gone. Now spread out before him was a long row of ships at anchor.

What?

"You turned the ... we were ..." Draven pointed back to the docks, looking for words as his senses failed him. "Now we're not there."

How is this possible?

"Quickly now. Our appearance didn't go unnoticed, and it won't take them long to dispatch guards." Nellonah spurred her horse to a fast walk. The others followed suit. Loken took Draven's dangling reins and guided the thief's horse. Somehow, they all just accepted what happened as if it were normal. Draven put a hand to the saddle horn to keep his balance.

♥ *This is wrong! We should have obeyed the priest. How can Elisah agree with this?*♥

"Listen, Nellonah could get wiped out of existence. I could die. I trust Nellonah. You trust Elisah. No one has to die. Well, except Seguris and a few hundred bandits." Draven swayed from side to side, trying to find the horse's rhythm, but it wasn't going well.

A few minutes had them before a ship called *The Rose Bush*. Nellonah and Elisah were already off their mounts and ushering them to men on either side of long, wide gangplanks. Draven half-slid, half-fell from his own horse. It took a moment before he could balance after the rocking sway of his mount. Loken took him by the hand and all but dragged him up a different plank. Draven wanted to shake him off, but his grip on reality was still tenuous.

They made it to the polished deck where Nellonah talked to a man with a familiar face. Draven swore as he looked at Thistle, a smuggler he once traded with. Thistle now stood attired in a fine suit, with boots and a broad blue sash running from shoulder to hip while a tricorn hat hung from a precarious angle on his head. After a quick conversation, Thistle bellowed at his sailors, who flew into motion.

Yeah, get the lead out.

Draven came up to Nellonah and Elisah, shouldering between them. The tall knight-commander gave him an irritated glance. "I don't want to concern anyone, but the ghost is having a fit."

"He always was rigid. Don't worry, he'll fall in line. He won't unleash the power of the relic." Elisah frowned, staring at the cuff as if she could see the knight within.

"Why?" Draven thought he knew the answer before even asking the question.

"Because doing so would allow you to access the same power." Nellonah tapped a finger to her lips.

Draven smiled at the thought. He looked around the deck, trying to get used to a different swaying as the deck rocked back and forth. Draven had been on ships before, but never at sea. This he could handle. The captain ambled over and clapped him on the back.

"Draven, lad, good to have you on my decks again." Thistle gave him a gap-toothed grin.

"You've come up in the world."

"You, it seems, as well. You'd pale if you knew what this trek was netting me." He departed and went back to shouting orders at his crew.

Draven gave Nellonah a sideways glance, wondering if she knew who she was dealing with. Standing there with the sea air lifting her hair in a corona, Draven's heart did a triple beat.

I need to mend things with her.

22

Calm Seas

CALM BLUE SEAS SPREAD out on either side of the bow, too calm. Draven leaned over the railing, wishing the wind would pick up. He liked the salty air, and the calm sway of *The Rose Bush* relaxed him. Captain Thistle cursed his men and called for oars.

Draven rubbed at the cuff, trying to slip a finger under the metal with little luck. His skin itched beneath it, driving him mad.

"You're doing that, aren't you?" As usual, the more he tried to pry Heart Master away from his skin, the tighter it contracted.

♥*It is a minor inconvenience, and no, I am not responsible for your dry skin.*♥

He turned to see Nellonah saunter past Thistle. Amber hair whipped past her in the light breeze, and her eyes, now cobalt, looked at Draven over a wistful smile.

"You'll want to watch talking to yourself around sailors. They can be superstitious."

"I swear the ghost knight has it in for me." Draven curled his hands over the wood of the bow.

"He's likely not the only one." She drew next to him, putting her back to the railing.

"Still undecided?"

"My feelings for you are more complicated than even I can fathom."

"That's better than hating me, I suppose." Draven looked at his boots.

"I don't hate you. I never did. But I hate what you did. The way you abandoned everything. Did you believe you could keep running forever, first from me, then the church, and finally the guild?"

"I never thought much about it. I lived for each day, because yesterday was full of ghosts."

"I'm one of those ghosts." Nellonah's finger crept along the railing toward his own.

"I know. You were never far from my mind. How could you ever gaze upon me again? I couldn't stand to look at myself." He raised his hand, the cuff throwing diamond glints off the metal. "I regret it took this to bring me back."

"Does that mean that you will leave again when it's bound to Elisah?"

Draven whistled, wishing he knew the answer.

"I wish I knew. It's safe to say I won't be welcome in Sharazin for some time. I'd like to stay until I understand my purpose."

"I don't hate that answer." She took his hand, rubbing her thumb along his knuckles. "Mind you, if you disappear again, I will hunt you down this time."

"I'm more worried about you disappearing. The cuff and the world be damned, I'd throw it away to keep you here."

"Even gods die, Draven, but I hope my creator will allow me to flourish for a while yet. If we are successful, she may even grant me my freedom. Who can say?"

"None of us will let her take you." He brought her hand up, kissing it.

They drifted into a comfortable silence. Draven enjoyed the sounds of the ship and the roll of the waves. Nellonah's touch reassured him there was enough reason to stay in one place. His thoughts drifted to a life removed from thieving, and he wondered if this was magic on her part. Draven gave her a long look, taking in her sweet smile and honeysuckle aroma.

Don't ruin it.

♥ *The goddess will do as she wills, and you must accept it.* ♥

Draven ignored the voice and slid closer to Nellonah, putting his arm around her. To his surprise, she didn't protest or turn him into a newt. Rocking in time to the waves, she was more god than mortal.

"You're still not forgiven, you know." She murmured the words against his skin, much like a kiss.

"What must I do to earn that?"

"Oh, I don't know?" Nellonah trailed a finger along the inside of his arm. "Fight a god? Face up to those you've hurt? Stay with me?"

"I think I can manage that."

"Making peace with Loken is the best way to start."

"And I suppose you have a magic spell for that? He thinks dying was a blessing, so that he no longer had my poor example to follow." Draven frowned as he recalled how deeply Loken wounded him with that remark.

"Words have little meaning after so long. You need to speak with your actions. This is a good start."

"Do you think there's time for me to make amends?"

Nellonah looked at him, an eyebrow raised.

Draven shook his head, irritated that he couldn't find words for the vague impressions eating away at him. "I struggle to see a future where any of us survive."

"You might not be wrong. I can't evade the goddess forever... I'm overdue to merge with her as it is."

"You think she will absorb you then?" He suppressed a shudder, trying to get the words out. Even the thought of her merging with Nerys turned his guts to ice. Imagining that such a union might take Nellonah from him forever was more than he could bear.

"She created me for one purpose. Nerys tasked me with finding Heart Master and binding it to a champion worthy of its power. Her need for me ends when the cuff is bound to Elisah. I hope for more ... yet the goddess can be merciless."

Draven bit back a retort. It would do no good. He pulled her tight, pressing a kiss to her lips. Nellonah didn't resist. Did she tremble, or did he? Draven couldn't tell. Over her shoulder, Draven could see Loken looking on with a neutral expression. Thistle made a rude gesture, and Draven rolled his eyes.

"Then we need to show the goddess you can serve more than one purpose. You've changed so many lives, and maybe we'll need more than enchanted weapons to fight this Seguris. A goddess-born sorceress couldn't hurt."

Her lips against his cheek turned upward into a smile. "Accepting anything is not your strong suit."

"Hey, I'm not—okay, yes, I am. But I'm trying to find it within me to make amends. Let's start with your impending doom."

Nellonah licked her lips before answering. Green faerie light danced around her blue eyes. The effect mesmerized him. "My doom could be your doom, too. If the goddess judges I'm to blame for this mess, she could just as easily decide it's easier to remove Heart Master from your corpse."

♥ *The judgment of the goddess is final. You must abide by it.* ♥

"The cuff isn't on our side. Or at least the ghost isn't. I really don't know the difference."

"The difference is immense. Heart Master is imbued with the power and knowledge of twelve gods. The Order of Twelve chose Ansalon to guard it. You cannot access its power without him, but it is not his alone to control."

"Good to know, otherwise he would have roasted me first thing." Draven beamed her a cheeky smile. "Why can't the goddess just wish this thing off me and put it onto Fairoaks?" He tilted his head in the knight-commander's direction. Elisah sparred with the sailors, one arm tied behind her back. The sailors didn't look to be gaining much from her encumbrance.

"Twelve gods. No one god commands it. The rules are complex, and impossible to comprehend, even for me. They exist for a reason. High-Father predicted a need for authority beyond a single god. Heart Master was to be that authority."

Draven stopped and thought about it. "Then... it could protect us both if Ansalon agrees."

"He is not likely to go against the decree of the goddess." She took his hand and led him around the railing to a low bench. Nellonah shoved him down and plopped into his lap.

Draven could have sworn his heart stopped for at least a beat.

23

HEALING OLD WOUNDS

 ORED WITH DAY UPON day of inaction, Draven took to the rigging of the ship for some much-needed exercise. The coarse fibers of the ropes dug into his hands as he pulled himself up to the spar. Sweat trickled down his back. Muscles burning, he swung around and looked at the deck below. Bare-chested sailors milled about their duties in the heat of the afternoon, cursing their captain, the gods, and anything else they could think of. Nellonah was nowhere to be seen, although Loken and Elisah conversed, heads close together. Draven smiled, enjoying the exercise. The wound on his back was now only a distant memory.

It's not the rooftops of Sharazin, but it's close.

For the first time since stealing the blighted cuff, Draven reveled in staring down at the world. No one chased him, that he knew of, and they were only days away from the ancient priest that would solve all their problems. There was still the business with the warlord, but Draven had little doubt Nellonah and her champion could handle him.

No harm going along for the ride.

He and Nellonah could start fresh in a new city. He wouldn't even mind if Loken joined them.

Well, not much.

Loken turned his head skyward as if the man were telepathic. He shouted and waved at the wiry thief on the ropes.

Draven sighed, wondering what new history lesson or myth he was supposed to commit to memory now. Shaking his head, he wound his way down to a rope with a weight attached and rode it to the deck. Draven tied off the weight and trudged his way over to Loken. As soon as she saw him approaching, Elisah walked off to spar with the sailors. The knight-commander never got bored with combat, whether it was with swords or grappling. Day and night, she would entice the unwary mariners into a mock battle.

I'd like to see how she fares against a real challenger.

♥*I'm sure she would happily split you from chin to navel.*♥

I'd last a few minutes at least.

Ansalon refrained from commenting, but Draven detected smugness rippling off the cuff.

As Draven approached him, Loken hobbled over and took a seat on a wide bench against the main cabin. Draven looked at the planks, dreading any conversation with his former protégé. He couldn't be sure, but he thought the spymaster struggled more than usual with his false leg. Loken motioned for Draven to sit next to him. Rolling his eyes, he sat as instructed.

Draven waited for Loken to speak. Sweat stood out on his brow. Gulls screeched overhead, and he found his attention wandering away from the looming conversation with Loken.

"Put your hand on my leg."

Draven's mouth fell open. Whatever he'd expected from Loken, this was not it. "We may need to mend fences, but there are limits."

Loken dropped his head and laughed. When he recovered his senses, he said, "It's for my leg."

"Your leg?" Draven still didn't connect the dots.

"My magical leg. The one that replaced the one I lost because of you."

Draven snorted. *I still think your lack of dexterity had more to do with it.* He kept the thought to himself for now. "You want me to rub your magic leg?"

Loken frowned and swore. "Not rub. Here, look." He yanked up the leg of his trousers, revealing a limb of dull gray metal resembling a human appendage. Where the kneecap should have been, two sparkling gems pulsed with pale light.

"Wait, are those—?"

"The Eyes of Nerys? Yes. Nellonah said if there was a sufficient power source, she could craft a leg that would function as well as the original. I replaced the jewels with counterfeits in the temple. Very good fakes, mind you." Loken regarded Draven with a sneer.

The breath left Draven's body, and he couldn't replace it. "You bastard! You stole the same jewels I went after, replaced them with fakes, didn't get caught, and you did it without a leg?"

"And an eye. You taught me well. I just apply those skills with a bit more subtlety than you do."

Draven huffed and folded his arms over his chest. "I don't believe it."

"Believe what you will. People, even temple guards, ignore you when you're maimed. It was easy to hide in the temple, do the deed, then hide till the doors opened the next day. When I heard of your theft, I laughed for days till Nellonah told me Heart Master had gone missing as well."

Still fuming, Draven cocked an eyebrow at Loken. "None of this tells me why I should touch your fake leg."

"Nellonah charges the gems, but this unfortunate affair has her distracted."

"And when the gems run out, you can't walk?"

"In a way. The gems will draw my own life, since I have no magic of my own. I could take it off, but then I'm back to being a cripple. Even then I can hobble a bit, just not as agile as I do when it's working."

"So you want to suck my life out instead?"

Loken smacked Draven's head open handed. Hard enough, his ears rang.

"Heart Master, you dolt. It has the power, more than enough magic to charge the gems."

Draven whistled, not entirely mollified. "Fine, I suppose I owe you that much. I still can't believe you stole the eyes first. Makes it even more tragic." He took a breath and placed his palm over the gems. *I should steal the cursed things right out of his leg. It'd serve him right.*

♥*Heart Master was never intended for parlor tricks.*♥

"The knight doesn't approve. That makes it worth it. You'd think he'd be happy to help the lame to walk or to heal your eye."

Loken shook his head. "The goddess demanded a price for my resurrection. The fall may have taken my leg, but she took my eye."

Draven rolled his eyes, noting a subtle blue glow from his cuff, and the stones in Loken's knee flared to life. Loken smirked, deriving some enjoyment out of the exchange. Whether it came from the magic or Draven's chagrin, the thief couldn't discern.

"You and my lady appear to have renewed your relationship."

"I'm hoping, still not sure we have one, but it's a start."

"You were awfully close earlier." Loken's metal leg flexed beneath Draven's hand, sending a shiver up his arm.

"And yet she likes to remind me I'm not forgiven. Can't figure out if she's serious. You know how she is."

"I do not know if anyone living knows how she is." Loken laughed at a hidden jest.

Draven shrugged. The salty sea air warred with the stench of ozone from magic sizzling the air. The twin gems in Loken's leg surged and glowed a steady brilliant green. Draven removed his hand just as Thistle wandered by. It didn't keep the captain from hurling a rude comment their way.

"I'd do anything for Nellonah, but I don't know how to apologize for abandoning her." Draven scrubbed his face with his hands as if he could wipe away the years.

"Abandonment takes time, and so do amends. You're off to a start just by being here ... if you're genuine."

"I am; I swear it. I don't know how to fight a god, or even a warlord, but I'm game to try for you both."

Loken smoothed his pant leg down over the gray metal. "I can't speak for my lady, but you're here. Your presence after the metal is removed will be telling."

Draven nodded his head.

"When did you become so wise?"

"When I stopped listening to you." Loken stood and walked away.

Draven shook his head, trying to tame the war of emotions that waged within him. He sought to regain control of his fate, but the longer Heart Master was on his arm, the less he believed it was possible.

Thistle dropped next to him, giving Draven a gap-toothed grin. The old smuggler might have cleaned up, but he still smelled like a plague rat dipped in rosewater.

"Gods, you smell even worse than I did after a night in the sewers." Draven's nose curled. "Have you ever bathed?"

"Only when I get knocked into the sea. What's the point?"

"You may dress like a captain, but you're still a pirate to the core, aren't you?"

"Aye. So, you favor the gimp, or the spy-lady?"

"I won't even dignify that with a response."

"Want to join my crew? I could use someone with your skills, and I can hide you from the church."

Draven thought on the offer. The darker part of him leapt to the surface. A scheming, selfish, jealous part. Once free of Heart Master, he could join up with Thistle, sail the seas, and steal enough to fill the hold of this ship. He shook his head, thrusting the thoughts away.

No, I'll not lose what little I've gained with Nell and Lock. I'm through with taking the easy way out.

"I think my fate lies on dry land, with Nellonah, Loken, and Fairoaks."

"Suit yourself. Offer's open if you change your mind. Up to you if you want to go get yourself killed. Deserts and disasters, boy."

24

Looking for Direction

Afternoon rains turned the dusty prairie humid, and Helena wiped at her brow. Heat crawled along the muddy streets of the sleepy hamlet of Thallen like a silent thief stealing what little energy the residents possessed. Farmers returned from their hard work to late dinners, while those of lower standing drank alcohol in the tavern.

Peeling paint flaked off the shutters and cracks ran up the wall. An open door offered the cool comfort of forgetfulness within. A slender man lounged by the side of the entrance, picking at sores on his arms.

"Damn it, we've told you not to do that filthy crap where people can see! You're the damned cook!"

The man grunted, sucked in his lips, and spat on the ground.

Helena looked at the pair and her stomach heaved. She tied the reins of her horse to the warped post in front of the seedy establishment and smoothed her robes before striding over to the man.

"Stables?" She hitched her knife belt around so the blade was within easy reach as she looked down on the man. Wispy strands of auburn hair hung limp against her forehead in the oppressive heat.

"You looking for a stallion?" he asked, punctuating his meaning by licking his scabby lips.

Helena didn't so much as breathe before driving her fist into his sunken mid-section. Her knee came up as his head fell, meeting with a guttural cry. He coughed and choked, his body drawing in on itself. His legs shook, but before he went to the ground, her other hand grabbed him by the throat, forcing his head up to meet her gaze.

"Stables." Her inquiry turned into a demand.

"That way." His right arm pointed around the corner of the tavern. Spittle trailed past his lips to a pointed chin.

"The goddess bless you." She released her grip on him, and he slid down the cracked wall.

By the time she returned from the stable master, the slender man nursed a goose-egg on his forehead, looking at her with a mixture of fear and ire. She snorted and ambled past him into the recesses of sin.

Fading light slanted in through the open door to show a dilapidated ruin. Rushes covered a dirt floor to soak up the smell of urine, vomit, and alcohol with only moderate success.

The narrow room led back to a long, low block of wood serving as a crude bar. Tables ranged from new lumber to rickety furniture more fit for a fire than holding drinks. There were no servers in evidence, only a stout-looking man with short, graying-blond hair plastered to his forehead. The heat overwhelmed even her vaunted stoicism.

To Helena's surprise, a half-dozen men mulled over drinks. Normally, she sought answers at the nearest chapel, but the only temple here was to the moody mountain god, and she'd find no welcome there.

Her entry caused every eye in the place to turn and appraise her. Helena let a hand drop to her knife belt and walked to the bar, head held high, gaze imperious. She rested one calloused palm on the scarred wood while running her gaze over the desperate lot. The barman raised an eyebrow at her as if daring her to order a drink.

"We have no wine here." His manner was just as gruff as his looks implied.

Helena's mouth became a thin, hard line. "Mead will serve. Or ale, if you have none." She clicked one blunt nail twice on the counter. A wooden cup appeared with some brown liquid that smelled of honey and berries.

"The clergy doesn't drink for free here."

In response, Helena slapped a copper coin on the sticky wood of the bar. "Velleris does not reward cheats." Her eyes narrowed, giving him the hardest stare she could muster. Her heart fluttered. This was not her element, and she knew it.

The Goddess decrees, and the faithful must follow.

"Is it some boy-whore you're trying to locate? We've none of that." He turned and spat on the floor, uttering some epithet that was lost to her.

Her stomach tumbled anew, but she continued to glare.

The barman glared back with an equal intensity. The conversations in the tavern quieted as the patrons scented the possibility of violence. All of those who still had the strength were spoiling for a fight in this heat.

"Information." A knot of tension settled in her shoulders while her fingers beat a staccato on the worn top of the bar. Somewhere behind her, she heard the stuttered screech of a chair thrust back from a table.

"Mayhap your arse is better tender than your coins." A voice called from behind her. She spun, murder in her eyes. A lanky man of middle years rose to his full height and settled his hands on his hips. Helena's fingers itched to draw the blade at her belt and filet the bastard, but he might possess the information she sought.

She let her arms fall to her side and took a step toward him. Lust and evil shone from his eyes. He doffed a wool cap and cracked the knuckles of his right hand.

Helena filled herself with the breath of the goddess, and power surged. Rage echoed through her at every indignation she'd faced and manifested itself in righteous fury. Hot blood surged in her veins as she lashed out with half a dozen rabbit-quick blows that left the man reeling. He landed one meaty fist to the side of her head, but she took no notice.

The wrath of the goddess was upon her. A few more well-placed punches and kicks had the man down. The other patrons looked down at the big man on the floor, trying to rise with only minor success. Her wild-eyed grin was enough incentive for them to reclaim their seats.

"What information?" The bartender was calling from over her shoulder.

"Seguris. A bandit. Or warlord. Where may I find him?" As she spoke to the barman, she marked the location of every man.

"South and east of here. Far south. They say he scours the old cities."

"Are you lying?" Her hand rose to smooth the errant strands of hair that came loose from her bun in the scuffle.

"No need. Don't owe them a damned thing. Nor you. Bandits with wagging tongues drift through, seeking to join him in his mad quest to rebuild the Mek-twin empire."

"My thanks." She walked back to the bar and drained the revolting mead in one long gulp. She wiped her lips with the heel of her hand, regretting the way it twisted her gut. "Temperance in all things, men of Thallen. Even moderation."

The patrons gave her a wide berth as she strode out.

25

CHAMPIONS MEET

KELL FOUND ACQUIRING A horse was easy, but mastering it was difficult. Getting used to the animal's rhythm took patience. Every step of the horse's hooves jarred his spine, and his legs ached from squeezing them together to stay in the saddle. He regretted not learning horsemanship, but it was rarely necessary for mountain raiding. He reined to an awkward halt as he came to a small city.

The sun beat down like a hammer on the muddy streets, sending the pungent aroma of animals and sweat up from the ground.

His long, blond hair hung damp and stringy as he wiped his brow with a cloth and thrust it back into his saddlebag. He missed the cool breezes that blew through the mountain passes. Just as he missed everything about the mountains. This flat land still made him nervous.

No trees obscured his view, and he could see leagues in any direction. Beyond the buildings in the town center, homesteaders raised livestock and grew food on the barren land.

It still struck him as odd that no one carried weapons here. Nearly everyone he observed walked unarmed and unconcerned. He made a note that if the warriors of the Veil mountains ever made it this far, it would be ripe for plunder, but then again, maybe these people possessed nothing of value.

He slowed his big black stallion to a walk. Spotting a stable near a run-down building that could only be the village tavern, he dropped his animal off. He wondered how Nala was faring back in her training but cast thoughts of her aside.

Once my task is done.

Ignoring the tavern, he made for a church bearing the sign of the sunburst at the edge of town. Drunks, he'd found, were unreliable sources of information. Violence sufficed when all else failed but was best used in moderation. He'd aroused the ire of an entire ale shop the day before and barely gotten out of the place with his skin intact. He hitched his ax higher on his back as it chafed against his sweat-soaked shirt.

The symbol of Regnir stood proudly atop the small chapel. He shook his head in wonder that anyone worshiped the mountain god in such a tiny building. Didn't they know the great god preferred towering edifices like the craggy peaks Regnir called home? Still, it was better than the mewling fools who bent a knee to Velleris.

He found the cramped room empty of everyone except a priest in brown robes of rough material. He noticed an enormous boulder had been converted into a makeshift pulpit with a row of simple benches leading to it. This made Kell smile. A sunburst like the one emblazoned upon his chest stood out on the face of the rock. At its heart clenched a fist. Mortared stone walls led up to it, empty of ornamentation. For the first time, Kell realized the seven-pointed star of Velleris bore similarities to the sunburst of Regnir. He wrinkled his nose at the realization.

The priest turned, revealing an aging man with a bushy, black beard. "Welcome, worshiper of the great one."

"Light of the day, dutiful father." Kell followed the greeting with a slight nod of his head.

"Welcome. Welcome. You are a big, strapping lad. Not from here, either. The mountains?" The priest's voice echoed from a barrel chest.

"Yes. I walk in Regnir's path." Kell scrubbed at his face, unsure how to continue.

"What troubles you?"

"I am on a pilgrimage." He pulled his shirt and vest open to show the brand of his god. The priest didn't quite go down to his knees, but the younger man could tell he wanted to.

"Holy Father." The priest's eyes went wide with reverence, but he recovered quickly, smoothing his coarse robe. "But where are my manners? I am Klast. A simple son to the father, and father to his faithful. Not so blessed as you, my boy. How can I help one of the chosen?" Klast pounded Kell's shoulder as if to test how sturdy he was.

"Chosen? I feel the call, but I don't understand what I am called to do. I've prayed and asked at every stronghold, but no one seems to know. Do you?" Kell resisted the urge to take hold of the man's robes. The continual burning, gnawing drag of the god-mark left him wayward and exhausted. Every time he stopped, the call pulled, dragging him to some unknown destination.

"Alas, I do not. But it must be of no little import. I have only heard of one other god-touched. He slew a demon, or so the stories go. We cannot always trust stories, though. Come. Sit. We can speak and seek enlightenment through discourse." Klast pulled him to a bench, and Kell launched into a long-winded explanation of how he came to this village. The priest listened, as priests do, nodding at all the right times, and keeping his counsel until Kell finished. "And where does this mark call you?"

"That is the blight of it. It changes from day to day. Oftentimes it is south, others it's west, then east. I can make no sense of it." Kell struggled to keep his hands still in his lap.

"Ah, and do you know what lies to the south and to the east?" The older man's eyes held a glitter.

"No. I am not versed in geography. My life was raiding and hunting before this appeared on my chest. I'd barely even put a foot on flat land before this."

"Wonders and terrors, young man. South and east are the old kingdoms, now claimed by the deserts. You will find dusty tombs, empty palaces, and paltry lords clasping at their fallen glory. West of here is the port city of Risell. Mayhap Regnir wishes you to reclaim some lost prize or keep others from doing so. Follow the path set before you." Klast placed his hands over his broad chest, ignoring Kell's crestfallen look. "Don't lose faith. I can offer you some guidance. Stay true and remember your faith. You are not the only one that has come calling about a pilgrimage. One of the faithful mentioned a belligerent woman seeking information about a warlord. She may have clues to your destiny if she hasn't already departed. Though she is a worshiper of Velleris, she may still aid your mission."

"But the watery-veined Vellerians are useless."

"I believe, from all accounts, you will find this Vellerian anything but watery-veined," Klast said with a chuckle that shook the bench they sat upon.

Kell nodded and rose to depart, thanking the priest. He noticed for the first time that within the confines of the church, the call remained silent.

The weight in his chest returned in full force as he hurried along the short street back to the stable, the mud baking into small peaks on the ground.

A sign from Regnir? Little mountains forming from the mud so like my home.

A second heartbeat pulsed under his skin in cadence with his own. Mud sloshed under his boots as he turned the corner to the stables to see a wisp of a woman dressed in an off-white robe cinched at the waist by a knife belt.

Despite her beauty, her mouth turned down in a grimace. A stone skipped beneath his feet, and her head whipped toward him. Errant wisps of reddish-brown hair escaped a severe bun. The glare she shot him gave him pause.

"Peace, warrior. I mean you no harm." He raised an open hand to her.

"What now?" She leveled him with an even more baleful glare. "If you've come from the tavern on behalf of your friends, I'm more than happy to show you the same courtesy I did to your friend."

"I come from the church." He dropped his hands to his sides.

"Goddess save me. A rock-hugger." She clasped the last strap on her saddle and started checking all the buckles, still keeping a wary eye on him.

"I have no quarrel with you. I, too, am on a quest. Do you know the Southlands?"

"I've toured them on missionary work. What kind of quest? I do the work of the goddess to save the world from chaos."

"Regnir has called me, but not with words." He opened his shirt once more to show the god-mark. "I was with my people in the mountains when this appeared on my chest."

"Convenient."

"I've no knowledge of the roads I travel. We could journey together. I've a stout ax, and there is safety in numbers. Mayhap we are on the same side." He touched his heart in a sign of trust. "My name is Kell."

"Helena. We could just as easily be enemies. My prize lies with a warlord named Seguris. He leads a band of murdering, raping thieves."

"I have no truck with such men. It seems on at least one point we agree."

"I leave within the hour. If you wish to ride with me, I'm not averse, but mind you, I'll have one eye on you the whole time. If you cross me, I'll gut you." The knight fixed him with a look. "I will wait briefly for you on the western road to Risell. There is a priest there with information I seek." She took the reins of her steed and walked it around the corner.

"Our journeys will be legendary, Helena." His voice rose. "Oh, the stories that will be told." Kell hurried back to see to his own mount, more confident than he'd been since he set out on this mission.

26

BARBARIAN AND KNIGHT

HELENA AND HER BARBARIAN companion threaded their mounts through piles of littered rubble with Helena in the lead. The rock-hugger from the north could barely control his mount, but at least he hadn't fallen off yet. Tiny puffs of dust rose in the air as remains of the keep settled in the dying sun. What few people remained alive busied themselves with sorting through the wreckage of their homes.

A lump formed in her throat as she looked into their soot-stained faces, bringing back memories of that first nameless village she'd visited. Tears and sweat traced thin tracks through the dirt on their cheeks. Behind her, Kell erupted in a series of curses that made her blush. These people looked at her with renewed hope, others with undisguised enmity. She had little doubt if they weren't so well armed, they'd find themselves at odds with these survivors. Helena ached to give them something, but her supplies were running low and Kell had even less than she did.

As much as she wanted to help, there was little they could do. Despite the burning in her eyes, they kept riding until the remains of the town became a sad memory. Kell pulled his steed in beside her own and continued his string of epithets.

"We should do something." Kell gestured with his hand as if she couldn't see the devastation for herself

"What?" She jerked her reins to put some distance between them.

"I don't know. Are you devoid of pity, Helena?" His anger was plain. It mirrored her own.

"And do you think those people seek my prayers, or your curses? We have limited supplies, and the goddess only knows how long our journey will take." Helena shook her head, irritated at taking out her rage on someone who didn't deserve it.

I swear to you, Velleris, when we find this devil, he will pay.

Kell opened his mouth, then hesitated and dropped his head to his chest, swaying in his saddle, and Helena noticed again how inexperienced he was. She wondered if he had ever even left home before being called by his pagan mountain god.

"I just want to do something. So much suffering. If only our enemies were within reach of our blades." He hung his head again before offering her a wan smile.

They rode on in silence, letting the leagues fall away as if it could ease their frustration over the sacking of the city. The sun dipped below the horizon, and the pair made a sparse camp in a copse of trees. A sputtering fire offered more light than warmth, but the anger in their hearts provided plenty of heat.

Helena stared into the flames, watching them turn in on themselves, consuming the deadwood they'd fed it. Yellow tendrils snaked around the dry limbs. It mirrored the raging flames in her chest. What began as a mission from a goddess had become personal with the people she met. Helena ground her teeth, willing Seguris and his god to dust.

"Did you know it would be like this?" Kell tossed more fuel on the fire, disturbing her reverie.

Helena looked up at him, his rough features knotted in frustration. She blew out a breath, noting that she'd curled her fingers into her palms till red crescents appeared.

"No. My missions from the church are usually more straightforward. Liberate a town. Bring in a criminal. Wage warfare against infidels. This..." She gestured her hand around the empty horizon. "This is new to me. But I will not fail Velleris or her faithful."

"I admire your resolve. Both in your goddess and yourself." He poked at the fire with a long stick, moving the burning embers around. "I have naught but questions. For my god and myself. For whatever dread circumstance we are about to face. Though I've seen battle many times, I've never had to deal with the aftermath. It makes me question everything."

"You do not seem sure of your mission. Do you lack faith?"

He laughed a long time before replying.

"You might call me an unwilling participant in this horror. Before I awoke with this mark, my sole ambition was to be chieftain one day. I cared for no one really, and mayhap the god thought I needed to awaken to destiny and my selfishness at the same instant." Kell tossed his stick into the fire, tearing off a piece of hard biscuit from his pack.

"Regnir's choice did not honor you?" Helena was aghast and couldn't keep the emotion from her face.

Kell made a production out of chewing for a long while. "No. I was angry, irritated, and wayward as a child. It took a new friend, and the god himself, to straighten me out."

"And now? You feel differently now?" She leaned forward, wondering if his lack of faith should anger her. Still, there was something about this loud, unclean savage that intrigued her.

"Somewhat. I recognize the need. I may never be as pious as you, but then again, Regnir demands little from his followers beyond following their hearts." His strong, white teeth ripped into the stale bread, chewing like a wolf.

"Piety gives grace in the shadow of evil. It can be your sword and armor if you let it. Velleris fills me with joy and goodness. She stills the anger that has always been at war within me." As soon as the words passed her lips, she snapped her mouth shut.

Kell's face softened into sympathy as he chewed. Finally, he tossed the biscuit into the fire and gave her a sly wink. Somewhere a bird cried in the night. The shrill sound gave a wordless critique of their discussion.

"We all have our sins, Helena. Mine was ambition. Or maybe still is. I wanted glory. Where I come from, that means being the best hunter, best warrior, and, if you're lucky, the best chieftain. I coveted all those things. I had forgotten what I was fighting for."

"Like your god?" she quizzed him.

"People and the moments shared with them. The rise of the sun and the arc of the moon. The flowers that bloom and die before their time. It was a hard lesson. I didn't want to learn it, but it has made a difference. More so, as I've passed through all this destruction. If my hand or even my death will end this, then I am honored." He rummaged through his pack and resumed his meal with gusto.

"Our hands..." She stared at the fire, choosing her words with care. "I have always spent my life in duty to the goddess. I have no friends outside my order. It is... frowned upon."

"You've made one now."

Had they been closer, Helena knew she would have received one of his now familiar claps on the back. It puzzled her. He regarded her with fondness, but not the slightest hint of lust.

She stared at him, speechless. "You assume I want the company of an unwashed barbarian lout. That presumes much. To an end, you are a means. A companion of convenience." Her arms crossed below her breasts, and she stared at him.

To her surprise, he only laughed as he did at almost everything she said.

"You're a queer one, Helena. I like you. And you like me. I can see it in your eyes beneath your jabs. I'm honored to be your sword-mate too." He winked at her.

Winked!

It made her want to smile despite herself. "You wield an ax, while I wield a mace." Helena turned her head but couldn't keep the tiniest hint of a grin from wrinkling the corners of her mouth, and soon it built into a laugh she could not contain. "Fine. I suppose you are not the worst, foul-smelling, filthy, uneducated barbarian I could ride with on this journey. Also, following your god-mark is no doubt easier than beating directions out of the locals."

Kell showed her his bright teeth in another winning smile and tossed her a mostly inedible lump of bread.

Great Velleris, what have I gotten myself into? Despite her misgivings, she too broke into a smile as they ate. Beside her, Helena noticed the kite shield shimmered in the dim light. An assent from the goddess? Was this a sign the blighted relic was warming to her? Would Helena soon be able to harness whatever powers it possessed? She hoped Kethek would have answers for them both.

27

CALL OF THE ANCESTOR

S EGURIS AND HIS MEN moved at an easy, league-eating pace looking for their next target, the city of Cadden. Although reputed to have a vast horde of magical weapons, a map leading to the Tower of the White Rose was, more importantly, said to be hidden in the cathedral dedicated to Velleris. The steady rhythm of hoof beats pounded in his temples. A subtle tingle spread up his arms and into his neck. The sensation was not new to him.

Magic. Something powerful. Something familiar. It's Mektwin. I'd bet my future kingdom on it.

Though it was just past midday, he threw up an arm and bellowed for his men to halt. Seguris wheeled his horse around to face them, leaning over the pommel of his saddle. The source of the power tickled his senses.

"Spread out into the trees. Make camp. Station sentries. I have business with our god." Seguris closed his eyes and inhaled, breathing in the earthy scent of the forest. His blood roared in his ears.

Seguris stared west. "We are not far from the port city of Risell, is that not so?"

Ethan sidled his mount a step closer to him, ever eager to serve. "Aye, Lord. It lies to the west, but there are no citadels or libraries to loot."

The call niggling at his brain throbbed in disagreement. "Send men out to bring down game to replenish the stores. It may be several days."

"How many men do you wish to go with you, Warlord?"

"None, good Ethan. See that the brothers and sisters do not stray. This is a matter for me alone."

Seguris wheeled his horse around. "Be ready to march upon my return. Ghedryn will soon grant us another boon." He galloped into the forest at a steady pace. The tantalizing surge of energy called him to another victory.

A few days later, when Seguris rode through the gates of Risell, he did so with a broad grin on his face. Though a dozen barons sought the Free Riders, because of their anonymity, he could still ride through the gates of any city with none the wiser.

"Come, come, Mektwin heir. Claim your destiny."

Pain lanced the back of his neck, causing him to clench the reins till his knuckles turned white. Seguris cursed, grinding his teeth till the sensation passed.

Who was this mysterious voice, and could he trust it? He waited for the voice to offer him more information, but nothing came. The call, though it was still present, only teased at his senses.

Seguris made a few turns, following the spider web of energy back to its source, his hand on his sword the entire time. In his saddlebag, The Fist of Heaven pulsed.

A warning? A confirmation of my destiny? Is there another divine relic close? The possibilities were endless. No matter, Seguris was ever ready to step into legend. Despite his bold claims, Seguris couldn't dismiss the nagging doubt that he followed the wrong path. Did he ride toward damnation or glory?

The only way through was forward. Seguris continued to follow the winding trail of magic through the streets of Risell until he came to an open market. He took a deep breath, inhaling the scents of roasting meat, sweat and a myriad of others. Shadows slithered across the stone cobbles like serpents ready to strike.

His gaze darted from one person to the next, but nothing in this place suggested powerful magic, until his eyes came to rest on an old man in a sable cloak, despite the heat.

Who wears a cloak like that in the heat but a wizard?

Seguris slid from his horse and looped the reins in a complicated knot around a post. A shopkeeper started off on a diatribe about leaving his animal to block the customers, but a baleful glare from Seguris silenced his protests.

Taking no chances, Seguris flipped open his saddlebag and withdrew The Fist of Heaven. He smiled at the way it appeared as nothing more than a battered brass gauntlet when not sheathing his meaty forearm. The warlord slipped the rough metal over his arm, watching as dull brass became gleaming gold. The shopkeeper's eyes widened in amazement. Seguris noted the tall man in the sable cloak turned to regard him as well, a wooden expression on his face.

The old man dropped the fruit he'd been scrutinizing and stepped out of the stall, favoring Seguris with a scowl. He brought a single, long finger to his lips as if commanding the king of the next Mektwin empire to hush.

Seguris's hand went to his sword belt, and he stepped into the center of the street. The people in the market gave him a wide berth, eying him as if expecting a fight.

They're not wrong.

The older man squared his shoulders. "You have no business here, relic holder. The god of conquest holds no sway with me." Seguris swore something moved beneath that lustrous sable cloak.

Could that be what I seek? Something about it tickles my senses.

"You have something I need." Seguris took another step. Now only a few strides separated the two, and the people of Risell formed half circles on either side of them.

"Know you face Kethek, the eldest of the inner circle of The Order of Twelve, perhaps even the last of that noble group. I say again: there is nothing for you here."

"You think I'm a stranger to pain, old man?" Seguris cast off his own cloak in a savage movement that ripped the clasp and fabric alike. He didn't plan on needing that cloak again. Seguris raised his hand, flexing his fingers inside The Fist of Heaven. Ruby light curled around his forearm.

"Please. I beg you. Do not force me to harm you. I only wish for peace. This burden is mine to carry. I assure you, you do not wish it upon yourself. The Trappings of the Wild are cursed." The old man twitched his fingers, and a staff carved with intricate runes and sigils appeared from thin air. Kethek struck it against the street, and the cobbles rippled under the blow.

Unimpressed, Seguris slid his curved blade from its sheath and whirled it in an impressive arc to show Kethek, a priest well past his prime, he would not intimidate a mighty warlord.

"By all means, test me. I have endured the lash for many years. I can handle a sable coat, old man."

"As you wish, south man, but remember I warned you." Kethek twirled the staff and held it across his body, awaiting Seguris's attack.

The warlord rained savage slashes on the old priest's staff. When steel met wood, sparks of red and white erupted from their respective weapons. The air itself thrummed with power, and Seguris struggled to keep his balance.

The adversaries fell into the rhythm of attack and defense. Seguris struck again and again, but the old man was more experienced and blocked the blows with only a modicum of effort. He also made use of that curious coat. Any strike against it turned the warlord's blade like a dozen hands shoving the sword to one side. Sweating, Seguris redoubled his efforts, and despite Kethek's skill, the warlord could tell the duel wore on the priest.

As desperation bloomed on Kethek's brow, the old man resorted to magic, hurling bolts of white light at Seguris. The warlord grunted, moving with the speed and strength of years of hard labor. Those he couldn't dodge, he caught and crushed in The Fist of Heaven.

His strength growing with every slash, Seguris snapped the magical staff in twain with a blow that drove the crowd back with its sheer fury. Kethek went down to a knee, air rasping from a chest that appeared too old and wizened to even draw breath. Seguris dropped his sword and resorted to his fists, battering the old man into submission. It didn't take long.

Seguris leaned over the old man, who at this point choked on each inhalation, and grabbed one clasp of the sable cloak. As soon as he touched it, a world of sensations echoed through him. He couldn't tell if they were his future or someone else's past. If Seguris could marry this power with The Fist of Heaven and Blood Thorn, even Ghedryn would have to kneel before him.

Kethek's gnarled fingers curled over his and looked up at him through watery eyes. Blood ran from his mouth and nose. "It is not too late. You can still stop. This thing will consume you if you dare use it."

Seguris snarled. Some part of him rebelled against it, but he disregarded that lone call of sanity. The warlord pressed the releases on the wolf-head stays to free the cloak. He pulled, and the old priest rolled out of it, his head striking the street with a dull thud.

Exultation coursed through him, just like in Ghedryn's arena. No, better. He whirled the cloak around his shoulders, the sable settling across his back like a cool wind. Inside it raged dozens, perhaps hundreds, of souls dancing along his skin. The touch exhilarated him, and he relished it. Within it, one spirit was dominant, and its power deafened him. A name whispered in his ear, telling him who.

"Khyris."

Khyris, the last emperor of the Mektwin. The greatest of Great-Grand Fathers. The man who tilted with gods and won. A better role model Seguris could not ask for.

A troop of armed men thrust through the terrified milling crowd, startling Seguris out of his reverie. Simple, leather breastplates and rough-hewn spears denoted them as city guards.

He paid them little heed. Seguris stared at the old priest, wondering if he should end his suffering. He considered it for a couple of heartbeats, but then shook his head. Failure should be punishment enough for Kethek. To think that the wretched man had caged the mighty spirit of Khyris for so long.

He turned to face the guard. At the thought of fighting them, the cloak turned hard against his skin and erupted in long, barbed spikes. The soldiers paled, but did not retreat. One stepped forward to bark orders at him.

Seguris laughed.

Dark spirits erupted from the spikes, shooting like missiles at the unwary soldiers, ripping the souls from their bodies. These spirits joined the others under his command and shot out again to seek others in the market. Wraiths shot out to all points of the city, toppling buildings and taking souls wherever they went. At will, they consumed dozens of lives. On some level, Seguris knew it was wrong, knew he should resist, but he couldn't bridle the power at his command.

When the carnage was done, the spirits returned to his cloak, and the spikes receded, leaving only the simple sable it had been before. He looked down at Kethek, but the old man had vanished as if he had never existed.

28

DIVINE JUDGEMENT

A SHUDDER RAN THROUGH the hull of *The Rose Bush*, jerking Draven from a light slumber. Blinking sleep from his eyes, he rolled out of his hammock and landed on the balls of his feet just as a thunderclap sounded, shaking the vessel. Footsteps sounded outside the door to his quarters. Thunder roared again and again, louder each time. He yearned for a porthole to see if they were approaching some monstrous squall, but Thistle had consigned him to a room just large enough to string a hammock. Draven couldn't complain. He was a late addition.

Sweet goddess of thieves. It sounded as if the sky was at war with itself. Stupid gods. It could be the case for all he knew.

♥*Do not blaspheme! The goddess is nigh.*♥

"This... can't be good." Stray hairs rose on static electricity to dance of their own volition as he shook his head. Draven pulled on his boots and raced to the main deck.

The scene that met him was like something out of a nightmare. A black sky loomed overhead. A curtain of absolute darkness descended, blotting out the stars. Just as his eyes adjusted to the gloom, a bolt of light arced across the sky, kissing the water close to the port side of the ship. Too close for his comfort.

Loken and Elisah appeared next to him as if by magic. Looking back, he could see Thistle barking orders from the helm. The wiry sea captain shouted to trim the jib and heave to. Draven noticed the man's trembling hands on the old wheel. Their eyes locked for a moment, and then Thistle was back to shouting, for all the good it might do them.

"She can't claim Nellonah without a fight!" Draven made fists, ready for a fight.

♥*The goddess will judge her, thief. Do not make an enemy of Nerys.*♥

"A pox on gods and goddesses both!" Draven advanced across the deck toward Nellonah with Loken and Elisah not far behind. "So far, they've done me nothing but harm."

♥*Ask yourself how you are still alive. Ask how many times poor decisions ended with you not being dead. Then offer your judgment of the goddess.*♥

Ansalon's smugness seemed to emanate from the cuff in waves, and Draven had to admit there could be some truth to the notion.

"It seems my period of grace is over. She is close." Nellonah offered a weak smile, and they stopped dead in their tracks as if held by an invisible wall. "My maker can be harsh but also just. Whatever transpires here, swear you will continue to Kethek to honor your pledge."

Loken and Elisah dipped their heads without question. Draven looked at them as if they were mad. Anger and frustration left him mute. He knew arguing with fanatics was pointless. Draven turned back to Nellonah, straining to push through the barrier, but it held him fast.

"Fires of Heaven, Nell, we have to do something. We can't just take this. Let us fight for you. I can't lose you." Before he finished uttering the words, a fire burned along his arm. It took all his strength to stay upright. "Bugger you, Ansalon! I won't let her go without a fight!"

"Drav," Nellonah said, her eyes moist. "You are about to see why gods create shards. You think all of this," she waved her hands to the roiling heavens, "is because of her anger. It is not. This occurs in your world when one of the gods manifests."

The barrier fell away, and they spilled onto the deck. Nellonah favored them with a wistful look. Spectral green light flared around her body and spread to every corner of the ship.

"The aura will keep the ship from splintering. That is what you consider going to war against, Draven." Nellonah stepped forward, touching Draven's cheek. He thought she wanted to say more, but she turned, thrusting her arms in the air.

More of that peculiar green fire shot into the sky in twin pillars. "Nerys, Goddess of Luck and Death, ride this beacon to your emissary, so that I may answer your questions and present our champion."

Draven looked from Nellonah to Elisah, the purported champion. The knight just gazed back at him, her mouth a thin, hard line.

"Is that necessary? Giving the goddess a giant target?" Draven asked.

"No, but it lessens the impact of her presence in the world, otherwise she might cause a maelstrom." Nellonah chided him as if he were a child.

Draven shook his head. *What madness have I brought down on Nell?*

♥Destiny, young thief. Destiny. I think your presence here is more design than debacle.♥

Draven shook his head, concerned there was no scorn coming from the knight inside Heart Master, only calm sincerity.

Emerald light exploded above them, dispelling the darkness and bathing the crew in eerie light. A pulsing wave of energy coruscated down the twin pillars of flame being projected by Nellonah. A shudder ran through Draven's entire body. Even his bones and teeth hummed with the power on display.

An eternity passed in a heartbeat.

The energy coalesced into a woman of epic proportions. Twice Draven's height, Nerys towered over even Elisah Fairoaks. Pale, green-tinted skin shone with that same disturbing light while hair the color of milk fluttered behind her. Draven sought a witticism to make light of her appearance, but words dried up on his tongue long before he could utter them.

Nerys gave him the briefest of glances, disdain turning the corners of her mouth, before regarding the other members of their group. Draven glanced over his shoulder to see Thistle and his crew frozen in place. He couldn't tell if it was magic or just shock.

Do goddesses smile? Or do they just glare?

"If I smile at you, you could not speak for days, pretty thief. Your antics are not unknown to me." The voice of the goddess became an errant whisper along his spine that made his skin crawl.

"Forty hells." Draven shook his head, attempting to clear the beguiling effect she had on him. Even Ansalon seemed to shrink into himself inside the cuff on Draven's arm.

Nerys favored each of them with that haughty, disapproving glare, and they all wilted just as he did. From their reactions, he wondered if she spoke to them as well. His ears roared too much for him to catch any words.

"Daughter." The word whistled out like an arrow to his battered ears, and everything fell quiet. Nerys extended her arm, pointing a slender finger toward Nellonah. For a moment, her skin shimmered, and Draven saw the hand was bare, bleached bone rather than green-tinged flesh.

Nellonah took a step forward, hands on hips, and looked up at her creator with an all too familiar expression of serenity.

"Nerys, goddess, harbinger of fortune and renewal, I welcome you to the world of mortals. How may we serve?" Nellonah flashed a hint of a smile, and Draven could swear she winked at him.

"Is she mad?"

♥*No. She, too, is divine. Do not forget, she is more than a mortal woman to moon over. She walks with the* gods.♥

Draven gulped, chastised. He blinked to clear his senses. Heart Master thrummed at his wrist, and a bluish glow crawled up his arm.

"Damn it, Ansalon, not now!"

♥*This is not my doing. The relic is reacting to divine magic. I may keep you from abusing it, but I cannot control it. It may even protect you from the goddess. But that seems unlikely given your character.*♥

If Nerys and Nellonah heard their exchange, they gave no notice. Instead they were staring at each other as if daring the other to make the first move. To Draven's surprise, it was the goddess who blinked first.

"Nellonah, I believe an accounting is due."

"Aye, Nerys, I owe you. You have my apologies, but there were complications, and I sought to deal with them before addressing you."

"The gods are at war, Ghedryn marshals an army behind a zealous warlord, and you call this—" the goddess's arm snaked out, latching onto Draven's wrist, "a complication?"

Draven blushed. Nellonah rolled her eyes. "Yes. The relic should not have recognized him. The ceremony to anoint Lady Elisah was only days away. As goddess of luck, I thought you might have had a hand in this." Nellonah curled an eyebrow at Nerys.

Oh, sure, blame it on the goddess. I love that woman.

"Capricious I may be, but I would never send this petty thief to his doom against one such as Seguris. You well know what's at stake." Nerys tossed his arm down, and Draven spun into Elisah Fairoaks, of all people. Loken broke into a hearty laugh, then slapped a hand over his mouth.

"We have much to discuss on how to rectify this most egregious error." Nerys's voice echoed like crashing rocks.

Nellonah squared her jaw and stared back at Nerys. A subtle shimmer of red, then purple light rippled across the sky, and both shard and goddess went rigid.

"Something has happened. Something terrible." Nerys looked to the heavens and for the briefest moment, Draven swore he saw fear in her eyes.

29

DESTINY THROWS THE DICE

THE EERIE GREEN LIGHT of the goddess cast lurid shadows over the deck, turning the churning waters of the sea in deepest jade. Electricity danced across the water. Looking over to Nellonah and Nerys huddled together in hushed conversation, Draven wondered what new cataclysm loomed on the horizon.

Maybe it's just me, but things are about to go horribly wrong.

He called to the spirit in the cuff, but only silence greeted him. He spoke Ansalon's name aloud, but the knight still refused to answer. He clicked his tongue against the roof of his mouth and banged Heart Master against the mast. He repeated this every few seconds until he got a response.

♥ *You are the most infuriating rogue.* ♥

"Surely you can hear something."

♥ *When a goddess wishes a private conversation, then I assure you, no one short of another god can listen in.* ♥

Draven sighed and cast his eyes around the deck. Captain Thistle and his crew remained frozen. He wondered what might happen if he toppled one of them.

♥ *Thief!* ♥

"Hey, I wouldn't do it. I was just thinking about it. Fiends' blood, this is boring. I've got to pass the time somehow."

Beside him, Loken chuckled.

Draven cast his eyes back to Elisah, the once and future champion. She remained stock still, arms crossed, a scowl on her face. He thought her frozen as well, but for the slow rise and fall of her chest. All attempts to elicit any information from her fell on deaf ears.

Draven huffed and crossed his arms, too. Loken placed a gentle hand on his arm. It took all his restraint not to saunter over and interrupt the discussion between Nellonah and her creator. "I carry the damned relic. I should be able to hear whatever this fresh development is instead of standing around twiddling my thumbs."

"Best not to involve yourself in the affairs of gods, brother." Loken clenched his hand around Draven's shoulder, locking him in place.

"Are you a mind reader, too?" Draven turned to look at his brother-in-arms with a scowl.

"Fear not. This must end soon. If Nerys stays much longer, she'll rip the skies asunder." Loken pointed to the heavens. Lightning raced along the sky, striking horizontally rather than vertical. "No god can stay on earth for long without causing chaos. This much, at least, I learned from Nellonah."

"I would have been knowledgeable, too, if I'd stayed."

"I would have thought a footpad like you would be beyond guilt by now." Loken beamed at his brother.

Draven wanted to wipe that knowing smile off Loken's face with a right hook, but figured Ansalon would just stop him, and he'd look an even bigger fool.

"No one is beyond guilt, least of all me. I've a world of regret, and I can't make amends by standing around like a muttering monk."

Loken laughed. "Draven, that is how amends start."

Their discussion came to a halt as Nerys and Nellonah turned to face their champions. Draven noted that the longer Nerys remained, the more Nellonah's features melted into that of the goddess. His stomach churned, wondering if this was the end of Nellonah. Would he ever see her again?

"We must hurry as Nerys's time on this plane must end soon." Nellonah waved her hand to the boiling horizon. "Our situation has become more dire."

Draven grunted, hoping his annoyance was plain. Heart Master constricted on his wrist.

"An ancient enemy has arisen to threaten the entire world. This is no longer just a squabble between gods. This old enemy makes Ghedryn's bid for power almost moot." Lightning strikes punctuated Nerys's words.

He prepared a sarcastic rebuttal, but Elisah clamped a hand over his mouth and squeezed till he believed the bones of his face might break.

"So now we have two enemies to face?" Elisah asked, her face even more grim than usual.

"We do not know, child. A great turbulence of magic erupted in Risell. That is all I know for certain. And Khyris is awake. The god killer is loose upon the world once more." The goddess grew silent, letting them digest the import of her words.

"Khyris? No! It cannot be!" Elisah's countenance now grew slack in shock.

Draven scoffed. "But that god killing is all just a myth. Khyris was just some Mektwin tyrant. Everyone knows they executed him, then dismantled his empire, and the people dispersed across the kingdoms." Draven scoffed again, certain he knew more than the goddess before him.

Nellonah sighed, rubbing the bridge of her nose. "Alas, my silly thief, those were lies told by the successors. Khyris killed two of the gods. Only then was he captured through the cooperation of gods and their human champions. That battle was how Ansalon earned the honor of becoming one with Heart Master. But Khyris was too powerful to kill. The best they could achieve was binding Khyris into a cursed object called The Trappings of the Wild."

"So, how do we find him?" Elisah resumed her crossed-arms stance, spoiling for a fight.

"It is a mystery, even to me. An enemy bears his prison, undoubtedly Seguris, Ghedryn's champion. Kethek was the guardian of The Trappings. You must continue to determine if he still lives. His life thread is faint, but he may still be of use in the coming fray. You must do this without my shard." Nerys grew quiet, letting her words sink in to those assembled.

There it was, the judgment of the Goddess.

Draven launched himself forward, anger clouding his thoughts. "No, you will not have her. Don't take her. We need her. I need her."

Nerys raised her hand, and a wave of green fire spread out from it, enveloping him. Draven could feel Ansalon's resistance, but Heart Master listened to the thief instead. Glowing blue energy wafted out of the cuff, hardening to armor that threw back even the flames of the goddess.

Draven struggled, his muscles straining to reach the goddess. Emerald sigils filled the air, blinding him. Electricity erupted from his cuff, fighting back the magic of the goddess. He was inches from her now, even if his hand only reached her abdomen.

I will not give up on her.

So intent on reaching Nerys, Draven didn't see the blow coming from his blind side until it was too late. Violent eddies of energy exploded, and despite the power of Heart Master, he was driven to the deck. He whirled to face whoever dared to curb his vengeance. When his eyes alighted on Nellonah, his heart sank, as did he, to his knees.

"Nell," he said, reaching out to her, the magic fading, receding back into the enchanted cuff.

"Drav, it's not what you think. Get up and stop being melodramatic."

Nellonah along with Elisah hauled him to his feet. The glimmer of a tear lurked in the corner of his eye before he dashed it away with the heel of his hand.

"Nell, I can't lose you." The world slipped away, and he wrapped his arms around her, even as something inside him broke.

"You are not losing her." Nerys laid a hand that burned with magic on his head. A warmth engulfed him, filling him with an indescribable emotion. "Perhaps now we see Heart Master's choice."

He stammered, barely able to fit words together. Much more of this, and he suspected drool would spill from his lips instead of words.

"I have my own duties to discharge, silly thief. With Khyris in play, Nerys thinks we need her Chaos Masque, which only I, as her shard, can claim. You and Elisah will continue to Risell, and eventually to The Tower of the White Rose. Loken and I will seek the Chaos Masque. Elisah will need both Heart Master and the Chaos Masque if she is to beat Seguris and Khyris."

Draven looked up at her, then over to Loken with a jealous glance. His cheeks reddened again. He shook his head, muttering apologies. Even though she wasn't being absorbed by the goddess, a well of emptiness threatened to swallow him whole. After just finding them again, he was losing Nellonah and Loken to travel with a complete stranger who despised him.

Loken went to stand beside Nellonah. Nerys laid a hand on both of their shoulders. The heavens trembled again and lightning rent the sky as the goddess exercised her power.

Loken looked back at him, proud and beaming. "Fear not, brother, I will look out for Nellonah. As I always have."

Loken's words stung him, even though Draven believed they should cheer him up. Nellonah merely looked at him with a pained expression. The skies continued to churn as power swirled around the trio.

"Draven, I will return when you need me the most. This I swear."

"Thief, champion, find Kethek. Get Heart Master where it is needed. I charge you. Nellonah must complete her mission and make her own choice. The world depends on you both." Nerys smiled, a benediction.

And just like that, the trio of Nerys, Nellonah, and Loken disappeared. Calm skies of white clouds looked down upon the ship.

Elisah gave him a contemptuous glare and turned on her heel, stomping away.

Somewhere behind him, Draven heard Thistle's voice. "Where'd the witch and the cripple go? I could have sworn they were right there."

Draven didn't answer. He was too busy looking for answers within his empty heart.

30

SIEGE

SEGURIS LOOKED OUT OVER fields of grain trampled by horses' iron-shod hooves. Thick impressions of their shoes littered the earth as fires spread from home to home. A swath of destruction cut through rows of uneven huts and mud-brick buildings. Men on horseback milled around the dead and dying farmers. Up ahead, survivors fled in all directions with what scant possessions they could carry. Harsh cries and laughter followed their flight from the men in mismatched armor. A line of six men sat astride strong steeds.

Seguris cantered up on a dark mount with white dappling its coat, almost an affront to the dominant color. His fist, encased in the golden gauntlet, held the reins. Dark curls fluttered behind him in the hot wind. Two men sidled left to make room for him without a word.

"What news?" Seguris kept his tone neutral despite a raging desire within him to see this town nothing but a pile of broken, burning timbers.

"The fools spent too much time harrying the peasants and gave the lord time to secure the gates. It's a siege now." This commander of his spoke as if telling a grand joke.

"A siege," Seguris repeated quietly, as if his lieutenant hadn't spoken. Eyes like basalt glared forward, as if he could batter down the stout timbers by the sheer force of will.

"Yes, my lord. I will gather the men and start planning an assault. The walls aren't that high, and they used wooden supports where they ran out of stone. It should only take a day or two to have them down, depending on their counter-measures." The man never even saw the fist that whipped around, and laid him out in the saddle, his stirrups the only thing saving him from being unseated. Ethan smirked as he watched his fellow lieutenant wobbling on his mount.

"Whoever allowed this has earned my ire." Seguris's tone was ice. A muscle jumped in his face, the only outward sign of his anger. A small smile threatened his lips when he saw how the other men blanched. Imagine if he'd hit the fool with his gauntleted hand. Seguris laughed, a cold, hollow laugh, and his followers found it within themselves to go even paler. "I will not have a siege." His steed pranced in place, dust caking its flanks.

Why did I do that? Weren't they my brothers just weeks ago? Now I treat them as servants. Ethan says I must act like a king, but I cannot quell this newfound rage in me even among my faithful. Now I wonder ... whose rage is it?

"As you say, chief. We await your order."

Seguris didn't recognize the voice, but he did appreciate the trembling in the man's voice. Seguris relished the fear emanating from the men. It warmed the bright yellow metal of his gauntlet. Still silent as a ghost, he dismounted. He liked to think he could feel the ground tremble as his heavy, dust-caked, black boots came into contact with it.

Even the earth recognizes my royal blood and my divine right to claim my destiny. Even if the cost is my soul.

His bushy, black brows knit together as he undid a complex series of knots that bound his saddle bag taut. A whoosh of air heralded the power within, and a flash of ruby light blinked in the noon-day sun.

"See to my horse," were the only words he uttered as he stepped away after withdrawing a garment of sable. He shook it out, the feeling of exultation coursing through him every time he handled The Trappings of the Wild. A long coat of silky hair, the expanse of black-tipped brown fur danced with a life of its own. Powerful hands twirled the coat around.

The passage of time ceased as the robe settled about him, and his fingers clasped the chains that ran from the wolf-headed buckles decorating either side of the robe. As soon as the signature snap-click of the stays sounded, a thrum of power echoed. He was sure it must sound like thunder to those around him.

Seguris relished the all-too-familiar weight of the old king welling in his breast, imbuing every muscle, nerve, and sinew with undreamt-of power. Shaking his unruly locks out, he observed that his stalwart aids withdrew to a safe distance.

"Warlord, shall I signal the men to fall back?" a familiar voice called. His most trusted lieutenant, Ethan, fought to keep his mount under control.

"Aye, Ethan. I have this in hand." A devilish smirk lit his face as he brought the golden glove crashing into the earth, sending a shock wave into the center of the village and nearly reaching the gates. From behind the wooden ramparts, a score of arrows sailed forth in reply, falling just short of his position.

"That's far enough, devil. We've magic of our own, and we've no trouble sending you back to whatever hell you crawled out of." A voice from inside the fort challenged. *The lord? A knight?* He knew the location of the white tower lay buried somewhere beneath that pile of stone and timbers.

Seguris threw his head back and laughed, then walked forward, paying no heed to the defender's threat. He would test his magic against theirs any day. Didn't Ghedryn himself support him? There was little chance anyone in the keep could boast their magic came from the gods. As if called from the ether, the now familiar form of the grim-faced god appeared at his side.

"Ghedryn, do you come to bless my latest conquest? You're early." Seguris inclined his head to the god, noting that neither his men nor the defenders showed any surprise at the form beside him. *So... only visible to me.*

"Is your ego so fragile you need my blessing?"

Seguris bristled but remained silent.

"What is this remnant of the past you clothe yourself in? I have given you a weapon of the gods. You no longer require trinkets made by men." The god scowled at him with distaste. Seguris turned a questioning eye toward Ghedryn, his curiosity piqued.

"A recent acquisition. I favor it. It hearkens back to the Mektwin Empire, and its power intrigues me." Seguris ran a finger along the chain binding the cloak. A wicked smile spread across his lips, although doubt snaked up his spine, belying his casual words.

"Cast it away. Vellerian priests created this rag out of your last emperor, and his madness curses it. It is an affront to your people's history, and all that you are about to achieve. While The Trappings give great power, it will demand much more in return. It will bring you ruin."

Seguris turned to retort, but the god faded away. *What was that about?*

A golden lash of pure electricity arced across the ground toward him. Dirt and rocks flew up in his face, causing him to shield his eyes. The tumult stung his eyes, fueling his already simmering temper.

A question for another day. For now, focus on the enemy in front of you, Seguris.

Seguris reached out with his gauntleted hand to catch the writhing, sparking serpent and crush it in his grip. A heady rush of power bloomed within him, as it always did, knowing that one day soon, he would grind his oppressors into dust. He smiled that smile that came from knowing he was unstoppable.

As he passed the village, consumed by flames, his rowdy band of brigands milled around. A few moved to his side, while he eyed the stout walls and whatever defenders perched behind them. Seguris waved them back, his disdain evident. There would be hell to pay later for forcing him into the battle, but for the moment, they could hold on to their miserable hides.

A voice cried out from inside the wall, calling for archers. The brawny warlord steeled himself. Men appeared along the wall, brandishing bows with barbed arrows. His vision focused on each one of them, the eldritch powers he commanded bringing them into perfect clarity. The familiar, gnawing hunger grew within him, demanding sustenance. The Trappings gave him great power but demanded payment in souls. Was it The Trappings or Khyris that demanded souls?

Either way, it wasn't a trade that Seguris minded paying. Swift points arced from the walls, seeking his life. Seguris did not fear.

The shafts whistled in the air, but before any could land, a swirl of darkness rose from The Trappings. Eddying currents of inky-black strands surrounded Seguris, forming an impenetrable shell that caught and snapped the shafts like so many twigs. The blackness coated him in a second skin, magnifying his form to twice his normal height. Wicked spines of the blackest night grew over his back. He heard the voices of dozens, if not hundreds, of damned souls lending their strength to him. Seguris devoured all the surrounding light and lumbered forward, an inevitable juggernaut.

Only a hundred yards from the portcullis, the archers withdrew, and a trio of mages replaced them, their flowing robes embroidered with symbols of power. They poured fire down on him, sucking even the flames from the burning huts to bathe him in an inferno.

It didn't matter. Obsidian armor absorbed it all. Death shrouded him from head to toe. The fires burned themselves out while the surrounding ground scorched and melted. Little sign that life ever existed on this blasted patch of land remained.

I will be victorious. Fate called me to this unlikely appointment. Destiny will not let me die before my people rise again.

Maddened by blood-lust, Seguris could contain the power he commanded no longer. He broke into a loping run, gaining mass from the shadows as he went.

The defenders lobbed anything and everything at him they could while their mages wove spells to thwart him. It mattered not one bit as he crashed into the walls. Stone shattered. Wood cracked. Metal fittings buckled.

Men screamed as they were flung headlong from their protective barrier. Blood ran in rivulets among the broken stone, and what could burn burned while he ground the rest under his heel. He threw his arms about like a raging behemoth, smashing everything within his grasp. Seguris raged, and The Trappings of the Wild fed on his carnage.

Drink deep, Khyris. I will keep your thirst slaked, and you will convey the power to raise our people up from their chains.

31

THE ROAD TO THE WHITE ROSE

T HE SMELL OF DEATH lingered in the air for days after the siege. Seguris smelled it even in the comfort of his pavilion as he lounged in a chair covered in furs. Sandalwood burned in a censer, but it did little to help. He didn't mind. The aroma of dying men and burnt bodies meant another step closer to the throne. Soon his campaign against the priest-kings of the middle kingdoms could begin, but first he must raze the blighted Tower of the White Rose and claim its singular prize.

Up till now, he had been just an irritation to the priest-kings, a noisome gnat that buzzed and nipped at any exposed flesh, but that would not last. After his inevitable victory, he would return to seek vengeance for the legions of wrongfully imprisoned Mektwin slaves. His countrymen would rise and flock to his banner. The hated Vellerians would die by the hundred score. Then, and only then, would he assume the mantle of emperor of the next great Mektwin age.

I doubt I need Blood Thorn with the power of The Fist and The Trappings, but best not to let it remain in the hands of those weak-kneed priests. As Ethan loves to remind me, never leave an enemy at your back.

Seguris pulled The Fist from his meaty forearm with a modicum of effort. It whispered power through the open spaces of his tent, a subtle change in the air's pressure. The guards on either side of the entrance didn't notice. He uttered a soft laugh. Being of ancient blood and dallying with the god made him more than mortal. Being of Mektwin blood made him sensitive to even the smallest amount of magic in his presence.

It matters little. As long as it means the return of my people and my ascent as their king.

He massaged the skin of his wrist. It always ached when he took off The Fist. Wide bands of scar tissue encircled his arms at irregular intervals from years of wearing chains. He relished that fateful day when he took his freedom and left a pile of corpses in his wake.

Could that have only been months ago? To you, Caldor, you miserable bastard. I salute you and your eternal damnation.

On that day, and every day since, he swore to throw down the priest-kings and restore the glory of the Southlands. His people yet whispered of the days when they ruled the world, even centuries after its destruction.

Soon I will raise the crowning city of Mekta from its ashes. Though the world now reviles us, I will see a golden age where not only the Mektwin but all races of men can flourish beneath this guiding fist.

Seguris dropped his hands to his lap as the guards admitted a slender youth shepherded by the ever-faithful Ethan. They both waited at the entrance, Ethan still as a block of stone while the boy fidgeted with a black lacquered box. Seguris appraised them, smiling at the boy's dusky skin. He waved him forward. Ethan offered a crisp bow and turned on his heel, departing without a word.

Ethan is well trained, but not of the old race. This youth, on the other hand, bears closer scrutiny.

The child stood before him. Seguris leaned forward, his hand stroking the gauntlet at his side. He thought he recognized this courier. His darker skin echoed a memory. Seguris was certain he was of the old race... his race.

Why would Ethan send the boy in to deliver it personally? Curious. I must speak to him about this irregularity.

"I've seen you before, have I not?"

"Yes, sir. I've brought you messages before. Usually in the field. This is the first time they have dispatched me to your tent."

"And your name?"

"Drin." The boy shuffled his feet, causing the box in his hands to tremble.

"You're Mektwin, aren't you?" Seguris reached out a calloused hand, and the boy proffered the box.

"As much as anyone can be, now. My mother had the dark skin of the Mektwin. My father, who knows?" A sheepish grin lit his features.

"Good. Good. Our people will return to glory. I will reward the faithful."

Drin bowed until his head touched dirt. "I am yours, Warlord. You shackle none and reward the lowest of us. I will follow you to death."

Seguris eyed the boy carefully. The words were right. The expression was right, but there was something off about this child. Perhaps he'd just grown paranoid. The Trappings whispered that all hands would be against him till he met his goals.

"Let's hope it doesn't come to that. At least for those of us who carry the old blood." Seguris rose to clap the boy on the back, sporting a devil's grin. "Now run along. I think this box contains the secret I've been searching for." A twinge ran up the back of his neck, making the hairs there stand up, reminding him of Ghedryn. He waited for some terse rejoinder from his god, but none came.

It was odd to feel his presence without so much as a word. Was it a silent reminder to heed him? A wordless warning to stay on his path? Seguris shrugged and set that concern aside for another time. He'd soon feed the god enough deaths to sate Ghedryn's grandest desires.

The courier turned and dashed out of the pavilion, squeezing past the guards. Seguris chuckled as he sat back and ran his hands over the wooden box. The lid bore the unmistakable seal of the bitch-goddess, Velleris. He thumbed the catch, but it refused to open. It was warded.

I thought I detected the subtle aroma of magic. That explains why Ethan sent it via a courier instead of presenting it himself. He loathes even the magic of the gods.

The brass glove rose and floated up to enfold his right hand. Veins of reddish power coursed over its surface. Seguris willed energy toward the box, and a web-work of golden lines appeared on the surface. More power surged from the glove into the ward, and the lines flared, growing brighter as the seconds ticked by.

Resist all you want. Your secrets will be mine.

Lines of energy flared, and the box disintegrated into ash, leaving a parchment in his hand. It bore no seal, but it stank of Velleris.

He unrolled the creamy vellum with care to display a map, faded by time. At the base of the paper, he discerned the image of a tall tower with a tiny flower on it. A rose. Beside it ran lines of script in his own language, a language that could now only be read by a few outside libraries and schools of magic. It took him a moment. It had been so long since he had seen Mektwin writing.

The wording was flowery and phrased in archaic verse, but the meaning was clear. Blood Thorn lay in The Tower of the White Rose. The White Tower, the last fortress of Mektwin kings before the priest-kings overthrew them. He laughed to himself.

All this time, and that which I seek lies within my homeland. I suppose they considered it ironic. I'll make them pay for this jest.

"Up. Up, I say. We are moving." Seguris strode around their encampment, kicking men out of their bedrolls and rattling tent lines.

The sun barely crept over the horizon, casting diffuse light in the early morning haze. His lieutenants took his cue and picked up the cry. Soon, the sprawling maze of tents collapsed one by one as the Free Riders leapt into motion.

Seguris caught up to Ethan, thrusting the rolled parchment into the man's hand.

"Never mind the writing. Can you follow the map?"

Ethan unrolled the vellum with care and nodded. "The Rose is our destination. A few of the landmarks have changed, but the path is clear. Deep in the Southlands. Provisions might be a problem. Do I have your leave to use the magical items for replicating and storing what we'll need?" Ethan eyed the map as if already calculating supplies, rate of travel, and half a dozen other things in his head.

"When have I ever denied you, old friend? This is the prize. After we seize this tower, victory is ours. No one can oppose us." Seguris clapped the man on the back with a lusty grin.

"Then it will be done so long as I don't have to touch the blighted things. The going will be slow, especially after we get into the sand, but I foresee no issues. The Vellerians will chase their tails trying to deduce where we've gone." Ethan rolled up the map with a bark of laughter. "I never once doubted your leadership."

"Knowing I was the right hand of a god could not have hurt in that regard." Seguris fingered the dull brass gauntlet at his belt.

Ethan smiled back at him.

"Aye, 'tis truth, Warlord. Hard to believe months ago we were both slaves. Shortly you'll be king, and I'll command your armies."

"With your mind and soldiering experience, there's none other I'd have at my side." Seguris turned back to the coming dawn, welcoming the coming light. A tingle started at the base of his spine, and he knew Ghedryn commanded his presence once more.

Soon not even he will command me. The power of The Trappings of the Wild grows with every life I take—and with it, so does my own.

"Get to the preparations. I must commune with Ghedryn." As he spoke the words, the air shimmered and the world of men faded. Inky blackness enveloped Seguris, and a shudder ran up from his stomach. Then light returned, showing a room with pitted, gray stone walls decorated with tattered pennants and weapons notched from use. At the head of the room, resplendent in gleaming brass armor, reclined his god on a throne of dark velvet. Ghedryn's mouth was clenched in a tight frown as he looked at Seguris.

Seguris strode forward, making no effort to bow before his deity. Whether this pleased or annoyed the god he had never been able to tell. *I fought in your arena for this chance, I'll bow to no one, not even a god.* He still did not know if Ghedryn could read his thoughts, but his god spat out a laugh, and leaned forward.

"You have made excellent progress in your pursuit of the prize." Ghedryn clenched a gauntleted hand over the arm of his throne.

"If you ever doubted, I would not be your man. The treasures I need to claim my kingdom will be at hand soon enough. You have no cause for concern."

"Be sure overconfidence is not your downfall, Mektwin. As it was for the last who held the throne of your people."

He fought to keep his temper in check. The god knew the fate of his people was a sore point and sought to rile him. Seguris offered him a tight smile.

"I measure my adversaries before each battle, so that victory will be assured. It hasn't failed me. I employ strategists to help keep the course. Is there some reason you have brought me here today?"

"Do not underestimate others who seek to claim the prize. This I have revealed to you. Regnir's warrior is as strong as an oak, and Velleris will employ her stoutest knight— if not an army of them. Don't doubt they'll have blessings of their own. And as for Nerys, whomever she uses will be both deadly and cunning. I have given you significant power, but do not dismiss that which is subtle." Ghedryn leaned forward, his gaze sharpening till Seguris thought it might pierce his breast.

"I bear both The Fist and The Trappings. There is little I can see that can challenge my power. Though my men aren't all experienced soldiers, my generals train them daily. How better to stop an assassin than with an army of them?" He barked out a slight laugh, but his god did not join in.

"The Trappings. I see you have not cast aside that devilish rag. Did I not warn you of its singular curse? There are reasons aplenty why the Mad King was overthrown."

"The Great King Khyris whose blood flows in my own veins? Aye, my god, you did." Seguris tried to keep his expression neutral even while his mind whirled with curiosity. His band had pillaged magic across the continent, and none had piqued Ghedryn's interest. Until now. He wondered what was so special about it that made Ghedryn want him to get rid of it.

Could he be right? Or did even the gods fear Khyris? This gives me much to consider.

"Why have you not heeded me?" The words were thunder.

Is he furious... or concerned?

"The Trappings are a useful tool. They are worth possessing for the more fortified cities. I'll not discard a weapon I can use just for an enemy to pick it up.

What if the Vellerian champion were to gain it? How much more powerful would they be? At the very least, I keep it out of the hands of others."

This seemed to mollify Ghedryn: his brow unwrinkled, and his iron grip relaxed. "There is some wisdom to that." Ghedryn stroked his beard, considering Seguris's argument. "But take care. The old king was mad as a hare, and there was no telling the influence he could exert on the unwary. The same power that can topple stone walls can also shred the mind of a mortal. And that is not taking into consideration the countless other damned souls contained within the blighted thing. I have invested a great deal in you. I'd not see you become a blithering idiot."

"Your concern for my well-being is touching." The urge to wink back at his god was maddening, but through a massive effort, he suppressed it. Even he could only dare so much.

"Now, away with you and back to your mission. Bring me the relics and destroy the other champions. Let your conquest echo through the world and into the heavens."

Seguris clapped a fist to his breast in response. Even as reality shifted again, his mind was in motion.

Ghedryn fears The Trappings, and I have them. Seguris is as good a name as Ghedryn.

32

ANSALON MAKES A CHOICE

D RAVEN STOOD AT THE bow of the ship, watching the waves crash against the hull, reflecting on those he hadn't thought of for years prior to the recent events.

Ansalon stewed within the cuff, offering neither counsel nor condemnation. Heart Master glowed almost continuously, a warm, constant reminder that destiny had stepped into his life, altering it forever.

Elisah joined him, settling beside him with her usual dour expression. She gave him a look Draven could not decipher.

"Your moping does no one any good." She turned, resting her elbows on the bow, and faced the ship's mast. Wind whipped her red hair into a mass of flaming serpents.

"I'm not moping. I'm grieving the loss of people I care about." His reply struck even him as petulant.

What does she even know about me? Does she know my suffering??

♥*Much more than you. You're still thinking of no one but yourself.*♥

"Could have fooled us." Thistle sauntered up, chewing on his pipe.

"You too, Thistle? I thought you might at least back me."

"Back you on what? Milling around like a doe-eyed youth about his lost love?" Thistle took the pipe from his mouth, wiped the stem, and stuffed it into a vest pocket. The aroma of stale tobacco wafted in the air.

Draven turned as if to confront his tormentors, but held up his hands and gave up, tucking them under his arms, and remaining stubbornly silent.

Why can't they leave me to my sorrow?

♥*Because danger looms, and you must prepare.*♥

Draven wanted to run, as he always did, but this time there was nowhere to go. Yet his abandonment of Nellonah and Loken had caused this in the first place. Otherwise, it could have been him accompanying Nellonah on her errand instead of Loken.

"You care deeply for people you gave no thought to a fortnight ago." Elisah raised an eyebrow as she hitched up her sword belt.

"Damn your eyes! Don't you think I know that? I put myself here. I stuck everyone on this path. I'd be going with Nellonah if I hadn't stolen this thing. If I hadn't run..." He trailed off, unable to complete the thought.

"But you did, and now you are on the cusp of destiny."

"I'm only important till this thing comes off. I'm just a placeholder for you." He beat at Heart Master with his left hand, having nowhere else to direct his frustration.

Elisah snorted. "What if you're not?"

"What if I'm not what?"

"A placeholder. What if it chose you for a reason?"

Ansalon had something akin to an apoplectic fit inside the cuff. It was the first thing to bring a smile to Draven's face since Nellonah's departure.

But he demurred. "No. I can't think of that. Ansalon won't even let me light a candle. He hates me. If your priest can't free this thing, we're doomed." Draven turned away, casting his gaze over the horizon.

"Draven. Listen. For all we know, Kethek could be dead already. Even if he is hale, he may not have the strength to release Heart Master. More to the point, Heart Master chose you for a reason. The relic itself must choose. We tested fifty knights, and Heart Master rejected them all before it agreed to Ansalon. I have seen much, so I can envision a thief's rise to champion. The High-Father may be dead, but his wisdom lives on in Heart Master."

Ansalon railed within the cuff, yet it pulsed in agreement with Elisah. Draven shook his head. "Then what should I do? I'm no fighter, and Ansalon would never allow it."

"Prepare. Find an accord with Ansie. He may be stubborn, but he's no fool. Get off your arse and give some thought as to whether you can be more than a footpad who takes flight when it gets too difficult." Elisah turned on her heel, and walked away.

Thistle fell into a fit of laughter and staggered off in the opposite direction. Draven heard him sharing this jest with the crew members, which drew even more laughter.

Draven sulked in silence.

♥*Do not even consider it, thief. I will not have it. No matter how many of the faithful we must test, I will not have it.*♥

"Wait. What?"

♥*It is of no consequence.*♥

"Elisah wasn't the first, was she? This wasn't an accident. Nellonah tested others, didn't she?" Draven sputtered the words, finally understanding.

♥*They tested many when I claimed Heart Master to fight Khyris for the first time. They can find another.*♥

"So... how many exactly?" A sly smirk lit Draven's face. The rage emanating from the knight became waves crashing onto a craggy beach.

♥*The exact number... eludes me.*♥

"Then round up. I have a right to know."

♥*Near... a hundred.*♥

Draven laughed. He couldn't help himself. "A hundred. And then you sought the champion, is that right?"

♥*Not—exactly.*♥

Realization hit Draven like a rampaging bull. "They tested Elisah before. That's why she's willing to concede Heart Master."

Ansalon fumed within the cuff. Heart Master pulsed and turned a solid blue. The cuff then extended to a gauntlet that ran from fingertips to elbow. Strength surged into Draven like he'd never imagined until Ansalon regained control and choked it off.

♥*It matters not. With the additional power of the goddess, it would have worked to bind Elisah to the relic. We* must *bind Elisah to the relic or we are lost.*♥

Draven couldn't help himself. He broke into laughter again. He wailed, slapping at his leg until he regained his composure. Then he slid down the bow and held up his right hand. Despite Ansalon's control over the magic, it remained a gauntlet.

"Ansalon, you have my leave. I didn't mean to jape. Well, not completely, but we have to consider this, don't we?"

♥*What is to consider? Will you fight Khyris? Would you take up arms and kill for the gods?*♥

Draven had to admit the questions were sobering. It was one thing to imagine himself riding to Nellonah's rescue; it was another to picture himself in battle, putting his own neck on the line for people he'd never even met. He took a breath.

"I don't know if I have what it takes to fight for an entire world, but I can tell you this. I know I can fight for Nellonah and Loken. Maybe that's all the goddess can ask of any man."

♥*That is not the speech of a champion... but it's a start.*♥

"Then you'll let me use this thing? I'd rather Elisah be the champion, but at least we can prepare for the worst. Which, in this case, is me." Draven barked out a short laugh as he tapped a finger to the edge of the gauntlet. The metal warmed and became supple beneath his touch.

♥*All right. We will begin. I will educate you in using Heart Master. At least what I learned to fight Khyris, but even I do not understand its true potential. Why else would I volunteer to shed my body to protect it? But—I will not allow you to misuse it.*♥

"Can't guarantee I won't try, but you have full permission to scold me if I get too greedy. I'm the last person I'd trust with this thing." Draven snorted and got back to his feet. "So, what's first? Flame? I'd really like to set something on fire. We could start with Thistle's arse."

♥*First, I will show you the past so you might understand how this came to be.*♥

"Always starts with a lecture. I should have known." Draven leaned his head back and closed his eyes as mists enveloped him. Memories not his own filled his mind.

♥♥♥

Ansalon looked upon the deposed king, Khyris. The freshly quarried white granite walls of the newly constructed Tower of the White Rose were a stark contrast to the devilish figure before him. They had stripped the Mad King of his armor, and he shook with unbridled fury. Chains bound his arms and legs to grommets embedded into the marble floor. Steel lances ran through the flesh of his chest, further constricting any possibility of movement. Yet the broad-shouldered, dark-skinned devil surged against his fetters, causing the lances to bend.

Sweet Goddess, he's not human. We've stabbed him, beaten him, starved him, yet he goes on.

"Come closer. I'll rip out your heart and feast upon it!" The Mad King's words were a guttural snarl.

Ansalon retreated a step despite himself. A white-robed priest of Velleris finished another warding spell, and a ring of white light flared on the polished floor in a seven-pointed star.

"Your days of murder and rape are over, Mektwin-scum. As is your empire." Ansalon clenched his fist, the enchanted bracer digging into his arm as his muscles expanded. He sorely wished he possessed the courage he boasted. The Mad King terrified him, and every night he woke from grisly nightmares of the battle that had toppled Khyris from his throne.

Another priest, this one in the gray robes of Nerys, laid a hand on his arm. "We are not without resources to deal with this problem, good knight. Despair not." Ansalon turned to him, raising an eyebrow.

Ansalon regarded Khyris again, marveling at how anyone could contain such power. "How can you be certain? We failed to kill him, and bound as he is, he seems as if he could burst free at any moment. Will the gods not imprison him?"

The old priest shook his head, sending wispy, white hair fluttering.

"We have prayed on this. The gods remained silent until last night. Khyris is the product of men, and it is our duty to bind him."

"Mantle of Velleris!" Ansalon swore under his breath. "You have a plan?"

"Velleris has offered us guidance. He will never know freedom again."

The Mad King thrust at his chains. The lances quivered as he threw his strength against the bonds. The ring of protection flared, but the chains held. Barely. A few of the links bent under the onslaught. The white marble beneath his feet turned black.

"At the very least, we have relieved him of his relics. We will hide the shield, gauntlet, and sword so they are never again used to enslave. Not even the gods will know their locations. We will also hide Heart Master."

"Aye. 'Tis the most powerful of the relics. Being hidden may not be all that is required. It should have a guardian." Ansalon rubbed at the enchanted cuff, which had become so much a part of him. "I will, of course, volunteer."

The priest nodded. "Time enough for that later. The Ceremony of Trapping must begin."

True to his word, dozens of priests filtered into the room. White-robed Vellerians, gray-robed Nerysians, dark-clad Regnirians, and the mail-clad Ghedrans gathered. Other priests of lesser gods filed in until there was scarcely any air to breathe. At last, two men entered, bearing a heavy fur robe that they draped over the thrashing Khyris. He snapped at them, and they fell back.

The priests chanted, low at first, then rising until it became a din. Ansalon's ears ached from the volume. His knees threatened to buckle, and he had to clench his fist and bite his lower lip to keep from going to one knee. Power rose from the very stones of the room, moving from one person to another. The gauntlet on his arm responded, channeling blue fire into the mix.

Khyris howled as the magic in the room swirled around him. Gold clasps on either side of the cloak around his shoulders snapped shut of their own accord. The dancing lights built to a crescendo and exploded, driving Ansalon to his knees. Blackness blotted out his vision. When he opened his eyes, Khyris was gone. The robe they had trapped Khyris in writhed with darkness. Despite the absence of the Mad King, his presence clung to the air in a dark miasma.

The old priest helped Ansalon to his feet as others collected the cursed garment. The trapping was complete. Ansalon prayed to the gods the world would be safe from Khyris's monstrous designs.

"Are you certain he cannot escape?"

"So long as one of the faithful guards him. For Heart Master—were you in earnest about becoming its guardian?"

"I would offer my life to safeguard this treasure. As resolute as my faith is, its power has tempted even me." He wrapped a hand around the gleaming silver, a shiver running through him.

"Then follow. Your life is not required, but your soul will be." The priest led Ansalon away.

He led Ansalon into a small circular room with a dozen men and women spread out against the walls. The knight inhaled sharply when he noticed each bore a relic from a different god. One held Blood Thorn in a quivering hand, another the golden Fist of Heaven. A wizened man in the leathers of a thief held the mirrored Chaos Masque of Nerys, and so it went. Ansalon fought the urge to go to his knees.

"It's about time, Kethek. We've been waiting an age," said a sallow man in aqua robes, gesturing with the Sea Tooth, an artifact of the first god the Mad King killed.

"Peace be with you. Some things take precedence over even the binding of Heart Master. I bring good tidings. Khyris is caged."

A chorus of cheers erupted from the assembly, then fell silent. They all looked at Ansalon with curiosity. He felt like an interloper.

"They informed us that one of our order would fill the role of guardian. Yet you bring us a bloody-handed knight, covered in the gore of conquest." The Vellerian priest who held Hallowed Verity spoke.

"Curb your tongue, priest of Velleris. Your only complaint is that Ansalon forsook Velleris and now bends a knee to Nerys. You opposed it when Heart Master recognized him as champion." A fury of voices erupted as they all argued.

Ansalon nearly choked, imagining what would happen if any brought their relics to bear.

"Please, if I might say something," Ansalon said. "I have fought for you. My blade avenged the nameless who died by the hundred score. I have bled for every one of your gods. Heart Master chose me to bear it against Khyris. I would lay my life down one more time. Even if it is my last act, I weary of the blood, the killing, and above all, the conflict. I seek peace, and guarding this relic is a burden it would honor me to take on." Ansalon raised the arm with Heart Master, wan blue light illuminating the arguing faces in the room. As one, they ceased their discourse.

"Well spoken, knight." A woman stepped forward with a relic he did not recognize. She bore a gleaming silver crescent. Ansalon besought his memory, trying to recall her name, but came up empty. "This knight speaks well. I say if he makes this sacrifice, then we should allow it. I second Kethek's nomination."

A quieter discussion ensued, this time with the majority assenting. Kethek motioned for quiet, and everyone nodded. "Ansalon, this is final. Do you need to make your farewells? Seal your affairs?"

Ansalon shook his head. "All I loved is dead. All I owned is dust. I have nothing but my life to give."

Kethek nodded, his face going wooden. "Then we shall begin. Stand in the center of the room and hold Heart Master aloft. Let us begin the incantations."

Ansalon held his arm up, his muscles aching as the chanting went on for eternity. Colors swam and power surged, such that he thought the walls would crumble. Time lost all meaning. Ansalon lost all sensation, and he could no longer tell if he still held the relic or if he even possessed arms.

The last thing he heard was the clinking of Heart Master falling to the floor, reverting once more to a plain band of iron and silver. His consciousness expanded, and for the first time, he saw with more than his eyes. From some far-off place, he noted his body laying inert on the chamber floor. His time as guardian had begun. He would not fail in his last duty to The Twelve Gods.

♥♥♥

"You're an idiot." Draven whistled through his teeth, trying to still his pounding heart after experiencing Ansalon's past.

♥*I would not expect you to understand my sacrifice.*♥

"Oh, I understand it. I just don't agree with it. I may fight for you lot if it comes to it, but don't expect me to follow in your footsteps."

♥*After you learn Heart Master's secrets, you may change your mind.*♥

A tingle of dread crawled up Draven's spine and not for the first time.

33

REVELATIONS OF IMPOTENCE

WHEN THEY ARRIVED IN Risell, the port city was in shambles. The harbormaster appeared before they even had the chance to disembark, giving them a frosty reception until Elisah presented a sheaf of papers. Draven assumed they must be authorizations of some sort to allow her passage anywhere in the known world.

Damned priesthood can do what they like when they like.

♥ This comes with being ruled by a theocracy. ♥

"Bugger that." Draven followed Elisah off *The Rose Bush,* eager to be rid of Heart Master. They halted at the end of the gangplank where Elisah turned to speak to Thistle.

"Mind you, Nellonah passed me the token she held over you. Attempt to leave without my consent, and you'll find your beloved vessel at the bottom of the ocean."

Thistle grumbled and spat in her direction before turning to climb back aboard the ship. Draven had wondered what they had over the smuggler to get him to forgo his nefarious operations in favor of a quest to save the world.

Draven walked side by side with Elisah in silence, caught up in a riot of emotions he couldn't voice. He marveled at the quiet workers who went about their tasks as if awaiting their executions. Few people spoke, and those who did whispered to themselves as if any louder noise would bring forth some fresh calamity. Elisah asked after an older priest, but the only answers she received were sullen silence or pleas of ignorance.

They made for the center of town, and devastation greeted them like an old friend. It was as if Ghedryn's own fist had smote from the heavens to flatten an entire section of the town. Buildings lay in absolute ruin, while others teetered on the brink of collapse. Elisah could not find out much about the attack, other than it was carried out by a stranger who suddenly appeared and disappeared. Even the soldiers posted at every corner appeared nervous.

"Any idea how to find our mysterious all-knowing priest? If he knew all that much, he'd have left a reception committee."

"You are assuming he still lives—and wants to be found. With destruction like this, he very well may have perished, taking our answers with him." Elisah shook her head, looking around at the rubble. Guardsmen still pulled bodies from the rubble for burial.

Gods, is this what I'm supposed to fight? Something that can level entire cities?

♥*Take heart, thief. Heart Master possesses great power, too.*♥

Draven swallowed, hoping Ansalon was right. Just then, he felt a tug on his arm. He looked down, expecting some hungry-eyed child, but there was no one. Still, something pulled at his arm. "I don't know if it's Heart Master, but something says to go that way." He pointed down an intact street, winding its way into the distance. Elisah shrugged and followed him.

They followed the relic through a series of winding alleys till they stood before a bleak two-story building fronted by stout double doors. Elisah looked the building up and down, wary of potential traps. "Your relic doesn't believe in straight lines." Elisah strode up, banging on the door with the heel of her hand.

"Mayhap it didn't want anyone to follow us. Especially if this Seguris already got the best of the priest once." Draven shrugged his shoulders as they waited for a response. None came. Elisah knocked on the door again, this time with the pommel of her poniard. Still no answer from the silent dwelling.

"Nothing ventured, nothing gained." Draven pulled forth his pouch of picks and went to work on the lock, his eyes sparkling. "Keep an eye out for any spectators."

Elisah rolled her eyes before scanning the street in both directions. "Go ahead. There doesn't seem to be a soul on this avenue, and from the look of the buildings, we're not likely to run into anyone other than thieves." She waved her hand about, and he had to admit the rest of the buildings looked poorly maintained, with shutters either hanging or nailed shut.

Draven sprung the lock, and the door creaked inward. He gestured for her to enter first. Given the dark interior, he'd rather risk her neck than his own. As usual, she just grunted, squared her shoulders, and marched in like she owned the place.

Draven followed behind her, overwhelmed by a dozen warring scents. The dusty smell of moldering books competed with body odor and stale sweat. He sniffed again and could also detect the faint, metallic trace of blood over the pungent aroma of rotting food. He motioned caution to Elisah, but she barreled through the house as if she were a wild boar rooting out truffles.

The trail of blood soon became visible, and they followed it upstairs, Elisah taking the lead. Draven drew his own weapons: one, a stout falchion; the other a dagger with teeth on the dull side, designed for catching and breaking swords. He wished his hands didn't tremble, but he was far outside his realm of experience. Sword play was one thing, but demons, gods, and mages were quite another.

"Why am I leading the way? You are the one bearing a relic of The Twelve."

"Because you're a hero, and I'm a coward?" Draven favored her with a weak grin.

Elisah shook her head and continued to ascend the steps. They came upon a man lying prone in the hall. Blood stained his face and robes. Elisah knelt down, holding her ear over the man's mouth.

"He breathes still. He's alive." She tilted his chin, and the man sucked in a shuddering breath.

From his wrinkled, sallow face, Draven assumed he must be the priest they sought. Kethek looked as if a giant had thrown him from a great height. Blood covered every inch of visible skin. His breath came in gasps, and despite Elisah's attention, he still hadn't come to yet.

They found a sleeping chamber at the end of the hall. While the knight-commander carried him there, Draven fetched water and clean clothes, although clean, in this case, meant less filthy than other garments. For a chaste man of the goddess, Kethek was not fastidious.

Draven and Elisah bathed his wounds and tended him as best they could, waiting for him to awaken. After what seemed like hours, Kethek coughed and attempted to sit up. He failed, of course, but with some help from Elisah, Draven propped him up on a pile of cushions purloined from other areas of the ramshackle abode. Draven gave the man credit: he didn't seem alarmed that there were two strangers in his home washing him like a babe and binding his wounds.

"You came before I passed from this world. I had hoped you might," Kethek sputtered, coughing again before settling down and drinking some water. "The champion from another world and the bearer of the talisman of The Twelve."

Well, he at least won't require lengthy explanations I'd rather not relive again.

Draven and Elisah exchanged a glance of disbelief before turning back to Kethek. The old man patted Draven's right arm.

"Ansalon, old friend. I hoped we might meet again before I died." The old priest uttered a few words, and a ghastly apparition appeared in the blue light that streamed from Draven's gauntlet. Heart Master hadn't reverted to the cuff or bracer forms since he'd activated its power with Ansalon days back. The shimmering form of a man of medium years with long, dark hair regarded them with a surprised expression. "A minor projection, so that we might all talk together. I can maintain it for only a short time, but I wanted to look upon Ansalon's face again."

Ansalon went to his knees before the recumbent priest, uttering words of comfort.

"I doubt I'd be as nice to the man that sucked me into a cuff for eternity." Draven rolled his eyes at Elisah, who regarded the scene with tears at the corners of her eyes.

"This is a reunion. Kethek, Ansalon and I are all who remain of the prior champions when gods died and cities crumbled to ruins, and we thought we'd all die under the boot of Khyris." She, too, knelt beside the bed, which left Draven the unwanted interloper.

The three old friends talked for some time, recounting the past when they fought together for a common cause. Kethek gave them a brief account of his battle with Seguris, and how he'd crawled here before his injuries overtook him.

They spoke of battles, both past and future. Draven stayed for the whole thing, although he withdrew some distance away to give them a modicum of privacy. The thief knew if he departed, it would deprive them of Ansalon.

Which is a shame because this would be a fine time to make a break for it... if it weren't for Nell, Lock, and this damned relic.

Draven looked on Ansalon as a man for the first time, and his dislike of the spirit crumbled, seeing him as a person instead of an obstacle. He shook his head, thinking of what it must take to give up your body just to protect a thing, an enchanted piece of metal that sucked up lives and gave nothing in return but death.

He noticed the trio fell silent, and the old priest beckoned him to the bedside. He stumbled over, picking a spot beside Elisah near the foot of the bed.

"We did not mean to leave you out. You will be vital in the coming days, and before you even ask, no, I cannot remove Heart Master. I doubt anyone can until your task is done. The powers imbued into the relics select the bearer, and not even the gods can change that. For whatever reason, no matter how mad any of us thinks it is, you, my young friend, will be Heart Master's bearer until you are not."

Draven's shoulders slumped, and he sagged against the bed. Somehow, he knew that would be the old man's answer. In his heart, Draven knew they would force him into the role of hero.

"I don't know that I can shoulder this burden." He bit at his lower lip.

"Neither did I." Hearing Ansalon aloud, rather than in his head, still unnerved Draven.

Elisah gave him a stern look. "None of us ever do."

"But we do, for someone must stand against the darkness and the terror that crawls across the land to ensnare men's souls." Kethek fell back against the pillows, exhausted. Ansalon's image disappeared.

Draven looked at Elisah. "Does your wisdom tell you what we should do now, oh former champion?"

Elisah's only reply was a sour expression that invited no comment from the thief.

34

CHAMPIONS UNITED?

AFTER A COUPLE OF dusty days on the road, Helena and Kell arrived at the gates of Risell to find them barred. It took showing her writs of authority and flashing her seal of office as a knight of Velleris to get them inside the city. Kell, as expected, was little help, blustering like an oaf, and brandishing his ax like a hill-bred savage.

Which, I suppose, is what he is. Madness that I chose him as a traveling companion. Still, the kite shield has only shown signs of life around him, so Velleris must favor him.

Helena laughed at the idea of Velleris favoring an unwashed barbarian from the mountains who prayed only to her brother, the god of emotion.

The goddess herself had been strangely silent since Kell had joined her, and he said he'd received no more visits from his mountain god, either. If he told the truth. All men lie. This she'd learned in her life. So what if he was painfully direct and always spoke his mind? He did not differ from any other man who had tried to use her for his own gain. Yet despite herself, Kell's surly temper and ribald wit had grown on her. He still smelled, but Helena found she didn't abhor him as much as she thought she might. Long talks into the night before they slept revealed him to be of a more intelligent stock than she had expected, though he was completely illiterate. And, for now, whatever Kell's agenda was, he kept it to himself hidden behind amiable smiles and good humor.

Beside her, Kell winced and rubbed at his chest again. She offered a silent thanks to Velleris that her orders came verbally rather than through physical pain.

"We're getting close. I can feel it. Deeper into the city and toward the northeast corner." The warrior spoke through clenched teeth, his knuckles white as he endured yet another wave of agony from his savage god, Regnir.

She shook her head again. After leaving the sad excuse for a town where they'd met, Kell had cried out in pain and nearly tumbled from the saddle. He said his god didn't impart any messages to him but also declared the pain meant they could not tarry and must ride hard for Risell. So they did, as fast as Kell could travel. He still wasn't much of a rider despite Helena's tutelage.

Moving toward the center of the city, she understood the need for haste. Many buildings lay in ruins while others were under various stages of renovation. No one would speak regarding what happened except for a great battle between wizards that had killed and maimed scores of people.

Soldiers and guardsmen marched everywhere. Men with pikes bearing the city's symbol stopped the pair, interrogating them about their reason for visiting the battered seaport. Helena told them only what was needed, so that she and Kell would be on their way. A flash of her seal was enough to silence even the most strident of the lot. Kell's hulking frame and even more hulking ax didn't hurt either.

They left their horses and a silver piece with a stable master.

"Here. The man we seek is here." He pointed toward a well-maintained town house in a rundown section of the city, veins bulging in his well-muscled arm. "Make haste! The mark is pulsing like an avalanche."

Helena rolled her eyes but kept her own counsel.

Kell strolled up to the house, unlimbered his ax to keep it within easy reach, and attempted to open the door, which was stoutly locked. He stood before it as if deciding whether to chop it down with the ax.

"Imbecile." She shoved him out of the way and banged on the heavy door with the pommel of her dagger.

The door opened, and Helena looked into the brown eyes of a man of middle height, dressed in supple leathers such as a thief might wear. His eyes bored into hers with the intensity of a serpent.

"You're no priest," Kell said before she could silence him.

"Quick, that one." The odd man put an arm across the door to bar the entry. "Kethek is not well, not giving out alms or blessings or whatever you've come for. Move along." The apparent thief tried to shut the door on them, but Kell and Helena both grabbed it in twin iron grips. The thief struggled before giving in, but still didn't welcome them inside.

"We must speak to the priest no matter the condition he's in. We are on an urgent quest for the goddess. Whether you believe it, the world itself is at stake from a slave-turned warlord."

"Sweet goddess, there are more of us. Elisah! I think this one belongs to you." The thief turned away from the door, allowing Kell and Helena entry into the house. "Elisah and I can use the barbarian, but we've already got a knight."

Kell gave Helena an inquiring glance. She returned his expression with grim certainty.

The strange little man catapulted himself up the stairs as if on springs. She took one tentative step. Kell exchanged another look with her, and she paused, unsure about following their host. A litany of curses erupted from the second floor so profane that even the barbarian blushed.

She tossed her head and raised her chin as she proceeded in the argument's wake. She didn't bother to look to see if Kell joined her. She heard his heavy tread behind her causing the old wood of the risers to creak. Helena made sure her dagger was within easy reach, not sure of what she was about to walk into. The thief and a woman clad partially in plate armor stood in a short hall, arguing. Spittle flew from the woman's lips while the man who'd let them into the house appeared indifferent to the epithets and ignored her as best he could.

"You do not know who they are! They could serve Ghedryn for all you know!" The woman gestured to Helena and Kell, her face red with anger. Her sheer size impressed even Helena.

"Ansalon says they're okay. That's good enough for me. Also, the relic would have gone all blue and glowing if they were enemies." The man tapped his arm.

Helena observed a brilliant shining gauntlet of silvery-blue metal peeking from beneath his sleeve. Behind her, Kell sucked in a long breath and expelled with more effort than necessary.

I'm sure his silly god mark is pulsing in time to their argument.

The woman threw her arms up in frustration and stalked off to the end of the hall next to an open doorway. The man turned back to Helena and Kell, rolling his eyes. He made a flourishing bow to Helena.

"I'm Draven. That moody servant of Nerys is Elisah Fairoaks, knight-commander, champion, and eternal guardian of something or other."

If that woman is a knight, then I'm a handmaiden to Velleris.

"We're attempting to save the world. Want to assist? It's probably certain death, but it promises to be a delightful ride." Draven punctuated the question with a sly wink.

Helena looked the man up and down once more, wondering how a man such as this could be called to serve the gods. Still, despite his height, there was steel to him. Also, she could not discount the intelligence behind his fierce eyes, and he had invoked the name of one of the great Knights of Valor who had served not one but all twelve gods before being slain in the Mektwin war. She imagined Kell crossing his arms and raising an eyebrow behind her, as was his wont when hearing anything he disbelieved.

Have I grown to know this brute that well in just a few days? The big warrior swept past her before she could respond and shook the man's hand with what must have been a crushing grip, judging by Draven's pained expression. She'd learned over the past few days, Kell did nothing by half measures.

"I am Kell, called by Regnir, and this is the fair knight Helena, bound to the whims of Velleris. Despite this, I find her a stalwart companion. If you speak true, we would offer our blades. My god mark tells me you are part of our quest to defeat Seguris and Ghedryn, the vile God of Conquest." Kell thumped Draven on the back, nearly knocking the smaller man to his knees, while the Fairoaks woman looked on in disgust, before disappearing into the doorway she leaned against.

"As this oaf conveyed, I am Helena, in service to the goddess Velleris. To which deity do you kneel? You are an unlikely warrior." Helena attempted to keep the disdain from her tone but doubted any success.

"Ha," he barked out a short laugh. "None, but you might say the knight-commander and I are here at the behest of the Goddess of Luck and Death. She's big on the death part."

An unfamiliar voice issued from the room Elisah had disappeared into. "Warrior, come. I fear my time is growing short." Despite its quietness, it offered a stern command that resonated in Helena's bones.

"Come." Draven gestured them both toward the room. "I didn't joke about the priest. He's in a bad way. Only the gods can keep him breathing much longer."

"I believe I can assist." Helena followed Draven into a spacious bedroom.

The roomy bedchamber became cramped with the four of them clustered around a wide bed occupied by an ancient man with more wrinkles on his face than Helena had ever seen. His breath rattled in his chest. Mottled bruising covered the man's face, and blood seeped from a dozen cuts to his scalp.

Sweet Goddess, how does the man even draw breath? And how old can he be? His skin is akin to aged leather, and his eyes, even half closed, hold the wisdom of the ages.

♥*Kethek was old when the war with Khyris raged across the land. His devotion to the Twelve called him to guard The Trappings of the Wild. Though cursed, the mantle kept him young. Age is catching up with him.*♥

Helena looked around to see where the voice had issued from. Surely not the old man.

"That was the knight in Heart Master. He seems to think you can hear him. Hey, maybe the relic would like her better than me, if she can hear Ansalon." Draven tugged at the silver gauntlet which flowed before Helena's eyes into a cuff, as the thief attempted to pry the silver-blue metal from his wrist, but other than flashing an unnatural light it didn't budge. "Hells. Anyway."

"Aye, I can hear him. It is strange; only the goddess has spoken to me before." Helena dipped her head in thought, wondering if this was some new blessing from Velleris to make up for the relic that failed to work for her.

"Sorry for that. He's a chatty old bastard." Draven flicked the silver metal and uttered a raucous laugh, amused at his own joke.

"The wisdom of a knight is nothing to mock." Helena stood back, glowering at him for his insolence.

Draven crossed his arms and sneered. "Try living with him. It's no banquet."

Helena looked over to Elisah, who sat by the priest's bedside, mopping his face with a damp cloth. Concern marred her scarred visage.

"I can try to heal him. It is one of my blessings from Velleris." Helena stepped forward to stand closer to the head of the bed, jostling Kell aside.

"What? Can you heal wounds? And yet you listened to me complain of the sores I developed from riding and said nothing?" Kell threw his arms wide, his face a mask of disbelief.

"There is no way under the heavens I will ever lay hands on your backside, barbarian. The gifts of Velleris are for need, not for your piggish comforts." Helena attempted a disapproving glance at him but could not keep the hint of a smile from creeping into her expression.

Kell muttered some epithets and sulked off to lean against the doorway.

"Kethek, will you allow me to heal you?" She held up her calloused hands to him, and the old man's eyes fluttered open.

"You may attempt to do so. I cannot guarantee you will succeed. This body is old and fading by the day." Kethek coughed, clutching at his chest. Blood ran from the corner of his mouth.

"Harm him, and I swear I'll gut you where you stand." Elisah rose from Kethek's bedside and backed away, her hand stroking the pommel of a dagger at her belt.

"Don't mind her. She's always in a foul temper. I think she's still insulted that Heart Master likes me best. Holy knights don't relish their relics in the hands of a footpad. Even an exceptional footpad." Draven straightened his jerkin as if proud of his admission.

Helena huffed out a breath and glared at Draven. Ire rose along her spine, filling her with rage. She clenched her hand, and the desire to strike out at the thief nearly overcame her. Kell laughed, which only infuriated her more.

"Heart Master will just protect me. You may break your dagger, and that would be wasteful. Besides, I know little about healing, but I believe you are supposed to be serene and filled with inner peace or some such rot."

Helena bit her lip, about to frame a retort, when Kell stepped forward and laid a hand to her arm. She whirled, staring daggers at him.

"Brash he may be, but he is correct. You've ample time to beat him senseless once the old man recovers."

Damn their eyes, damn all their eyes, but they are correct. I need to rein in my temper.

Helena closed her eyes and counted in time to the beat of her heart. When peace descended over her, she opened her eyes and exhaled. Out of the corner of her eye, Draven's arm rose, pointing in her direction. The thief looked mystified. Helena couldn't help but notice it was the arm bearing Heart Master. The cuff seemed to pull him toward her against his will.

"I swear by Nerys, this isn't me." Draven pulled at his other arm to no avail.

"I would posit a theory that Heart Master wants you to touch it while channeling your healing." Kethek struggled to sit higher on the bed.

The ignominy knows no end. Helena reached out, grabbing Draven's hand and pulled him closer till they stood shoulder to shoulder. Grimacing at his touch, she slid her hand up to hold onto the cuff which now covered his entire forearm. Whorls of detail she couldn't make out crawled over the surface in a moving metal tapestry. *What secrets this relic must hold.*

Helena winced at the oily texture of the metal and how it moved under her hand. A shiver ran up her spine, and a sick, queasy feeling roiled through her stomach. She steeled herself and wrapped her hand around the thing. She swallowed hard, refusing to give in to revulsion.

"I should warn you that I'm spoken for, so don't go getting any ideas." Draven sidled closer to allow her to grasp the holy relic without stretching.

Her hand shot out toward his jaw, connecting with bone. Draven's head rocked backward, but it did nothing to erase his good humor. He rubbed his chin with his free hand, offering her a grin.

"Nice shot. It only protects me when I'm not being a rogue." He gave her another annoying wink.

"Can we get on with this? The priest needs our help and we do not have time for this idiocy." Elisah glared at them, but Helena detected fear for the old man as well.

Then she realized: Elisah had known him. Helena suddenly felt small in the presence of ancients.

Kethek said nothing but assayed a weak grin, almost as if to show sympathy for the immaturity of Heart Master's bearer.

Helena cleared her throat, put her hand on the relic again, and reached her other hand out to the old priest, touching his forehead with her fingers. She stilled her thoughts, stilled her heart, stilled her breathing until she became an empty vessel. The power of the goddess rushed in to fill that void with warm golden light. Her eyes remained closed while tingling warmth radiated down her arm to Kethek.

Heart Master added a distinctive energy. Ever changing, it was warm, then cold, and finally burning like a fire. Her body ached with the magic flowing through her to Kethek. The old priest shuddered and went rigid beneath her touch. Through their link, Kethek's pain became Helena's, his injuries became her injuries, but also a creeping darkness that clawed at the old man's soul. Dark, cold, unknowable magic—no doubt that of Nerys, the goddess of death—crept through their link. She didn't know its source, but if she hadn't had the strength of Heart Master on her side, she would have perished alongside the old man.

In some dim, distant way, she was aware voices spoke around her, but she could not understand the words. Her legs buckled, but muscular hands supported her. Tears ran from eyes that could no longer see. She knew only the struggle, the healing and finally, an explosion of light that sucked the world from her mind. Before the void claimed her, an evil voice called to her.

Come to me, child of Velleris. I will drink your soul and devour your goddess. Whether the voice belonged to Ghedryn, Seguris, or some other entity, Helena had no idea.

35

KETHEK SPEAKS

D ESPITE THE DAZZLING FLASH of light that blinded everyone in the room, Draven and Kell caught Helena before she blacked out. Draven exchanged a knowing glance with the brawny man he'd met only minutes before. As they eased her into a chair, she mumbled something about Velleris and evil.

What a truly odd pair these two are. Him I can't help liking. He's big and odd, but he smiles about everything like a simpleton. Her I can't figure out. Loud and angry. Elisah must love the competition.

"Sorry, big man, Kethek's got the only bed in the place. I cleaned off a couch downstairs that we might lay her on. You wouldn't believe the shape of the place when we got here. Old Kethek's a bit of a pig."

"I heard that, thief."

Draven turned to regard the old man, who sat up on the bed with a modicum of help from Elisah. The oozing gashes in Kethek's face had disappeared, and his bruises had faded to mottled yellow. Healthy color replaced the pasty pallor his face had sported only moments before.

Draven shook his head at the transformation. "Good, because you're a damned embarrassment to the clergy. Would it hurt you to wash a dish once in a while?"

The old man crossed his arms over his chest and turned his head away.

Kell reached out a hand to caress the unconscious woman's jaw and looked at her a bit too long for Draven's comfort.

"I do not think we should move her. I have never seen her heal anyone before, but if Kethek speaks and she is in another room, she'll want blood." Kell rubbed

Helena's arms as if friction would bring her to. "And to think she could have healed my saddle sores, and she said nothing."

Draven shook his head, turning to consider Kethek again. *It was to be hoped that he wasn't too weak and too old to remember anything useful.*

♥Mind how you speak of Kethek. His burden was greater than yours, and he carried it far longer.♥

Draven gritted his teeth and cursed to himself, wondering if it might actually be worth it to chop his arm off.

"The knight will soon recover. She is strong. I have witnessed many healings in my day, but this is the first I have been subjected to myself." Kethek favored them all with a lopsided grin, assessing his new health by raising his arms and twisting his neck until it popped.

True to his word, Helena stirred and shoved Kell, who nearly tumbled onto his arse. He leapt to his feet as if his legs were springs.

"What happened? Is the priest healed?" Helena surged to her feet as if expecting an attack. Kell took her hand and pulled her back to the chair.

"I am fine, good knight, retake your seat. We have much to discuss." Kethek sat up, taking stock of himself, nodding his approval. "Not as hale as I was with The Trappings but still fit enough to advise you." He paused, struggling for words. "Champions, I am in your debt. Were it not for the company present, I would not have survived Seguris's attack."

"You do owe us. Coins, if nothing else. We also cleaned up the place." Draven resumed his spot beside Elisah, who looked piqued again. "What? If I'm traipsing around the world, I should get something for my trouble."

Elisah did not bother with a reply, turning back to Kethek.

"And for that, I suppose. The pursuit of knowledge compels my interest more than mundane tasks, and until late, I carried the burden of keeping the Mad King imprisoned. Now he is free, and combined with a new enemy. This event could spell doom for our land." Kethek scratched at his face, which sported the beginnings of a beard.

"Like the knowledge of how to get this thrice-damned thing off me and onto the proper champion?" Draven paced around the small room, scowling. "How can you say you can't transfer Heart Master to Elisah, or this other knight, without even trying?"

Elisah jerked her head, giving Draven a sidelong glance of disgust.

For someone who was ready to stand aside and let me bear this thing a while ago, she's awfully touchy about it going to another knight.

"You know the truth of it already." The old man folded his hands on his lap and stared back at the thief.

"No, I don't think I do." Draven crossed his arms and thrust out his chin.

"I suppose I must make it plain then. Heart Master is born of The Twelve. All twelve gods. It follows only its own rules. It does not answer to the gods simply because they created it. It answers to its own needs. For the time being, you fill that need."

Helena could only hold her tongue for so long. "That is absurd. He is a thief. There is no hint of holiness about him. Even in the short time we've been here, it's clear he's a feckless lout."

Kell laughed, and they all turned to stare.

He rose and stepped forward. "None of us chose this. I certainly didn't. We were chosen. Some of us by gods, some of us by relics. I may not know this man, but if this trinket chose him, then there must be a reason."

"The warrior of Regnir speaks the truth. There are times a sword is called for, other times a lock pick. Who and how Heart Master chooses is still a mystery to me." Kethek pinched the bridge of his nose. "Enough of that. There is a much bigger issue we must address."

"Seguris." Draven spoke the name, but everyone nodded in response.

"Yes. There are other forces at play, but Seguris is the immediate threat. You must reach the tower before him."

"What's so important about the tower?" Draven asked.

Across the room, Kell's mouth snapped shut as if he were about to ask the same question.

"Blood Thorn." Helena uttered the words, but Kethek inclined his head in agreement.

"Blood Thorn by itself is powerful. If he combines it with the power of The Fist and The Trappings, then I fear not even Heart Master can stop him from realizing his dreams. And the longer he wears The Trappings, the darker and more twisted those dreams will be."

"What are these 'trappings'?" Kell asked, leveling an accusing finger at the old priest.

"Yes, the goddess did not mention these. Are they another relic?" Helena leaned forward in her chair.

Across from her, Elisah remained silent but her expression was haunted.

"Nellonah has that in hand, or she's supposed to. Nerys sent her after the Chaos Masque. It's supposed to even the odds. Right, Fairoaks?" Draven turned his head to Elisah, waiting for a response. It was a long time coming.

Finally, she spoke. "Assuming she is successful. There are no certainties now. The new Mektwin warlord was enough of a threat with The Fist of Heaven. With Khyris on his side, it's impossible to gauge our chances." Elisah's expression turned grim and pensive, giving away little of what actually spun in her ancient mind.

"Hells. We let Nellonah go off for Nerys, and we don't even know if she'll succeed. I thought the Chaos Masque was a sure bet. You don't even know if it will work?"

"Nothing can be certain when the gods war, young man." Kethek reached up to pat his arm. "But the reasoning is sound. Much like Heart Master, the Chaos Masque is shrouded in mystery. It may disintegrate The Trappings. The question is, can it do so without releasing the evil trapped within? Over the years, thousands of souls have become trapped within it, an unintended consequence of binding Khyris into that cursed object. I believe, though, that's a concern for another day." The old man's features became pinched.

"So where do we go from here?" Helena's simple question echoed through the room as they turned back to Kethek.

"The tower—with all haste. I can help you now that I am healthy again. If we can charter a vessel, I believe we may yet arrive at the tower before Seguris." Kethek rose from the bed, testing his legs as if for the first time. He teetered and Elisah offered him a steadying hand. Then he breathed out slowly and bustled past Kell and Helena. "Give me a hand with packing a few things, young knight."

Helena and Kell rose to assist Kethek as he thrust a pair of leather bags into their hands and began throwing things, seemingly at random, into them. Clothes, trinkets, journals, old books, and jars of unlabeled herbs clattered, filling the bags till their seams threatened to burst.

Wonder if I should tell him about my satchel? Draven smiled and kept that little secret to himself. *As if I want some old wizard rooting around in my pretties.*

♥*Kethek is more than just some wizard. He deserves our trust. And respect.*♥

Draven rolled his eyes at Ansalon. "No fear about the ship. We have one anchored here, unless that unreliable wharf rat has abandoned us."

"If he tries to sail without us, his ship will be so much flotsam." Elisah held up a small, silver medallion that glinted even in the dim light of Kethek's bed chamber.

"Then let's be off. Every moment we delay puts Seguris one step closer to the tower. If we do not beat him to it, I fear the world may end." Kethek's pronouncement chilled even the hard-edged Draven to the core.

36

THE TRUTH OF HALLOWED VERITY

KELL HUNG HIS HEAD over the railing of *The Rose Bush,* waiting for his current bout of nausea to pass, watching frothy white waves form as the ship cut through the clear blue sea. The old priest, Kethek, stood at the front of the ship, his hands thrust above his head, blue light dancing off his palms. Kell shook his head and retched again.

May Regnir blast his soul to ashes. I dislike boats. And I am certain he is making it worse with his infernal magic.

His god-mark surged, and the roiling in his stomach abated. *Is Regnir finally showing me some mercy? Or does he simply realize if I do nothing but spill my guts, I'll be no use in the coming battle?*

He took a shallow breath and pushed himself up from the railing. Though his body may be recovering, he worried his spirit was not. It had been a boon to be joined by Helena. Now that they were part of the larger company of Kethek, Elisah, and Draven, Kell found himself wondering what he could offer that the more experienced champions could not. Draven and Helena both bore relics. Kethek and Elisah had been fighting evil for centuries. Kell... had an ax and a god-mark that left him weakened. What use would he be in their cause?

Elisah and Draven spoke in hushed voices by the big spoked circle the captain said steered the vessel. Draven was a fair companion, but the knight-commander barely acknowledged Kell and Helena. She glared at them as if they had no place in the company.

The ways of the holy were strange indeed. What carnage she must have witnessed in her long and bloody life. She'd forgotten more about combat than the rest of them would ever know.

Helena didn't appear bothered by Elisah's silence. Although perturbed by the thief carrying the holiest of relics, she gave no notice to the older woman. When he asked why, Helena tossed her braid and muttered about Elisah Fairoaks being a relic herself, and one who served the wrong goddess.

As if beckoned by his thoughts, Helena approached, walking as nimbly on the swaying deck as she did on dry land. Kell still didn't trust his steps on the ship unless he had something to steady himself with. Although unarmed, she bore the shield that occupied so much of her time. When she didn't think he was watching, she spent hours staring at the thing as if her willpower alone could bring it to life.

Without warning, she threw the shield at him. It wobbled on an odd trajectory, but Kell caught the relic with some difficulty. A soft golden glow surrounded it and he dropped it as if scalded. The shield clattered to the deck, the sound reverberating in his ears. He looked to Helena in confusion, while she glared at him as if blaming him for some unintended slight.

"Go ahead. Pick it up." She leveled a finger at him.

"I don't want to." Kell regarded the shield as he would a serpent about to strike.

"Why?"

"It makes my skin crawl. It may suit you fine, but it feels odd to me. I can hear the metal singing to me if we stand too close." Kell shivered over the hunk of metal. "Is it magic?"

"It is Hallowed Verity," Helena stated, looking down on the embossed shield decorated with a single white tower. Roses crawled up the edifice like greedy fingers.

"Wait. Is this the tower we now seek?"

"It is supposed to be magical. Velleris bestowed it upon me prior to my journey, but it has remained nothing but a lifeless piece of metal." Helena lifted the edge of the shield with her boot and let it drop back to the deck. "Until I met you."

"'Tis obvious. If it is a gift from your goddess, it recognizes me as an enemy. Regnir and Velleris have always been at odds. He is the heart while she is the law. They are opposites." Kell attempted to speak with some certainty, despite a wriggling doubt in his stomach.

"And yet... we are friends." Helena bit her lip, looking at him through eyes half closed as if her own words surprised her.

"Are we, Helena? Or are we just companions with a singular goal? 'Tis what you've said since we met." Kell looked from her to the shield. Contrary to what he had said, he wanted to pick it up. For once, the cursed god mark lay silent on his chest.

"If you're looking for some heartfelt confession of love, you'll not find it here, but yes, I consider you my friend. Mayhap my only friend outside the order. We don't know how far we can trust the others. You and I must be on our guard."

Kell beamed. He had expected Helena to bond with the female knight-commander and shut him out once she found someone more like herself to confide in.

"You should have a shield to guard your back when I cannot." Kell flicked his eyes downward at the curious item winking in the noonday sun.

"Or you." She joined him at the rail, her words little more than a whisper.

"What? No. Your goddess gave that to you, and I'm a warrior of Regnir. We do not favor shields." Kell found himself lost in a sea of words, unable to pick the correct ones.

"Test it. Pick it up." Her words were forceful, but Kell could detect something else behind her expression.

"But your goddess gave you this, I cannot. I should not."

"You can, and you will. Both my goddess and Kethek say that the shield responds to stillness, balance, and yet I am filled with rage, always rage. I fail my goddess in that, despite my attempts to quell it and act always as her hand. You, however, are content, even amid chaos."

If she only knew the doubts I have.

"Helena?" Kell reached down, but inches away from the metal, he froze, torn between loyalty to Helena, and his desire to hold this thing that called to him.

"Just pick it up. It won't bite you. We need to know if the gods really meant this for you." She nudged the shield toward him with her boot, and the closer it got, the more of a golden sheen the relic took on. "And in case it bites you, I will heal you. Probably." Suddenly Helena winked at him in a most unsettling manner.

"Fine. I will, just to test it, then I will return it to you. I swear." Kell wondered if he was lying to her or himself. No part of him believed he had any claim to a relic of Velleris, but he also wondered if perhaps the shield sought to claim him as Draven's cuff had done. The realization did nothing to soothe his frayed nerves as his anxiety returned a hundredfold.

Will she hate me if this works? Will she still call me friend if her shield chooses me over her? Kell offered Helena another uncertain glance and knelt down, his fingers only inches from the golden metal. He squinted as the roses around the tower bloomed, a few petals falling to be carried off by the wind. Radiant light sprang up from the metal, pulsing in time to the crash of waves against the ship.

Helena gave him a shove, forcing his fingers to touch the enchanted metal. As soon as his hands met the shield, the light intensified, enveloping them both in its glory. Emboldened because it did not, in fact, bite him, Kell took Hallowed Verity in his hand and rose. Across from him, Helena beamed, which surprised him. He thought she'd be furious.

"I—I don't know if this is a good thing, Helena. I don't carry a shield. I'm not even sure what to do with one in combat. It would hinder swinging my ax." Despite his words, he held the shield reverently, its face toward him. The image of the tower and roses came to vibrant life as if he looked through a window on the tower itself.

"Learn. This is a blessing. Though I wish it were for me, I am ecstatic to see this stubborn piece of metal come to life. Mayhap I will wield the cursed blade, or simply the power of my goddess." She trailed a finger along the studded edge of the shield, her mouth agape in delight. Kell thought he detected a note of sadness underlying her joy.

Who would want to wield the cursed blade of Regnir, a weapon meant only for anger? And how will I fight with a shield on one arm?

In response to his thoughts, Hallowed Verity vibrated. Helena snatched her hand back as if shocked. The metal turned soft in his hands. Kell tried to drop it, terrified by what might come next, but the shield held to his hands, flowing over his arms, and settling around his chest.

Kell spun, trying to dislodge it, but try as he might, it stuck to him like a second skin. Out of the corner of his eye, he spied Draven and Elisah running toward them. Helena gaped but stood stock still. The metal hardened beneath his touch into a golden breastplate, still showing the same tower and creeping roses. For the first time since it appeared, the god-mark went silent. If he listened closely, Kell fancied he could hear Regnir laughing at him.

Helena reached out to touch the metal again, this time with a wry smile. Elisah and Draven stopped just short of them. The would-be champion arched an eyebrow while the thief who bore Heart Master laughed at his predicament.

"Ha! It's about time someone else got stuck with one of these rotting relics. Does yours talk?"

Kell found himself at a loss for words. "No. Not as I can tell. It just feels cool and peaceful. This is madness. I am sworn to Regnir. How can this be?"

"The gods have a capricious sense of humor, and their relics more so. Everything is on its crown." Elisah shook her head in disbelief.

"That's not fair. I have to listen to a noisome knight, and he gets peace?" Draven shook his fist at the sky and walked away in a huff.

Kell turned back to Helena. "Do you hate me for this?"

"Armor of Velleris. I wish I could. I'm passing jealous, but I have no anger for you. I'm saving that for Seguris. At least someone is going to get some use out of this blighted relic." Helena rapped her knuckles against the chest plate. Golden light winked beneath her hand. "Now you can stand on the frontline to keep the rest of us from getting slaughtered." She walked away laughing, leaving Kell more confused than ever—but he could no longer question whether he belonged in this company.

37

AN UNEXPECTED DETOUR

THANKS TO THE OLD priest and his magic, Draven and his companions arrived at a small beach shortly after daybreak. Thistle maneuvered the ship as close to shore as he could, and they unloaded the gear and disembarked with the horses.

Kethek assured them it was less than a day's ride to reach the tower from this isolated stretch of sand crowded by cliffs on either side. Draven cinched his saddle girth strap and checked it over a dozen times. Riding did not come naturally to him and saddling horses even less so. Around him, the others did the same, though with practiced ease compared to his nervous fumbling.

What in the nine hells am I doing here?

♥*We are attempting to avert disaster. Even if it is a fool's errand.*♥

"You, maybe. I'm just trying to save the woman I love, and my skin. Maybe Loken if he's nice. The rest of the world can rot."

Ansalon refrained from answering, though scorn radiated from Heart Master at his comment.

Nellonah. Just the thought of her brought back the same familiar remorse. Odd that they'd only reunited for a short time, but her absence now resembled a leagues-wide trench where his heart should be. *Please, let her return safely from her thrice-damned errand, and, for all our sakes, let her be on time.*

Elisah went around to each mount, adjusting straps, or nodding her approval as if she were the general of the smallest army in the land. When it came time to check Draven's, Elisah shook her head with bemusement. "Backwards." When she finished she looked at him. "Three hundred years, maybe four." She moved on to the next horse.

This is real. I am going to fight a warlord with nothing but this relic and my wits. We are all going to die.

Thistle came down to speak with Elisah, who finally relented and gave him the medallion that hung from her neck. He smiled from ear to ear and shoved the ward into his belt.

I think he's about to dance a jig.

Their farewells with the captain and his crew were short. Thistle wanted nothing more to do with this mad endeavor, and Draven couldn't blame him.

I wouldn't mind being shut of this mess myself.

♥*Cease your prattling. It would be an honor to be called into this conflict. Show your mettle, if you have any.*♥

"Hey, I can prattle to myself if I want to." Draven noticed every eye on him as the rest of the company mounted up while *The Rose Bush* weighed anchor. "Let's see how any of you would enjoy having a knight stuck in your head." Draven clambered up onto his horse with less grace than usual.

"It's a race now." Elisah punctuated her words with a sharp whistle and thundered away, sword held high. One by one, the company followed her.

♥*She was always one for drama.*♥

Draven shook his head and squeezed his knees together, urging his horse to follow. "You're one to talk."

They rode in relative silence for the next hour. The lush beach gave way to a vast desert that spanned the horizon. Winds whipped across mountainous dunes, and Draven could scarcely believe such a desolate environment could exist so close to the ocean.

♥*This is the work of Khyris and his damned war. Mekta was once a verdant paradise. The killing of the gods, the raging battles to defeat the Mad King—the land was scarred in such a way that it is unlikely life will ever flourish here again. I know. I was there. Some of this is my fault.*♥

Draven swallowed hard, sadness and sorrow creeping into his heart. He said nothing, but turned his eyes to the horizon, wondering what devastation they would leave in their wake. What fresh horrors would this battle with Seguris let loose on the world?

A shiver ran up his arm from the enchanted cuff, then a burning sensation that jerked his arm, pulling the reins to the right. He willed his arm to comply, but to no avail. His horse now moved perpendicular to the rest of the party. He looked over his shoulder to see the other riders slowing.

"Hey, Ansalon. Seguris is the other way. What in the goddess's name are you doing?"

♥*This is not me. It's Heart Master. It senses evil and seeks to combat it.*♥

"Look, we've passed by plenty of other evil, and it's never done this before. How do I stop it?"

♥*Heart Master has always been capricious. Mayhap you just awakened its power. Only a supreme act of will can override it. I suggest you accept it. The alternative is excruciating pain, both physical and mental.*♥

"Brilliant." Draven tried pulling at the cuff with his free hand, but the metal heated till it scorched his skin. He relented, and the pain faded. The other riders joined him, Elisah pulling abreast of his mount.

With a heroic effort of willpower, Draven reined his mount to a stop. Fire crawled up his right arm, his breath now came in labored gasps. The other riders clustered around him in a circle as Draven clutched the cuff to his chest in agony.

Kell studied him, concern etched in the smooth lines of his face. Helena just looked annoyed while Elisah and Kethek favored him with quizzical expressions.

"It's not me. Heart Master is in control. It says, in no uncertain terms, we need to go this way. Ansalon says it senses some unknown evil." Draven winced, sucking breath through clenched teeth. Sweat poured down his brow as he hunched in the saddle.

"We have no time for this. Get your cursed relic under control. The battle is this way." Helena thrust a finger in the direction they had been heading before Heart Master pulled them away.

"You think I don't know that? It's burning my blighted arm off. I don't think I have any choice. It took all I had just to stop."

Kethek pulled up, laying a hand on Heart Master. He pulled it back as if it was burned. The enchanted metal flowed down to cover Draven's fingers in a bluish gauntlet, and up till his entire arm was armored. Blue flames rippled around him.

"Whether we have the time or not, Heart Master sets the course. Though we may not fathom it, I trust in Heart Master. Lead on, thief." Kethek laid a hand to Draven's arm, careful not to touch the relic again.

Draven scowled at him. He didn't like to lose. Especially to some blighted piece of god-metal. "Fine. Lead the way, Heart Master."

The company followed, though Draven could hear Helena complaining the entire time. They rode hard, Heart Master compelling them to ever greater speed. It didn't take long to learn why the relic diverted their course.

They came to the top of a large dune. Looking down over the shifting sands, Draven spied a disorganized caravan. A group of fifty men in billowing garments bearing curved swords stood guard over many men, women, and children chained in a line.

Some distance away from the primary group, a single youth ran with a pack of a dozen swordsmen on his trail. The pulsing of Heart Master pulled his arm toward the runaway, who fled as if his life depended on it. Even from a distance, Draven could discern blood coloring the boy's dusty garments.

"Slavers." Elisah spat on the ground before Draven could even frame the thought.

"Heart Master is pulling me toward the boy." Draven uttered the words, a cold ache in his heart.

We don't have time for this, but there's no way we can leave them. Damn this cursed thing.

"Draven, you and I will save the boy," Elisah said. "The rest of you, guard our backs. Those are steep odds, but we are champions. They will not see another day."

"Oh, aye, ten to one. I'm sure it will be fine." Draven looked at the others, but they didn't appear concerned.

♥ *Take heart, thief. You are champions. This rabble will be as chaff before the scythe.* ♥

"Bugger." Draven spurred his horse forward, his guts crawling. Every instinct in his body revolted against riding into a fight he could pass by, but slavers were the worst filth the world offered. Elisah fell in behind him, as did Kethek, Kell, and Helena. "Well, this should be fun."

Blue fire raced up his arm as Elisah and Draven galloped toward the boy, who turned on his pursuers, brandishing a long, slender knife. The sun glinted angry fire off the metal. A livid purple bruise ran the length of the youth's face while a cut on his cheek dripped scarlet roses onto his dusty garment. Draven admired the boy's courage.

"I'm done. I'd rather die than be your plaything." The boy's voice cracked on the final syllable.

Draven pulled closer and leapt from his horse, already pulling knives from his jerkin to lob at the closest slavers. One went wide; the other buried itself into the back of a bearded man, who whirled, glaring at his unseen attacker.

Draven drew his falchion with one hand, and his toothed sword breaker with his other, just in time to ward off the slice of a scimitar. Heart Master blazed. His return cut snapped the desert blade as if it were glass, continuing down to cleave through the man's shoulder.

Hells. Draven couldn't help but marvel at the power, even while being sickened at the gout of blood spurting from the neck wound. He caught a glance of the boy, who looked back at him with defiant curiosity.

Draven didn't have time to ponder this as another slaver rushed forward, attempting to skewer him on a curved blade. Elisah's steed crashed into the man, trampling him beneath the horse's iron-shod hooves. A swipe of her great broadsword ended another man's life.

Shouts rose behind him, warning him that reinforcements would soon be on their way, but he could only trust the others to meet that charge as two men confronted him. Draven parried and spun while Heart Master sent waves of blue fire at the men, burning hair, fabric, and flesh with ease. The flames reduced the men to charred caricatures in minutes. Bile rose in his throat, but he choked it back.

Thunder exploded behind him, and he risked a glance to behold Kethek calling lightning from the sky to end more lives. Helena and Kell worked together like parts of the same machine, killing slavers with a disturbing economy of motion.

It's like they have been doing this for their whole lives. The way the pair of them move together is uncanny.

♥*Thief! Attention!*♥

Draven shook his head and brought his knives together with a clatter of metal, sending a thunderclap of sheer force into four men advancing on Elisah. The knight-commander had remained mounted, raining down blows on any who came within reach. The boy stabbed men from behind or slit their throats. Draven swore at the way the boy's eyes lit up as he did so.

Still, I don't know what he's seen. Who am I to question? My life before Nellonah was no feast.

Draven turned back to the fight, wreathed in azure fire, his knives moving with inexplicable precision. Men died, and part of him died with them. If this was the life of a champion, they could keep it.

♥*Mind you, Draven. These men do evil work. This is a service to gods and men alike.*♥

Draven sighed and went back to killing.

The last slaver died at the hands of either Kell or Helena, Draven couldn't tell which. He gazed over the battlefield with a heavy sigh, fighting the desire to fall to his knees and heave his guts into the bloody sand. The boy gazed at him, menace lurking behind those dark, glassy eyes, so out of place on a boyish face. Stringy blond hair fluttered in the breeze.

The rest of the band busied themselves unlocking fetters or tending to what injuries they could. Helena laid hands on some, healing injuries while calling to her goddess. A wan golden glow encompassed her, and he could not reconcile her with the same woman that had dealt death without mercy only minutes ago.

I can't help appreciating the irony of freeing slaves while on the way to kill a slave-turned-warlord.

Draven couldn't take his eyes off the boy. He saw something there. Something both familiar and unsettling. The boy didn't move, not even to clean his knife, which he gripped so hard the knuckles of his hand showed white beneath his tanned skin.

He reminds me of me, and Loken, back before Nellonah. Back when survival was at the point of a knife, and gnawing hunger haunted every waking hour.

Memories flooded back to him of pain, betrayal, and worse. Before Nellonah rescued him, life on the streets was not kind. Draven viewed himself reflected in this battered boy's eyes.

"You don't own me, you know. Just because you killed them." The boy spat on the ground, fingering the knife's edge, testing how keen it was after slitting so many throats.

"No one owns anyone." Draven wondered what words would have mollified him at that age.

"Were that true, none of us would be here. I'll still not be your toy or mule, or whatever you want me for. I'll gut you like the rest of them." The boy stooped to retrieve another knife, this time a long-bladed poniard as if he were ready to take on Draven and all his friends.

He probably is.

Draven laughed, rubbing a hand over his face.

"We wish you no harm. Something warned us there was evil here, and we came to root it out." Draven frowned at how bizarre the words sounded coming out of his mouth.

I have definitely had this thing on my arm for too long. I sound like Ansalon.

"Why weren't you chained like the others?" Draven cocked an eyebrow, almost afraid of the answer.

"I was their plaything. Slavers always seem to like little boys. I thought their coin was worth it, but when they started pummeling me, that's where I draw the line."

Draven's heart leapt to his throat. His knees grew weak at the implication.

"Do you have a name?"

"I've several. What do you care? My mother named me Tarn, but each new uncle likes to call me something new. Drin. Lacre. Mak. Pick any you like. If you've a coin, then I'll consider it, but nothing rough, unless you want this pig-poker in your eye."

Draven raised his hands in front of him, palms out, while shaking his head. "No, nothing like that. No one will try to harm you or, ah, touch you. Like that. We're not that way."

Tarn shook his head, barked out a short laugh.

"Oh, so you're one of those holier than the goddess doers of good deeds, then? They just want it kept in the shadows. Make yourself feel better helping the poor little waif."

"Look, you guttersnipe, we want nothing from you but to free you. Then you can let the wind carry you where it will. Goddess only knows why Heart Master pointed us this way."

"So, your motives aren't pure after all. You want something from me or one of those puking slaves." Tarn crossed his arms over his chest, chin raised with a haughty expression.

Fate saved Draven from another stumbling reply by Helena joining him.

She gave the boy a curious look and snarled at Draven. "We've freed the slaves. They'll be taking the camels and horses and making for a settlement. Goddess, bless their path. Boy, get whatever possessions you have and join them. They plan on setting out soon."

"No." Tarn's answer was simple and unequivocal. Draven surmised there would be no point in arguing with him.

"This is not the time for recalcitrance. They say they'll help find you a place to live and someone to take care of you." Helena turned to go.

"You think I'm going to throw in with a bunch of poxy ex-slaves. You lot in the church are as mad as they say."

Helena glared at the boy with a vein in her forehead pulsing.

"I'm thinking I'll throw in with your band. At least you know how to defend yourselves. According to the scarecrow here, you're not a bunch of buggers."

Draven's mouth dropped open. He didn't expect that. He figured the boy wouldn't trust anyone after the slavers and would strike out on his own.

"Don't speak foolishly. We are going to war. It's no place for children. We seek the white tower to keep a relic of great power out of the hands of a madman." Helena frowned as if wondering why she imparted all that to a perfect stranger.

Kid's got charm. I'll say that.

♥*There is... something about him. Mayhap Heart Master sees an opportunity in him.*♥

Oh, sure, to be killed, maimed, and dismembered along with the rest of us. Heart Master's just rife with opportunities.

"The white tower, you say? Sounds like some place filled with riches." The boy's eyes lit with avarice.

"You." Helena leveled a finger at Draven. "Do something with that." She jerked her head at Tarn and then stomped off, apparently too furious to continue the discussion.

Draven turned back to the boy, who gave him a wry grin.

"We're stuck with you, aren't we?" Draven couldn't decide if it was a question or a statement.

"Oh, aye. I'm with you till something better comes along."

As if we didn't just save you from slavers.

"Think well before that caravan leaves. Helena doesn't jest. We ride into mortal danger." Draven attempted to sound stern, but from the expression on the boy's face, he failed.

"War produces spoils. And if you lose, I can join up with the winners."

"Come along. I suppose you can ride with me." Draven waved his hand, and the boy followed him.

I'm going to regret this.

♥Of course you will. He's the image of you.♥

38

DEFENDERS OF THE WHITE TOWER

TRUE TO KETHEK'S WORD, they arrived at the White Tower the following morning while the sun was just ascending into the sky. The tower was a marvel. It stood like an alabaster nail driven into an expanse of yellow desert. White sandstone buildings sprawled beneath it, and around those were an imposing wall, also bleached of color. Emerald vines crawled up the tower from base to spire, with reddish blossoms. As mad as it seemed, they resembled roses from a distance.

Can a rose bloom in a harsh environment? In Sharazin they take cultivation. More magical mummery, I'll wager.

As the company drew within bowshot of the walls, billowing forms erupted from the sand, bristling with crossbows and curved scimitars. The defenders of the white tower stood stock still, ready to pepper them with shafts.

Draven tensed, wondering if Heart Master would respond to his commands against these white-clad phantoms. Kethek urged his horse forward, and Draven imagined fingers tightening on triggers and bow strings. The old wizard thrust his hands to the sky, fingers splayed outward, intoning some litany in a language Draven didn't recognize. Sweat rolled from Draven's brow, but he refused to release the grip on his knives to wipe it away. *Well, this would be an embarrassing end to an already doomed quest.*

♥*Fear not. The faithful will recognize the litany.*♥

Easy for you to say.

Kethek's voice took on a melodic quality, rising as if the elements themselves harmonized with the old wizard's gravelly voice. When Kethek finished, Draven's heart sank as if lamenting the end of the old man's song.

What in the nine hells was that?

♥*It is difficult to translate. It is both a blessing and a promise. The litany is a covenant between mankind and the gods. I do not truly understand it myself,*

but all who pledge themselves to The Twelve must learn it.♥

Well, we aren't dead, so it must be doing something.

As they looked on, the weapons of the white-cloaked defenders of the tower dipped. No one moved until a pair of them stepped aside and an older man emerged from between them in a robe so white it nearly blinded Draven. He raised his voice to address Kethek.

"You've been away a long time, Holy Father. My great-grandfather bid you farewell before I was even born. Does your return bode fair or foul?" The old man's flowing beard moved in the wind as if by the hand of a ghost.

"I wish I could say I come with glad tidings, but I do not. Ghedryn has nominated a champion to bring his name to greater glory."

"The god of conquest has always supported this order. How does he now threaten the white tower?"

"Ghedryn has directed his champion to claim Blood Thorn. The champion, as much as I dislike calling him such, already possesses The Fist. To make matters worse, he has taken possession of The Trappings of the Wild."

The white-robed priest hissed a word beneath clenched teeth, spitting into the sand. Draven couldn't make out the word, and Ansalon kept his own council.

"How are you called, great-grandson of Oonan?"

"I am Lovar. Fourth to hold this position since your departure. What do you propose, Holy Father?"

"With me are the champions of Velleris, Regnir, and, ahem, Nerys. They need to secure Blood Thorn before he can claim it. Elisah Fairoaks and I will assist you in defending the tower from his bandit horde until they have the prize. Then we can defeat this assault here, putting an end to Seguris before he becomes another Khyris." Kethek leaned back in the saddle, his face grave.

I am not ready for this. I'm no hero.

♥No amount of preparation can make you a champion. Your actions will. Heart Master didn't choose you because you can swing a sword. It chose you for your cunning. Stand when you must and skulk where you can, or just lay down and die.♥

Lovar's eyes narrowed as he looked at Draven. Those eyes bored into him like burning brands, but Draven stood his ground.

Draven rolled his eyes. *I'm done being intimidated by old men and holy missions.*

"They may try, but powerful wards guard the relic." Lovar's eyes burned with suspicion. "A wave of those gnarled hands will not dispel them. No one scion may enter. It must be a conclave. Do these champions know the penalty for failure? Or did you build some secret way that you could exploit for your own needs?"

"I made sure that I did not. In the event Khyris overwhelmed me, I didn't want him to have easy access to the cursed blade. But the gods will guide the three. I have faith in them. They have overcome much already. They will not break when the time arises."

Draven studied Lovar. The wise old priest was apparently far older than Draven realized.

He's no more convinced than I am.

"How soon will this attack come?" Lovar asked.

"Far sooner than I'd like. I do not know Seguris's location with any certainty, but we can't be more than a day ahead of him."

"Hey! No one mentioned penalties," Draven interjected. "Is this some sort of test? And what does it measure? Have you been holding out on us?"

Kethek raised his hands for silence. "Do not worry, there is a test of sorts, but it is only to ensure the gods agree. No one person can claim the thorny rose of the tower."

"And the penalty Lovar mentioned?"

"Oblivion," Lovar said. "If the gods judge you unworthy, they will eradicate you from existence."

"I feel like that would have been an important detail to mention." Draven leveled a searing glance in Kethek's direction.

"Take heart. The gods favor us. They would not see us burn. Every step of this journey has been perilous. What's one more test?" Kell clapped Draven on the back, giving him a hearty laugh.

Draven scowled, scanning the horizon. His eagle eyes perceived no dust cloud, but then again, if they wrapped their horse's hooves, there might not be one.

♥*Cease your fears. The defenders of the tower are legendary. All will be well till we claim the cursed blade.*♥

The company dismounted and let the men in white cloaks lead their horses away. Elisah and Kethek went with Lovar to plan their defense. Draven didn't care for the odds. There couldn't be more than a few hundred here, assuming they were even proper soldiers. The men in white looked more like priests in their billowing robes. Tarn disappeared around a corner, almost as soon his feet touched the sand.

Great, what's he up to? Probably casing whatever treasury these people possessed.

Heart Master remained silent but tingled on his arm. Draven understood only a fraction of the power it contained. Would it be enough? And if it was—what would it cost him?

He looked over at Kell and Helena, still relative strangers to him, even after traveling together. They huddled together in hushed conversation. He would have to rely on Kell and Helena for his life, though he barely knew them and wasn't sure if he could trust them. Draven shook his head, sidling over to them.

Helena gave him a sidelong glance as she and Kell separated. She looked irritated. Of course, she always looked angry, except in the heat of battle or the few times when she shared an inside jest with the big oaf.

They look like shield mates, but according to Kell, they just met. I wish Loken or Nell were here. I'd dearly love an ally to confide in.

Kell broke the silence first. "Draven, we were discussing our odds. We don't like them. If Kethek speaks truly, then we will have to be quick in the tower. Pray this test is not a long one."

"Draven will obviously fail without our piety, and you're a toss-up, oaf." Helena offered Kell a sneer, but Draven detected mirth in the jest.

"I trust he is up to the task, being favored by the goddess of luck," Kell said.

"And death," Draven added. "Don't forget the death part. From my experience, Nerys is as likely to kill me as help me. She was none too pleased for me to wield Heart Master. Can't say I blame her. I don't feel like a champion, even with Ansalon prattling away in my head."

"You may be a thief, but you have kind eyes, and I don't doubt your heart. You've even taken a ward."

Draven's face reddened at Kell's jest.

"Ward? Really, Kell? More of a street hustler who's dying to pick over our corpses."

Tarn appeared as if by invocation, nodding his head. "'Tis true. I will. That breast plate looks as if it might go for a penny. Is it real gold?"

Draven shoved Tarn behind him, but out of reach of his purse. "Don't mind him. He's a compulsive opportunist. Mayhap we're kin."

"You wish, old man." Tarn sauntered off, probably to case the tower.

Draven smiled while Kell laughed, and Helena rolled her eyes.

"So what's the plan?" Draven attempted to get back to matters at hand, but not before scanning the horizon again.

It's ironic. In another life, I'd probably be riding with Seguris rather than this holy contingent.

Heart Master froze on his arm, icy metal searing into his skin. His fingers went numb, and he cursed while trying to shake sensation back into his hand.

"What's the matter, Ansalon, can't take a joke?" Draven rubbed away the cold with his opposite hand.

Before Helena or Kell could frame a reply to his question, another priest walked up to them. This one was younger and carried an armload of scrolls. Unlike most of the other white robes, he sported a full head of hair and a pair of spectacles perched on the tip of his nose. He clasped a hand to his breast then offered them a curt bow. "I'm Velay. I'm here to help you prepare."

When Velay attempted to gesture with his hand toward a massive gate of iron-bound timbers, a few scrolls dropped to the shifting sand at their feet. He blushed, giving them a wide-open smile of apology. He knelt to retrieve the errant scrolls, only for two more to topple from his grasp.

Helena stooped, gathering them in her arms as if they were newborn babes. "Mayhap we should help you with those."

Draven rolled his eyes and took a few scrolls while Kell scooped up the rest, leaving Velay empty handed. "Thank you." Velay picked at his robes with his suddenly empty hands. "I had little warning, so I gathered as many as I could. Please follow me, and we'll begin."

"Auspicious beginnings." Draven tapped a finger to his lips, following Velay, one step closer to either his destiny or his demise.

Don't be late, Nellonah. You're the only one I can rely on here.

♥ *You forget me, thief. I may not approve of you, but I shall not desert you.* ♥

"As if I could ever forget about you, you old ghost."

39

Best Laid Plans

Helena, Kell, and the thief followed Velay through the massive entryway, past a series of sprawling sandstone buildings. They eventually entered a blockhouse with a plain unadorned door consisting of hundreds of irregular pieces fitted together and hammered in place with more nails than Helena could count. As they passed through an entryway with symbols of The Twelve gods, she noted the lack of white-robed followers.

Perhaps they're all being pulled away for the defense, as we should be. Kell and I should be on the front lines defending the tower instead of rooting around for the cursed blade. If Seguris dies at the foot of the tower, we won't need Blood Thorn.

Velay led them through several disused rooms until they came to a wide chamber with a massive table, twelve feet long and made from wood so dark it seemed to devour the light. The scholar spread maps and scrolls on the table in a spiderweb of ancient parchment. When he was done, barely an inch of wood remained visible.

Helena gave them a cursory glance. She didn't want to find that cursed blade. Did it call for her, even now? *Velleris warned me against the blade. What if I lack the faith to wield it? It is the product of Regnir. How will I face the goddess after this? Am I still a worthy servant of Velleris, or will the wards refuse me?*

Velay pushed his spectacles higher on his nose while his nasal tone rambled about the tower and Blood Thorn's resting place. Helena gathered her thoughts, focusing on the map that described the elaborate corridors leading to the pinnacle of the tower.

Velay cleared his throat. "According to the ancient chronicles, Blood Thorn rests at the very apex of the tower. Getting there will be easy enough. We have maintained the halls and passageways as near to new as possible."

"Then The Twelve will test us. How is that accomplished?" Helena smacked her palm onto a map of the tower clearly older than all of them put together.

Velay blanched at the rough treatment of his documents. Guilt nibbled Helena for her outburst, followed by shame at losing control of her temper.

The scholar smoothed his robes. "There is a large room at the top of the tower with twelve doors, one for each of The Twelve. Penitents can only enter through the door of their patron. To enter any other door would mean almost certain death. Whether there is a further test inside, no one knows. There are no records of the contents of the reliquary, most likely by design."

"That's it? Just walk through the right door? That sounds easy enough." Draven traced a slender finger around a map of the tower. "This room seems to extend upward by nearly a hundred feet. Why? We should be ready for anything."

"I'm an ancient studies scholar. I know little about architecture." Velay pursed his lips, pointing to a worn vellum scroll with writing so tiny Helena could make out only the occasional word. The scholar steadied himself before continuing. "This is a covenant of The Twelve, nine really, as some of The Twelve had already perished. It specifies that only a conclave of The Twelve may remove Blood Thorn from the tower safely."

Helena scowled. "Don't you mean ten? I thought only two gods perished at the hands of Khyris?"

"It's a matter of some debate as to the fate of the god of death. Some say he was killed by Nerys, others claim it was Khyris. Only the gods know for certain."

Helena blinked in surprise. Not till that moment did she realize everyone they'd met at the tower bore the same dark eyes and skin of the Mektwin. "And by 'safely', you mean without being blasted into cinders."

"But we are only three? Is that sufficient?" Kell leaned over the table, his expression unusually dour.

Velay went silent for several moments before answering. "The covenant specifies that three or more champions of their respective gods should suffice. If you are united in your goal, then you should survive, and Draven represents the aspect of two of The Twelve. That should help."

"'*Should* suffice?" Helena wanted to rip her hair out by the roots. Getting answers from this mousy priest was akin to counting the hairs on a running dog.

"I cannot offer you a guarantee any more than I can tell you what to expect, but if the gods favor you, they will see you through any obstacle."

Kell laughed. "You must worship a god I've never heard of. Regnir makes his followers work for their destiny."

"Doesn't matter. We have no choice." Draven clenched the edges of the table as if it kept him upright. "We will tear this tower down to the foundations if required. I have come this far, and it's my only hope of seeing Nellonah again."

"That's assuming much, thief. I'd rather stay at the base and kill Seguris so we don't have to climb the tower." There, she'd said it. She felt her mouth turning to a hard thin line, daring anyone to argue.

"I'd love to get out of this mess, but I don't think fate's going to be that kind," Draven said. "We find the blade while Elisah and Kethek turn the bandit army into a pile of carrion. You're welcome to wager your life in that battle. I'm not. At least, not until we exhaust the sane options." Draven crossed his arms over his chest. "We'll inform Kethek and Elisah. They should at least be apprised where we're heading, assuming they don't already know."

Kell nodded at Draven's words.

"Fine. Lead the way, priest." Helena kept her reply short, afraid they would see her cowardice. *Goddess, spare me from the cursed blade.*

Velay led them back out of the building, across the inner courtyard to a larger edifice with a second story. Dozens of white-robed priests milled around this building with even more armored men filing out, clad in snow-white plate armor, bristling with weapons.

Perhaps they are capable of a better defense than I'd imagined. If only I were joining them. Praise Velleris, they will be enough.

Once inside, they entered a wide rectangular room where Elisah and Kethek stood over a large map of the tower complex and the surrounding desert. Flanking them was Lovar, and half a dozen unnamed followers of The Twelve, all appearing resolute, and all decidedly Mektwin.

I wonder if they realize they're going to war against a fellow countryman?

"We are just finishing our plans for the defense of the tower," Kethek announced. "Lovar informs me his scouts have spotted the oncoming army. Larger than expected, but we hold out hopes for a successful defense. The tower has stood for many years, and one follower of Ghedryn will not change that in a day." Kethek was now clad in black robes with silvery embroidery, almost the complete reverse of Lovar's cassock of white with gold piping.

"How many defenders?" The question was out of Helena's mouth before it registered in her mind.

Elisah raised an eyebrow at her impertinence. "Around three-hundred knights and archers with a dozen battle clerics besides the faster moving assassins. Kethek will, of course, coordinate the clerics, while I will command the knights and rogues."

Countenance grim, Elisah turned to face Helena and her comrades. Helena could tell the knight-commander harbored no illusions. If Helena, Draven, and Kell failed, those at the base of the tower would die for nothing.

"I'm leery of not sending support troops with you," Elisah told her. "But we're stretched thin already. It'll take a smart woman to keep these two louts on point and, if necessary, wield Blood Thorn to keep it from Seguris."

There it was. Helena's fear had been given a name and thrown back at her. She nodded her head as she ground her teeth in frustration. *I will not take up the blade. I. Will. Not.*

"You two, come along now." Kethek waved his hand, beckoning her and the thief through yet another doorway. "I will prepare wards to assist in the battle. You can help power them with Ansalon's assistance."

As if my best use is as a vessel for the goddess. What am I other than that, just a woman with too much anger? The perfect receptacle for a cursed blade fueled by fury. I never stood a chance.

She wished for a denial from the goddess, but Velleris was silent.

Helena followed as Kethek led Draven around rack after rack of weapons. Draven laid his relic to sword or shield, while Kethek muttered words in the lost tongue of the Gods. Power pulsed from the item, and they moved on to the next one.

It was tedious work. Kethek did not excuse Helena from it. She did the same thing as Draven, but without Kethek. She knew the old tongues, and she worked with the power of a goddess. Draven was merely a conduit. Helena was divinity itself, favored by Velleris, rather than by blind chance. Draven's eyes glazed over, and her lips twitched at the thief's discomfort.

I'd rather be on the battlefield, but if it makes the thief ill at ease, it's worth some tedium on my part.

Guilt gnawed at her that so many would die, so that they could search the tower. Helena spent her entire life in combat, only to stand by while others went to war while they combed a dusty ruin. And for what? A cursed sword that could be her doom. She didn't like the odds for any who crossed her this day. Whether it be the thief or Seguris, they'd find her ready.

Draven glanced over at Helena and smiled one of those self-serving smiles. She sneered back. Helena refused to give him whatever satisfaction he sought.

Draven jerked back from a suit of armor as if burned. Helena raised an eyebrow, wondering what his problem was this time.

"What do you mean, explode, old man?" Draven backed away, giving Kethek as wide a berth as possible.

Kethek coughed into his hand to suppress a chuckle. Helena couldn't help but snicker at Draven's ignorance.

"You are in no danger. Heart Master protects you. The wearer can only trigger the immolation ward in ancient Mektwin." Kethek shook his head, holding the bridge of his nose.

"Why would you want a knight to burst into flames?" Draven asked.

Helena rolled her eyes and shared a look with the long-suffering priest. "As a last resort."

Draven shuddered. His narrow face went white at the implication.

Has he no honor? Is he really that craven? Helena considered how strange this must be for the faithless. *He is adrift without belief.* For a moment, she almost felt sorry for him.

Kethek called a halt when the scouts returned, announcing Seguris was within hours of reaching the tower. They assembled again in the map room. Helena made one last, vain attempt to convince Elisah that they needed her at the foot of the tower.

"Knight-commander, you know you need me. I'm worth two or three men, at least."

"Do you not understand your instructions? You are a soldier of The Twelve. Act like it. We stand when called. I'll not have you throwing your life away when we need you to open the reliquary." Elisah offered Helena a pat on the shoulder that failed to assuage her in the least.

"Do you want to die sooner? Granted, both options are a death wish." Draven smirked at Helena, baiting her again.

"There is honor in battling a foe to protect others. Don't judge me till you've walked my path, rat." She crossed her arms, huffing.

"The spurs wouldn't fit my manly feet."

Were it not for Elisah, Helena might have disemboweled him. She noticed Tarn milling around the assembled, never staying in one place for more than a few moments. Draven might look upon him with fondness, but there was something about the boy-child that rankled Helena.

Kethek called them to attention with a voice that boomed like thunder. Helena's pulse quickened, knowing the time for arguments was long past.

"Friends, our time grows short." Kethek called the room to attention with a voice that boomed like thunder, and Helena's pulse quickened, knowing the time for arguments was long past. "The enemy is at the gates," he continued. "Our outlook may appear grim, but fear not. The gods are with us, and they have elected champions to sway the tide in our favor after reclaiming The Rose of the White Tower. The Order of Twelve has never faltered, and we shall not start now." Kethek let his works sink in. He transfixed each with a gaze, wilting any objection. "Defenders, we must hold the line against the forces of evil, and hold it we shall, with Elisah Fairoaks commanding the troops and myself assisting the clerics with my magic. Champions, ascend. You carry our hopes for victory in your hands." Kethek closed his eyes briefly, giving them all a curt nod.

I will not let fear be my guide. I will face my destiny, whatever it bodes. A rusted chunk of enchanted metal will not command my fate.

When the last of the clerics filed out, Kethek and Elisah turned to the three champions with grim smiles. They stood like titans from a past age, the room reverberating with their shared power.

"You are our last hope. Do not fail us," Kethek said. "You know what is at stake. I owe you all my life. I would not be standing here without you. I swear to spend it giving you the time you require." He turned on his heel and strode out.

Elisah barked, and Velay appeared as if by magic. Helena tried to imagine the bookish scholar taking part in the defense, and she grinned.

"Take them up the tower, show them the way to the sword, then get back here," Elisah told Velay. "We all fight today."

"All but us, don't you mean?" Helena wished she could bite the words back when Elisah fixed a baleful glance her way.

"Oh, you will fight. You will surely fight this day, Helena. Part of being a champion is knowing when to pick your moment. We are the feint and the parry. You are the stroke that takes the head." With that, Elisah departed, leaving them alone with Velay.

"Scholar, lead us to our destiny." Kell swept past them, hooking Velay by the arm. Helena shrugged and followed with Draven picking up the rear as if he trudged to the gallows.

"Hold up, where's Tarn? We should take him into the tower to keep him out of the fight." Draven looked for the boy, but he was nowhere to be seen. "He was right here."

"It doesn't matter. The tower is no safer if only the chosen can enter. He'll turn up." Helena marched, caring little that Draven wandered off to look for Tarn.

Helena and Kell followed Velay to the foot of the tower, which was wider at the base than Helena would have thought when she observed it from a distance. Up close, it looked as if they could have fit their entire army within.

Why didn't we just huddle them all inside, but I suppose they wanted to distract Ghedryn's lackey from his prize.

There were no battlements as far as she could see. Just smooth white walls with nary a window in sight. Only the climbing vines and occasional blooms of crimson clung to the surface.

Velay twisted a series of decorations set into the base of the tower. The stone of the wall groaned and slid away to reveal a massive entryway into a wide-open room decorated in colorful banners. Tapestries depicted verdant forests, sweeping mountains, and free-flowing rivers. Knights clad in ivory armor with a variety of religious symbols did battle with beasts while the heavens raged above.

The scholar led them to a recessed stairway, motioning them to follow. Helena fell in behind him, noting that Draven rejoined them, having given up on Tarn.

"Let's not dally. If they're right, it may be up to us, but I doubt another of these cursed relics is going to do us any favors." She brushed past them into the winding stairway. She took the steps as quickly as possible, which wasn't much, as her pauldrons scraped the edges of the narrow stairwell.

"Is there no better way to reach the top of the tower? It will take an age to get through this rat's warren. Seguris will be old, fat, and retired by the time we get back down. If we get back down." The restricted nature of the passage gave Draven's words an eerie, otherworldly quality.

Helena held her tongue at the complaint, thinking it futile to try and silence the thief. Draven was the smallest of them, but he was also the whiniest. Kell suffered any indignity with equanimity, barring saddle sores.

"To where we are going, no. There are wider ascents for the mundane parts of the tower, but not to the reliquary. As you might imagine, there was a desire to restrict access." This voice was thin and reedy. Almost certainly Velay.

"Why do the gods never make anything simple?"

That rat loves to squeak. She smiled despite herself and continued her ascent. Even her sturdy legs ached with the strain, as it seemed as if they'd been on the stair for hours.

"The gods protect their secrets, even from the faithful." Helena stumbled on a broken stone and put out a hand to protect herself. "Mind yourself, some of these steps are brittle with age." She waited for a reply, but it never came.

Gone quiet? Or he's died of his own whingeing. Helena smiled again, this time with pure delight, and her steps seemed lighter.

After an eon of half-walking, half-crawling up the shallow stairs, they came to a door bound in heavy, brass fittings disused and discolored by age. Helena put her shoulder to the old wood. It swung open with a squeal. The wood left scratches on the marble floor. She stepped aside to let the others pour out of the passage.

Marble tile spread out in alternating colors, as if it were a massive game board. An ornate curved wall dominated the center of the room, leading into a smaller circular room. Doorways stood every few feet, each with a sigil of the gods. Inky blackness swallowed all the light from within the entrances. From her vantage, Helena discerned the sigils of the dead sea god and of the mountain god Regnir, to whom Kell owed his allegiance. She assumed Velleris had one as well, somewhere outside Helena's field of vision. Kell whistled, and she wondered if he perceived something in Regnir's portal she could not.

"You must enter only the door for your patron. Any other could lead to death." Velay stood back against the wall.

A wry grin twisted Helena's mouth.

"Let's find out." Without another word, she spun, grabbed Draven's arm, and whipped him into the portal for the sea god.

Blue light erupted in a deafening thunderclap. Draven hung frozen, writhing in the void before flying back in a crash of metal on stone as Heart Master sheathed the thief's entire body in holy armor. He lay there panting and cursing before rising.

"Or maybe not." A light chuckle escaped her lips even as a subtle tingle of guilt wormed its way up from her stomach. *Stupid thief had it coming.*

"What in the frosty hells was that?"

"Just curious to see how lethal the doors might be." Helena turned to hide her laughter. Draven replied with curses that were music to her ears while Kell looked on with a frown. Velay stared with open-mouthed horror. Another twinge of guilt wriggled in her gut, but she swept it away with a shake of her head.

"Well. That was... interesting. I fear I can be of little use to you now. From here, it is between you and the gods. I will rejoin the rest of my order. May the Twelve guard you." Velay bowed and turned to leave.

"Die well." Helena turned to face the group. The mousy priest's footsteps faltered before shuffling out of the room, leaving the three champions to their fate. Helena fought the urge to join him.

"So, all at once, or one at a time?" Draven quirked an eyebrow.

Kell stepped forward, jutting out his chest. "Let us not tarry, all at once. We should act as one, instead of in competition as we have been." He leveled a meaningful glare at Helena, then to Draven.

As if he's innocent. Big oaf.

Draven nodded. "I've already been half-immolated already. What's once more in the name of a good time?"

Helena found the doorway bearing Velleris's sigil and stepped into the inky blackness without bothering to see if the others followed suit. *It's not as if I need them, anyway.*

Her world exploded, then it all went black. No air. No sights, smells, or sounds. Only oblivion. Then another world rushed back in, overwhelming her senses. Helena would have dropped to her knees if she could touch the ground, but she found herself propelled through a landscape of myriad colors and cacophonous sounds.

"Renounce your anger. Renounce your passion. Know only The Law of Twelve." The voice of her goddess came from everywhere and nowhere. It crashed into her, crushing the breath from her chest. Helena squeezed her eyes shut, willing her lungs to function, but her throat closed to a pinprick.

Desperate, she recited the litany in her mind, fighting to rid herself of any emotion. On and on, the words paraded through her mind even as her body screamed for oxygen.

> *The goddess is just. The goddess is kind. The goddess is wise.*
> *The goddess is the law made manifest.*
> *It is only through the law that we find salvation.*
> *It is only through salvation that we may ascend.*
> *Until we ascend, we are naught but beasts.*

The pressure eased. Still, she did not stop chanting the Law, even as she gulped in air. On and on, she recited the rede. Until at last, spent and panting, she grew quiet. The menacing pressure relented, cradling her instead in a lovely golden glow.

"Go forth Daughter, and mind the lesson to master your emotions, else they could be your undoing. Only in order will you find salvation."

Gravity returned, sending Helena crashing into a floor of glistening marble. Her senses disappeared into blackness for the second time.

40

ARMIES COLLIDE

SEGURIS SAT ASTRIDE HIS stallion, overlooking the battle line drawn between his Free Riders and their enemies in white. Bodies lay scattered across the ground on both sides. His own men sported motley armor cobbled together from the best their victims offered, and though differing in style, the mismatched plate gave them a sinister aspect that inspired dread. Defenders of the tower gazed back, apparently unperturbed, in their billowing robes of white and gold or burnished armor painted bright ivory.

He looked across the lines to the priest he'd neglected to kill the day he'd claimed The Trappings of the Wild for himself. The dark-robed old man cast spell after spell at him, which Seguris, or one of his own wizards, countered and returned with deadly effect.

Magically speaking, they were at a stalemate. Arrows and bolts were equally useless. Each side had magic enough to erect shields against mundane attacks. In this struggle, his Free Riders were dwindling as the defenders refused to come out to meet the aggressors.

One or the other would need to commit to the field. That would need to be him. The defenders could hunker down inside the tower and presumably weather a siege, while he'd have a problem keeping his army fed. Time was of the essence. Seguris needed to get to the tower and its treasures. Normally he would have no problem calling a charge, but one thing bothered him.

The enemy were Mektwin. Not all, but most. Enough to make him wonder. To make him ponder why the people he sought to free from bondage were fighting for the same gods who put the rest of their race in chains.

How can this be? They should cheer me, throw down their arms and join me, but they array themselves against me. They are holding fast to their banners of The Twelve. How can I tread my own people under my heel?

"My Lord, the men are growing weary of this stalemate, and in the battle of magic, we are shedding our numerical superiority. We must charge soon if we seek to wipe them out." Ethan reined up beside Seguris, peering deep into his eyes for unspoken answers.

Seguris nodded, still lost in his thoughts. "It will come soon, faithful Ethan."

Ethan turned his mount to ride the line, keeping their men in formation.

As if bidden, Ghedryn appeared next to him, the god's shape lacking substance. "Have you lost your backbone, Seguris?"

"Of course, I haven't, but I am puzzled. The Mektwin do not flock to my banner as they should. How can I slaughter the very people I am sworn to liberate?"

"These are not the Mektwin you seek to save, my champion. They are weak in slavery to the Twelve. They are but spineless lackeys. Let them be the chaff that must fall for your own people, your genuine people, to rise."

"As you speak it, it shall be. But I am uneasy about this." Seguris scratched at his beard, unconvinced.

"Charge now, or I will do it for you." Ghedryn's words rumbled in his mind like a thunderstorm.

Seguris tarried no longer, booming out orders for his men to charge at his mark. He deflected a lightning bolt meant for him from one of the white robes and raised his sword in defiance.

"Ride them down, my Free Riders. Grind them into the very sand until their bones are the foundation for our empire."

His men did not need a second command. As one, they charged, riding out ahead of their commander, eager for blood. Where the white-robed defenders lacked mounts, they spoke words of power to create their own from the blockhouses and low sandstone walls. Massive gryphons of earth arose under the defenders to bear them like unearthly steeds. Soon, all was chaos as warriors clashed in the ring of steel.

The Trappings writhed about his shoulders, hungry for fresh souls, but he held it in check, calling orders to make sure his Free Riders went where ordered. It was tougher work than it should have been. His men had only weeks of formal military training, but his word was law and his voice thunder.

Seguris kept the wizard in his sight because he was the greatest threat on the field. Now, he also spied another that gave him pause. A fierce knight, tall and broad of frame, swung a great sword like felling wheat. He ordered more men to bring down the knight, even if it cost him a hundred soldiers.

Shaking away the last of his doubts, he spurred his mount to fulfill his destiny. Right or wrong, the course was now set, and it would only find its conclusion in the blood of those arrayed here.

Seguris's shamshir rose and fell in crimson arcs, taking lives with every swing. He caught killing blows on a shield of air, courtesy of his elemental ring, and returned incinerating fire. It was a recent acquisition from the ruins of Cadden and complemented The Fist of Heavens nicely. The Trappings of the Wild collected souls by the dozen as the battle raged on, but he hesitated to release its power just yet. He knew that when released, it would take him over, surrendering his considerable will to the power of Khyris, the Great. Each time he did so, he feared losing himself.

How long till I can no longer keep Khyris from overwhelming me?

His Free Riders fought well. One on one, they were no match for the better trained guardians, but their sheer numbers overpowered the white robes. Seguris let Ethan take the lead in that battle, while he worked his way inexorably to the magic-wielding enemy who slew his men by the dozen. The old wizard was their greatest adversary in this mass slaughter. Bring him down, and victory was assured.

Seguris could not help but think this battle meant nothing. He was sure the actual battle was being fought up in that tower, and with every second that ticked past, he was in greater danger of losing it. Seguris swore it was a battle he would not forfeit.

Another ivory-armored knight went down, placing Seguris within twenty paces of his target. He couldn't remember the old man's name, but he'd make sure his head was on a pike by the end of the day. He dismounted his horse before it completely halted, and ran toward the wizard. Meanwhile, another lightning bolt hurled his way. Seguris only just deflected it with the power of The Fist.

This man's power is legendary. If he'd used The Trappings, I never could have bested him.

Seguris rained fire at the wizard or priest, whatever he was, who swatted it all away as if it were a summer's breeze. Seguris barely recognized this force of nature as the battered, old man he'd left for dead in Risell.

"Time for you to die, old man. I brushed you aside once. Now, I'll stamp you out." Seguris wreathed his body in flames. A low growl escaped his clenched teeth.

The old wizard responded by waving his arms, stirring up a small tornado that caused sand to dance around him.

"I am Kethek, wizard without peer, and you will not prevail. Even if I fall, the champions of the tower will turn Regnir's cursed blade against you and your master." A blade of light streaked out toward the warlord. Kethek invoked more words of power, raining down cataclysmic forces of nature on his enemy.

Seguris caught it in The Fist, but it drove him to one knee until he could unleash a bolt of lightning of his own, causing the wizard to stumble.

Sand erupted around them in a whirlwind as the two titans threw elemental energy at each other, neither giving quarter. Thunder clouds gathered overhead, roaring in protest at the energy being unleashed between priest and warlord.

Lightning careened once more over Seguris's shield, a tiny tendril searing the side of his face while a funnel of air ripped Kethek's robes to shreds.

"Give up this madness, Seguris. I sense there is still a man somewhere inside you. A man that loves his people. Turn aside from Ghedryn's mad conquest." Kethek threw his hand up, and a funnel of pure white light poured into him, suffusing him with even greater power.

"There is one thing you have forgotten, old man." Seguris beat at his chest, stirring his anger to a boiling point.

"And what's that, warlord?" Kethek glowed with eldritch energy, laughing, his features devoid of pity.

"I'm not alone in this fight." Seguris grinned.

Kethek's mouth fell open.

Seguris tilted his head back and let The Trappings take over, let Khyris take over. The wraiths poured from the ermine pelt in a tidal wave of darkness. They cut through the whirlwind of sand like a hot knife, hungry for the old man's blood. Lost spirits darkened by The Trappings coated Kethek from head to toe in a black, inky morass. The old priest slew them by the dozens, but their tide was legion. Kethek died screaming, his soul falling victim to the very relic he spent his life guarding.

Somewhere deep inside Seguris, another part of his soul gave way to the powerful entity bound inside The Trappings. Another shred of Seguris fell aside, and Khyris grew ever stronger.

How long until there is nothing left of me? How much will I pay for raising my Mektwin empire?

Everything.

He couldn't tell if the answer came from himself, or Khyris.

41

PLUCKING THE ROSE'S THORN

D RAVEN LAY ON A cold, slick floor that chilled him to the bone even with the protection Heart Master afforded him. He put his palms to the stone and pushed himself upright, despite reeling senses and uncooperative muscles.

♥*Up, thief, up. Men die for every moment you tarry.*♥

"Devil take you. Don't you remember the skulls? The torture I've just been through. I deserve a moment at least."

♥*What skulls? What torture? One heartbeat we were outside, the next we appeared here.*♥

"How utterly criminal. Nerys spared you my test of wills with that bitch goddess?" Draven snorted, trying to even his breathing enough to stand. His muscles quivered as if he'd just finished a fight for his life, and he had, with all the horrors Nerys could throw at him. "Never mind, I'll live, but after this I'm done with that monster I call a goddess."

He looked around and perceived his companions to be in a similar state. *Hate to imagine what that prude Velleris came up with for Helena, but she deserved it for trying to kill me.*

♥*The goddess of the Law is just. Velleris does not punish so much as instruct.*♥

I'm sure. The gods teach us to be better people. What rot.

Draven cast his gaze toward the center of the room to determine how difficult it would be to claim their prize and found it curiously empty. He stood in a round room thirty feet across. White marble with inlaid ebony formed a spiral on the floor. Puzzled, he stepped into the center of the room, wary of unseen traps.

Draven was almost disappointed to see nothing but open air. No traps. No sword either.

Then he looked up.

Well, hells. Blank, white walls rose fifty feet to a ceiling domed in a massive work of stained glass that depicted either a knight grasping a red rose, or a goat being immolated by a dragon. Draven surmised the latter interpretation was not correct. *Infinitely more amusing, though.*

A sword hung suspended from the glass work by wires and hooks. It gleamed a dull red as colored light filtered through the glass, throwing a sparkle of rubies from it to dance along the walls, like writhing serpents.

"Well, that's just grand," he said, putting his hands on his hips. He chewed his lower lip, still worried about the boy. Surely Elisah or Kethek would keep him out of harm's way, but it was hard to focus on this blighted artifact when Tarn could be in danger.

And just why does Tarn occupy my thoughts? What is it about him that pulled Heart Master to him and compels me to worry for his safety?

Draven shook his head, trying to center his thoughts on the problem before them.

Helena sidled up next to him. "I don't suppose Heart Master comes equipped with wings."

Draven replied with a sneer and wondered if it might be possible. It was magic, after all.

Ansalon, is it possible? Can it fly?

♥*Don't be absurd. It's no magic wand to fulfill your desires. Find your own way to the sword.*♥

"The sword could be a trick." Draven remembered to speak aloud so Kell could hear him, too.

♥*I sense the power from here. The rage of the blade is unmistakable.*♥

"Great." He wanted to see what the others offered. *Better their necks than mine.*

♥*Craven.*♥

"How do you think I've stayed alive this long?" Draven licked his lips, casting Kell and Helena a sideways glance.

Kell ran his hand over the smooth walls. "There are no handholds to speak of. It would be folly. The shield might save me when I fell, but there's no purchase. I could scale any mountain back home with ease, but these glassy walls would be impossible even on my best day." Kell shook his head.

"How about you, any wings to go along with that self-righteous halo?" Draven shot Helena his most infuriating grin.

"Nay, I can slay any fool, but my armor is not suited for climbing. Mayhap we raze this tower to the ground and pick up the pieces."

Draven couldn't tell if she was joking. He walked over to Kell and ran his fingertips over the stone, which seemed to be a mixture of granite and marble tiles. Smooth, but not perfectly smooth. He pulled the falchion out and banged the pommel against this wall, happy to see a few chips fall away.

I can break it.

He held up his fist, and willed Heart Master to manifest a thick gauntlet with elongated talons covering his fingers. He did the same thing with his other hand. Finally, he covered his feet in boots with hooks, like a bird's talons.

He smiled, pleased with himself, and rammed a claw into the wall. Draven worked his way up. It was tough going, but he made steady progress. Below him, Kell whistled and laughed. He turned to face the two below him.

"No worries, I'll be back with this thing in mere moments." He grinned, proud of his ingenuity. That's when a piece of stone erupted from the wall, knocking him into open space. Draven crashed to the floor in a heap of tangled limbs. Heart Master protected him from injury, but the wind sailed from his lungs.

"Hells and bloody damnation," he swore as Kell helped him to his feet.

"Probably want to avoid that on your next attempt." Kell brushed him off, and Draven couldn't tell if the words conveyed guile or empathy.

"If it's even possible?" Draven wondered aloud, craning his neck upward, failing to see the seam in the stone block that erupted from the wall.

Damned magic.

Draven repeated the exercise twice more at different sections of the wall, with similar results. When he reached around the ten-foot mark, a piece of stone would magically jut out of the wall, sending him tumbling back to the ground. One thing he knew now, it could attack from any spot on the walls, which made the climb impossible for a normal man, but Draven was anything but normal.

Ansalon, can Heart Master augment my strength as well as protect me, help me jump higher and further?

♥*Yes, of course, but not to clear fifty feet in a single leap. Remember, it can cushion the blows, but enough of them are going to incapacitate you.*♥

"Helena, Kell, do you think you two would be able to throw me up a dozen feet for a good head start?" Draven inquired, just imagining the host of replies they would have.

"We'll toss you to the sun if necessary. You might not have noticed, but there are no doors out of this place. If we don't solve this puzzle, then we're going to die a slow death."

"Great, let's skip the sun part. I don't want to go that high." He attempted a grin, but the immensity of the task took much of the bluster out of him.

Draven perched on their shoulders, feeling their muscles coiled underneath him. "Ready whenever you are," he called out, his stomach already flipping over. The pair uncoiled, releasing him like a massive spring, sending him at the wall some twenty feet up. He kicked out, catching himself in a crash of stone and sparks. Draven drew a breath and kicked again at an angle.

He knew he couldn't leap straight across, but going at angles, he should be able to scale the wall before it lashed out at him. It worked, and he began a torturous upward spiral around the room that left him dizzy from the relentless pace.

On his second pass, a massive fist of stone awaited him, but Heart Master came through, melting the stone fist in a shower of blue flame. Now he pivoted in a zig-zag pattern. He made his ascent as random as possible, making it impossible for the magical trap to guess where he'd leap from or land.

Shattered stone rained downward, and he hoped Kell or Helena wasn't in its path. All he could think about was leaping, catching himself, leaping again, and lashing out with Heart Master when a stone projection outguessed him.

The ascent was nothing short of grueling. He had to give up ground to dodge sudden outcroppings of granite that moved like lightning, but finally he was within a few hand spans of the target. From this vantage point, the blade looked pitted and rusty.

"If this is just some ruse, I'll reduce this tower to the foundations." He swore curses at Nerys with every successful jump. Draven could picture it now, his next leap, and he would grasp the hanging blade with all the grace of an eagle wheeling through the air.

As usual, Nerys was both with and against him. Out of nowhere, a projection of stone hit him from behind on what should have been his last leap. It knocked him into the wires. The razor-like cables wrapped around his arms and legs. Only Heart Master's ethereal armor saved him from being cut to pieces. Draven hung there, staring down at the floor in a panic. He fumbled for the arcane blade but only knocked it from its hook. Draven missed catching it by a handbreadth, and it sailed into open space.

One by one, the cables snapped under his weight. Draven uttered a prayer, and hoped Heart Master could protect him as he followed Blood Thorn toward the floor of the chamber. He heard a distant clatter and hoped the blade was indestructible or they'd wasted their time and his life.

At least I didn't impale anyone.

Draven shut his eyes. He didn't want to see the end coming, but a glowing golden light raced up, snaring him in its grasp.

What new deviltry is this?

He found himself lowered to the floor. The golden glow disappeared back into Kell's chest plate. The big man stared back at him with an embarrassed grin.

"I think this is something I had a right to know." Draven stooped, retrieving the rusty sword that was obviously not meant for him. The dull, evil blade rested across his palm with no hint of the magic it contained.

"Alas, I did not know," Kell said. "It would have made things easier."

Helena turned her head, refusing to look at their prize.

"Do we need a wizard to activate this thing, or just dumb luck?" Draven balanced the point of the blade on one finger.

All eyes turned to Helena.

42

CHAMPIONS COLLIDE

THE TRAPPINGS RECALLED THE spirits, covering him in ebony armor festooned with spikes, and Seguris's spirit reclaimed control of his body. He had no memory of what had transpired, but the battle still raged around him. Around them. Khyris prowled just beneath his conscious mind, waiting, watching for his time to take over again. Of Kethek, nothing remained save for a pile of bones picked clean of any flesh.

Seguris shuddered, staring over the battlefield as yet more souls poured into The Trappings. *Will any number of souls satisfy Khyris?*

A white-robed soldier charged at him, sword swinging wildly. Seguris side-stepped with ease, enhanced by not one, but two holy relics.

Seguris looked at the soldier again. This one didn't sport the ivory armor of the knights, and was little more than a child. The spectacle-wearing youth wielded a sword as if it were a carving knife. A Mektwin boy.

Seguris's eyes moistened in regret as he reached out, grabbed the boy by his neck, and choked the life out of him. The look of betrayal as life faded from those eyes was something Seguris would never forget if he lived through the ages.

Why? Why am I killing the people I pledged to save? My people fall at my hand, purer of blood than any Mektwin I've ever met. Am I mad?

Out of the corner of his eye, he spied the knight who had been mowing down his Free Riders like chaff. All doubts flew from his mind as he saw another pair of his soldiers go down before that bloody broadsword.

Seguris angled toward the knight, knocking men and women of both banners out of his way as he went. A man in white surged toward him, dropping his weapons as he went. Seguris narrowed his eyes as he prepared to cleave the man in twain. Instead of attacking, the man grabbed at his waist. Seguris suspected a trap and wrestled the man, breaking his grip. The warlord tossed the man as far away from him as he could just in time for the man to explode in a wave of holy light.

Madness. They waste their lives just for the chance to kill me. Seguris shook his head in disbelief. Surveying the battlefield, he saw the scene repeating over and over. And it appeared to be working. White robes immolated themselves, but for each of them who died a dozen or more Free Riders perished in the conflagration. His massive army dwindled.

For a moment, he stood torn between his men and the whirlwind of steel before him. Another man ran headlong at him, and Seguris burned him to death with fire before the zealot could get within a dozen paces of him.

The visor of the knight's helm lifted and Seguris saw the face of the knight for the first time. Soft lips parted while cool blue eyes took him aback as they locked on him.

A woman. Remarkable.

She whipped her broadsword, dispatching another of his Free Riders in an arc of crimson. Her current assailant dispatched, she turned her gaze back to Seguris. He met that gaze with equal fire as he took a step forward, trusting Ethan to defend against the suicidal tide.

"Seguris." The woman uttered his name as if it were an obscenity, wiping her blade on a dead man's tunic. One of his own men, he noted.

"What is the name of the woman I am about to kill?" he asked with equal scorn.

"In this world, I am known as Elisah Fairoaks," she replied as if it were normal to live in different worlds.

"You do not differ from any other lackey of the priest-kings I've slain. You all realize how pointless that faith is in the end." Seguris flicked his sword, sending droplets of blood through the air.

She threw her head back with a hearty laugh. "You'll find I am nothing like others you've faced." She cocked one hip, a broad smile on her face.

"Then you're not one of these defenders. You're something different."

"I trained their grandfathers." She wiped a thumb along the edge of her blade and balanced the sword on her shoulder.

"And will you beg me to relent as the priest did?" Seguris's sword twitched in his hand. At his back, The Trappings hissed, ready to strike.

"What point? You are a lap dog for that creature on your back. It's your leash. I am here to fight the master, not his pup."

Seguris's face went livid with rage.

"It's not a relic or a holy object, you know. It's a prison to contain a criminal so evil he threatened the gods. You're just a skin suit he's wearing."

"I am a slave to no one. No one will ever chain me again." Seguris fingered the clasps of The Trappings of the Wild, impatient to release the wraiths. And yet, he wondered if some truth rang in her words. How much of him remained and how much was now Khyris, the god-slayer?

"Look at you now, fingering that thing like a woman's breasts. Tell me again how you rule. First Ghedryn, and now Khyris. Before that were there other masters? You're still a slave, Seguris, you've just taken on different chains." Her full lips twisted in a sneer.

"That's Great King Seguris, blood heir of our Great King Khyris. No one owns me!" He beat at his chest with the pommel of his sword as if it could chase away the truth.

"Prove it. Fight me as a man without your baubles." Elisah drove her sword into the earth and pulled off her helmet, letting it drop to the ground in a clatter.

Seguris sneered back. It would be so easy to let loose the wraiths, to rain glimmering energy at her from The Fist. The temptation overwhelmed him, and his knees shook with the effort of controlling it.

"Only a fool doffs their armor when facing a woman claiming to be older than the sands on which we fight, but I'll use no magic or relics if that suits you.

The end will be the same." He swung his sword in the air, and the pair marched forward, daring each other to make the first move.

Seguris broke the stalemate with a sideways slash to her ribs. Elisah's broadsword rose and blocked it, as if she were brushing away a cobweb.

"Are you growing tired? Surely, you can do better than that." Elisah side-stepped, her feet never crossing.

Seguris admired how a woman her size could move so fast, and with so little effort. Her sword leapt out, an adder looking for a throat to pierce. A swift parry, a turn, and then a riposte.

The world around them disappeared. Seguris could no longer tell one blow from the next, as they devolved into a ringing cacophony. The two of them moved as one in a whirling maelstrom of death.

A Free Rider barreled into Elisah, sending her careening away from Seguris. He took that moment to catch his breath as Elisah batted the man away with a backhand slash that opened his stomach. The stench of blood and offal arose, making Seguris's eyes water. Another rider flew forward and fell before her blade, then another. He lost count of the men that fell beneath her blade while he recovered, but his soldiers soon lost their nerve and turned back to easier pickings.

Elisah whirled to face him and aimed an overhead strike at Seguris, her breath coming in ragged gasps. His shamshir rose to block it, and the blow left his blade ringing and his arm stinging from the force. Then they were back at it. Elisah opened up a gash across his cheek, and he feinted to break her momentum. When she charged in, he scored an equal blow, opening her armor, rending a shallow wound along her ribs.

They went on like that for some time, trading blow for blow. The difference was stamina, and Seguris could feel his flagging. The holy woman possessed an inexhaustible supply of both skill and stamina. He was running out of time. With every moment that ticked by, the zealots in the tower inched closer to victory.

Another unsuccessful series of blows left Seguris with blood flowing down his cheek, and he could hear Ghedryn in his mind. The voice echoing so loud it almost drove him to his knees. "Finish her. Destroy the meddling bitch once and for all."

Seguris parried her thrust and channeled every bit of electrical energy he could up her blade, along with scarlet energy from The Fist. Elisah Fairoaks convulsed and fell to her knees, smoke curling away from her hair and face. Twisted lines of dark energy ruptured beneath her skin. She looked up at him with a sly grin.

"You have won. Yet this only heralds your inevitable defeat." Her sigil-encrusted broadsword fell from nerveless fingers. Elisah's hand rose once more and a bolt of holy fire raced toward him, wreathing Seguris in white flame. A moment later, the fire died out, leaving his hand scorched and his elemental ring blackened. He sought to call the flames to finish her, but found the metal dead and useless. The Fist of Heavens smoked and it took several heartbeats until it crackled to life again.

Shaking his head, Seguris drove his shamshir into her abdomen and ripped up with all his strength, cutting through bone, muscle, and sinew. He pulled free his blade, waiting for The Trappings to do their work, knowing her soul would be a priceless addition. A brilliant beam of light crashed down from the sky, immolating the knight's body. Somewhere in the wind, he heard a voice.

"Her soul is not for the likes of you." A wicked female laugh echoed in the wind, and he cursed in disappointment.

Seguris turned back to the battlefield to find his army decimated. Of the thousand or more soldiers he started with, only a few dozen remained. As far as he could tell, Elisah was the last defender of the tower.

"It will take too much time to search the spire." Speaking more to himself than any remaining followers, Seguris raised his arm and shot a bolt from The Fist. He followed it up with most of the wraiths from the Trappings. "I'll pick Blood Thorn from the rubble. The mangled bodies of those champions will decorate our camp." Another blast of power rocked the tower while the wraiths swarmed around it, tearing bricks out one at a time. It would be only moments before he claimed his prize.

43

RAPID DESCENT

KELL LOOKED ON AS Draven traced circles in the air with Blood Thorn. The pitted dagger, however, showed no signs of life. It remained exactly as it had looked from the outset, a broken dagger that appeared as if it would splinter at the slightest touch. Kell sighed but said nothing.

The relics always change when they find their user. He's not the one. Mayhap it will sing for me and spare Helena.

"Perhaps Heart Master could ignite its power?" Helena's question sounded more desperate than hopeful.

Kell leaned against one wall. "More likely Draven lacks the warrior's heart to wield it."

"Fine." Draven tossed the dagger to him. Kell caught it awkwardly. Rage seethed in the metal. Anger roiled up Kell's arm and it sparkled in his grasp, but it did not come to life as Hallowed Verity had.

She doesn't want to hear it any more than I want to say it.

Just then, the room shook as the ship had when they were on the ocean. Kell reached out an arm to steady Helena. The dagger flamed a bright red, and Kell had all the confirmation he needed.

Draven yelped in surprise. "What is that?"

"Reminds me of a rock rumble. We get them in the mountains. The elders say it is the mountain god's way of speaking to his shamans."

"And what's it saying?" Draven fought for balance as another tremor swept through the room. "Perhaps how to open the door?"

"Do I look like a shaman?" Kell held the dagger as far from Helena as he could, but it pulled in his hand toward her.

Kell reached out with his senses but felt nothing. There was no pulsing in his chest, or any sign at all, that Regnir was with him. The dagger did, however, make the shield on his chest thrum uncomfortably.

"The goddess is just, the goddess is wise, the goddess is kind."

Kell turned to look at Helena, but she continued muttering the words. Kell looked at Draven, hoping he might know.

"It's some kind of prayer or something the Vellerians do. Not sure what it's for." Draven tried to poke Helena in the chest, but she grabbed his hand and twisted till he yelped.

"Never touch me, alley-bred filth." Helena locked eyes with Draven, and Kell could swear she was attempting to kill the thief through sheer willpower.

Another rumble and dust and glass fell from the domed ceiling high above them. Whatever force Seguris used would not take long to bring the tower down.

"Helena, we both know this belongs to you." Kell offered the dagger to her, pommel out.

"We know nothing of the sort. Regnir is your god. It should be yours."

"Just as we knew Hallowed Verity should be yours. These relics are upside down."

Helena shook her head. He couldn't tell if she denied him, her goddess, or fate. Then she stilled, and the words resumed, louder than before.

"The goddess is the law made manifest."

Kell peered into eyes that had gone hazy with religious fervor. He'd seen it often enough in Martok, his shaman, to know he'd need to snap her out of it somehow.

"I hate to interrupt a tender moment, but may I point out the tower is shaking, and there is still no door? A lock I could pick, but even Heart Master is having a tough time getting through these walls." Draven pulled at Kell's arm, but the big warrior shrugged him away.

As if to punctuate Draven's words, a massive sheet of glass and lead fell from above. If not for Kell's relic, their quest might have ended right there. A golden barrier appeared above their heads, sparing them from an avalanche of broken glass.

Cursing himself, Kell grabbed at Helena's hand and pried it open. She did not resist. Her entire body went limp as a leaf on the wind. He shoved the relic into her hand and closed her fingers around it. Lurid red light crept from between her fingers. The ugly little dagger grew into a dull, curved blade, dripping blood.

Helena screamed, and the rectangular outline of a door appeared on one wall. Inside the rough shape, a massive oak tree grew with dozens of branches chiseled into the stonework. Draven launched himself at it, but pry as he might, he could not find any purchase.

Kell's stomach somersaulted, unsure how to help his friend. *Have I betrayed her?*

Her arm came up and batted him away as if he were a child. When he looked up, that dim red light seeped from her eyes, surrounding her whole body. Helena sank to her knees, crying tears of blood. She brought the blade to her forehead. He raced forward to stop her, but Draven caught him by an arm and pointed to the uncooperative door. Each branch radiated the same blood-red light as her blade. Realization dawned on him.

"This is her fight now. We can't help her. It's between her and that damned thing." Gone was Draven's quick wit and amiable smile, replaced by grim certainty. "She must master the relic on her own, just as we did. And I'll wager it's the only way to open that portal back to the rest of the tower."

Kell's heart ached as something buffeted the tower again and more stone fell around them. Helena roared and lashed out with the blade, striking golden sparks against Kell's breast plate.

"Your prayer, Helena. Hold on to your prayer." Tears ran down his cheeks, wanting nothing more to crush her in his arms and tell her all would be well, but he could not. *Nothing will ever be well again.*

"Blood." The single word hung in the air, fouling the lungs of all that breathed it. Kell couldn't tell if it came from Helena or from the sword. "Until we ascend, we are naught but beasts." The words started out a guttural growl and then softened into Helena's normal measured tone. A thin silver line outlined the cursed sword, and all the tension went out of Helena's body.

"Are you well?" Kell wasn't sure he wanted to know the answer.

"I'm not mad, if that's what you mean. For the moment, I have caged the beast. Also, I know how to raise the door." She offered him a wan smile.

The tower shook again, continuing to crumble. Masonry fell all around them. Kell blocked the pieces he could, but his attention could not be everywhere. Helena slashed out with Blood Thorn, which elongated or contracted, more like a whip than a blade, cleaving massive blocks in twain. She darted over to the outline of the door and jammed the base of her blade to the roots of the tree. Helena closed her eyes, and her face screwed up in an expression of intense concentration. Slowly, the branches of the tree depicted on the wall filled up tendrils from the blood sword.

"Hate to be the bearer of bad news, but this place won't last much longer." Draven raised his voice over the tumult of falling stone as the floor buckled underneath them. "On the upside, it doesn't seem like it will take long before the upper part of the tower becomes the ground floor."

"Hold steady, I've almost got it!" Helena shouted over the crash of stones.

Kell watched as the entire tree filled with blood. Once more, almost by prophecy, the world tilted. One half of the room sank lower than the other, and the shaking did not cease this time. A section of wall separated itself, falling away, revealing open air and a long distance to the ground. For the briefest moment, the door slid away, but another ripple of the floor sent Helena sprawling. She cursed in languages Kell didn't even recognize.

"No time. Lock your hands with mine. I will attempt to use the tower breastplate to protect us from, um, the other disintegrating tower." Kell braced himself as the section of floor they were on tilted, threatening to spill them over the ledge.

"I could really use those wings, Ansalon!" Draven hooked his arm around Kell's waist.

The warrior projected his will into the relic on his chest. Kell imagined soft arms to hold them and a shield overhead to protect them from what little of the tower remained above them. Golden light surrounded them. Blue and red ribbons from Heart Master and Blood Thorn joined his gold ones to act as one.

Kell smiled even as the world turned upside down.

Finally working in concert, and all it took was the complete destruction of a landmark that has existed longer than the three of us have been alive.

Moments later, the tower did indeed come crashing down. Rubble bounced off the shield overhead even as the light below gently lowered them toward the ground.

The strain was unimaginable. Sweat beaded his brow. Even with the help of the other two relics, Kell found his mind stretched to the breaking point as if it were his own sinews that protected them.

Somehow, they made it to the sandy ground at the base of the tower, and Kell could release his hold on the magic. He slumped to the ground, blackness threatening to overcome him. He looked back and saw the once indomitable tower was nothing more than a smoking pile of rubble.

Pray Regnir the world does not join it.

After so many leagues traveled, it seemed a bitter irony that he could prove too weak to even take part in the fight with Seguris's forces. Kell ground his teeth together, marshaling what little strength remained in his body.

Finally, he made it to his feet with the others. A host of armored men formed up some ways off. All of them bore the motley arms of bandits. There was not a single white-robed defender to be seen. None alive, at least. Their bodies, along with many more of the warlord's men, lay in the blistering sun.

Kethek... Elisah. They can't have fallen so soon.

Off to one side, Kell thought he spied the remains of Velay, the acolyte who guided them into the tower hours ago. He couldn't be sure as the youth faced away with a broken neck, but the hair looked the same. Kell was no stranger to battle, but the carnage before them turned his stomach.

Some are little more than children.

Kell turned back to the enemy, and saw the man who must be Seguris, muscled like a wolf coiled to strike. A sable cloak fluttered in the hot wind and it was impossible to miss the golden gauntlet glowing the color of blood. The warlord bled from a score of wounds from the battle they'd missed.

"Why won't you all die?" The man stood up to his full height. His remaining men were arrayed behind him, waiting for orders.

Kell lifted his weapon high. "Come then, wolves. My ax is ready to cut you down." A bestial growl erupted from his throat.

44

A Battle of Wills with Blood Thorn

Helena stood at Kell's side, staring across the sand at dozens of blood-mad bandits. Dead center of their ranks loomed a swarthy man who could only be Seguris. His black curls fluttered in the breeze, framing a fierce visage that burned holes in them even at this distance.

How curious this man has dominated our every waking hour, and this is the first time we are laying our eyes on him. A nervous giggle escaped her at the thought. Blood Thorn throbbed, a thirsty engine of murder just waiting to be unleashed.

She braced herself, waiting for the charge of the remnants of his army, but their leader held them in check. Blood Thorn itched to be fed. Helena did not relish her experience with the relic. Where she hoped for radiant, golden arms to cradle her, she found only a hissing, clawing thirst.

"Can either of you see any sign of Tarn?" Draven asked, casting his eyes around.

Helena and Kell shook their heads. There were so many bodies, it would be impossible to identify just one.

"We'll avenge him," she swore through clenched teeth. "We'll avenge them all."

Seguris moved out ahead of his troop and put his back to the champions to address his troops—if you could call a rag-tag group of bandits soldiers.

"Here it comes." Helena tensed, fighting the pull of Blood Thorn to race into the fight. Slender tendrils no larger than a strand of hair, wormed their way into the skin of her arm. Her stomach lurched, but power like she'd never imagined filled her.

"Stand down, Free Riders. Behold, three champions of the weak and impotent gods. Stand down, and bear witness as the might of Seguris, the next Mektwin emperor; Seguris, the Invincible, grinds them under his heel, this time for good."

"Well, that's unexpected." Draven shook out his arm, Heart Master slithering up to cover it in pulsating magic armor.

"At least there is some honor to this coward." Helena flexed her arm, Blood Thorn moving with her, an extension of her limb.

Seguris sprinted toward them, his boots kicking up sand. Helena planted her feet, ready to leap forward as well, only to see Draven sit down, crossing his arms.

"What? Like I'm going to waste my energy running in the sand when he's coming to us, anyway? Kell, get one of those shields ready. He looks annoyed."

Helena put face to hand and prayed to Velleris for the thief to fall first. Seguris stopped short, thirty paces away, brought up a heavy brass gauntlet, and let fly a wave of force. Only Kell's quick thinking with the shield saved them from being ripped to shreds. Sweat rolled down his temples, and Kell shook with the effort.

Draven kipped up to his feet, responding with a curtain of blue fire. Seguris raised his left arm, then thought better of it. Instead, he touched the stays of his ermine cloak. Fur turned to inky-black darkness, covering him in spiked, chitinous armor.

"Careful, I don't think this is just the prelude." Helena brought the cursed blade across her body. It thirsted for blood. The need became a weight dragging at her arm.

Seguris faltered and sank to one knee. The champions of The Twelve turned to look at each other in surprise. The warlord climbed back to his feet, but subtly changed. Milky white eyes devoid of pupils glared at them, and the expression of grim determination became what she could only describe as manic glee.

"I don't think this is a good thing," Draven said, running the blades of his daggers against each other as if they could sharpen each other.

Helena nodded and looked over at Kell, who shifted the grip on his ax. Seguris stared at them with a soulless gaze that made her anger seep away like sand through a sieve.

Something has changed. And it does not bode well. Does Ghedryn now control his puppet directly? Or— even worse—Khyris, the Mad King?

Seguris waved his curved sword in the air but took no step toward them. "Kill them, my Free Riders. Kill them all in the name of Khyris, the last emperor of the Southlands."

Across the field, the warlord's men turned to each other in confusion. Weapons raised, they pivoted toward a man on horseback clad in well-polished, if dented, armor that contrasted with the more motley foot soldiers.

Helena couldn't make out the reply, but it must have been a confirmation as bandit-soldiers uttered battle cries and charged. The man on horseback held back, shouting orders from the rear of the mob, his face ashen.

Seguris continued to do nothing while never wavering in his glassy eyed stare as his soldiers flew past him on either side. Helena and her companions drew into a tight wedge.

Three against thirty, let's see if this sword earns its name.

Testing her new weapon, Helena flung her arm out and Blood Thorn stretched like a whip until it found a home in the neck of an oncoming attacker. She looked over to Draven and found that opalescent armor tinged in blue flowed over much of his body. He gestured with his arm and eerie fire flowed, maiming half a dozen of the men rushing toward them.

Blood and magic reigned as the enemy crashed into another hastily conjured golden shield. Kell sank to one knee, shuddered, and the shield buckled under the weight of scores of killers. Helena rushed to his side and pulled him up.

"We've got magic aplenty now. Let's whet our steel. Save your strength." Helena waved her cursed blade, its form writhing in her grasp. "Let us live or die by our courage."

Kell gave her a shaky nod, lifted his ax, and cleft the breastbone of an oncoming man. Blood sprayed. Blood Thorn drew in and absorbed the droplets.

Helena thought she spied that sneaky little waif Tarn moving around the ranks of the Free Riders.

Was he a spy all this time?

So lost in the fray, she almost didn't notice a contingent of Mektwin guardians slamming into Seguris's men from the side. There weren't many and most bled from injuries, but they fought like avenging angels. Their courage warmed her heart.

Helena blinked in surprise at how effective Draven was in a proper fight. Much of it was Heart Master, she supposed, but the slender man moved like a dervish, slashing with those long daggers.

Kell waded through the bandits, swinging the ax like he was felling saplings, his body sheathed in Hallowed Verity's golden light that protected him from blows that should have ended his life.

She shook her head, mindful she didn't collect one of those swords in her own gut. Unlike Hallowed Verity and Heart Master, Blood Thorn offered no protection, but what it lacked in defense, it made up for in pure offense. It slithered to find its way around shields and swords, searching for more blood, wending this way and that, often splitting into two or three forks to steal even more lives. And the more it found, the more its power grew. As effective as it was, the blade sickened her, and she longed to be wielding her trusty mace in its stead.

Blood Thorn roared in her head, seeping deeper into her soul till she couldn't tell where it ended and she began. It fed off the rage she normally suppressed and grew stronger. As the battle wore on, she knew she was less in control of the blade and increasingly under its control.

And through it all, Seguris didn't appear to have moved a muscle. He stood, staring on, a sick smirk turning his rugged face into a mask of sheer cruelty. Watching the remains of his army being butchered seemed to delight him. As Helena watched, wisps of smoke rose from the fallen, wending their way through the air straight to him as if he were drinking the dead.

Sweet Goddess Velleris, that is exactly what he's doing! He's increasing his power from the dying. We are killing ourselves by killing his men!

Finally, the battle between his chosen and the chosen of the gods, ended with the remaining bandits fleeing. Blood Thorn writhed, wanting to give chase, but Helena clamped down on the impulse.

The battle is here, you cursed snake!

The mounted man in the dented armor threw away his helm, and sword. His face was haggard as he gazed at the dead and then at Seguris. She saw, or imagined she saw, tears carving channels in the dust on the man's face. She expected him to charge, but he rode away as if wounded, his body slumped over the horse's neck.

She turned her attention back to Seguris, knowing the only battle that mattered was about to begin.

45

THE REAL FIGHT

DRAVEN STARED ACROSS THE field at Seguris, wondering if the warlord wrestled to control his relics, just as he did with Heart Master. The blood-stained sand reeked of death, and he struggled to keep from being sick. Somewhere deep within Heart Master, Ansalon reveled in it. Draven wished he could echo the ancient knight's enthusiasm. His own blood turned to water over the death he'd caused. Regarding the silent Seguris, he steeled his nerves for the battle that hadn't even started yet.

♥*Take heart, thief. Mighty though our enemy is, we outnumber him.*♥

I'm not entirely sure it's even the same man. Draven rubbed at his forearm. Though covered in the milky-blue armor of the relic, he could still feel his own arm beneath, chilled but still his own. Gooseflesh prickled the skin. The warlord leered back as if daring the champions to make the first move.

First error, more like.

Ansalon, as usual, was silent when the real work began, but a soothing coolness ran up Draven's spine and the holy armor extended to cover his entire body. Blue flame erupted from the armor, wreathing him in its ghastly light.

Great, now I'm on fire. Another first.

He was about to step forward when Helena and Kell moved in unison. It still boggled his mind how in sync the pair was. Much like he had been with Loken, once upon a time.

Kell whipped his ax in a vicious circle while Helena flicked her wrist, and that awful sword danced in the air, moving of its own volition. Drops of blood cascaded off its ruby sheen. Not to be outdone, Draven followed suit, and together they charged Seguris.

Seguris planted his feet and howled. The sound echoed even though there were no surfaces for the sound to bounce back from. The dark armor of The Trappings writhed in response. Black wraiths broke loose from the armor, which returned once more to a long fur robe. The shifting, black shadows shot at them like thousands of arrows.

So, it's armor or ghost army. Not both. That's good to know.

Draven, Helena and Kell skidded to a halt in the shifting sand, and Draven threw up his arm to defend against whatever horror was coming, only to see Kell was once more a step ahead of him. The long-limbed warrior brought his ax up in both hands as if he could slice through the wraiths and invoked another shield covering them in an arc of golden light.

"Protect the flanks." Helena sidled away from him to one side of Kell.

As if I didn't know that.

Draven and Helena raised their weapons to deal with any shadows that slipped past Kell's barrier. A quick look at Kell gave him pause and the warrior's muscles shook with the effort as the thick black shadows crashed into his barrier. Kell sank to one knee.

Can you cut a shadow? And how long can he keep this up? Through the veil of shadows, Draven observed that Seguris hadn't moved. In fact, the warlord seemed rooted to the spot. *Maybe he can't attack while using The Trappings.*

Draven and Helena fanned out to the edges of the golden barrier as the wraiths poured around Kell's shield, which wavered under the onslaught. Draven lashed out with the blue fire that leapt from his long knives, burning shadows to curling wisps of smoke. Sighs of anguish escaped those things as they burned. *Goddess, are those people? People I'm killing all over again?*

♥ *You are releasing them from an unholy servitude. Do not waver.* ♥

Draven gulped, hoping the spirit was correct. If anyone knew about spirits in servitude, it would be him. He still couldn't envision anyone chaining themselves into one of these relics.

Damned magic!

♥*Damned magic that is saving your life. Stop thinking about anything but the battle.*♥

Draven bit back another curse as he cut a black spirit into ribbons. He unleashed a gout of holy fire that sent another dozen spirits to the abyss.

"How many spirits can there be in that damned cloak?" Draven didn't really expect an answer.

"From this battle alone? Hundreds." Helena pivoted and lashed out with Blood Thorn in a wide arc, the blade elongating to an impossible length to protect her side of the barrier.

Just as things were turning in their favor, Kell fell to both knees and the golden shield flared, rippling a dozen different colors. Blood leaked from Kell's ears, staining his blond locks. The warrior's muscles strained as if he could keep the shield up through sheer force of will. Helena attempted to help him, but a fresh wave of phantoms besieged her. Draven parried to keep a wraith from his own throat.

The shield buckled, exploding in a flare that nearly blinded him. The force of it knocked him and Helena in opposite directions to land dozens of feet away from Kell.

Draven shook his head, trying to clear the ringing from his ears. Wraiths latched onto his side and back, eager teeth biting through Heart Master's armor. He screamed as the scrabbling phantoms made it through, tasting his blood. Ansalon, or Heart Master, he couldn't tell which, lashed out with a wave of fire. The pain receded as wisps of ash drifted up from him. The wraiths backed off, leery of joining their kin in oblivion.

When he rose, shaking, Helena was already racing toward Kell. Draven couldn't see the big warrior, just a mass of swirling shadows covering him. A cloud of scarlet flew from the pile of milling wraiths to be absorbed by Helena's blade.

Phantoms don't bleed. That must be Kell's blood.

The bones in Draven's body went to jelly, and he nearly dropped his knives. He waved Helena back, pouring every bit of strength he had into holy fire, bathing the mass till they peeled off Kell, returning to their master. They whirled over Seguris's head in a raging storm cloud until he raised his hands, and the dark souls settled once more into the sable cloak.

Kell tumbled to the ground. Somehow, the magical breastplate survived, but from where he stood, Draven could see it was now pitted and scratched with a massive furrow running down the front. Kell fared no better. Blood marred every inch of his body. Bone protruded through Kell's skin in so many places. His locks of tawny hair were gone, devoured like so much of his skin. Smoke rose from his shuddering body.

How is he still alive? Draven edged toward him, keeping a wary eye out for their enemy, who had yet to swing his sword. The cloak rippled, and Seguris was once more clad in that night-black armor with spikes extruding the length of a man's hand in some places. A long-curved blade magically appeared in the warlord's hand, but his face contorted as if from some inner struggle Draven wasn't privy to.

Blood rose from Kell's body, racing to Helena's blade, and the knight sank to her knees beside him, both hands going to the hilt. Her brow knit in anger and the flow stopped. She crumbled in on herself, panting for breath. Helena didn't pass out, but Draven could tell she'd just been through the fight of her life. He knew the feeling. At least Ansalon was on his side for the moment.

Draven turned to face Seguris. Tears gathered at the corners of his eyes, but he dared not shed them until the warlord had breathed his last. He cast his knives to the sand, knowing the time for mortal weapons had passed. Holy fire ignited a long, thin rapier at the end of his right arm. Along the other arm, Heart Master created rows of hooked teeth several inches long, making the appendage a giant sword-breaker.

"You stand alone, little man." The words boomed out of the warlord more like a thunder clap than speech. Venom dripped from the air at their utterance.

This can no longer be a man, more like some demon, spawned from the very pits of the underworlds.

♥ *You are not wrong. There is nothing left of Seguris. Khyris stands before you, as evil and malevolent as when he trod the kingdoms of the world under his iron heel.* ♥

And how many did it take to kill him last time?

♥ *We could not kill him. And you really don't want to know. Heart Master was the key then, and it will be again.* ♥

Inspiring as always. Come up with something witty for my tombstone. "My whole life, the world has been trying to kill me. The streets were my parents and hunger, my teacher. I am no more afraid of you than anyone else that's tried to take my life. Bring it, emperor of dust." Draven flourished his rapier in the air like one of those nobles about to duel, although his blood thinned by the minute and his bones turned to jelly.

Nellonah, if you're showing up with some new relic, now would be the time. He waited, half hoping that she would magically appear in a green fireball, but alas, only the still desert air met his senses. *Damned magic, anyway. Never there when you need it.*

46

THE TIDE TURNS

DRAVEN CHARGED. HE HELD his blade aloft as if going for a wild, overhead strike. Seguris, or whoever he was, angled his blade across his body, ready to fend off Draven's blow. At the last moment, the wily thief dropped low, cutting at his opponent's legs with his rapier. It was a move that had worked for him in the past.

This time, the results were sadly not as he hoped for. He had bowled Khyris over, but his blade failed to penetrate the armor. Draven leapt to his feet, swinging at Khyris, hoping to catch him off guard. His blow raked angry sparks from the Mad King's side, but again he did not penetrate that oil slick of a suit of armor. The thief back-stepped, wary of a counterstrike.

"You are quick. I'll give you that, but you cannot hurt me." The Mad King got to his feet, and Draven lost any illusion he still fought Seguris. The man had grown several inches, and his chest expanded into a gross parody of human musculature.

"Then I'll just have to see if my wit can cleave through to your black heart." Draven whirled his sword, driving Khyris back another step. He hoped the fear in his heart didn't eclipse his bravado. He lashed out with Heart Master's flames once more. "Or I can just cook you inside that shell of evil."

Khyris backed up with a roar, lashing out with a beam of light from The Fist. Draven dodged it, coming to rest on the balls of his feet some distance away.

"I guess being trapped in rotting fur for a few centuries has dulled your faculties." Draven spun, attacking with flame again. This time, he narrowed it to the smallest point he could. Draven's enemy bellowed as it penetrated the armor, but not mortally. Khyris failed to go down.

"I will tear your soul to shreds, little man!" The Mad King lashed out with another wave of force.

This time Draven failed to evade it and went flying across the sand.

On the upside, he was far enough away to gain his feet before Khyris was on him again. Draven noted the Mad King preferred magic to swordplay. Perhaps old Khyris was not as skilled as Seguris. Draven hoped that was true. He knew he'd need every advantage if he was to survive this fight. It seemed Nellonah and Loken were going to be too late to do any good, assuming they were still alive and not roasting in some hell contrived by Nerys.

Gods help us if I'm *the only one left.*

"My soul is already in tatters, but you're entirely welcome to try." Draven tumbled out of the reach of the dark blade Khyris wielded and tried a new tactic.

Draven used Heart Master to super heat his blade and struck a fanning blow at the sand, sending a stream of molten glass at his opponent. The Mad King attempted to block it but was only partially successful. Khyris's hair smoked, and more souls died within the Mad King's armor.

Draven attempted a repeat, but Khyris rushed in before his blade could land, seizing him by the throat. Draven battered him with the hilt of his rapier, with little effect. He raked the teeth of his armor's sword-breaker along Khyris's jaw, causing the Mad King's grip to slacken.

"Laugh this off, insect!" Khyris channeled power through The Fist of Heaven until it exploded into Draven.

The blow sent Draven flying. He crashed into the sand, throwing a plume of dirt up into the air. He fought for each breath, the world receding into oblivion.

The blow wasn't painful so much as it was a complete cessation of reality. Draven lost all feeling in his limbs, and Heart Master fared no better as the translucent armor faded, leaving his skin exposed to the hot sand underneath him. He did not know how far he'd fallen, but Khyris was little more than a speck on the horizon. Draven levered himself up on one arm. Pain ratcheted through his stomach, chest, and shoulder. Somehow, he found the strength to vomit on the pristine sand before falling back again.

"Sweet goddess, he broke something, maybe a lot of things." He considered praying, but he was pretty certain that Nerys could care less about his fate. Ansalon was a dim far-off whisper he could no longer hear. Since Khyris had not crushed him yet, he must be slowing, or Helena or Kell had rejoined the fight. "That's good."

The sun overhead burned his eyes, so he closed them despite a nagging sentiment they should remain open. The pain faded to a dim memory. Draven could no longer feel the sand beneath him, so that was good, too. Every sensation shrank until he imagined he floated in a warm bath.

"Ansalon, am I dying?" Draven tried to suck in air, but his lungs didn't seem to be working properly, and it failed to bother him in the least. His question didn't elicit an answer and even that did not concern him. "I guess I'm dying. Gave it a shot, Nellonah. For you, I gave it a shot." The world seeped away, one slowing heartbeat after another.

Pain slammed into him like a boulder. Something burned every nerve at once. Air returned to his lungs as if from a heated forge, and he swore he was melting from the inside out. Someone far away screamed, and it took a moment for Draven to realize it was him.

"You don't get off that easily, Drav." He recognized the voice, but he couldn't believe it was really her, saving him yet again.

Draven looked up at her through blurry eyes, truly seeing her for the first time. She sported no glamour, which was odd. He'd never seen her without one. There was no otherworldly glow about her, but the gaze he saw in her pale blue eyes filled his heart with warmth.

As the pain subsided, strength returned to his limbs, and with that also returned the memory of the battle. The Mad King was still out there. He squinted past Nellonah and saw Helena whipping at their enemy with Blood Thorn while dodging multi-colored bolts of magic. Alongside her now fought Loken with a fluid grace that belied his many missing parts. Their blows rang across the sand like angry bells. He could almost feel the gods warring overhead in an echo of their struggle.

Who knows, maybe they are?

His arm tingled. Then Draven sensed Ansalon for the first time since Khyris threw them across the sand. Power thrummed in his skull as the holy armor of Heart Master flowed over his skin once more.

Draven levered himself up to a sitting position, surprised his head didn't explode. Nellonah knelt beside him, her eyes expectant yet sad. He took her in an awkward embrace, what with his ghostly armor and her knife handles poking out of her leather armor at nearly every angle.

Since when does she carry weapons? She doesn't need them.

♥*She does now.*♥

Ansalon's answer hung like an ominous thunderclap in Draven's mind.

"So, time to whip out that divine relic and wipe this demon from the face of the world? You got the relic, right? The Chaos Masque?" Draven released her.

Nellonah's eyes watered, and for a moment, she said nothing. "I—Draven, I can't do that. The story is too long to tell, but it's not going to be that easy." Nellonah lowered her gaze, refusing to look him in the eye. "We managed to acquire the relic, but so far we've failed to activate it." She held up a band of black satin laced with a design so intricate Draven's eye couldn't follow the stitching. Silver feathers and skulls hung from the fabric, which made an unbroken circle. It glowed a deep eerie light in her hand. "The Masque turned into this when I claimed it."

Nellonah pressed the band into his hand with a wink. They both looked on in surprise as the band writhed, changing in his hand. The shimmering glow faded and left Draven with a mask of lead layered with hundreds of broken pieces of mirror. The metal sat in his hand, doing absolutely nothing but weighing it down. He shifted it to his offhand, thinking the proximity to Heart Master could be an issue, but it remained dull gray metal. The mirrors didn't even reflect the sunlight.

Draven exhaled, steeling himself for whatever horror this new relic might bring. Putting it on, he clenched the muscles of his face, imagining the shards of mirror burrowing their way into his face. Still, nothing happened. Nothing changed. He took The Masque off, eyeing it dubiously.

"Maybe it's meant for Loken?" He turned the mirror-encrusted mask this way and that, looking for an inscription, but found nothing.

"No, we already tried." Nellonah shook her head in resignation. Blond hair whipped in the wind, a delicate curtain of gold.

Draven got to his feet, surveying the battle raging across the sand from them. Helena was weakening, and Loken had disappeared completely. Khyris rampaged like a nightmare, wraiths dancing around him in a never-ending maelstrom.

"Well, this is going to be a problem." Draven looked over to Nellonah for answers, but her ashen countenance offered only silence.

47

Chaos Unleashed

THE BATTLE RAGED CLOSER to them as Draven regarded Nellonah, who glared back with a mixture of anger and frustration. He turned the Chaos Masque over in the evening sun, tempted to toss it, but with his luck it would end up working for Khyris. "We're running out of time. I need to get back into the fight. Kell is down, probably dead, and Helena can only hold the Mad King for so long. Pretty sure Khyris has taken over Seguris." He tossed The Masque to the ground in disgust. "What's it supposed to do, anyway?"

"Nerys said it induces chaos. That it should work to weaken the trappings if we can get close enough. The ultimate expression of the goddess of luck. It should have been perfect for you."

Draven eyed her, wondering if he should take offense. "Like Heart Master was for Elisah? Maybe we've got this all wrong. Maybe they seek opposites? Or maybe they exist to teach us a lesson." Draven beamed, proud of himself for the insight while Ansalon scoffed from within Heart Master.

"That's not as intended." Nellonah shook her head with a displeased expression.

"None of this is as anyone intended, Nell. None of it. It glowed when you had it." Draven nudged The Masque toward her with the tip of his boot, dreading the thought that he might be right. He wouldn't wish one of these relics on anyone, much less the woman he loved.

Yet another disappointment reminded him he had failed to protect Tarn, whose body lay either in the tower's rubble or among the heaps of corpses. Draven imagined his tousled hair, bloodied, falling over a face caved in by heavy boots.

Not to mention Kell, who likely gave his life that he and Helena might continue to fight. Tears formed in his eye to envision Nellonah having to enter the fray.

Nellonah stooped to retrieve the mask, and it went through the same transformation. Once again, it shimmered with life, resembling a black silk band. Light crept all along her hand where it touched her. She gave him a helpless look.

"I still don't know how to activate it." She stroked the material, peering intently, her forehead wrinkled in concentration.

"Try thinking chaotic thoughts." It was half jest, but he had little to offer on the relics. "The others just took over. Mayhap this one needs an invitation."

"Draven, that's absurd. That's not how the gods crafted the relics to be used, but we are also out of time."

Draven could see she was right. Khyris raged ever closer to them, while Helena attacked, rebuffed either by black armor or swirling wraiths. Draven took heart that at least someone wounded the brawny Mektwin as blood seeped from his neck and leg.

Nellonah closed her eyes, mumbling words that were too low for him to hear. *Probably in some dead language, like sorceresses do.* The seconds ticked by, and without warning, the band slithered up her hand. Nellonah flinched, her arm shaking. Up and up it winded while her body convulsed.

Draven raced over to catch her before she fell. The Chaos Masque settled around her throat. It stretched over her skin, tightening like a garrote. Draven pulled at it with one hand, trying to dislodge it. His fingers could find no purchase, and then a blow from behind threw him wide.

Spitting sand, he turned to find Khyris leering at him. Helena took the opening to slice across that black armor, and the Mad King almost went to one knee. The insane eyes flickered for a moment. Khyris backed up, and for a single heartbeat, Draven thought he saw Seguris again. Anguish tore at the warlord's features before Khyris returned, his face melding back into a mask of lunatic rage.

Draven turned back to Nellonah, heart in his throat, but she stood on her own now. Dark green energy wound around her body, forming a pair of wings that lifted her a dozen feet into the air. The band at her throat morphed again into the glittering mask of mirror shards hiding the features of her face, but for her eyes. Her eyes burned with that same fire, eclipsing the irises altogether. If ever anyone resembled the fury of The Goddess of Luck and Death, then it was Nellonah at this very moment. His heart swelled in his chest.

Now that's my kind of angel.

"Fear not, my love. I'm in control, and I think I understand. The world is a web of laws, with chaos biting at them like so many gnats." The voice that issued from the Chaos Masque was Nellonah's but tinged with a thicker timbre that sent a chill down Draven's spine.

Rage boiled across the sand as scarlet energy from The Fist threw Draven and Helena like rag dolls and Khyris's madness erupted. Nellonah managed to take flight and avoid the worst of it. Draven could detect no sign of Loken or Kell, whose fate was still unknown.

Please don't let them be dead. The silent prayer was all he had time for as Khyris unleashed another wave of wraiths at them, which Draven countered with a wall of blue flame. The number of damned souls had gone down from infinite to just more than he could count.

That's something, at least.

Nellonah raced down from the sky too fast for his eyes to follow, blasting Khyris with a wave of energy the hue of a sheet of malachite. The Mad King uttered a howl that vibrated Draven's bones. The whirling wraiths touched by Nellonah's divine flame disappeared in sparkling, coruscating light.

Khyris sucked in air, drawing the myriad souls back into his armored form. He staggered and withdrew for the first time since this onslaught began. The Mad King's eyes darted back and forth, as if unsure which of them presented the greater threat.

Helena pressed the attack, lashing out with Blood Thorn, raking sparks off of the armor. She cleaved a few spikes from the dim, black metal, and the Mad King howled again. Khyris responded with a back-handed blow from his gauntlet that sent the knight reeling, where she crumpled in a heap.

Draven charged in, willing the blue-flame rapier to thicken into a proper saber. He struck a flurry of blows, forcing Khyris to parry in defense. Draven locked swords with the big man, trusting in the power of Heart Master to match the Mad King's strength.

He wanted to look up to see if Nellonah would seize the moment to attack Khyris from behind but didn't dare. Nellonah soon rewarded his hopes as she latched onto the Mad King's back with hands that had grown into curved talons. Spikes shriveled and died, turning to dust as her magic did its work. Souls flowed up from the dense, black armor through Nellonah to disappear in sparks of light.

Ansalon stormed within Heart Master, and flames whooshed in response. Draven feared burning Nellonah, but the holy fire appeared to strengthen her. The spikes fell faster, and the souls flew away like chaff on the wind. Khyris heaved, his guard faltering.

For a moment, the maniacal glint faded from Kryris's eyes and his expression filled with anguish. Tears drew tracks in the dust and grime on those dark features.

"Kill me."

The two words were spoken so softly Draven strained to make them out. Then the inhuman glare returned, and the thief knew Khyris reigned once more.

Draven swung his flaming blade, attempting to do just that. Somehow, Khyris caught it in The Fist's grip. Powerful muscles wrenched the blade, surging ruby-red magic up the length, blasting Draven back. He stumbled, going down, his side aching as if at least one organ had ruptured and all his ribs had splintered.

Khyris threw his arms wide. Wild, dark energy whirled around him, and a single massive spike erupted from his back, impaling Nellonah. When she fell to the ground, the mask dissolved from her face, flowing back down to a band at Nellonah's throat. Draven shouted, struggling to rise to her aid, but his body failed him, dumping him to the sand.

"Now I will wrench that wretched bauble from you, even if I must tear your arm from the socket to do so." Khyris strode toward Draven, every step filled with menace. Waves of power rippled off the Mad King. Sand melted into glass beneath him.

Draven managed to stumble to his feet. His side burned as Ansalon and Heart Master labored to repair whatever damage The Fist had done. He was out of clever rejoinders. The flames coating his armor flickered.

Resorting to more mundane weapons, Draven whipped a half-a-dozen slender knives at Khyris. Three skittered off the armor, but then it shimmered, turning back to a cloak as the remaining three blades sank home in the Mad King's chest.

Khyris ignored them as if he were immune to mortal damage, but The Trappings hung in tatters that danced in the wind. He pulled the knives out as if brushing aside biting gnats.

Draven gulped and willed the rapier back into his hand. For a moment, he thought it might fail him too, but it remained trusty as ever, while Heart Master's flames grew stronger by the second as if the relic found some new reservoir of energy.

Khyris raised his hands, sword now discarded for raw power, when a familiar scarlet magic encircled him, whipping the Mad King around like a rag-doll. Helena reappeared, wreathed in an angry red light.

"This fight is far from over, unholy tyrant. I am the arm of the goddess, and she wills you to die."

48

THE FATE OF TARN

"I NEVER THOUGHT I'D be so happy to see you." Draven wiped the sweat from his brow, relieved to see Helena back in the fight. Her armor hung in tatters while her hair whipped in the breeze. Blood seeped from Helena's scalp before darting off to soak into her blade.

Draven took her reappearance as an opportunity to slash at Khyris's back. This time the blade tore through The Trappings, slicing through the fur, leaving a dark red weal on the Mad King's back. Khyris did not even turn. He waved his hand, and another arc of light from The Fist crashed into Draven's blade, rocking him back.

A dozen dark souls took off from The Trappings, possibly the last confined there, and leapt toward Draven. His blade sent one to the afterlife. He parried the talons of another, but the pain on either side brought him to one knee again. Nellonah staggered toward him, an arm outstretched. A flick of her wrist wreathed him in flame, sizzling the remaining wraiths in golden dancing light.

"There is only one soul left, my love. The one we don't want out." Nellonah sank to the sand, obviously exhausted but still alive. His heart screamed at him to rush to her, but Khyris animating Seguris's scarred body still menaced Helena. The weary knight traded blows with the god-slayer, neither giving quarter.

♥ *This fight is far from over. The goddess will watch over Nellonah until our duty is done.* ♥

As if I believe that for a moment, but I can't abandon Helena. Despite Draven's concern for Nellonah, he continued to battle, knowing they were all doomed if

Khyris triumphed. He stared past Helena, hoping in vain Kell would magically return to the fray, but the big man remained absent.

Not much chance he survived the wraiths. I'll raise a pint to you, Kell. And to Elisah, and Kethek, and Tarn, and all the other poor bastards who died this day.

Movement caught his eye. Tarn appeared, running straight into the fray with bloody daggers in each hand. Draven dropped his guard as he waved the boy off and received another spine-jarring blow from Khyris. He flipped back, regretting the pain in his aching ribs, and noticed Loken crawling toward his bow, having lost the use of his crafted limb.

He never did know when to quit.

"Brother, leave the fight to us. Help Nellonah if you can." Draven limped back into the fray just as Helena's Blood Thorn crashed down into The Fist of Heaven. The two relics detonated in a kaleidoscope of energy. Tarn leapt forward, driving a knife into the Mad King's leg. Draven rubbed at his eyes in disbelief.

Am I mad, or does he seem bigger?

♥ *You are not mad. This boy is far more than he appears. Guard your flank.* ♥

"You're a fool to join this fight, but I'll dine on you later." Khyris swept the boy aside, sending Tarn through the air to land a dozen feet away.

Odd, when he hit me. I went flying like a shooting star. Maybe the Mad King has a soft spot for children.

♥ *Khyris has no soft spots. There is something greater in play here than mortal eyes can discern.* ♥

Draven shook his head. No time for that now. When he turned back to the battle, Helena went down again. The knight was on one knee, gasping for breath. Draven channeled fire along his blade and launched into a flurry of blows designed to distract the Mad King. Khyris batted most of them away with The Fist, but he slowed with each one. *Looks like his pet Mektwin is wearing thin.*

The body of Seguris bled from hundreds of wounds. Small tears in his skin leaked blood and some sort of dark matter Draven couldn't identify. It wafted in the air for seconds before plopping to the sand to bubble away into the earth. One leg was nothing but a mass of torn tissue. Draven couldn't imagine what kept him on his feet with such damage. Breath flew in and out of that ruined body in ragged gasps.

Another wave of energy sent Draven into a rolling dive, and his return blow scored a slash down Khyris's chest, severing the gold chain that held The Trappings. The remnants of the sable robe fell from the Mad King's shoulders. Or was he Seguris now? Blood Thorn erupted from the enemy's chest before being pulled loose, and Seguris's body sank to the ground, unmoving.

"Did we win?" Draven asked. He wasn't certain anyone survived to answer him. He glanced around searching for survivors when his eyes locked with Helena's. No longer the holier-than-thou champion she once was, the weary knight gave him a berserker-worthy grin. She looked every bit like a maddened demon now with Blood Thorn writhing in her hands, lusting for another victim.

I really hope I'm not next. She never liked me much to begin with.

Draven knelt to make certain the Mad King was truly dead when slender arms appeared from behind Helena. A curved blade slashed across her throat, spraying blood down her chest. Helena's eyes went wide, and Blood Thorn dropped from her fingers. The cursed blade reverted to a rusty dagger as it thumped to the ground. Helena stood transfixed, her expression serene, before slumping to join her cursed blade. Ruby-red petals of blood blossomed in the sand around her head.

Tarn stood over her, holding a bloody knife. Draven struggled to find his voice but failed. Tarn winked at Draven and his face lit with glee. He stooped to retrieve the dropped relic, and as he did, he changed. Tarn's slender arms filled out, and he grew tall, taller than Draven. A beard erupted from a face now craggy with the ages while his ratty clothing became dented armor of brass and gold.

"Thank you, thief. I've been looking for this for some time. I didn't relish facing Khyris again, and now I have all I sought." The voice that elicited from the giant's lips boomed like thunder. Similar to Nerys's, but deeper, and filled with untold anger. Overhead, the sky raged with violet thunder and the ground shook, throwing sand into the air.

"Tarn." Draven fumbled for words as he raised his sword, coiling his muscles to react. He never got the chance as a bolt of energy issued from the god's hand, and Draven went flying yet again.

I really need to work on my landings.

♥*Beware, Draven, this is a god you face. Ghedryn, unless I miss the mark.*♥

Damned gods. I'll have his holy hide for killing Helena.

Ansalon failed to reply, and Draven couldn't help but wonder at the knight's loyalties.

Ghedryn stood over the fallen Seguris, looking at him with disdain. "You were a poor champion. I will choose better when next I select a scion for my wrath." He fingered the rusty knife that was Blood Thorn just moments ago. "Now, I'll take my gauntlet back and be gone after I dispose of the rest of these fools."

"I put down one monster. I have no problem slaying a god to fill out my day." Draven lacked any conviction he could fulfill that prophecy, but he was game to try. Helena and Kell were dead, Loken couldn't stand, Nellonah was out cold, and he could scarcely lift his arms.

Ghedryn stooped to retrieve The Fist of Heaven from Seguris, who somehow clung to life, hugging the relic to his chest even as blood seeped from wounds too numerous to count. The god's foot trod on the remains of The Trappings of the Wild, and that was his undoing.

The sable cloak came to life, wrapping around Ghedryn's leg, crawling upward, stretching and morphing as it went. Ghedryn screamed. The sound echoed everywhere, vibrating Draven's bones with the power. The ground shook, and the sky grew even darker. Brooding clouds rolled across the horizon. As one, Ghedryn and the trappings exploded in blood and bone. White light erupted across the sand, leaving Draven shaken.

When the dust and smoke cleared, Ghedryn had disappeared, killed or consumed, and in his place stood a withered, hunchbacked figure with emaciated limbs and a cadaverous leer. Draven could hardly understand how he remained upright. His hands shook, but Draven sensed immeasurable power from this being. Wispy hair reaching to his skeletal feet stirred in the dry wind as the clouds dispersed, bringing back the scalding desert sun. Seguris gazed up at his ancestor, still clutching the fist while snaking his hand out to keep Blood Thorn from the Mad King.

So that's the Mad King... he doesn't look like much.

♥ *You stand before the true form of Khyris, the last emperor of the Mektwin Dynasty. He is free, and we are all doomed.* ♥

The eternal optimist. I treasure that about you. A limp breeze could topple this old relic.

Khyris took a step toward them, and his body nearly collapsed in on itself. Glaring hatred at them, he tried again and fell to one knee.

"Damn you all. Years of imprisonment may have weakened me, but I shall return to slay the rest of the so-called gods, and remake this festering land."

Draven channeled fire down his blade, but before he could hurl it, the Mad King waved his arms. His hands described symbols in the air that hung like angry rents in the world's fabric. The Mad King's body dissolved into the sand. All went still, and Draven whistled through clenched teeth, surveying the carnage the ancient king left in his wake.

"So... not the end, then?" He fell to one knee, wondering exactly what this victory had cost them. "Damned magic, anyway."

49

THE FALLEN

Draven got to his feet after what seemed like an age, his mind reeling with the implications of a centuries-old tyrant who could consume gods walking the land once more. But that was a worry for tomorrow. Nellonah was all that occupied his mind at the moment. The need to get to the woman he loved consumed him.

Loken sat with her head in his lap, Nellonah's chest rising and falling slowly. Loken favored Draven with a look somewhere between heartbreak and happiness. Only a trickle of blood flowed from the wound, and that left room in his heart for jealousy that Draven's brother held her instead of him.

"I think she'll be fine. Her breathing is better, and the bleeding has stopped. I think it's the relic." Loken looked up at him, hope filled his tired eyes. "For all their harm, they seem to let you take enough punishment to kill any dozen people and keep going."

"Damned magic. Still a little amusing that the master planner is stuck with a relic devoted to chaos." Draven ran a hand through his blood-matted hair.

Loken laughed in reply and Draven kneeled, cupping Nellonah's cheek in his hand. Her eyelids fluttered open, and Nellonah took a deep breath, smiling up at the brothers who shared no blood but everything else that truly mattered.

"The battle?" Nellonah's voice was little more than a croak, but she shoved Loken away and sat up with only a token complaint.

Draven related the pyrrhic nature of their victory, Ghedryn's demise, and the Mad King's strange departure. He plied her with questions about her new form, but she waved him off once again. He wondered how much she had sacrificed to take part in the fight against Khyris. Draven spared a moment for the once-petty thief who picked pockets and fleeced merchants, without a care in the world. Should he shed a tear for that Draven, the one now dead, replaced by a repentant wielder of a holy relic who fought with gods? He shook his head.

Nay, that Draven was a coward. I think I much prefer this version of myself. Especially if it means keeping my brother and Nellonah close.

"What of our friends? Are they all gone?" Nellonah looked around in disbelief, laying a hand on Draven's arm.

"I rushed to you as soon as it was over. What I know for certain is that Ghedryn, in the guise of a boy, killed Helena. And the wraiths of The Trappings devoured Kell. Of Kethek and Elisah, I cannot say, but since they were not standing when the tower came down, they must have perished with the defenders." Draven hung his head, suddenly ashamed that he and Heart Master, for all of its vaunted power, could protect none of them.

"Any chance one of you could power my leg? All the magic flying about somehow rendered it as inert as Draven's honor."

Draven made a rude gesture, channeling power from Heart Master, hoping his brother got singed a bit. To his disappointment, the magical device swallowed all the power he aimed its way. They both got to their feet and assisted Nellonah. Draven couldn't help being unnerved by that moving band of black silk around her neck, more like a spider's silk than any natural fabric.

I wonder if that's how others feel when they see Heart Master crawling up my arm.

♥*Heart Master is a holy relic. The Chaos Masque is something else entirely.*

Mystery cloaks this relic. Their bearers rarely share its secrets.♥

"Damned magic. Damned gods. Thrice-damned Fate."

"So many dead..." Nellonah spoke as if she hadn't masterminded this whole affair. Draven took her hand.

She may be a devilish schemer, but she's my devilish schemer. She gave his hand a reflexive squeeze as if reading his thoughts.

"There is death, and then there is a realm beyond." They all turned to behold a being of golden light with the barest hint of female features.

Draven squinted and thought he could make out the shape of Helena's mouth and nose in the blinding visage. He turned to see if her body had disappeared, but it still lay there, blood drying in the heat of the sun.

"That is merely a husk. I no longer require it." Her words came from everywhere and nowhere, though Helena's lips did not move. "Velleris noticed my passing and elevated me to one of her Divine Guides. I will advise you in the trials to come, such as I am able. Do not worry for me. I am happy now. The rage left me in death as if it were an affliction of the body. This is what I always aspired to, but before I leave you, there is one more task I must attend to."

Helena floated across the battlefield. They followed as best they could. Because of Nellonah's and Draven's injuries, it wasn't quick. Loken opted to remain, standing guard over Seguris, who still rattled breath into his lungs.

The golden glow shimmered a short distance away from where Kell lay. The big man's chest rose and fell beneath the magical breastplate. Blood seeped from hideous wounds that should have marked the end of his life. Bone protruded in places it shouldn't. His broken limbs bulged as if they'd been decaying in the sun for days. Draven's stomach turned, looking at Kell, wondering how it could be possible the big warrior still lived, and what kind of life he could ever have in that miserable shell?

Helena's golden light settled over him, blinding Draven and Nellonah, who could only get within a dozen paces before falling back. Gradually, the glow dimmed enough they could approach once more. Kell lay transformed. His clothing still hung in tatters, but the Hallowed Verity breastplate now gleamed as if newly forged and Kell's body was healed of all but the most superficial wounds. Kell lay reclined on one arm, speaking to Helena's ghost in hushed tones.

Helena's glow continued to dim until it disappeared entirely. Kell searched the ground, looking for something. His search fruitless, he stood facing them with a sullen expression.

"The thrice- damned shadows ate my ax, blade and all. I loved that ax." Kell smoothed his hair out of his face, sauntering over to join them. "Helena says she'll be back when we need her." An errant tear traced down the warrior's unlined features. "It will not be the same in her absence. She took a piece of my heart with her to the heavens."

"I'm sorry, Kell," Draven said, finding his voice. "We would never have survived this without her. I can't say I liked her all the time, but she was a force." Draven clapped his hand to Kell's shoulder and led him back to where Loken awaited them.

"What now? Hel tells me there is yet one villain who remains alive."

"Now?" Draven's expression turned somber. "Now, we slit the warlord's throat, drink a cask of ale each, and then, if we've strength in our bodies, we bury our friends."

When they reached the fallen Seguris, they found him much improved, trying to sit up with Loken pressing the edge of a knife to Seguris's throat. The point dug into the flesh of Seguris's neck, causing blood to trickle down the dark, scarred skin.

"We should kill him quick, before he heals anymore." Loken tightened the blade against the warlord's skin, and Seguris spasmed.

"All in favor? I say aye." Draven wondered at how callous he'd become in such a short amount of time.

Seguris glared daggers at him, but either would not or could not say anything in reply.

"Stop!" Nellonah's voice boomed at them. "We need him. As much as I'm loath to admit it." She tugged at the spider silk that cut into her neck as if it choked her.

"For what?" Draven knew what her reply would be before she uttered it, but still itched to cut the warlord's throat.

"He knows Khyris. The Mad King inhabited his body. He may know something that will help defeat the god-killer." Nellonah tapped a finger to her lips. Draven knew the gears of her mind were already turning over possibilities.

"You should have killed me when you had the chance." Seguris struggled against Loken's knife.

"You've got a point. He's a complete charmer. I'm sure he won't slit our throats at the first opportunity." Draven threw up his hands in disgust.

Nellonah knelt beside the defeated warlord, pulling Loken's knife away. Loken did not release his grip easily. "Simply put, do you hate Khyris?"

"The Mad King? With every drop of blood in my veins." Seguris held so tightly to his relics they cut into his hands, causing them to bleed anew.

"Will you fight with us to get your revenge?" Nellonah's voice was a silky purr.

"If I must. I harbor no illusions. I cannot kill him without help, and it seems my god is dead." Seguris struggled to put the words together. "I'd make a good replacement." He smiled at his own jest.

"I don't like it." Draven and Loken spoke as one and looked at each other. Then the pair shared a chuckle.

"Nor do I, but Helena said it would be necessary to befriend our enemies. Mayhap this is what she meant. Even if it was his god who killed her, I'll stay his death for now." Kell extended his hand to the former warlord, who took it with some hesitation.

"I only wished to free my people. To give them a kingdom, then I found them here defending my enemies. I thought his blood flowed in my veins. I was wrong. My people's blood is in my veins. Khyris must die. Only then can my people be free." Seguris wobbled a bit when he got to his feet. The big man stretched his limbs, causing fresh blood to seep from injuries that healed before their eyes. The Fist of Heaven glittered in the harsh desert sunlight as he slid it back on his hand. He held Blood Thorn in his hand, eyes devouring it and the blood started to turn as it did with Helena.

"No. That's not going to happen." Draven snatched it out of Seguris's grasp before the transformation could complete. "I'll be damned if we come to the end of this, and he gets to keep Blood Thorn." Draven opened his enchanted satchel and thrust the cursed relic inside. "It'll be safe from peering eyes until we elect a new champion. No hand but mine or Nellonah's can open this bag and retrieve it."

Seguris gave him a stern look, but then roared with laughter. "I'm going to like fighting by your side, champion. You're a man I can respect."

Draven whistled at the man's vitality. Seguris had bled enough to kill three men.

Nellonah pulled Draven away from the small group to gaze at the sun setting, an ugly purple hue. He watched the muscles of her neck pulse against the fabric of the relic. She put a hand to it as if embarrassed.

Nellonah looked him straight in the eye and took his hand, placing it on her breastbone. "You know, I'm not divine any longer, not a part of the goddess."

"And what does that mean?" Draven searched her expression for answers, but really only wanted to crush her in his arms.

"Nerys has no hold over me. I don't have access to her power. I'm just as human as you." Nellonah cracked a grin and winked at him. "I just make it look good."

"I think I can live with that. Poor Lock will have to start using your name though."

"It will do him good. I'm afraid, Drav, but it was worth it to find my way back to you." Nellonah blushed, tilting her face down.

"What happens now?" Draven ran a finger along the tip of her chin.

"We mourn. Then we avenge... and somewhere along the way we make time for this." She pulled his face to hers in a kiss that melted all complaints. His arms rose to embrace Nellonah, her heart beating a rhythm against his chest, the sound sweeter than a siren's call. He kissed her, long and thoroughly, worshiping her with lips and tongue. In the timeless language passed down through the ages, he staked his claim to a piece of her soul. By the time they finished, the sun had dipped below the horizon.

They turned to rejoin Loken, Kell, and Seguris. Draven marveled at the motley company and wondered how they'd make it even a day without killing one another.

"Are you ever going to tell me about Nerys and this collar?" Draven ran a finger along the narrow band of silk at her neck, then flinched back at the unnatural texture.

"In time, my beloved, all stories are told, and all prophecies fulfilled." Nellonah winked at him as they went in search of rest before beginning the arduous task of caring for the fallen.

Damned magic, anyway.

Somewhere inside that haunted relic, the old knight laughed.

THE END

Acknowledgements

There is a commonly held misconception that a single person is responsible for creating a book. It takes a village, or in my case, a mid-sized town. I'd like to recognize just a few of those people. First off, my devoted wife who has been a stalwart champion even when I doubted I'd ever get to the end of this novel. Next up are my editors at Dragon Street Press, Scott Macmann and Audra Morrison. Working with DSP has been nothing short of stellar. I'm honored they chose Heart Master.

Supreme thanks must go out to Jenni Cornell who became a huge fan of Draven even as I was about to shelve the book in favor of another project. She fell in love with this crazy, mostly inept thief I created decades before and refused to let me give up on him. Thanks again, Jenni, this book literally wouldn't have happened without your enthusiasm.

Wendy Vogel is, bar none, the best editor and writer I have ever had the honor to work with. Her skills as a developmental editor are second to none. She possesses the heart of a fighter and the soul of a sorceress; if you have any love for Seguris in this book, it's because Wendy continually challenged me to do better. Wendy, apologies if Seguris bears a striking resemblance to Adon the Black; he was a sizable inspiration in evolving my antagonist. Also, huge thanks must go out to Pamela Holdren, a dear friend who is also a fabulous line editor and is always there when I need a sounding board or a devil's advocate. Also, thank you, Jeri Fay Maynard for continually being there to offer words of support and critique when I needed them most.

Thanks to everyone from Cincinnati Fiction Writers who have helped with critiques and edits over the years. This group of writers dedicated to each other's success has been essential to me. Joining up was my best decision as a writer, and one I've never come to regret. I'm truly honored to have worked my way up to be a member of their leadership. John Burris, thanks for that brutally harsh first critique. That experience opened my eyes to what it means to be a professional writer. Thank you as well to my continuity readers John Hagen and James Angne.

My heartfelt thanks to my family back in West Virginia who supported me over the years even though they didn't have a clue what I was talking about most of the time. I can never forget where I hailed from. Honorable mention to Walt, Becky, William, and James Mick who helped me get started on my first professional short story back in the day. It was a painful choice to switch from typewriters to word processors but ultimately necessary.

In closing, I would like to thank writers like Robert E. Howard, Edgar Rice Burroughs and Fritz Leiber for inspiring a young boy to dream that one day he could reach out and touch the hearts of others with his humble words. And finally, dear reader, thank you for coming along on this epic journey. I hope you will enjoy reading this book as much as I did writing it.

-Nikolas Everhart

ABOUT NIKOLAS EVERHART

Nikolas Everhart was born in WV many moons ago. He developed a love of writing at an early age beginning with the speculative writers of the 1930s. It wasn't long until he was chronicling his own stories of sword-swinging heroes and rapacious villains.

His hobbies include mentoring other writers, yoga, tarot, and weaving chain mail. He has been a prominent member of the Cincinnati Fiction Writers group for nearly a decade. Nikolas currently resides in Cincinnati, Ohio with his beloved wife, Teri, an army of cats and one very angry bird.

Grab Your Free Book Now!!!

Dragon Street Press is pleased to offer digital versions of our current Grab Bag Anthology Series free of charge to DSP Friends & Family. If you haven't already joined, then today is the day.

You'll also get access to news, cool supplemental content, and opportunities to be part of select reader groups with exclusive early-access to new releases.

Grab your Free Stuff at...

https://dragonstreetpress.com/about-free-books/

ABOUT DRAGON STREET PRESS

DRAGON STREET PRESS (DSP) publishes fiction of high quality with special emphasis on speculative genres such as fantasy, science fiction, alternate history and dystopian.

DSP believes in critical thinking, the power of imagination, the value of knowledge, and the intrinsic worth of every member of our communities.

Based in Cincinnati, Ohio, DSP is a proud member of the Midwest Independent Publishers Association (MIPA) and the Independent Book Publishers Association (IBPA).

Find out more about us at https://dragonstreetpress.com.

www.ingramcontent.com/pod-product-compliance
Lightning Source LLC
Chambersburg PA
CBHW060521160726
47991CB00001B/126